C₁

Cherry Hollow

ISBN:978-1-7374960-3-8 E-book
ISBN:978-1-7374960-4-5 Paperback
ISBN:978-1-7374960-5-2 Hardcover

Cover Design: Kristy Hoy

Edited by: Kate Matson

Cherry Hollow

Melissa Roos

Dedicated to:

To the girls who knew me when we were young, to the exceptional women you have become.

So privileged to have you through the years,
to have that connection, that bond.
Whether it's been one year or thirty, you will
always be my group, my click, my classmates,
but most importantly my friends.
No need to mention names, you know who you are.
But look at me, I'm a name-dropper after all!

Joy, Amy, Jessica, Shelly, Jeni, Stacy, Marie
"Bust a Move"

PROLOGUE

Black gossamer trailed behind her as she ran over the frozen ground, chilled to the bone. Her breath came out in hot puffs of white. Suddenly she stopped, her feet buried in snow. She stood in the quiet of the forest with flakes drifting down all around her and listened. Tiny crystals fell, virgin white and pure, lazily floating, stacking softly on each other like angel's breath.

The winter wonderland around her was serene and enchanting, but she knew just beyond her vision, just beyond her reach of hearing, someone waited.

She spun at the crack of a twig, biting her bottom lip to keep the cry that was lodged in her throat from coming out. Weak knees and legs of jelly made it almost impossible for her to stand as fear coursed through every vein. She didn't know what direction it would come from, but she knew an attack was inevitable.

Steeling herself, she prepared to do battle with the unknown. She wouldn't cower behind a tree or go out without a fight. Determined to face the demon in her nightmares, she waited. It only had to show itself.

CHAPTER 1

The sun had set hours ago behind the vast autumn woods and music pumped out of the speakers from the stereo Charlotte had hauled out of the house. Some teenagers danced, others ate and talked. They clustered in groups and mingled among themselves in the small clearing behind the large stone house where the bonfire raged.

Cami was late for her own party. Correction: to her twin sister's party. Her back hurt, and so did her feet. The restaurant had been busy, and she had stayed an hour over her shift because Finn's was swamped.

She walked toward the music, tied her light green hoodie around her waist, and grabbed a soda out of the cooler. Cami wove her way through the throng of students giving hugs and saying hello until she found her close group of friends.

Tanya gave Cami a hug. "You look exhausted."

"I am. I really didn't want to come." She acknowledges this with a shrug of her shoulders. "And yet here I am."

"Well, we're glad you did. It wouldn't be the same without you."

"We were just about to roast some marshmallows. Do you want one?" Joselyn asked.

"No, but I'll go over and sit while you roast yours."

"Find a spot and we'll be over."

The little glade was cozy even though the night was dark, the moon constantly peeking out from behind drifting clouds of steel gray. Surrounded by trees it gave the clearing a sense of enclosure as the edge of woods danced with firelight.

Cami's eyes searched the faces that were illuminated by the light of the flames, looking for one in particular.

A little discouraged when she didn't see him, she scooted a log closer to keep warm. All she had wanted to do was go in the house and crawl into bed, but instead she had forced herself to come out back just to see if he was here.

Cami's heart soared as she spotted him on the other side of the bonfire. Luke Warner, the quarterback, heartthrob, and the keeper of her heart. But to him, she was nothing, just one of the gang.

He didn't have any idea he held her heart in his hands, and had since ninth grade biology. His wispy blond hair and gray eyes had all but rendered her speechless from that moment on.

Her heart plummeted as she saw who he sat next to. Her twin sister. A twinge of betrayal surged in the pit of her stomach. It was tonight or never. She had to let him know how she felt before Charlotte did. She couldn't be sure that her twin had been kidding when she'd teased her on the way home from school about Luke, giving her an ultimatum, daring her to tell him or else. Cami could only hope it wasn't already too late.

Charlotte wiggled in close, leaning in to whisper in his ear. He smiled, looking up and catching Cami's eye. He straightened and gave a brief nod.

"Are you sure you don't want one?" Joselyn waved a roasting stick in front of her face, breaking her eye contact with Luke. "You can't turn down a marshmallow. All that warm, sticky goodness."

"Yeah, sure. I guess." She took the stick from Joselyn and stood, glancing back over at him. *Was it her imagination or was Luke watching her? Did he know?*

She fidgeted with her stick and pulled at her black t-shirt, wishing she had gone into the house first to change instead of coming directly from work. Without a second thought, she stuck the marshmallow over the fire.

She felt a tug on her sweatshirt as Kevin came to stand

beside her. "You gonna burn that thing to a crisp before you eat it?"

Cami looked at Kevin. "What?"

He pointed a finger. "Your marshmallow. It's on fire."

"Oh, shoot!" Cami gasped, glancing at the ball of flames on the end of her stick. She waved it frantically, trying to put the fire out.

Kevin doubled over in laughter. "You look like an idiot."

Cami stuck her tongue out at him. She pulled the stick toward her and blew the flame out. All that was left was a charcoaled lump.

"Are you going to eat that?" someone asked from behind her.

Cami wrinkled her nose and turned toward the voice to find Luke standing there. Cami took a step back. "Umm...no. Do you want it?"

"Sure. I like my marshmallows well-done."

Cami held out the stick and in one slow, graceful gesture, Luke pulled the entire burnt glob off the stick and popped it into his mouth. She looked on in awe, unable to say anything.

He smiled at her. "Thanks." Someone called his name behind them. He turned and waved over. "Be right there." Then he looked back at Cami. "If you burn anymore, let me know."

"You bet. I'm all yours."

Luke cocked an eyebrow at her, and Kevin gave her a little jab. Joselyn gasped while Tanya looked at her in horror.

Cami cleared her throat, registering her mistake. "Oh, I meant...what I meant was they...the marshmallows...burnt ones...are all yours."

"Right." Luke smirked, walking off to join the other football players.

Cami smacked herself in the forehead. "I'm such an idiot," she hissed.

"No argument there," Kevin chuckled. He pulled off the rest of his sticky white marshmallow and licked his fingers.

"Is there a hole somewhere I can go crawl into and die? I

can't believe I just said that."

Tanya patted Cami on the arm. "It really wasn't that bad."

"It wasn't?" Cami asked hopefully.

"It was an absolute train wreck," Kevin commented, pushing another marshmallow on his stick. He balanced his graham cracker and chocolate bar on his leg, the makings of his s'more.

Cami snagged the chocolate. "I think I need this more than you right now." She broke off a piece and stuck it in her mouth.

"Hey! That was for my s'more!"

Cami shrugged and popped another piece. "Chocolate helps heal embarrassment and humiliation."

"Then you're gonna need more than just one."

"Who asked you?" Cami glared at Kevin as she bit off another piece.

"Is he the only one that's not aware you're in love with him?" Tanya asked, hands on her hips.

"Well, if he wasn't, he is now after that comment."

"Be quiet, Kevin. Cami can't help she gets all tongue-tied when he's around," Joselyn said.

"Some guys are so clueless," Tanya added with a slight shake of her head.

"Why is it you're fine with him when we're in a group but one-on-one, you're a disaster?" Kevin asked, stifling a laugh.

Cami wasn't able to respond as her twin sister, Charlotte, walked over and stood next to her.

They were the same height, willow thin, the same fine arching eyebrows, slender nose, and high cheekbones. They were almost identical except for their coloring. Cami had honey brown hair and hazel eyes, while Charlotte took after their mother with sunshine, blonde hair, and blue eyes.

"It's about time you got here. I was worried you weren't going to make it at all. Did you see? Luke's here." Charlotte wiggled her eyebrows at Cami.

"Oh, she saw him alright," Kevin snickered, but it was quickly followed by a grunt as Cami's elbow connected with his ribs.

Charlotte raised an eyebrow. "What's that supposed to mean?"

"It's nothing." Cami pulled Charlotte close and whispered in her ear. "You didn't say anything to you-know-who did you?"

Charlotte smiled deviously. "Not yet."

"Please don't. I'll find a way to do it myself." A look passed between them, only sisters would understand.

"You're off the hook for now," Charlotte said. "I'm glad you could finally make it since I did this mostly for you and that *thing* we talked about on the way home from school. I had to set up all by myself, you know." She glanced down at Cami's outfit which consisted of her black Finn's t-shirt, blue jeans, and her favorite hoodie tied around her waist. "I guess you didn't have time to change?"

"You knew I had to work late."

"Work, work, work. That's all you ever do. You're no fun, lately."

"So what if I actually want to work for my money instead of having it given to me by Daddy?"

Charlotte flicked her silky mane over her shoulder and her signature fragrance of white rose drifted around her. "I can't help it if you have a conscience where money is concerned. Daddy has lots and doesn't mind sharing." She patted Cami on the shoulder. "If you didn't work so hard, you might have time for other things." Charlotte's eyes flitted in the direction Luke had gone.

Kevin chimed in, "She has a point. You don't have to work if you don't want to."

"Exactly. You work because you want to. I guess it's your idea of fun. Not me," Charlotte glanced at Kevin. "I'm the essence of fun." Charlotte looked around. "And I think that's what this party needs. Something fun. Something to shake it up a bit." She squealed with delight. "We need to play a game. And I know just the one."

"Not one of your games, Charlotte. I'm too tired."

"Lighten up, Cami. This game has a twist. Even *you* will enjoy it. And it could work in your favor." Without warning, Charlotte climbed up onto a stump near the fire and clapped her hands together to be heard over the music. "Can I have your attention, everyone?"

People sitting by the fire, and standing over by the snack table turned in her direction, but the glow-in-the-dark corn hole game didn't stop. She tried again, clapping louder. "Listen up everyone."

The music was turned down.

"We're going to play a game."

"What are we going to play?" someone shouted.

"I'm glad you asked." Charlotte was always one for dramatics, so she paused. "Hide-and-seek, with a twist."

"I don't think that's such a good idea, Charlotte. What if someone gets lost in the woods?"

"Relax, will you? No one's going to get lost. We've done it before and it's been fine."

"Yes, but there are a lot more people here tonight than in the past."

"What's the twist?" someone else asked.

"I'll tell you," Charlotte said, ignoring her sister, giving her attention back to the gathering crowd. "But first we need to make sure we have even pairs. One boy for every girl. If you don't want to play, you don't have to, but we need even numbers. Boys over here," Charlotte pointed. "Girls over there."

There was a shuffling of feet. Bodies moving from one side of the fire to the other.

Charlotte surveyed them. "Now, let's count to make sure we have enough. How many boys?" She waited while they counted off. "And girls?" She nodded. "Okay, we need two more boys."

The guys called a couple more over.

"Like I said before, we are playing hide-and-seek. The first time the boys are going to hide in the woods and the girls are going to find them. Girls, you can only find one boy. When you find someone, and it doesn't matter which boy, kiss them on the cheek and bring them back to the fire with you."

There was a chorus of moans and giggles at the announcement.

Charlotte smiled elegantly, as if she had expected this. "Now, now. Let's give it a try. Guys, are you ready? You'll have to the count of thirty to hide."

Cami hooked Charlotte's arm. "Charlotte," she whispered, "tell them not to go too far. We can't have someone wandering off and getting lost."

"Okay, fine. If it will make you feel better."

"It would."

"Fine. Don't go too far into the woods. Make sure you can either see the fire from where you're hiding or hear the music." She glanced at Cami. "Better?"

Cami nodded.

"Here we go. On your marks...Get set...Go!" she shouted as the boys took off into the dark woods.

Tanya squeezed Cami's hand. "Maybe you'll find Luke in the dark."

"I couldn't get that lucky," Cami said back. "Besides, he wouldn't want to kiss me, anyway. My hair is a mess and I smell like hamburgers and French fries."

"Your hair isn't a mess. You look fine. And you smell like the fire now. We all do."

"Count the last ten with me," Charlotte shouted. "Ten, nine, eight, seven, six, five, four, three, two, one!"

"Ready or not, here we come!" sang a chorus of voices.

Charlotte gave one last command: "You have to kiss the first boy you see!"

The girls all darted out across the little clearing in groups and disappeared into the woods. Voices were hushed as they went into the darkness created by the looming trees, quickly turning into giggles as the girls fanned out and located the boys. There was a loud roar as boys came out, scaring the girls and chasing them back.

Cami, Joselyn, and Tanya stayed together, searching. The moon had come out from behind some clouds, was full and shining brightly, filtering through the thick fall foliage casting an eerie glow across the uneven ground.

They spotted three guys from the chess club easily behind an outcropping of rocks.

Cami elbowed Tanya. "There's three over there."

"Let's do it. We could do worse."

They kissed them good-naturedly on the cheek and followed them out of the woods back to the bonfire.

Kevin came out on the other side with someone he barely knew, looking uncomfortable. He sought them out quickly.

"Well, that was awkward. How about you guys?" Kevin asked.

"We found half of the chess club hiding behind some rocks," Tanya answered.

"We should have some sort of signal so we can find each other if we do this again. And knowing Charlotte, we will."

"Speaking of which, it looks like she got lucky," Joselyn said, pointing. Charlotte emerged from the trees with Brock Gibson, the captain of the football team, on her arm. She smiled, leaned in close, and kissed him on the cheek, right in front of the fire for everyone to see.

"Ugh. Can you believe it? She got so lucky," Joselyn said, sounding a little jealous. They watched as she laid her hand on Brock's chest, flirting and laughing. "She probably already kissed him in the woods."

Kevin frowned. "I thought they'd broken up."

"They did," Cami answered.

"Are they back together?" he asked.

Cami shrugged. "Hard to say with those two."

"Why does it matter?" Joselyn asked Kevin.

"It doesn't."

"Hey, everyone!" Charlotte waved as she looped her arm through Brock's. "We're going to play again as soon as everyone gets back. This time, the girls are going to hide."

"Like, how does that happen?" Joselyn asked, pointing as a bunch of football players came out of the woods near them. She grabbed a soda out of the cooler. "Practically every one of them was found by a cheerleader."

"They probably cheated," Tanya said.

"Whatever," Cami motioned, throwing her hands up. "Let's do the signal thing. In case anybody hasn't found us."

"Okay," Kevin said. "What's the signal?"

"I know! We hoot like an owl."

"Yeah, that's good. I like that," Kevin replied.

Cami spotted Luke coming out of the woods with a girl she had seen only a handful of times at school but was hard to miss. Her hair was green and spiked in a mohawk, and she had more piercings than Cami could count. She wore black leather and a spiked collar.

"Not everyone on the football team got a cheerleader."

"Ouch. Looks like Luke didn't fare well. That girl is definitely not his type," Tanya observed.

Kevin laughed. "How do you know Luke's not into leather and spikes?"

"Because he hangs out with us."

Cami wrinkled her nose, trying not to show too much interest. "At least our guys were good sports."

"The only problem with your plan, Kevin, is there's only one of you and three of us." Tanya wagged her finger at the three of them.

"No problem, I can just kiss all of you," Kevin beamed. "You know you all want my body."

"That's wishful thinking," Joselyn chided, taking a sip of her soda.

"Josie, I'm wounded," Kevin said, winking at her.

"Find a couple of other guys. *Decent* guys from our regular crowd to give the signal to," Tanya strategized.

"I can do that," Kevin nodded, looking around.

They turned as Charlotte stood perched on her stump clapping her hands again. "Looks like everyone is back. Places people. Girls, over here." She waved them over. "Brock," Charlotte said, keeping a possessive hold on him, "is going to start the countdown for the guys."

"Ladies, if you will," Brock called. "On your marks… Get set. GO!" The girls took off. Cami ran alongside her friends as they disappeared into the dark woods with one last look at Kevin.

Charlotte ran up laughing and stopped next to them. "Hope the chess club finds you."

"We could have done way worse," Tanya said.

"And you probably will," Charlotte answered on a laugh.

Joselyn turned sharply, tripping over a branch. She stumbled and fell forward into Charlotte, covering her in soda.

Yelling in disgust, she said, "You're such a spaz, Joselyn."

"I'm sorry! I tripped. It was an accident."

"I'm soaked!"

"It's not that bad, Charlotte."

"Easy for you to say. I'm the one that's wet and sticky." She shivered in the dark. "And now I'm cold." Charlotte pulled her wet t-shirt away from her skin, thoroughly disgusted. "I can't believe you, Joselyn."

"I said I'm sorry."

"Here." Cami unwrapped her favorite hoodie from around her waist and held it out to her sister. "Take my sweatshirt."

"It's your favorite, I can't."

"Take it. Then you won't freeze."

Without hesitating, Charlotte pulled her wet t-shirt up over her head and tossed it on the ground, then snatched the sweatshirt from Cami's hand and pulled it on. "You guys' better hide. Unless you *want* to get caught by the chess club,"

Charlotte said smugly, then took off at a sprint, veering off to her left.

"Sometimes your sister really pisses me off," Joselyn said, watching her disappear into the dark woods.

"Charlotte is just very competitive, that's all," Cami said, switching back into game mode as voices carried toward them. "Quick, hide there," Cami pointed to Tanya. "Joselyn, there should be a spot just behind that pine tree. See there? Right where Charlotte went."

"Yeah, I see it." Joselyn dashed off.

Cami hurried through the moonlight, stretching the limits well out of range from the clearing. She could no longer see or hear the party. She squatted behind a large boulder, peering out into the dark woods, knowing full well no one had ventured out farther than her, except for maybe her twin sister.

These were their woods, Charlotte's and hers. They had been in the family for generations, and Cami had run amongst them since she could walk.

Giggles, screams, and laughter filled the night air as girls were found. Minutes ticked by. Cami tensed as she heard footsteps and looked up to see Brock Gibson staring down at her.

He smiled. "Hey, Cami."

"Hi, Brock." She stood.

"I hope you won't take this the wrong way, but I was looking for your sister. No offense."

"None taken." She pointed to her left. "Try over in that direction. You better find her fast before someone else does."

He grinned broadly. "I'm trying. Thanks."

"No problem." She leaned against a tree and watched him disappear.

Time stretched, and the voices all around slowly diminished, and all together retreated. It seemed everyone had been found, but her. Just as she was about to step out of her hiding place, she heard a long drawn out *who* that carried on the night air. She smiled. What a pathetic owl Kevin would make. She answered back. It came again, closer this time. With it, the crunch of footsteps on dry leaves. She answered and stepped out from behind the tree.

"An owl you are not," she smiled as he neared.

"No, but it worked. I found you," Luke said, walking toward her.

"Oh, Luke. I… I wasn't expecting you." Her pulse quickened at the mere sight of him.

"Disappointed?" he asked, stopping a few feet from her, tucking his hands in the front pockets of his jeans.

"No." She shook her head. "But how?"

"Kevin."

"Of course." Cami was nervous, awkward, standing in the dark facing the boy of her dreams. Her palms started to sweat. Wiping them hastily on her jeans, she said, "You don't have to kiss me. It's okay, we can just go back." She moved and so did he.

He gently took her arm and stepped in closer. "Now what fun would it be if we didn't abide by the rules? And kissing was a rule."

"Oh… of course," she said, flustered. She leaned in close so he could kiss her cheek. With his fingertips, he turned her head slightly and kissed her fully on the mouth.

He tasted like marshmallows and smelled like burning wood. Cami melted like butter from the pressure of his warm, enticing mouth. He pulled back, smiled, and she had to catch herself so she didn't fall forward into him.

Her fingertips went to her lips. "I think that was technically against the rules," she whispered.

He smirked. "Sometimes I like to bend the rules." Luke hesitated, watching her for a moment. "We should probably head back."

She nodded and fell in step next to him, her heart soaring. Her mind raced to come up with something to say, but all she could think of was that kiss. That brief electric encounter.

"So, are you still working at Finn's every weekend?" he asked. Luke held out his hand. Placing hers in his tentatively, he helped her step over a fallen log.

"Yeah, hours are terrible, but the tips are good. How 'bout you?"

"I'm still at the golf course for a few more weeks. We're getting ready to close for the season." He tucked his hands back in his front pockets. "It's mostly just Saturdays and Sundays now anyway, since football is in full swing."

All too soon, they came out into the clearing, walking the last few yards in silence. Cami noticed the fire was dwindling and the guests were fewer.

Spotting Tanya, she waved, unsure if she should walk toward her or stay with Luke.

"Hey, looks like the guys are going to take off," Luke said, turning to Cami. He gave her a long, slow smile as his eyes flicked down to her mouth. "Guess I'll see you around?"

"Sure," Cami said, trying to seem casual, but inside her heart was thumping hard against her ribs. Giving him a last glance, she turned as Charlotte's face flashed through her mind...Cami reached out into thin air... a scream ripping, ricocheting off the edges of her mind... She pressed her hands to her ears as a sharp pain pierced the back of her head. There was an unbelievable pressure on her chest, making her gasp for air. Cami swayed holding her head as images drifted through her mind.

"Hey, are you okay?" Luke asked.

She saw eyes, white light, and then there were two of him. Her stomach clenched. "I think I'm going to be sick."

"Here, sit down." He guided her to a log by the fire.

"What's the matter?" Tanya asked, coming up beside them.

"I don't know. She acted like she was going to faint."

Their voices floated around her.

Tanya squatted down. "Are you okay?"

Everything went dark.

"Cami!" Tanya shrieked. She shook her hard, and Cami's eyes fluttered open. "Somebody get her some water!"

A crowd gathered around them, and they thrust water forward.

Tanya forced a bottle to her lips. "Drink!"

Cami did as she was told and took a sip of the warm water. She swallowed hard and forced the bottle away. "I'm fine."

Tanya scowled at her. "You don't look fine and you just blacked out for a couple of seconds."

"I did?" Cami's eyes rolled back in her head again. Charlotte's face floated through her mind. "It's not me," she hissed. "I...we can't breathe."

"What do you mean?" Tanya asked, holding Cami's face between her hands so her eyes focused on hers.

On the edge of hysteria, she shrieked, "Something's happened!" Cami gulped in air. "I think Char..." She could barely bring herself to think it, let alone utter the words. "Charlotte's dead."

CHAPTER 2

(Ten years later)

The low stone wall built with rocks gathered from the earth ran the border of their land and flanked either side of the driveway. Cherry trees grew wild at the edge of the Pennsylvania woods, mixed in among the predominant pine trees of hemlock and white pine, creating an emerald forest tinged with gold and scarlet. The orchard that once was cultivated on the north side and kept in neat rows had now multiplied savagely. Vines twined around and through the cracks in the stone wall and stretched toward the trees. Cami stopped at the entrance, windows down, air teeming with the scents of autumn, and took it all in. It was beautiful, rugged, and wild, just like she'd remembered.

She took a deep breath, relishing what she saw, missing it like a long-lost friend. On a sigh, she drove past the wall and around the bend in the drive. The manor came into view, looming large, dark, and ethereal against the cornucopia of fall colors. The facade was a dark stone harvested from the very ground it stood on, with a shake roof dripping moss off the edges. There was a small, high-pitched porch dead center of the house that protected a heavy wooden door that beckoned to her to come home, as the house sprawled out from it in both directions.

The manor had withstood time, weather, and five generations of Parkers. It bore witness to joy in the lean times and the prosperous, to love at weddings and births, and it had seen its share of sorrow in death and tragedy.

At the center of the circular drive was a fountain, a statue of two girls dancing arm in arm, connected and frozen in time, reflecting the happiness that once lived here.

Cami shut the car off and got out. She was home. Her heart ached at the sight of the house, the forlorn feeling of time passing, and the manor falling to neglect.

Emotions and memories swamped her. Her stomach clenched as those last weeks and days came rushing back. She told herself on the way here that she could walk right in but now...being here...it was different. Swaying a little, she reached for the SUV, leaning on it for support, and let the memories flood in.

Everyone in black. White roses cascaded over the coffin. Her sister's porcelain face. Her mother weeping. Her father stoic. Herself numb, going through the motions. She remembered the long line of mourners, friends, family, neighbors, and classmates. Then after...the nightmares, the rush of tears and the packing of boxes.

In the blink of an eye, she had lost so much: her twin sister and the only home she had ever known.

In their haste to get away from the tragedy as fast as possible, her parents had moved to New York City. Something so foreign to her she couldn't even comprehend it. They had forced her to go with them, leaving behind her friends and the rest of her senior year.

Cami wasn't sure how long she stood there, letting the memories come, barely coping as they engulfed her. Her heart longed for Cherry Hollow and all the years lost in the unending woods of her youth. And yet, not once in ten years had any of them been back. Not until today. She was the first to return.

She could still hear her mother's voice.

"Why do you want to go back there? There's only pain and sorrow. Your sister's memory is there waiting around every corner," she'd sobbed.

"That's exactly why I have to go back," Cami had said. "I love it there. I want to have a home at Cherry Hollow and a business. I had hoped you'd understand." But her mother never would. Maybe she never could. She needed to go back for herself, for Charlotte, and to stop the demons that haunted her.

"Understand? How could I? I lost everything that night. I barely survived. And now you want to rip open an old wound. Why? Why would you do this to me?"

"You lost a lot, Mom, but you weren't the only one. And you didn't lose everything. You still have Dad... and me."

Her mother waved her off and sniffed. "Yes, but your sister... She was such a force." She dabbed at her eyes.

Cami had been about to relent, seeing the pain her mother was in, not wanting to cause her more.

"A business in that little ramshackle town will never succeed. No, I forbid you to do this, Camilla."

That last comment had set the wheels in motion. Her sister may have been her mother's daughter, but she was her father through and through. And the Parkers? No matter what, they were never forbidden to do anything. And failure wasn't an option.

Cami had a good solid business plan in the front seat of her SUV. She'd calculated her risks, crunched numbers, and done her research. Now all she had to do was implement. After five years in the event planning industry, she had solid connections and long-lasting friendships where she could get anything supplied to her on a moment's notice. Cami would make this work. She had to, if for no other reason than to prove her mother wrong.

Pushing off the small SUV, she walked to the porch and stood nervously outside, keys in hand, afraid to go in.

Cami swallowed, pressing down nerves and weighing her options. There was a hotel in town where she could get a room for the night, come back first thing in the morning when she wasn't so overwhelmed. *Don't be ridiculous,* she scolded herself. *The movers were coming.* Her hand shaking, she inserted the key and turned the lock. "I need to do this, Mom," she said out loud.

Before she could change her mind, she lifted the old latch and the door swung in. Dampness and mildew accosted her. The scent of something long closed off had her stifling a sneeze. Dust motes swirled up and drifted across the floor as the outside air stirred in.

A feeling of déjà vu came over her as she stepped across the threshold into the dark house. Her eyes swept the grand foyer. Everything was exactly as she remembered. The high ceiling, the arching openings, and the big structural beams all in a heavy, dark walnut wood commanded attention but couldn't compete with the imposing staircase that swept the center of the space. She took in every detail, turning a slow circle, missing nothing.

"I'm home," she called out. Her voice rang into the empty house and echoed back to her. She smiled. She swore she could hear the house itself sigh with relief. "I'm home," she said again on a sigh of her own.

Cami flipped the switch and the grand chandelier came to life with fifty tiny light bulbs. It sparked and flashed, flickered off, and then went back on. Cami jumped as a few bulbs popped like firecrackers and burnt out. She laughed despite herself.

"Looks like I'll need light bulbs. I'll have to make a list." Cami glanced at her phone. "Movers will be here in a couple of hours," she said to no one but herself. "Better check the house. Bedrooms first."

She slowly ascended the stairs, trailing her hand along the banister, clearing a thin line of dust. She pictured Charlotte and herself laughing as they ran up the stairs time after time. Chasing, racing, and playing with each other. A chill raced over her, giving her the sensation of something brushing past her on the stairs. She shivered despite herself.

At the top, she hesitated. *Which room should she choose?* She went straight to her old bedroom and opened the door. Sun spilled in through the dirty windows, casting the room in a cheerful light despite being void of any furniture and the walls bare except for nails that had once hung her favorite pictures. When she left ten years ago, she had taken every item, not wanting to leave anything behind.

She crossed to the window and looked out at the front yard. Her room had a view of the driveway, the fountain, and in the winter when the trees were bare, a glimpse of the main road.

Cami went back into the hall. The east wing where her room was located had two other bedrooms, which still held the furniture that had graced them when she was a child, only now they were covered with sheets, looking abandoned and forlorn.

She wandered back down the hall to the center of the house and opened the double doors to her parents' bedroom. The doors swung noisily in to reveal the big empty room. Crown molding and an enormous fireplace defined the primary bedroom, but the real focal point was the view.

The far wall was all glass and opened out onto a small balcony that faced the forest. She walked toward the French doors, opening them wide as she was greeted with the fresh scent of pine. She inhaled deeply and relaxed, taking it all in.

This was such a change from the hustle and bustle of the New York streets. It was void of city noise, the rush of cars, horns honking, the bustle of people. Here, there was only the rustle of branches, the chirping of birds, and the sigh of the wind. This was what she wanted to wake up to everyday.

The crunch of tires on gravel carried through the trees, reaching her in-tune ears. "Who could that be?" Cami pulled her phone out of her back pocket. "It's too soon for the movers."

She pulled the French doors shut and made her way downstairs just as there was a knock. She tugged on the heavy wooden door.

"Tanya!" Cami squealed, engulfing her friend in a hug.

Tanya held on tight for a minute, then released her. Keeping her at arm's length, she said, "Girl, aren't you a sight for sore eyes! It's been over a month since I saw you last."

"I didn't expect you to come by until tomorrow."

"I wanted to surprise you, plus I figured there would be more than enough cleaning to do before the movers get here. I came prepared to work." Tanya was in jeans and an old faded red t-shirt. Her long black hair was swept up into a messy bun. She winked and held up a bottle of wine. "And to catch up when we're done."

"Perfect."

"Let me grab my cleaning stuff and we can start in whatever room you want."

"You're a lifesaver." Cami followed her out to her car. "I was just walking around upstairs. I'm going to take the main bedroom as my own."

"Is there a lot coming on the truck?"

"It's mainly just my bedroom furniture and a few other pieces. Living in that tiny flat in New York City, I didn't accumulate much."

"I know. I saw your apartment. Neat, and very minimalist. Not one thing out of place and nothing extra sitting around." She grabbed a bucket. "That should make it easy for us, then. Looks like there's plenty of furniture left here, anyway." Tanya tucked a long ebony strand of hair behind her ear and handed Cami a basket full of cleaning supplies. "I brought a broom and vacuum cleaner, too. Didn't know if you'd have them."

"I do. Mine's in the back of the SUV. As much dust is in the house, we'll probably need them both to make a dent before the movers get here."

They unloaded everything and climbed the stairs to the primary bedroom.

"It's nice there are hardwood floors throughout the upstairs instead of carpet; I'd forgotten that. Can you imagine how gross it would be after ten years of dust?" Tanya said, heading to the bathroom to fill a bucket of water, not afraid to make herself at home.

"I know. They'd all have to be ripped out. I'm pretty sure there are area rugs in the attic that my mom had wrapped and sealed before we moved out."

"Hey, you have hot water," Tanya commented.

"I had a plumber come in yesterday."

"How did you manage that?"

"Do you remember Mr. Bontrager that lives down the road?"

"Yep."

"He's been watching over the place all these years. He has a key," she shrugged. "I asked him to get a plumber in here and make sure I had running water before I came. He plugged in the refrigerator and said it still works."

"That's great. What about heat and electricity?" Tanya asked, wringing out her sponge.

"I have an electrician lined up to come over tomorrow morning, as well as the plumber coming back and the HVAC guy. I'm sure nothing is up to code, but we have it at least. Half the bulbs blew when I turned on the lights in the foyer."

"Let's hope we don't blow a fuse using the vacuum."

"Fingers crossed," Cami said, plugging it in. She tapped the switch with her foot. It came to life, and she started in the far corner of the room while Tanya started scrubbing in the bathroom.

***

He drove down the road with his windows down. The October air was warm and held the hint of fall in the breeze. The leaves had started to change. Everything was muted green, mixed with amber and gold. He enjoyed the drive meandering down the back roads, up hills, around curves, and driving beside tiny brooks that ran alongside.

As his left hand rode the wind outside his window, he felt relaxed. He hugged the edge of the road as he made the curve so he could continue his leisurely drive but had to tap the brakes as he came upon a big moving truck. After easing off the gas, he drove along behind it until the truck turned onto a country road. His heart did a flip. *Where were they going?* The only houses out this way were the Bontrager's and the Cherry Hollow Estate. *Was that old couple moving? Or had the Parker's finally sold Cherry Hollow?*

He turned and followed the truck at a safe distance. His heart dropped even farther as he watched it turn into the driveway of the estate and disappear around the bend. Slowly he drove past, waiting to see if it came back out. Managing a three-point turn right in the middle of the road, he slowly inched by, trying to get a glimpse of the truck or any other vehicles coming and going.

Nothing was visible from the road, the foliage too dense. Weighing his options, he tried to decide if he should simply pull in and see what was going on. Dashing that idea quickly, he determined that would be too obvious. No, he needed to steer clear of the property until he figured out just who was in the house and why.

No one had inhabited Cherry Hollow since the Parker's had moved out. He cursed himself. He had had every opportunity to go into the abandoned house, but hadn't. As time marched on, the need to do so had ebbed. He thought he was safe, convinced himself he was. The Parker's had left and the case of how Charlotte Parker had died remained a mystery.

People had speculated over the past ten years about her untimely death. Everything from an accident to premeditated murder had been whispered about, rehashed, and gossiped over. No one, not even the police, had any leads. And if he could help it, it would always stay that way.

Putting his foot on the gas, he sped down the rest of the road, wanting to get as far away from Cherry Hollow as fast as possible.

CHAPTER 3

The movers were long gone. The main bedroom was clean, furnished, and the bed made. They unpacked Cami's clothes, and with the bathroom spotless they put away her toiletries.

They were both exhausted by the time they flopped down on the sofas in the freshly cleaned drawing room.

Feet up and a wine bottle in her hand, Tanya stated, "I'm going to crack open this bad boy. But first we should eat. I'm starving."

"Me too. I haven't eaten since this morning." Cami pulled her long honey-brown hair out of her elastic band and ran her fingers through it, smoothed it, and re-secured it. "I have cheese and crackers, half a gallon of milk, and yogurt in the fridge that I brought with me from the apartment."

Tanya wrinkled her nose. "Yuck. I say we go into town and grab something to eat. If we stay here, we will literally starve. Cheese and crackers? Really?" Tanya scoffed.

"You brought wine. Cheese goes with that." Cami laughed when Tanya forced a gag. "Let me grab my keys." She pushed off the couch and went in search of her purse. "Found them," she called, coming back into the room. "Ready?"

"Yes." Tanya unfolded herself from the couch and followed Cami out the door.

"I bet we are a sight, dusty and disheveled."

"To hell with how we look. Let's go to Finn's. I feel like a cheeseburger and ice cream."

"Yes, ice cream. I haven't had their ice cream in forever,

and it's so nice out. We can sit at a picnic table near the creek and eat. What a good idea."

"I'm full of them," Tanya said, pulling the door shut. They hopped in Cami's SUV and drove off.

Tanya adjusted the radio and found an 80s station. Madonna filled the air. Tanya started singing along as Cami rolled the windows down and the cool air blew through. Madonna gave way to Bryan Adams, and they sang along at the top of their lungs. The song died down and faded into a commercial.

"We had some great times in high school, didn't we?" Tanya asked, glancing sideways at Cami, tucking a stray curly black hair behind her ear.

"Yes, we did." Cami detected a note of sadness in Tanya. "We had fun last month when you came to New York, too."

"Yeah." Tanya hesitated, shifted in her seat, and then drummed her fingers on her leg. "I'm just glad you're finally here. It's hard to leave the coffee shop for any length of time, though, even for you. It's my pride and joy."

"I know it is. I'm so proud of you. You always had a dream to run your own place, be your own boss. And that's just what you did." Cami was proud of Tanya, and even envied her a little for taking the risk, branching out into the unknown. "That's what I want, too."

"And you'll do it!" Tanya leaned over. "Can I ask... Never mind."

"Ask what?"

"No, I don't want to ruin it."

"Ruin what?" Cami asked, noticing the question in her best friend's big brown eyes.

"This." Tanya waved her hand between the two of them. "Us. Our friendship."

"You couldn't. You're my best friend and always have been." When Tanya said nothing, Cami regarded Tanya. "Seriously, what's the matter? I just saw you last month and talk to you at least once a week. Did something happen that you didn't tell me?"

"No. Nothing's happened."

"Then what?"

"I guess it's you being here, being in the house again." Tanya swallowed hard. She hesitated.

Making a right turn, Cami could hear the uncertainty in Tanya's voice. Gently, she nudged her friend. "What?"

"I've always wondered, but never had the nerve to ask. But now that you're here, I can't help myself. Why didn't you stay with me for the rest of our senior year? We could have had so much fun. My parents mentioned it to your mom."

"Really?" Cami asked, clearly shocked. "I didn't know that. But it doesn't surprise me that she didn't say anything. You know as well as I do, though, there's no way my mom would have let that happen."

"Why?"

"You know why." Taking her eyes off the road, she looked directly at her best friend. "Or maybe you don't? I guess I thought you did. Why didn't you ask before now?"

Tanya shrugged and leaned back in her seat. "There was never a good time."

Cami sighed, suddenly exhausted after the long day. She didn't want to get into it, but felt Tanya deserved an explanation after all these years. *Wasn't that what this move was supposed to be? Rediscovering the past and righting old wrongs. Here goes nothing.* "I was having nightmares night after night. I'd wake up screaming, my mind filled with images of Charlotte, the feeling I was being suffocated, and this shadow lurking in the background, watching, waiting. My parents would come running, thinking I was literally being murdered in my sleep. Losing Charlotte and me falling apart had both of my parents on the verge of a nervous breakdown. The police were asking questions. My mom was trying to plan the funeral. It's no secret Charlotte was her favorite. It was just too much. They needed to get out of the house, away from it all." Cami pulled into the lot at Finn's and parked the car. "Can you understand?"

"I guess as an adult I do. But as the teenage girl who watched her best friend in the whole wide world move away and not come back, not even once in ten years..." Her voice trailed off. "It just hurt, you know?"

"Believe me, I know. It hurt me, too. More than you'll ever know." Cami placed her hand on Tanya's arm. "But I'm here now."

Tanya beamed. "You are! And we're going to make up for lost time."

Cami laughed. "This is why you're my best friend and always will be."

They got out of the vehicle and walked across the parking lot of the old drive-in famous for their ice cream. A few people called out to Tanya and waved as they got in line underneath the neon blue sign for Finn's.

"I've been meaning to ask you, whatever happened with Richard? Did you guys break it off before you left New York?"

They inched up as the line moved forward, and more people filled in behind them. "I did, then I gave my notice at work."

"Can I just say, he did not impress me the couple of times I met him."

"Yeah, we had nothing in common." Cami pictured Richard in his business suits and superior demeanor. He came across as polished and professional, but underneath, he was just plain arrogant.

"He seemed pretty self-absorbed."

"That's exactly what he was."

"You could do so much better. Tons of guys would love to date the gorgeous Cami Parker."

"Ha!" Cami laughed, glanced down at her dirty t-shirt and faded blue jeans. "Me, in all my glory. Thank goodness my mother can't see me now. She would thoroughly disapprove of my appearance. Looks like we're up," Cami indicated the empty window and the employee behind it. They debated quickly and settled on cheeseburgers, chocolate shakes, and split an order of fries. They ordered, paid, and slid over out of the way.

"There's a picnic table. Why don't you grab it before it's gone? I'll wait for the food."

Cami nodded and walked across the lot to the table. She was about to sit down when someone cleared their throat behind her.

"This looks like trouble," she heard them say. "Excuse me, but that's our table."

Cami turned on her heel and placed her hand on her hip, ready to argue. But when she took one look at the man, her mouth dropped open, and nothing came out. The image of his lips on hers some ten years ago came rushing back. And all the confidence she felt, the haughty comment that was on the tip of her tongue, vanished into thin air. Suddenly she was seventeen again.

Cami had pictured how she might run into him someday, but not once did she imagine she'd be standing in front of him in faded, dirty jeans, a ratty t-shirt, flip flops, hair hastily pulled up in a ponytail, without a trace of makeup on.

"Cat got your tongue?" he asked with a hint of a smile playing at the corner of his mouth.

She narrowed her eyes and really looked at him. His hair was the color of sand, just a shade darker than it had been in high school. His facial features had thinned out slightly, but his gray eyes were still the color of storm clouds on a rainy day. There was no doubt it was him. Luke Warner, her high school crush.

Swallowing hard, she found her voice. Mustering every ounce of confidence she could, she said, "I don't see you sitting there, or any of your food. Looks like this table is fair game." She quickly slipped in, staking her claim in the middle of the table. "But since I'm a nice person, we'd be willing to share."

"We?"

"Hey, Luke," Tanya said, walking over. "Are you joining us?" she asked, placing their food on the table between them.

He looked from Tanya to Cami. "I should have known *she* would be the other half of *we*. Don't mind if *we* do," he said, sitting. "Over here," he called over his shoulder. A couple of guys walked over.

"Hey, Parker," a big burly guy said, sitting down as the picnic table shifted under his weight. "Long time no see."

"I'm sorry. Should I know you? You look familiar but…" She took in his closely cropped brown hair, hazel eyes, and big broad build.

He grinned at her. "I'd know you anywhere. You look exactly the same. Let me give you a hint. One time, I picked your pretty little ass up and carried you across the end zone for a touchdown when the seniors were playing the juniors in flag football."

"Bobby Cannon!"

He beamed. "In the flesh, baby. You know who these other two bozos are?"

"Well, I recognize Luke," Cami said, then turned to look at the guy sitting next to her. He was tall and muscular with a shock of black curly hair on top of his head that made him appear three inches taller. "And where the two of you are, Aaron Phelps is usually close behind."

He bobbed his head but said nothing, simply sunk his teeth into his cheeseburger.

"Still a man of few words," Bobby answered for him, dipping his fries in his ketchup.

"What brings you to town besides Tanya over here?" Luke asked between bites.

"Hey, does she need any other reason?" Tanya demanded.

"Simmer down, your highness," Bobby interjected.

"And what is that supposed to mean? Why have you guys always called me that?" Then she realized. "Is it because my last name is King?"

Bobby tapped his nose. "Ding, ding, ding. We have a winner."

Aaron snickered; Luke smirked.

"Even I knew that years ago," Cami piped up.

"Did you guys have names for everyone?" Tanya asked, suddenly curious. She slipped her straw out of the wrapper and jammed it down into her shake.

"Not everyone," Luke answered.

Tanya pointed at Aaron. "What is his nickname?"

"Butterfingers."

"Why?" Cami asked, surprised. "I don't remember him dropping any passes?"

"He did in junior high."

"Drop one pass and they never let you forget it," Aaron said, shaking his head good-naturedly. "I always like the name we had for Joselyn Finch. We used to call her Birdy. Not just because of her last name, either. Those enormous glasses she wore made her look like an owl."

"I haven't seen her in years, but I doubt Joselyn would like to hear that." Curiosity peaked now, Cami asked. "What was Luke's name?" *Besides heartbreaker.*

Bobby laughed, "Warner." He shrugged. "They all can't be winners. Of course, I was Big Guns." He flexed his muscles, showing off his biceps.

Tanya rolled her eyes and poked at his large biceps. "I would have thought that nickname stemmed from your last name, not these puny muscles, but whatever." Her mouth twitched, trying not to smile. "Did you have one for Cami?" she inquired, wadding up her ketchup packet and dropping it on the tray.

"I'm not sure I would want to know."

Luke shook his head. "I don't think we did."

Bobby barked out a deep laugh. "Like hell man, you're the one that gave her the nickname." He nudged Luke with his elbow. "It was Double Trouble, remember? Luke always said Charlotte was trouble, but you?" He pointed directly at Cami. "You were twice that. You were double the trouble." He chuckled, then Bobby looked at Cami, realizing his mistake in mentioning Charlotte. The entire table fell into an uncomfortable silence. "Oh, hey, Cami, I didn't mean...I'm sorry."

She smiled at him. "Don't worry about it, Bobby. It's okay. It was a long time ago and I don't mind you mentioning Charlotte." She shifted her gaze to Luke. "You, on the other hand, aren't getting off that easy. Why would you think I'm double the trouble?"

His gray eyes shot holes through her heart when he looked directly at her. "My mama always said you gotta watch out for those quiet ones."

Bobby agreed and wagged a fry at her. "If that ain't the truth. Your highness over here, you always know what she's thinking, but you?" Bobby jerked his head toward Luke. "I'm with Warner. You gotta watch the quiet ones."

"Hmmm... I'm not sure if I should be offended or not."

"Nothing wrong with being quiet if you ain't got nothin' to say," Aaron chimed in.

"Touché."

"Thank you, Aaron, my thoughts exactly," Cami agreed.

They ate in silence for a few minutes as the line to order food went down and the people at the picnic tables thinned out. The sun had set behind the hills and the air was turning colder.

"So, you never actually said what you are doing here," Luke said. "Just visiting?"

Cami sipped her shake and shook her head. "No, I'm moving back."

"Permanently," Tanya added, and gave her a little sidearm hug.

"Really?" Bobby asked. "Where are you gonna be livin'?"

"At my house."

"Cherry Hollow?" Luke asked, surprised. "Why? I mean, that's a big house just for you."

Tanya was quick to jump to her defense. "She's going to open an event venue."

"Is that so?" Luke asked. He was quiet for a moment. "That place would be perfect for it."

"I thought so."

"Can't you just picture it? It's the perfect place for a wedding," Tanya said wistfully. Thinking out loud, she added, "Or an engagement party. You could host anniversary parties or retirement parties, even a class reunion."

"Exactly," Cami said.

That sparked a round of other comments. They laughed and talked until the lights flickered on the sign.

"Looks like they're about to close and we're the last ones left," Bobby commented.

Cami shivered. "It's getting cold, too. Guess we had better be heading out."

"It was good running into you ladies tonight," Luke said, scooping up his trash. "Guess we'll see you around."

"I guess so."

"You gonna give her a business card, Aaron?" Bobby asked.

"I don't have any on me," he shrugged.

Bobby fished out his wallet from his back pocket and thumbed through it looking for a card. "Here," he said, selecting a slightly crumpled one and handing it to Cami. "You need any landscaping done. Call them. Best damn landscapers in the county, let alone the state."

"Thanks, Bobby," Cami leaned in and gave him a hug. He didn't hesitate and returned it, lifting her off her feet.

"Missed seeing you around, Parker."

"I missed being seen." She turned to Aaron next and hugged him, too. "It was great to see you all again. This was a lot of fun."

Cami turned to Luke at last. He reached for her, hugging her tight. "Don't be a stranger now that you're back." He released her and socked Tanya playfully in the arm. "You either, your highness."

"Right back at ya. Good night, guys."

CHAPTER 4

Cami woke to the sun falling across her face, seeping in through the windows. Stretching cat-like, half-awake, she shivered as a light whisper trailed up her arm. She could have sworn that someone touched her. The soft scent of roses drifted past her in the air and made her think of Charlotte. Fully awake now, the sensation and the scent dissipated.

She had slept soundly for the first time in a while without dreaming vividly of Charlotte, of the woods, or that night.

Cherry Hollow had been a magical place for them as children, adventure hidden behind every tree. They played in the brook, climbed rocks, ran through the orchard, and ate cherries until their bellies hurt. Charlotte and Cami always carried around the highly coveted pail of cherries when they were outside, picking, sharing, and eating their precious fruit.

But as much time as they had spent in the woods together, Cami had spent just as much wandering it alone, building little forts out of sticks, searching for fairy rings, and reading books perched on fallen logs. Following butterflies as they flitted on the breeze, watching minnows dart in and out of shadows in the creek, or listening for the big, old hoot owl late at night, Cami loved everything about the woods and the orchard.

The orchard was comprised of Sweetheart cherry trees. They bloomed white and pink in the spring, and had deep green leaves shaped like hearts, which turned red and orange in the fall. But most important were the cherries. Bright red, tart and crisp. They lasted throughout the summer months. Even after they were picked, they were perfect for snacking and baking.

Easing out of bed thinking of Charlotte with a smile on her face, she went to the French doors and walked out on the balcony, taking it all in.

The deep emeralds of the pines mixed with sun-tinged golds of the maples, oaks, and deep reds and oranges of the Sweetheart cherries created a visual that rivaled the ocean as the wind sent the leaves rippling softly. She took a deep breath and inhaled the fresh autumn scent, relaxing for the first time in years.

The city had never been her thing and she knew it never would be, unlike her parents. Her mother thrived in the city; her father, too. But they did so for different reasons. Her mother liked the city because it was busy and noisy. With all her charity work, friends, and the hustle and bustle of the city, she didn't have time to think, let alone remember, what she lost.

Her father liked the long hours put in at work and even enjoyed the commute. He liked the board meetings he was a part of and the weekends spent at the country club where they belonged. He enjoyed going out at any hour and being able to get takeout or go to a nightclub.

Not Cami. She craved a simpler life. What she had once and what she had lost. Her parents chose not to remember, but Cami couldn't help it. She needed to remember. Charlotte haunted her dreams and images of that night still flitted about in her subconscious.

With a wistful sigh, Cami left the little balcony and headed for the bathroom, ready to start her day. She had so many plans, tons of ideas, and couldn't wait to implement them all. But first things first.

She stepped into the shower, mindful of her first appointment, the electrician. Followed by the plumber and then HVAC at noon. She needed to set up an appointment with the chimney sweep. There were five fireplaces in the house and she wanted to use them all, starting with a good cleaning.

She toweled off and made a mental list of other things she needed to do. Paint samples and a kitchen designer were on the top of her list. Cami needed a kitchen that she could use for big parties and easy catering. She slipped on capris and a loose tank top. Blow-drying her hair, the business card Bobby had given her caught her eye.

She hadn't really looked at it last night, just tucked it in her pocket. She examined it now.

The Green Zone. *Guys rushing to take care of your grass. We do it all: mowing, designing, and implementing the perfect landscaped area for you.*

That made her smile. She wondered who all worked there. Bobby and Luke? She should have asked. Then she remembered Bobby had asked Aaron for the card. So, maybe Aaron. Regardless, she'd call them.

She put the hairdryer away and walked to the window. If she was going to have an outdoor venue option, she definitely needed to hire landscapers. She'd have to call and get an estimate. If possible, Cami wanted to use locals or people she knew and help promote their businesses as well.

She walked through the upstairs, noting every room on this level except hers still needed to be cleaned, as well as most of the downstairs. The doors stood wide open to all the rooms except Charlotte's. Cami paused outside of it. Her hand lingered above the knob. Was she ready to go in? She wasn't sure. Maybe she should wait a few more days. She needed to be mentally prepared to see Charlotte's room, and to be in her space after all this time.

Then again, maybe sooner was better than later. She'd just take a quick peek while she had the courage. Kind of like ripping off a Band-Aid. She wouldn't touch anything, just look. She took a deep breath and turned the knob, but it didn't turn. Cami tried again, but the door was locked. *Huh.*

She didn't remember her parents locking the room after

Charlotte died, but they could have. Everything happened so fast after they found her body.

The house was old, and the doors had old-fashioned skeleton keys. She'd have to find the keyring and see if she could get it opened.

Shrugging it off, Cami went downstairs to eat something before the electrician arrived.

***

Luke sat at his desk and took his first sip of coffee, enjoying the slide of warm liquid down his throat. He set the cup down and looked around, still unable to comprehend his new promotion to detective. It felt surreal. Just last week, they had a retirement party for Detective Swanson, who had been the department's only detective for thirty years, and this week, he was moving his things in. In fact, it was so new he hadn't even unpacked his stuff.

He dug through the lone cardboard box that he had hastily thrown items in from his old workspace. Luke unearthed some pens, pencils, and a highlighter and put them in his Penn State mug he placed on his new desk. The desk itself was far from new. It was old and scuffed, like everything else in the room.

Reaching in again, he retrieved pads of paper, some sticky notes, a Hershey Chocolate World magnet, and a scarred football. He tossed last year's calendar in the trash and pulled out the new desktop month-at-a-glance his administrative assistant had given him. Luke looked up when there was a knock on the door.

"You all settled in?" Bobby asked.

Luke shrugged. "I guess. Don't have much to settle. Feels funny sittin' in here while you guys are all out there."

"You can come out and hang with us any time if you get lonely."

"Thanks."

Bobby eased his husky body into the office and leaned on the door frame. "You got much to work on?"

"Nothing new right now. Some old unsolved case files the chief wants me to look through, get a new perspective on." He shrugged. "I don't know that I'll be able to find anything now that the cases have gone cold, but I'll give it a shot."

Bobby nodded, then smirked. "I just have to ask, what did you think of running into little Miss Trouble last night?"

"I was surprised to see her. Same as you, I expect."

"Just as pretty as I remember." Bobby ran his gigantic hands across his finely cropped dark hair. "Hell, I haven't stopped thinking about her since I saw her walking across the parking lot. Hell of a note about what happened to Charlotte all those years ago. Seeing Cami brings it all rushing back."

Luke didn't want to admit he hadn't stopped thinking about Cami, either. So, he didn't. Ten years hadn't changed her much. She still had those all-knowing, intense hazel eyes, honey-brown hair, and had remained willow slim. Her quiet beauty radiated through even though he could tell she had been cleaning and hadn't bothered with changing before they had jumped in the car to grab some food, but in his mind, that made her all the prettier. It was all he could do not to reach out and rub that smudge of dirt off her face.

She was the last thing on his mind when he went to bed last night, and the first thing on it this morning, but he tried to act noncommittal. "It was fun catching up, all of us just hanging out like old times."

"Seems to me that once upon a time you had a little crush on Cami Parker. Still got it?"

"I don't think I ever said I had a crush on her."

"Some things don't need to be said, but are there for the seeing if you know where to look. I'd think you'd be keen on that, Mr. Detective."

Luke huffed. "Even if I did, that was ten years ago."

"Doesn't matter. She's still the same girl she was, only older."

Luke couldn't argue with that. "That was high school. This is now. I'm sure she's changed a lot since then."

"Didn't seem like she had to me. Maybe not as shy as I remembered her to be. Time flies by. Don't always get a second chance at a good thing."

"She probably has a fiancé, or at the very least, a steady boyfriend."

Bobby hooked his thumbs in his belt loops. "Maybe. But I didn't see a ring on her finger. And I've never known you to back down from a little competition." He shrugged. "Just saying, it might be worth looking into. Shouldn't be too hard for you to find out," he hesitated, and added, "Detective. Maybe that could be your next case."

"I'm sure the chief would love that."

"There was an awful lot of pretty there last night to look at."

"Sounds to me like you're the one with the crush."

"I ain't afraid to admit when my head's been turned." He pushed off the door. "But it wasn't Cami I was looking at. Gotta go. Are we still on for cards tonight?"

"You bet. Kevin's place right?"

"Yep. See ya later, Warner."

Luke turned his attention back to the box. Not much left in it: a pack of gum with one piece left, a dog-eared paperback, a first aid kit, and a small package of thumbtacks. He tossed everything in the bottom drawer, except the gum, that he deposited in the trash. In a matter of minutes, he was unpacked.

He stood, adjusted his weapon, staring out at the open field behind the station. *Might as well get started on the old cases,* he thought. With that, he turned away from the window and crossed to the big metal filing cabinet. Luke deliberately went down to the bottom drawer, which contained the few old unsolved ones, pulling out the file that changed the course of his life.

CHAPTER 5

Brock Gibson topped off the tank, checked the oil, and loaded the mower onto the trailer. He went back into the building, located the weed-whacker and the leaf blower, repeated the same process with both and carried them out to the trailer. Once he had them secured, he lifted the gate and fastened it. He loaded up an extra can of gas and replacement string. Brock knew Aaron had several stops to make, so he wanted to be sure he was prepared.

Aaron came out of the office with unruly black hair discreetly tucked under a ball cap carrying a clipboard, a water bottle, and his lunch.

"You have the new addresses?" Brock asked.

"Yep," Aaron waved the clipboard, then handed a piece of paper to Brock.

"Here's an updated list of estimates. One just came in. So I added it," Aaron said, stowing his lunch in the cab.

"Okay." Brock scratched his chin as he ran down the list with his eyes.

"Somethin' wrong?"

"Yeah, this new one, it's out on Sawmill Road."

"What about it?" Aaron asked, taking a long drink of his water, watching Brock over the bottle.

"Nothin'. Just, did you write that down correctly? Only two houses on Sawmill. The Bontragers and Cherry Hollow. The Parker place."

"Yep. That'd be the one."

"Okay," Brock hesitated. "Who called? Did you get a

name?"

"Didn't need to, already knew who it was."

"Who?"

"It's Cami Parker. Ran into her last night. She's back and apparently here to stay. Cannon gave her our card 'cuz I didn't have one. She called this mornin' while you were out here."

"What does she want?"

"A free estimate." Aaron shrugged. "So I added her to the list. Is that a problem?"

"No. It's just a blast from the past. Wasn't expecting…" He cleared his throat. "Just a surprise, that's all."

"Some surprises are good, others are not. You be the judge of this one." Aaron climbed into the truck, rolled down the window, and stuck his head back out. "Need to get movin'. See you tonight at Kevin's, if not before. Bring lots of money, 'cuz I plan on takin' most of yours." He started the truck.

"You haven't won in quite a while, my friend."

Aaron's dark brown face, the color of warm molasses, creased into a grin that encompassed his whole being. "I have a secret weapon today."

"And what could that possibly be?" Brock asked, intrigued. "You're crap at cards."

"Look at that list again." He waited. "Last appointment for the day is Cherry Hollow, right?"

"Yeah. So?"

"You take one look at Cami Parker and you won't be able to think straight the rest of the evening. If you can't think straight, you won't be able to focus on your cards." He tapped the side of his head with an index finger. "Smart on my part. You have a nice day now." Adjusting his cap, he pulled away before Brock could say anything else.

"What the hell was that supposed to mean?" Brock shook his head in disbelief. "Won't be able to concentrate tonight. Hell, I will not be able to concentrate all damn day," he mumbled to himself. Cami Parker. He hadn't seen her in ten years, not since… not since the funeral.

CHAPTER 6

Cami was exhausted. She flopped down on the sofa in the drawing room. Her arms and back hurt from scrubbing the kitchen from top to bottom, wiping the inside of the cabinets, sweeping the floor, cleaning the counters and the woodwork.

She repeated the entire process in the library, the dining room, and the sunroom. Doing all of this while she conducted the appointments with the plumber, the electrician, and the HVAC guy.

Pulling out her cell phone, she glanced at the time. She still had half an hour until her appointment with the landscaper.

She just needed to shut her eyes for a few moments or she wouldn't be able to function by the time he got there. Closing her eyes, the enticing warm blanket of sleep pulled her under.

In the early stages, she dreamt of Charlotte.

"Come on, Cami! Come swing," Charlotte called from beneath the big oak. She sat on the wooden board and pumped her legs. "Give me a push."

"If I do, are you gonna push me after?" Cami asked, looking up from her book.

Charlotte rolled her eyes. "Of course, I will. Better yet, I'll give you, my cherries."

Cami eyed her sister's full pail of Sweetheart cherries and decided it was worth it. She put down her book, came up behind Charlotte, pulled the swing and her sister backward as far as she could, then let go.

Charlotte giggled as she rushed forward, then swung back. "Give me an underdog!"

Cami shoved her sister forward and waited for gravity to bring her back.

She gave her another push. "Okay, make sure you're hanging on."

She waited for her sister to swing back and grabbed the ropes. As the swings' momentum shifted, Cami braced to catch the swing and begin the run. She ran forward with all her might, as fast as she could. Her legs pumped and just when she could barely hang onto the swing any longer, she gave one big, last shove and ducked under the swing, sending Charlotte as high as the ropes would go. Charlotte squealed with delight, and Cami flopped on the ground next to her book.

Cami draped an arm over her eyes and squinted against the sun as the rays filtered through the leaves. She lay in the long grass and watched her sister sail back and forth through the air over her.

"Do it again," Charlotte cried.

Cami popped a cherry from her sister's pail in her mouth, pushed herself off the ground, and ran around as Charlotte came sailing back. Cami didn't even hesitate. She grabbed the swing and ran, ducking under as her fingertips brushed the seat.

"Again!" Charlotte demanded.

Cami came around again and gave her another.

"Higher!" Charlotte shouted.

Cami rounded the swing again, running faster, and gave her another huge shove, ducking under and collapsing face-first on the ground, completely out of breath.

"Again!" Charlotte chorused.

"I can't," Cami gasped and rolled over, her chest heaving.

Charlotte sailed back and forth over her head, each time not going as high as the last.

"I dare you to jump out."

"If I do, I'll land on you!"

"No, you won't."

"Yes, I will."

"JUMP! I double dare you."
With a shriek, Charlotte let go.

***

Brock knocked and took a step back, waiting. He took in the entire house with one long sweep of his eyes. He hadn't been here since the funeral, he thought with a pang in his heart. The last image of Charlotte was seared in his brain. Her pale, lifeless face, so still, so fragile, looking as if she was lost in a dreamless sleep. He swallowed hard, pushing the image to the back of his mind. But before that, before the funeral, it seemed like almost once a month the twins were having bonfires, picnics, or parties of some sort here. It had been a lot of fun; some of his best memories of high school were made at Cherry Hollow and contained Charlotte and Cami in them.

Brock knocked again and caught movement in a second-story window. He lifted his hand to wave mere seconds before the door swung open wide. Cami stood on the other side, looking a little disheveled and sleepy. Her clothes were crumpled and there was a crease down the side of her face, but with the honey-brown hair and hazel eyes, he'd know her anywhere.

"Did I wake you?" he asked, surprised, thinking of her looking out the upstairs window, just seconds ago.

"Umm... yes, I guess you did." She stifled a yawn. "I'm so sorry. I sat down for a minute and must have fallen asleep." She tried to straighten her clothes and smooth her hair. She smiled up at him. "I apologize for my appearance." She shrugged. "So much for first impressions. I'm Cami Parker. Please come in."

"Hey, Cami. Long time no see." He stepped into the foyer and took a quick glance around. It felt like he had stepped back in time. Everything was exactly the same, minus the massive amounts of flowers that had been here the last time. He turned his attention back to Cami. "I take it then you don't recognize me? Aaron didn't tell you who was coming out?"

"Actually, I never asked, and he didn't offer. He's a man of few words."

Brock laughed. "That's for sure."

She looked at his face. "Don't tell me. I want to see if I can get it right, without help."

"Just so you know, if you guess poorly, the price of the estimate goes up."

Cami smiled at that. "Fair enough. I'll try not to hurt your ego." She slowly took him in.

He fidgeted wondering what Cami saw when she looked at him. Brock wished he'd gone in last week for a haircut. He knew it was a little long, the color of walnuts, Charlotte used to say, with brown eyes to match. Brock had a round face, that in his opinion had honed down as he had matured but the cleft in his chin remained. Six-foot tall, broad through his shoulders causing his white polo to stretch taut, wearing jeans and loafers, he still carried himself like the football player he used to be.

"Brock Gibson?"

"You got it." He reached out to shake her hand and was surprised when she opened her arms to hug him instead. He heartily hugged her back. "It's been a long time."

"Ten years. Seems like a lifetime, and yet just yesterday. If that makes sense?"

"I couldn't agree more. Imagine my surprise when I had your address added to my list this morning. I thought for sure Aaron had gotten it wrong."

Cami smiled at that. "I'm sure you did."

"Never thought I'd be back here or have a reason to come back."

"I'm sorry. I hope this isn't uncomfortable for you."

"It stung a little as I turned into the drive but I'll manage." He gave her a hint of a smile. "On to other things. May I ask? What brings you back?"

"Yes, you may. I'm starting my own business. Event planning, event venue. I want to breathe some life back into this old place and have it be *the* place to have an event, whether it's a wedding or a reunion. My major spaces will be the ballroom and an outside terrace. That's where you come in. You wanna head out back and take a look?"

"You bet. Lead the way."

He followed her down the hall, through the kitchen, and out onto the back veranda with his notebook in hand.

"So, you and Aaron are in business together?"

"Yep, he doesn't talk much, but that's not a requirement when you're using a shovel."

She laughed at that. "Just the two of you, then?"

"We have some guys that work for us, but Aaron and I own the business."

"That's great. I always figured you guys would stick together." She turned to encompass the patio. "I would like to use this existing area for outdoor dining. It would have to be enlarged, of course."

"How big are you thinking? How many guests?"

"About a hundred. Give or take." She looked down. "I love the flagstone, and it's still in perfect condition. I want to salvage as much of the original house as I can. Do you think you can still get this exact material?"

"We can easily get flagstone, but to match the color perfectly, I doubt it. What we could do is find something to complement it, lift out stones and intermix with the new."

"I love that idea. I would like the edge to be curving and organic."

Brock nodded. "Easy enough." He made some notes. "Are you okay if I take a photo of this existing patio and get some quick measurements?"

"Go right ahead."

Cami waited patiently while he measured, made notes, and snapped a couple of photos with his phone.

Finished, he looked up at her. "What's next?"

"Follow me."

They walked down the stone path that meandered

through the trees.

"I'd like to widen this path a little, make it large enough for two people to easily walk on, side by side." The path split in two directions. "If we go right, it will take us to the clearing."

He followed her in silence as they came into a small glade, and remembered Charlotte hiding in the woods, waiting for him to find her.

"I don't know if you remember or not, but this is where we used to have our bonfires."

"I remember."

"Of course, you do." She turned and smiled at him. "I'd like to put an arch tucked under those weeping cherries. I think it could be the ideal place for an outdoor wedding." She waved her hand, encompassing the whole of the clearing. "This area would be for seating. The path would continue and lead right up to the arch."

He made a few more notes, his mind already working out details, envisioning the total scene. "Here's what I'm thinking. Let me know if I'm on the right track."

She nodded.

"We should make the structure of wood and stone. I'm thinking of an archway with the columns squared, rustic, flowing into organic, so the top of the arch looks like branches. In the center, we could incorporate carved leaves, blossoms, and cherries." He studied the ground and saw that it was a mix of grass and moss. "We could take out the grass and plant all moss, keep the maintenance low, but the ground would still be a lush emerald green."

"So far, I like what I'm hearing. I would need some lighting here, too. But I don't want it to stand out. It should blend in and accent. Definitely set a mood, romantic and magical."

"I agree. What about fairy lights hanging from the branches?"

"I absolutely love that idea."

He jotted a couple of other things down. "Anything

else?"

"I have some other ideas. I can show you if you want to follow me in the other direction, but depending on the price of the first two projects, they may have to wait."

"Let's look." He turned and the scent of roses drifted past him. He looked around. "Wow, those flowers are fragrant."

Cami stopped. "I don't know where it would come from. There aren't any flowers out here. But now that you mention it, I smell it, too. It smells like roses. That was Charlotte's signature fragrance. She always wore it because of her..."

"Her middle name was Rose," he finished for her.

"Of course, you knew that."

Brock shrugged. "What can I say? Your sister and I were on-again, off-again so many times during high school. She was the first girl I ever fell for. My first real crush, my first kiss, my first real girlfriend, and the one I never could quite get over."

The scent dissipated, but the memory lingered between them.

A whisper of a smile twitched at the corner of her mouth. She swallowed hard and said, "Follow me. I'll show you the rest of my wish list."

CHAPTER 7

They sat at the round table, beer cans half empty, nachos gone, pizza boxes discarded, with red and blue checkered chips piled high in the center. Hard rock poured out of the speakers surrounding them. Kevin shuffled cards while Aaron pulled the entire pot toward him.

"Looks like you're on a roll tonight. What's your secret?" Kevin asked, dealing out the cards.

"No secret. I'm just not distracted like everyone else."

Kevin furrowed his brow. "Okay, what gives?"

Aaron took a sip of his beer and grinned slyly. "Brock is distracted because of his late afternoon appointment, and I figure Luke and Bobby are thinking 'bout the same thing. Either that or they've lost their magic touch."

"You wish," Bobby barked.

Kevin put the pile down and picked up his own cards, sorted them by suit and color. Looking at Brock he asked, "What am I missing? Where was your appointment, or should I be asking, with who?"

Brock scrutinized his cards. "You'll never guess where my last estimate of the day was." He pulled out two cards and discarded them. Not waiting for Kevin, he offered, "It was at Cherry Hollow with Cami Parker."

Kevin quirked an eyebrow. "Really? What's she doing back? Are they finally selling the place?"

Brock took a long pull on his beer, sucking it dry, and crinkled the empty can. "Nope. Cami's back to stay and startin' a business."

"What about her job in New York?" Kevin asked.

Brock shrugged. "Didn't get into all that. I was too busy writing down everything she wanted to do to the place. I hope she's got a big budget, because it won't be cheap."

"Talk about a blast from the past. I couldn't believe it when I saw her last night at Finn's. It was like taking a step back in time, especially with her and Tanya together," Bobby said. "She was just as pretty as ever, not in the made-up way Charlotte always was. No offense, Gibson. But in her own quiet way. Fresh. Natural. Didn't you think so, Warner?"

Luke looked at his cards, trying to avoid answering directly. To say his heart hadn't skidded across the pavement at the sight of her would be an understatement, but he wasn't about to admit that to these guys. "You could say that."

Kevin glanced around. "You've all seen her? How long has she been back?"

"Just a day or two," Bobby answered. "You seem surprised. I thought you guys were tight."

"We were. We are. But I guess it's been a few months since I've actually spoken to her," Kevin admitted. "Not since the engagement."

"Yeah, most fiancé's frown on regular contact with other hot chicks," Bobby commented. "They're funny that way."

"Guess we know who's whipped," Brock added with a chuckle.

Aaron stifled a laugh. "Looks like someone's on a short leash."

"Shut the fuck up, you morons," Kevin retorted, turning red.

"Lay off him," Luke chimed in. "He's the only one here who's actually got a woman."

"Thank you, Warner, the voice of reason."

Luke laid down a card and called for another. Kevin slid him one.

"'Course the only reason he still has a girl is because he weighed her down with a rock so huge she couldn't run, even if she wanted to."

"Yeah, what are you trying to compensate for, Kev? Ain't you got enough to keep her satisfied in bed? You gotta do it with a rock instead?"

"You're a bunch of assholes. All of you. Especially you, Warner, mister law-and-order. I expected better from someone who just made detective. Who's in?"

They all threw in a few chips.

"If I remember correctly, you had a thing for Cami," Brock scratched his head. "What was it you called her?"

"Trouble," Aaron supplied.

"That's it! How could I have forgotten?"

"One look at her and that's all you're going to get," Bobby called and threw in a couple more chips. "I'm stayin'. Who's with me?"

"I'm in," Aaron said, tossing in a couple. "Damn shame what happened to Charlotte. Detective Swanson leave the file behind for you?"

Despite the music, quiet descended over the group.

Luke looked up from his cards and glanced around the group. All eyes were on him, even Bobby's. "You know I can't answer that question. It's confidential."

CHAPTER 8

Cami wandered through the woods, first through the overgrown orchard, then following the worn deer path that meandered along the creek with no clear direction in mind. A patch of yellow shone brightly in the sunlight growing wild among the forest floor. She bent down, plucked a little buttercup, and twirled it in her fingers. Without warning, the memory swamped her.

They had searched all night. Searched until the moon slowly faded and the sun inched above the horizon. When they couldn't find Charlotte on their own, the police had turned to her.

She led the police through the trees, beyond the out of bounds they had set for the party, toward the rockier terrain. Walking on moss and around ferns, Cami could hear the babble of the brook as they twisted and turned, stepping carefully over rocks and broken branches, stopping short by a newly fallen tree.

There, in a dapple of early morning light, Charlotte lay flat on her back, still and lifeless, looking as if she were merely asleep. A police officer scrambled toward her, desperate to check for signs of life, but Cami knew in her heart that she was already gone.

She stood in that exact spot now. How she had gotten there, she couldn't say. The fallen tree was still there, only not fresh like it had been. It was rotten and aged by time and weather. Cami reached toward the ground where her sister's head had lain all those years ago and touched the sharp rock covered in moss protruding from the earth. The sting of innocence lost was at the sharp tip of the rock, and the scent of roses surrounded her.

"Charlotte? Are you here?" she asked.

The wind swirled and rushed through her hair, carrying the scent. It was almost like a hug or a caress, if the wind could do that.

"I've missed you." Cami eased back, sat on the rotten log, and ran a finger along the warm bark. "It's been ten years since I've been here. Nothing has changed, and yet everything has. What's it been like for you? Does time stand still or fly by where you are? Have you wondered where we've been? Why we haven't been back, not even once in the past ten years?" She sighed heavily, feeling the burden of the years seep out of her and leach into the fall air. "I wanted to, but Mom wouldn't let me. She wouldn't let any of us. It was too hard for her. She didn't even want me to come now. I swear I could have heard a pin drop when I first told her. Then all hell broke loose."

Cami straightened her legs and stood. "That night still plagues me. I relive it over and over in my dreams. I've come back, Charlotte. To end the questions that keep me awake at night. To find the shadow that lurks in the woods. I can't keep going on like this with you haunting my dreams. I need peace and closure. For you, for Mom, for Dad, and for me."

The scent of roses had dissipated and Cami wondered if she had just imagined it. She sighed and tried to shake the melancholy feelings that surrounded her. Today was fresh and beautiful. She wouldn't spiral down into a funk again. Starting back toward the house, she was determined to find the key to Charlotte's death. Her first step would be to unlock her sister's room. There had to be keys somewhere in the house.

Walking back, she smiled, watching squirrels dart in and out, scampering back and forth in front of her carrying nuts to store for the approaching winter. Birds chirped and twittered incessantly, fluttering from branch to branch, and in the distance a woodpecker drilled in rapid fire, echoing through the trees.

Coming out of the trees into the clearing behind the house, Cami heard the crunch of tires on gravel. "I wonder who that could be?" She rounded the house just as a man got out of the car.

"Kevin!" Cami called, waving at him.

Turning in her direction, he smiled. "Well, look at that. It is true. Cami Parker has returned to Cherry Hollow."

She threw her arms around him, and he hugged her tight.

"Imagine how I felt at poker last night when everyone at the table had seen you but me. I told them they had to be imagining it because there was no way in hell that one of my best friends since kindergarten could be back and not have called me. So, I drove out here during my lunch hour, mind you, to see for myself." He held her at arm's length. "And here you are, in the flesh, looking pretty as a picture."

She laughed. "It is so good to see you."

"It's good to be seen. Now what's your excuse for not letting me know you were back?" he questioned.

"I don't have an excuse," she said brushing her hair out of her face. "Except I just wanted a couple of days to adjust before I let everyone know. In my defense, you are on the very top of my list to call."

"I might actually want to see that list, but for now, I guess I'll believe you."

"Can you come in?" Cami gestured toward the house. "Have a drink or something to eat?"

Kevin's eyes flitted up to the house and returned quickly to Cami's face. "I don't think so. Like I said, I'm on my lunch break. There's an appointment coming in at two. I need to be back."

"At least sit for a minute." Cami linked her arm through Kevin's and they walked to the house. She pointed at the steps. "Please sit, just for a few," she begged.

He relented. "Only for a couple."

They sat.

"Nothing's changed here," Kevin commented, looking out across the vast front yard. "Do you think that fountain still works?"

Following his gaze, Cami looked at the fountain. It was old and cracked in a few places. Dirt and grime had built up in the creases since no one cared for it, but it still looked beautiful to her. Two little girls, arm in arm, caught in laughter for all eternity. "I don't know, but I'm going to try my hardest to get it going again."

He nodded. "What's on your agenda for today?"

"Going to the store. I need groceries in the worst way," Cami said. She looked at him. Took in his face. Gone was the boy she remembered, replaced by a man. He still had the same warm, brown eyes and dark brown hair, cut a little shorter than the last time she had seen him. She ached for the years that had passed without him in it. "So tell me everything since the last time we talked."

Kevin shrugged. "Not much has happened."

Cami scoffed. "Hard to believe, it's been like three months?"

"More like five."

She ignored the comment. "Whatever happened to the girl you were dating? You were a little unsure about her the last time we talked. Are you still dating her?"

"You could say that."

"Well? Is it serious? Or did you break her heart?"

"I guess it's serious," he hesitated. "We're engaged."

Cami gasped, reached over, and gave him a heartfelt hug. "That's so wonderful! What's her name? When do I get to meet her?"

"Oh, you've met her."

"It's someone I know?" she questioned, surprised.

He nodded.

"Who?"

"I'm not telling. You'll just have to wait and see. Have dinner with us tomorrow night."

"Seriously? When and where?"

"My house. I'm having a cookout. Most of the old gang

will be there."

"Text me the address."

"Sure." He pulled out his phone and sent it. He looked at her then. Really looked at her. "Why did you really move back, Cami? Last I heard, your mom didn't want any part of you coming back here, ever."

"That's true, she didn't. Still doesn't."

He stood and looked down at her. "Then what's changed? Why now?"

Her face softened, but she stared up at him. "It'll be ten years, Kevin. For once and for all, I need to know what really happened that night."

"Why?"

"I'm stuck. Stuck in the past. Haunted you might say. And I miss this place, Cherry Hollow, and you. All of you."

"We've missed you too. But Cami, what if you aren't able to find the answers you're searching for?"

Cami looked past him to the fountain, with her arm linked through her sister's. "I have to at least try."

"Maybe there's nothing to find."

"Maybe there's not."

"It could have been just an accident, like the police said it was."

"It might be."

He looked down at her and met her gaze with concern in his eyes. "Are you going to be able to live with that? Are you going to be able to let it go?"

She shrugged and gave him half a smile. "I'll have to, won't I?"

He pulled her up off the steps, wrapped his arms around her, hugging her tight, and placed his chin on top of her head. "Yes, you will."

CHAPTER 9

Cami searched the drawers in the kitchen but already knew they weren't there, since she had just cleaned them out yesterday. She searched the pantry, the mudroom, and the large hallway closet. Walking down the hall, she tried to think like her father. *Where would he put keys for safekeeping? The study. His desk. Why hadn't she thought of that before?*

She opened the heavy, wooden double doors and stepped into his domain. Everything was the same: the massive wooden desk, the old swivel chair, and the large fireplace that ran the length of the back wall.

Pulling back the leather chair, she sat for a moment and took it all in. Oh, how she missed coming in here, finding him buried in papers or a book, asking him to push her on the swing or to take a walk through the orchard with her. She even missed standing here begging for the car keys while Charlotte did the same. Fighting over them like two cats.

Her heart ached at the loss of her sister as she thought of all the times they squabbled over petty things. Why had they fought? Why hadn't one of them just relented and let the other take the car?

Because sister's fight.

The words came so clearly into her mind she could almost swear they were spoken out loud. Cami glanced around but didn't see anyone or anything. Reaching, she slid the center drawer of the desk open and found a ring of keys. She picked them up and turned them over in her hand. The skeleton key was there with the others.

Pushing in the drawer, she left the room, ascended the stairs, and went straight to Charlotte's room. The reality of what she was about to do sat heavily on her shoulders. Even though they had been twins and inseparable until they were teenagers, neither entered the other's room without first asking, a rule her mother strictly enforced.

Her hand shook slightly as she inserted the key and turned the lock. The door swung in. Cami stood in the doorway, afraid to go in, and slowly scanned the room. Unlike the rest of the house where dust had covered everything, here there was an absence of dust. Charlotte's white bedspread and plush white rug looked as if someone had just made the bed and vacuumed. *That's so bizarre*, she thought. *How could that be? Had the room just been sealed so tightly that air hadn't been able to circulate?* Cami couldn't explain it.

Before she could change her mind, Cami lifted her foot and stepped across the threshold, and like breaking a barrier, the atmosphere shimmered around her. She crossed and went to Charlotte's bureau, her white robe draped over the upholstered chair, waiting for her to slip it on. Cami's hand traced over her sister's things: her jewelry box, hairbrush, makeup, and fingernail polish. She stopped when her hand landed on a glass bottle of perfume. White Rose, Charlotte's signature fragrance.

At the center of the bureau was a picture of the two of them on their seventeenth birthday, only weeks before her death. Picking it up, she examined it and wondered if Charlotte had any idea that her days were numbered.

Cami placed the picture frame back on the dresser. Careful to put it exactly where she had found it. She surveyed the room. Everything was just as Charlotte had left it the night of the bonfire.

The police had asked if they could search Charlotte's room after her death as the investigation was in progress, but her mother wouldn't have it. Mom had much preferred to think of Charlotte's death as a horrible accident. Not once had she let the detective say otherwise. Daddy and Detective Swanson were good friends, but she remembered them arguing more than once. From the day they found Charlotte's body, no one entered her room after Mom closed the door.

Until now.

With a shaky hand, Cami pulled open the top drawer of the bureau to reveal Charlotte's things. The dresser was filled with clothing: camisoles, silk pajamas, jeans, and shirts. Everything was in its place, neatly folded and stacked just so. What Cami had expected she couldn't say, but not this. Not a bedroom that looked like someone might return to at any moment. Suddenly overwhelmed, Cami choked back a sob and ran from the room.

***

Luke walked down the street to Jolt, the little coffee shop, opened the door, and slipped inside. He greeted a few customers as he made his way to the counter.

Leaning on the counter as Tanya walked over, Luke gave a little wave.

"What'll it be, Detective? The usual?" she asked.

He smiled. "Too late in the day for my usual, too much caffeine. How about decaf instead?"

Tanya grabbed a tall to-go cup and poured in decaf, slapped a lid on it, and handed it to him. "That one's on the house because it's so boring, so keep it quiet. I don't want my reputation ruined for serving decaf."

He laughed. "You sure?" Luke asked, reaching for his wallet. "It's the best damn decaf in town, boring or not."

"Why, thank you, but I am. My treat." The door chimed and she glanced over. "Looks like we are both in for a treat." Tanya stuck her arm in the air. "Hey, girl!" she called out to Cami.

Cami came over, stretching over the counter, giving her a hug.

"After all these years, I'm not sure I'll get used to seeing you walk into Jolt."

"Well, you'd better get used to it, I plan on doing it a lot." Noticing Luke, Cami blushed slightly, instantly mad at herself that after ten years he could still make her pulse spike just by looking her way. "Hey, Luke," she managed to say.

"Hello, Cami."

Tanya smiled brightly at Cami. "What can I get ya? Name it, it's on the house as a welcome back treat."

"You don't have to do that," Cami protested.

"Who is in charge here? I can and I will. Now order." She held up her hand. "Wait, let me guess. You want something cherry flavored. How about my specialty and named just for you, a cherry blossom refresher?"

"Sold. What's in it?"

"Passion tea mixed with lemonade on ice with a double pump of cherry sweetener."

"That sounds wonderful."

"Give me a minute. And whatever you do, don't ask Luke what he's drinking."

As soon as Tanya turned her back, Cami asked conspiratorially, "What do you have?"

Luke motioned her in close. She leaned in and he whispered: "Black coffee, decaf."

Cami stifled a laugh.

"Apparently, it's too boring for Jolt so Tanya doesn't want anyone to know."

"Your secret's safe with me."

Tanya placed the drink in front of her. "Take a sip. Let me know what you think."

"Mmmm, pure heaven."

The door chimed again.

"Looks like after-school activities are done. Here comes a wave of teenagers. Wish I could talk."

"I have some errands to run, anyway. Thanks for the drink. Real quick. What are you doing tonight?"

"Nothing. Why?"

"Do you want to stop by after work, maybe have dinner?"

"Sounds great. I need a girl's night. I'll bring takeout. I've seen your fridge," she called as she moved down the counter. "Later, Luke."

They both walked to the door.

"Which way are you headed?" Luke asked.

"This way," she pointed.

"Me too. Mind if I walk with you?"

"Not at all."

"What brings you in besides Tanya and Jolt?" he asked as they strolled down the street together passing the florist and the local drugstore.

"Well, I need groceries if that wasn't just made obvious, but I actually came in to see Detective Swanson," Cami said, taking a sip of her refresher.

"Really?"

"Yes," she shrugged, not sure how to explain. "He's kept in contact with me off and on over the years, and I wanted to check in with him and say hello."

"You don't have to explain it to me, but can I ask, when was the last time you spoke to him?"

"It's been almost a year now. Why?"

"So maybe you haven't heard?"

"I haven't heard a lot of things," Cami laughed self-consciously. "Which may be surprising since I have spoken to Tanya almost every week for the past ten years. She's pretty selective on what she tells me."

"Are we talking about Tanya King, your best friend?"

"The one and only."

"Well, that's a surprise. Why is that?"

Cami twisted the cup in her hands nervously. "She's trying to protect me." Pursing her lips together she inwardly scolded herself. She'd never really admitted that to anyone before, but for some reason it just slipped from her mouth, and to Luke of all people.

"From what?"

Shoot. Now she was going to have to explain. She swallowed hard, pushing down nerves. "From myself."

They moved to the side to let a boy go by on a bike.

Great. Now he's going to think I'm fragile or worse. "Let me explain that."

"I'm listening."

"At first when I moved to New York Tanya tried to keep me up to date on the local gossip. What everyone was doing, who was dating who, where so-and-so went to college," she glanced at him. "I'm sure you get the idea."

Luke smirked, and nodded slightly. "I do. It's the way of the world especially in a small town, nothing to be ashamed of. We all do it." He tucked his left hand in the front pocket of his dress pants, sipped his coffee and asked, "So what changed?"

Cami adjusted her purse strap as she walked, stalling. "It just hurt too much. After Charlotte's death and the move to New York, I was very depressed. I longed to come back. Wanted it more than anything, but my mom wouldn't hear of it. I lived for news from back home, pumped Tanya for information, gossip, on anything and everyone. But after I talked to her, I would become even more depressed. I was missing out on so much: Cherry Hollow, you guys, this town, everything. My therapist advised me to stop asking, stop gossiping and only concentrate on moving forward. New things: people I met in New York, college, my classes, and new friends I made. It worked, I got better, moved on." Or almost, Cami thought. Suddenly Cami paused and sucked in a breath. "I'm rambling." She blushed, "I'm sorry."

"Don't be."

"So back to your original question, no, I haven't heard about Detective Swanson. Tell me, please."

This time Luke hesitated. "He had a massive heart attack about six months ago."

Cami stopped in the middle of the sidewalk, just outside the police station. "Oh no! That's terrible. I'm so sorry to hear that. Is he alright now?"

"He's better, but needs to slow down. He retired last week."

She nodded, understanding. "Who took over for him?"

"Why don't you come in and I'll introduce you to him," he said coyly.

"Are you a police officer?"

"I am." Pulling the door open, he indicated for her to go first. "Please, come in."

Suddenly uncomfortable, Cami took a step back. "I think I'll pass."

"You sure?"

"Yes. I just wanted to say hello to Detective Swanson. I'll meet the new detective some other time. Thanks, Luke." She turned on her heel and hurried back down the street to her SUV, leaving Luke holding the door.

CHAPTER 10

What was he going to do? After ten fuckin' years, Cami Parker was back, and in the one place that could lead to his ultimate demise.

Why now? Just when he'd felt safe, things were going his way, and the Parkers were only a distant memory. After all this time, he had pushed what he had done to the recess of his mind, forgotten and buried like Charlotte's dead body.

Darkness had descended as he crept closer. He stayed hidden and surveyed the big house that looked like a stone fortress in the dark. It held the night and everything that prowled around it at bay. The house was lit from within. The warm, yellow light was in such contrast to the ebony shadows, tempting him to peer in.

Without warning, the front lights came on and the door opened. Out stepped two women. Their voices carried in a sing-song way that a woman's does when they've been laughing and having a good time. He inched forward, desperate to catch even a snippet of conversation.

Both heads turned as a twig snapped under his shoe. The sound carried easily through the trees. He cursed himself and pressed back into the shadows.

A minute passed. Adrenaline pumped through him as raw fear. *Did they see him, or was he just another mysterious sound in the dark?*

He relaxed as they shrugged off the sound. They said their goodbyes. Tanya gave Cami a quick hug, went to her car, and climbed in. He shrank back even farther as the car rounded the fountain and the high beams swept through the trees. Cami stood a moment longer, watching the taillights disappear down the drive, glanced his way, then went inside.

He breathed a sigh of relief as he watched the lights wink out, one by one, all over the house as she made her way through. He tried to picture her progress as she closed up for the night. *Would she lock every door? Check every window?*

Slinking closer, he peered in a front window. It was dark, but the door to the room was open and he could see through to the grand foyer. *Did she know he was just outside? Did she suspect anything? How could she?* Yet he wondered, and that wasn't the only thing.

Did she suspect that her twin's death wasn't an accident like it was ruled all those years ago? There had always been rumors that Charlotte and Cami knew what each other was thinking, or how they felt. That they could sense each other's emotions and knew their very thoughts. *Had she seen him that night in her mind? Surely not, or he wouldn't be here now.*

The bigger question that absolutely terrified him: was it possible for her to remember? Being back in the house, in these woods with millions of memories around, could they trigger something that was buried deep in the recesses of her mind? For fuck's sake, he hoped not. That thought alone made him break out into a cold sweat. It would be the end of him.

He couldn't let that happen. He'd built a life, a reputation, come too far, and it had been too long to let the death of Charlotte Parker take him down now. The past would stay buried. It had to. He'd make damn sure of it.

Through the window he watched Cami ascend the stairs. Moments later, the light went out in the foyer. With the house dark, he slunk back into the shadows, determined to do whatever it took to keep the death of Charlotte Parker dead and buried.

***

Cami sat on the edge of the bed and watched her sister paint her toenails, her signature pearl white that glistened in the soft lamplight.

"It took you long enough to come back," she said without looking at her. "I've missed you."

"I've missed you, too. And I'm sorry. I meant to come sooner, only Mom wouldn't let me," Cami whispered.

Charlotte tsked. "Whenever did you let Mom decide what you can or can't do?"

"I always did. It was you that stood up to her," Cami answered. "You were the defiant one, not me. You always tested the limits, not me."

Charlotte's blonde hair hung loose down her back and shone like gold in the warm light. Cami's heart wrenched as her twin sister's seventeen-year-old face, frozen in time, smiled back at her.

"That's right, I did. You, Camilla Hope Parker, were timid and shy, always following the rules, doing exactly what you were told. I was wild and free. You were always cautious. Maybe if I had been more like you, I wouldn't be dead. Maybe if I'd listened..." Her voice trailed off. She looked back down at her toes and concentrated. "Did you come back to find the truth?"

Cami inched closer to her sister on the bed. Her heart hurt so much. She wanted so desperately to reach out and touch her sister, to hold her tight, but was afraid that if she reached out, she would disappear. "I did. Whatever that is."

"Good."

"Can you tell me? Do you know what happened to you that night?"

"I'm not sure. Everything is so...confusing."

Charlotte's image shimmered in front of Cami.

"What's happening?"

"I don't know," Charlotte answered. "But there's something in the dark."

"What do you mean?"

Charlotte's image became translucent, then solidified. "In the woods. Someone is watching. They don't want you to find the truth, but Cami," Charlotte pleaded. "You have to."

"I'll try," Cami promised.

"Be careful," Charlotte said. She got up from the bed and went to her bureau. She twisted the top on the polish, looked at her sister, and reached out to set the polish down. "In the woods, in the dark, the shadow waits."

Charlotte let go of the polish and the glass shattered as it fell to the hardwood floor.

Jolted awake by the sound of glass breaking, Cami sat up, her pulse skipping, disoriented in the dark, the smell of fingernail polish lingering in the air. It took her a minute to realize she was in her own bed, in her parents' old room, not Charlotte's. It had all been nothing but a dream.

The dredges of sleep still clung to her like a spider web when she walked through it. Charlotte's warning echoed in her mind, "In the woods, in the dark, the shadow waits."

The sound of glass had been so real. She shuddered. Maybe she should check the house.

Reaching out for the bedside lamp, her hand hesitated. Thinking better of it, she left the lamp off, grabbed her cell phone instead, and tiptoed out into the hall.

Moonlight filtered in through the wide windows, casting long gray swatches of pale light across the expanse of the upper hall. Every door off the hallway was open except Charlotte's. She turned to go in that direction but stopped when she felt a draft on her bare legs coming from the opposite end. She inched down the hall and peered into the first room. Nothing.

She could feel the draft more intensely, and the soft sound of fabric fluttering caught her attention. She peeked into her childhood bedroom.

Be careful.

The floor sparkled as moonlight shimmered over glass. Cami gasped. The window was shattered. Without thinking, she ran to the window and peered out into the darkness. A silhouette of a person stood just at the edge of the trees. Cami's blood ran cold as she lifted her cell and dialed 9-1-1.

CHAPTER 11

The fall air flowed through the Ranger as Luke drove the back roads toward Cherry Hollow. It was chilly, but he didn't mind. The crisp air invigorated him. To say he was nervous was an understatement. But he was. He pulled into the lane, saw the house that haunted his dreams. The good ones and the bad. The place where his life had changed. That night almost ten years ago, he had fallen further for a girl who he had been interested in for a while, only to have her taken from him. Trying hard to avoid the heartbreak, and the cold hard truth that Cami was gone, he refocused and looked toward his future. To a path, to a career, that would hopefully lead to helping someone else so that this never happened to them, or if he couldn't prevent it, at least give them closure. Helping others and solving crimes had been what he was meant to do. But unfortunately, it took that long ago night to put the wheels in motion.

Luke pulled past the construction truck and parked next to the fountain. Greeting the men up on the scaffolding, he made his way to the front door with a cup carrier from Jolt in hand, rang the doorbell, and waited.

Cami answered the door almost immediately. "Luke? Good morning," she said, opening the door wide. "What a nice surprise."

His stomach took a dip. He stood mute for a split second, his carefully rehearsed greeting all but forgotten at the simple sight of her. She looked fresh in the morning light despite the late night he knew she had. Her light brown hair was twisted up into a messy bun, and soft tendrils escaped and framed her face, setting off those hazel eyes. She was dressed simply in jeans and a pale green button-down shirt with the sleeves rolled up a quarter of the way. Finding his voice, he managed to say, "It's a beautiful day."

"It certainly is. What might you have there?" she asked, noticing the brown cardboard carrier with cups.

He smiled. "Thought maybe you might need a little caffeine after your late night. So I swung by Jolt on the way."

"You're a lifesaver," she said, ushering him in. "Please, come in." She closed the door behind him and led the way to the kitchen.

Twisting out the cup, he handed it to her. "A caramel macchiato Frappuccino for you, courtesy of Tanya. She said that's your favorite."

"Mmmm, it is. Thank you." Cami took a sip and savored it. "And what do you have? More decaf?"

"Not quite. A red eye."

She raised her eyebrow at him over her cup.

"Black coffee with a shot of espresso."

"Talk about a jolt."

He laughed. "It'll start your heart, if not your day."

"I guess so. Again, thank you." She raised the cup in a kind of toast. "I have to say, I'm surprised to see you."

"I thought you might be. Can we have a seat and let me explain?" Luke indicated the kitchen table.

"Of course."

"Heard about your little incident last night, so I thought I would come out and check on you."

"How did you know? I haven't told anyone." She hesitated, clearly putting it together. "Wait. I forgot, you're a police officer. Still trying to wrap my head around that fact."

"Hmmm, I'm not sure if I should be offended or not," Luke said with a laugh.

"No offense meant by that. It's just that I still picture you as the high school quarterback, not a police officer."

"I guess I'll let you off the hook. As far as being a police officer, I was, until a week ago."

"Oh?" she said, taking a sip of her frap.

Luke shifted in his seat. "I'm the new detective for the department." He watched her, waiting for a reaction, but her face remained neutral behind her coffee cup.

"So, you took Detective Swanson's place?"

"Yes."

"You forgot to mention that yesterday."

"Yes, I know, I'm sorry. I was trying to be clever, but clearly, I wasn't."

She said nothing.

He cleared his throat. "Do you want to tell me what happened last night? Officer Cannon gave me most of the details this morning, but he didn't have the whole report written when I left."

Cami set her Frappuccino down on the table. "There's not much to say, really. I was sleeping and heard something shatter. I got up to investigate and found the window in my old bedroom destroyed, glass everywhere. I ran to the window and saw someone standing at the edge of the woods. Right at the tree line." Cami shivered outwardly. "I dialed 9-1-1 immediately."

"How long did the person stand there after you called?"

"Not long. By the time I gave the dispatcher my name and address, they had slipped into the shadows. Leaving me wondering if I'd seen anyone at all."

"Do you think they saw you?"

"I can't be sure. I didn't turn on any lights, so it was as dark inside as it was out."

He changed the direction of the conversation. "I saw the guys are here replacing the window already this morning."

She nodded and ran a finger around the rim of her cup. "Yeah, Bobby called it in for me right away. They showed up bright and early to replace it."

"That's good. Do you mind if I look at the room?"

"Not at all." She stood. "Bobby said the grass was trampled down near the window outside the study, like someone stood there peering in." She pointed in the study's direction as she led him to the stairs.

"I'll check that out before I leave."

They ascended the grand staircase that swept up through the foyer with a curve of dark wood and wrought iron.

Running his hand along the smooth banister, he noticed the wainscotting, moldings, and the detail in the woodwork. Crown molding ran seamlessly along the ceiling, and cherry blossoms were engraved into the rich wood every few feet, giving the space a rich ornate feel. The sweep of stairs commanded attention in the grand space. There was a stained-glass window at the top of the landing depicting a cherry tree in full bloom. Not usually a romantic, he couldn't help but notice the light danced cheerfully through it. A kaleidoscope of colors cast the space in an enchanting glow, which made him think of magic and castles.

"This place is gorgeous, Cami. I've forgotten what it looked like in here." Without thinking, he said, "It's a place where you'd expect fairy tales to come true."

"A lot of fairy tales have a tragic ending," she added softly, giving him a ghost of a sad smile. "But I agree."

At the top, he caught her arm. "Oh, hey Cami, I'm sorry. I wasn't thinking."

"It's not your fault, Luke. This place was magical. Correction, it is magical, or at the very least could be again. That's why I came back. I couldn't resist the pull and the charm of this place." She looked down at his hand on her arm. "My room is this way."

Luke let her go and they walked down the corridor in silence. She stopped just outside the open door.

Glass sparkled in the sunlight, sprinkled all over the floor.

"Be careful. I haven't cleaned up yet."

His shoes crunched on pieces of glass as he walked

across the expanse of the room to the gaping hole where the window had been. The men were on the ground now, over by the truck, getting out the replacement window. Luke stood at the opening and scanned the front yard.

"Can you show me where you saw someone?"

Cami came up beside him and stood. "There," she pointed. "Right between those two dogwood trees."

He followed her finger with his eyes. "Did you see more than one person?"

"No."

"After they disappeared, did you hear a car start or see any taillights, like a car pulling away?"

"No, nothing."

"I saw the golf ball that was thrown. Cannon had it bagged for evidence," he said, thinking out loud. "It was nothing special. Could have easily been purchased at any sporting goods store." Several thoughts ran through his mind as he realized he couldn't see the road because the foliage was too dense. Maybe it was just some teenagers out for a little fun. "As far as most people know, the house is empty or abandoned and has been for almost ten years now." He sipped his coffee. "Have you had any other vandalism over the years?"

"I'm pretty sure we've had a few incidents. Mr. Bontrager down the road would be better to answer that. He's been watching the place for us."

"I'll check with him. This might be as simple as some teenagers out on a dare, not realizing anyone had moved back."

"That's possible. An empty house is a very tempting target."

Shifting mentally, Luke turned around and examined the room. "You said this was your bedroom. But it's empty. Where are you sleeping?"

"This was my room growing up. I'm staying down the hall in the main bedroom."

He nodded. "I'll check by the study before I leave and see if they overlooked anything last night. Although I highly doubt it, Officer Cannon is as good as they come."

"I know. It impressed me when he showed up last night. Who knew Bobby would turn out so great?" Cami said with a laugh.

Luke smiled. "Hard to believe any of us turned out halfway respectable." He turned from the window. "Can I help you clean this up?"

"No, it's fine, really. I'm going to wait until they're done installing the window and then get to it."

"Good enough." They walked out into the hall. Curiosity got the better of him and he asked, "Which room was Charlotte's?"

"She was on the other side of the house, in the west wing."

Luke nodded. "Is it hard being back?"

Cami shrugged. "It is, and it isn't. If that makes any sense?"

The corners of his mouth turned up. "It does." He followed her down the corridor, peering into the other rooms as they went. Every room still had sheets covering furniture except the one in the center of the house, which he assumed was Cami's now.

"I've missed this place, the house, the woods, and my friends. It's the only place I really have ever felt at home. I thought maybe being away for ten years would have changed that."

"But it didn't?" Luke asked.

She shook her head. "No, it didn't. Can I ask?" She hesitated. "Did Detective Swanson ever talk to you about Charlotte's case?"

He noticed she stopped in front of the only door that was closed. "He did. As a matter of fact, he left me the file."

"Have you read it?"

He met her hazel eyes and held her gaze. "I've glanced through it." For some reason, he wasn't prepared to tell her he had read every word the file contained more than once.

"Did you know my mom never let the police or Detective Swanson in to see Charlotte's room?"

"Yes, I'm aware of that."

Cami put her hand on the knob and hesitated. "This is her room. Do you want to see it?"

He almost couldn't believe what she offered. Detective Swanson had tried for years to get access. "If you want to show me?"

Cami hesitated for a second. "I do." Then twisted the knob, but it wouldn't turn. "Huh?"

"What's the matter?"

"It seems to be stuck."

"Here let me." Luke tried the handle. "It's not stuck, it's locked."

"It can't be. I was in there yesterday and I didn't lock it, just pulled it shut." Slightly flustered, Cami said, "I'll be right back with the key."

She was back in a matter of seconds. Shaking her head. "I swear I didn't lock it."

Luke said nothing, just waited quietly. He noticed her hand trembled as she inserted the skeleton key into the lock.

The door swung open, revealing the room. The contrast of this fully decorated bedroom to the others that were draped with drop cloths and covered in a thick layer of dust was almost shocking.

As if reading his mind, she said quietly, "It looks as if she'll be right back, doesn't it?"

"It does. Looks like you've cleaned in here already."

"But I haven't. This is how I found it."

"How does that happen? There's not a speck of dust."

"I don't have any idea."

Luke itched to go through the room. Investigate every inch, looking for clues, leaving nothing unturned. Instead, he crossed his arms, stood at the threshold and watched Cami hover just outside the doorway.

"We weren't allowed to go into each other's rooms

uninvited. My mom was a stickler on that. Even though we were close, and twins seemingly share everything, she wanted us to have our own space. Our own place that was private."

"Do you know if anyone has been in this room since Charlotte's death?"

"As far as I know, only my mother. My mom came in after finding out. I saw her sitting on the edge of the bed crying."

"Any other time?"

"To get clothes for the funeral."

"What about your father?"

"Not that I'm aware of."

Luke looked at her when her voice hitched, a million questions running through his mind. "I can't even imagine, Cami, what this must be like. I'm sorry."

"Don't be. Most of the time I feel like I'm over it, but every once in a while, the emotions of losing her just swamp me."

"I get it. I really do. My grandfather died a year after we got out of high school. I was devastated. We were exceptionally close. We went fishing all the time together. I still can't drive by a pond or a lake without thinking of him." He turned a slow circle in the room. "Do you smell that? I could swear I smell roses."

"Charlotte always wore a fragrance named White Rose. Actually, there's a bottle on top of her bureau." Cami walked across the room and picked it up. "See."

He crossed to her, accidentally brushing her arm as he reached for it. The bottle was empty, the liquid all but evaporated except for a tiny drop in the corner.

Standing next to Cami, he was all too aware of how good she smelled, but it definitely wasn't the overpowering scent of roses. Hers was sweet and tempting, like a warm, ripe cherry. He looked at her and noticed for the first time that her hazel eyes were more of a moss green, with flecks of gold and brown sprinkled throughout. They were mesmerizing. His gaze dropped to her mouth. For a second, he remembered the hasty kiss in the dark woods all those years ago that had left him aching for more. He cleared his throat and shifted backward, breaking the connection. "Where do you think it's coming from?"

"What?"

"The scent of roses."

"I don't know," she answered, her eyes scanning the room.

The fragrance was completely gone now. He didn't know what to think of it, either. Had they imagined it because they were thinking of Charlotte? Or was it just encased in the room, having been closed up for so long? It was possible it had saturated the room. Her clothes and bedding could have absorbed it while Charlotte was alive and overtime it slowly leached out into the air.

"Luke?"

"Yes," he said, looking at her, trying hard not to reach out and brush a strand of silky hair out of her eyes.

"Can I tell you something without you thinking I'm crazy?"

"Of course." Luke's phone chimed. "Hold that thought." Glancing down, he skimmed the text. "Looks like I'm needed back at the office. What did you want to tell me?"

"Never mind. It's not important. I'll walk you out."

"Could I come back sometime and look through her room? See if there's anything here?"

"Of course, just let me know and we can work something out," she said, walking to the door, followed closely by Luke. Waiting for him to pass through the doorway, she glanced back into the room, then hastily pulled the door shut behind him. Neither one heard the faint sound of the lock being turned as they walked away.

CHAPTER 12

The road curved around a narrow bend just before it came to the edge of town. Cami checked the address and turned onto the next road, stopping in front of a cute Cape Cod. There were several cars parked on the street and in the driveway, so Cami pulled up behind an SUV. Grabbing her freshly made brownies off the front seat, she walked up the short drive. She could hear music pumping out from behind the house so she ventured around to the backyard.

The yard was the size of a postage stamp and framed in with a little white picket fence. Kevin stood at the grill flipping burgers as smoke billowed out. A few guys hung nearby chatting and women hovered around a table arranging food.

Unlatching the gate, she let herself in, hoping to go unnoticed for just a few minutes.

Kevin glanced up as she closed the gate.

"Welcome, Cami!" he shouted over the music. "Come on in!"

Every head turned in her direction. Suddenly, Cami felt like she was right back in high school, awkward and shy. She felt like an outsider even though she knew practically everyone there.

"Cami, over here." Tanya waved. "Hey, girl! Look at you, looking fresh as a cherry blossom in that cute outfit." Tanya gave her a quick hug. "Whatcha got there?" she asked, eyeing the container in Cami's hand.

"The standard. Brownies."

"Good choice. Everyone likes brownies."

Cami shrugged. "Where would you like them?"

"You can put them on the far end of the table with the other desserts," Joselyn said, coming up behind her.

Cami glanced over her shoulder. "Joselyn? Is that you?"

"Of course. Who else, silly." She leaned in and gave her a quick hug.

Cami took her in. Joselyn had cut her hair since the last time she had seen her. Gone was the mousy brown hair, replaced by a flattering cut that angled around her face and hung like a satin curtain, the color of copper. Her soft brown eyes were no longer hidden behind glasses that were too big for her face, and her pale green dress accentuated her curvy figure.

"You look so pretty, Joselyn," Cami said, truly meaning it.

"Thanks." She turned and called over to Kevin. "Are those burgers ready?"

"Coming right up." He flipped the last one onto a serving tray and carted them over, placing them at the far end of the table he called out, "Everybody grab a plate. Time to eat."

Cami stepped back and let the others get in line.

"Hey, Parker. How's it goin'?" Bobby asked, coming up beside her.

"Hi, Bobby."

"Are you alright after last night?"

"I'm fine. Thanks for asking."

"Are you eating?"

She nodded.

"Let's get in line. After you," Bobby indicated for her to go first.

Grabbing a plate, she selected a cheeseburger and some potato salad. "Everything looks great, Kev," Cami said as she made her way down the buffet.

Kevin smiled as he placed a tray of hot dogs in the center of the table. "Good, because I've been slaving over that hot grill for over an hour now."

"An hour? Hell, for that long, I expect to get a steak out of the deal," Bobby joked. "Not a charcoaled lump of beef."

Kevin picked up a juicy burger and plopped it on Bobby's plate. "You'll eat a burger and you'll do it without complaint. Or next time you can have the cookout."

"Touchy, touchy." Aaron popped into the line to grab a beer. "Looks like someone's got their panties in a wad."

"You guys haven't changed at all," Cami laughed.

"Cami," Tanya called. "Get over here. I saved you a seat."

She snagged a soda and made her way to the long table set up at the back of the yard. There were a couple of women Cami didn't recognize sitting across from Tanya.

"Cami, let me introduce you to a couple of friends."

She heard Tanya say their names, but it totally went in one ear and out the other as Cami saw Luke arrive.

"Better late than never, Warner," Bobby called as he sat across from Cami. "The party is already started."

Luke came striding across the yard, confident and a little cocky. He stopped at the table, slapped Bobby on the back, and said, "You know the party doesn't start until I arrive."

"Warner, grab a plate and get something to eat," Kevin said pointing with his spatula at the long table of food.

"Will do," Luke called over his shoulder to Kevin. "Be right back."

Out of the corner of her eye, she watched him make his way down the long table of food, acutely aware that the only place left for him to sit was next to her.

He came striding over and glanced at the spot next to her. "Mind if I sit next to you?"

"Not at all. It's yours." Cami tucked her long hair behind her ear and tried to calm her racing heart as he slid in next to her.

"Look out, you know she's trouble," Bobby said, forking in coleslaw.

"I'm not afraid of a little trouble," Luke responded, giving her a heart-stopping smile.

To say he made her laugh was an understatement, but he did. Sitting next to him, she listened to him banter back and forth with Bobby and Tanya, yell down the table at Brock and Aaron, and compliment Kevin's grilling.

The gang told stories from high school, chiming in, filling in the gaps like old friends do. Cami hung on every word, longing for the years she'd missed with all of them. Some stories she remembered, but a lot she missed.

Losing so much so quickly, her sister, her home, her friends, and the boy she loved, Cami had done what her therapist had suggested, the only thing she could to survive: she locked them all away in a part of her heart she thought she'd never get back, vowing to keep them safely tucked away and avoid the hurt. But sitting here amongst old friends, an ache in her heart for the past and what she lost was slowly starting to subside. She rode the wave of the old and familiar, new and exciting, and dared to dream of what she might salvage from the years of absences.

She let her guard down and simply enjoyed the night. Listening to Luke talk to her and the others, she told him of the plans she had for Cherry Hollow and her new business.

The sky darkened as night fell. Kevin turned the music down so the neighbors wouldn't complain and then the inevitable happened. The conversation turned to Charlotte and the last party they had.

"Do you remember when we played hide-and-seek at Cherry Hollow?"

Cami stiffened suddenly. "We played hide-and-seek a lot. During the day and at night."

"Wasn't that Charlotte's favorite game to play?" Aaron asked, taking a sip of his beer. His eyes were glazing over. He slid down the table, getting closer to Cami.

"Yes, it was," Cami answered softly.

A hush fell over the group.

Tanya came to Cami's rescue. "Remember when we had the treasure hunts at your house? Those were the best."

Joselyn chimed in, "Your mom always had the best clues."

Aaron crinkled his can and chucked it at the trash can. Out of nowhere, he said, "Do you know I had nightmares for weeks after your last bonfire?" He snagged Kevin's beer right out of his hand and took a long pull, draining it.

He slammed it onto the table and Cami jumped.

"I kept dreaming I was lost in the woods and Charlotte was chasing me, covered in blood."

"Aaron, I think you've had a few too many," Kevin said.

"Too many? I haven't even started." He got up and walked over to the cooler, fishing out another.

Bobby stood. "Take it easy, Aaron."

"Did you know my mom kept me from going out for over a month after your sister died?"

Luke put his hand on Cami's arm. "That's enough, Aaron. You need to stop."

"I think she needs to know."

"What do I need to know?" Cami asked, tensing.

"That we were all dragged in for questioning. That we were all suspects in your sister's . . ." He put his hands up and made air quotes with his fingers: "'Accident.' The thing I don't get is, if it really was an accident, why were we all questioned?"

"I'm sorry, Aaron. I didn't know."

"It was a long time ago, Aaron. Let it go. Cami had nothing to do with it," Luke said, coming to her defense.

Aaron cracked the cold can he was holding and took a big swallow. He swayed a little as he stood at the end of the table. "What do you mean, she had nothing to do with it? It's because of what she saw that had us all being questioned. Gibson got the worst of it. Tell her, Brock."

Sick to her stomach and in shock, Cami turned to Brock. "Is that true?"

Brock shrugged his shoulders and gave her a weary smile.

"He's just too nice to say anything."

"And you've had way too much to drink." Luke stood and took Aaron by the arm, leading him away.

"I'm not finished," Aaron argued, yanking himself free. "How in the hell do you think you're going to make that place into a venue that someone's going to want to have a wedding at when everyone in the fuckin' county knows your sister died there?"

"It was an accident," Cami said, not convinced herself, shrinking back from Aaron, barely able to reply.

"Was it?"

He leaned in close, and Cami could smell the beer on his breath.

"It's not like your sister was nice. Popular, sure, but nice?" He laughed. "She was the perfect mean girl. Ask anyone here. I bet they would all agree with me."

"Don't you dare speak poorly of my sister. She wasn't a saint. None of us are but she was still my sister."

"That's enough. You're done," Luke said, easing in between them and forcing him back.

Bobby stood on the other side of Aaron, taking his arm and pulling him away from Cami. "It's time for you to go home."

"I don't wanna go," Aaron said, slurring his words slightly.

"You're embarrassing yourself. Move." Both Luke and Bobby escorted Aaron away.

"Your s-sister was a b-bitch," he called over his shoulder. "Plain and simple."

"Enough!" Luke barked and yanked Aaron out of the yard.

Cami looked at the others in disbelief. Brock avoided eye contact with her, and her heart dropped. "Oh, Brock," she whispered.

Tanya reached for Cami's hand, Kevin draped his arm protectively around her, and Joselyn stood nearby, shaking her head in disgust.

Tears welled in Cami's eyes. "I'm so sorry. I didn't know how hard it was for all of you." She stood quickly. "I think I should go. Kevin, I'm sorry I ruined your party."

"Cami, wait. You didn't," he protested.

"Let her go. Can't you see she's upset?" Joselyn said, coming to her rescue. "Let me get your container."

"Just keep it. I'll get it some other time." Cami turned to go, but Kevin engulfed her in a hug.

"I'm so sorry, Cami. I didn't know he felt that way."

"It's fine. Really. He's drunk."

"Still, he had no right to say those things."

"But he's right. Why were you questioned so thoroughly if it was an accident?" She pulled back, trying to keep the tears from coming. "I need to go." She turned and Joselyn handed her the plastic container that held what was left of her brownies. Cami reached for it hastily when the rock on Joselyn's hand caught her eye. "Joselyn, are you engaged?" Cami asked in surprise.

"Yes, didn't Kevin tell you?"

"I hadn't had the chance."

"Of course not. It's always been about the Parker Twins. Looks like nothing's changed."

"That was way out of line, Josie."

Hurt, Cami looked from one to the other. Swallowing a lump, she managed to say, "Congratulations. I'm happy for both of you." Then abruptly turned on her heel and left.

CHAPTER 13

Cami sat on the edge of her bed, trying to calm her racing heart. Her stomach was twisted in knots, making her feel queasy. How could she have been so stupid to think she could come back after ten years and everything would be alright? That everything would be the same. It couldn't. It shouldn't. Too much had changed. *They* had changed, and just as importantly, *she* had changed. She had, hadn't she? Sitting with them she was torn between who she used to be and who she'd believed she'd become.

She didn't realize what had transpired with the others while her family dealt with the aftermath of Charlotte's death, the funeral, and the inevitable move. Why would she? Her mother had protected her from the gossip, shut her away from prying eyes, and ultimately isolated her from her friends.

Had they really all been treated like suspects? Had the police and Detective Swanson interrogated them? That must have taken days because there had been like what, fifty or more kids at the party. Were they questioned in groups or one at a time? Cami hadn't given such things any thought, but now questions of what happened that night and the days to follow tumbled through her mind. And what had Aaron meant when he said it was all because of her?

It had hurt them, all of them. That much was obvious. More than she ever realized before. But maybe she could make it up to her friends. Or at least some of them. How to go about it was the real question? What could she do? She'd have to think about it.

She could start with Brock. No matter what he charged, she would go with the Green Zone, giving him and Aaron the business. It was the right thing to do. If…if he wanted to take the job. What if he didn't? What if Aaron refused to work at her house? Her gut wrenched. She'd cross that bridge if it came.

And what if Aaron was right? What if no one in the area wanted to have a wedding or a party here because of Charlotte's death? Her heart sank even further.

What a shame it would be if this magical place she loved so much saw no joy again. No, she wouldn't let that happen. She'd make Cherry Hollow the most spectacular place to have events. People would come from hundreds of miles around to have their special day here. She'd spend every dime in her savings to make it so.

"I know," she said out loud. "I'll throw Kevin and Joselyn an engagement party. Right here at the hollow." She wouldn't charge them; she wouldn't dream of it. She'd just offer the space and invite anyone they wanted, making it a grand affair.

Cami would try to use as many local contractors and local businesses for anything she needed. From florists to bakeries, DJs and bands, including bed-and-breakfast and hotels, she would make an all-inclusive package that showcased the best of the locals.

Her stomach was still in knots, but it satisfied her that she had a plan, a way to move forward. Cami changed for bed. She slipped on a cotton camisole and matching comfy shorts. Combing through her long hair, she pulled it into a loose ponytail, brushed her teeth, washed her face, and turned out the bathroom light.

Opening the window next to the bed, the breeze drifted in. Enjoying the cool, fresh night air, she crawled under the covers and switched off the lamp. Cami lay in the darkness and listened to the house settle around her, breathing in the fresh scent of pine and calming her nerves.

"They will know Cherry Hollow for grand celebrations, not Charlotte Parker's death," she whispered into the darkness.

Sometimes it was hard even for her to remember past the tragedy.

Laying down on the bed she flipped over her pillow, punching it twice. Breathing deeply, she calmed her mind and willed the stress of the evening to go away. There was nothing she could do about it anymore at this hour. As she lay there in the dark, her mind wandered to Charlotte, trying desperately to remember how it had been while she was alive. Slowly it came back to her. The long hours spent in the drawing room playing games or putting together puzzles, racing up the stairs to the attic to play hide-and-seek. Taking turns driving to school, hanging out with friends after. Cami's eyes became heavy and soon she drifted off.

Cami stood at her locker, as Tanya waited patiently for her to get her books.

"I can't wait for the football game tonight. The theme for the student section is White Out. I have those cute white jeans I bought last week I'm going to wear," Tanya said. "How about you?"

"I have that white sweater but Charlotte will want to borrow it I'm sure. So I could wear my white Penn State hoodie with a little white tank under it," Cami said, tucking her books in her locker. Hearing laughter she turned in time to see Brock lean over and kiss Charlotte before he slipped into Biology.

Charlotte caught her eye and smiled mischievously. Coming toward them she called out, "Ready for lunch, girls?"

"Almost, just waiting on Joselyn and Kevin."

"Never fear the gangs mostly all here," Kevin bellowed down the hall approaching fast. "I'm starving!"

"When aren't you?" Tanya asked.

"Always." Kevin leaned on the locker door and glanced at Charlotte as she craned her neck to watch Bobby walk by. "Break anybody's heart today?"

Charlotte tossed her hair and gave Kevin a wink. "Wouldn't you like to know."

Cami reached for her tote.

"All clear here?" Kevin asked, peering down at Cami.

"Yep," she said, shaking her lunch at him. Charlotte linked her arm through Cami's.

"Are you going to let me wear your white sweater to the game tonight?" Charlotte asked.

Cami stifled a laugh. "It'll cost you."

"Move it or lose it, girls." Kevin coaxes. "My stomach is growling." He slammed the locker door.

Cami sat up with a jolt, disoriented. The image was so real, the sound so loud. And the feel of her sister's arm linked with hers still lingered. Cami actually reached out, felt the soft comforter on the bed, over her legs, to remember she was home in bed not in the hallway at school. The dream made her long for high school and her sister.

She wished she had her yearbooks so she could look back through them and remember, but she knew hers were still in her room at her parents' house in New York. *I wonder what happened to Charlotte's yearbooks? I wonder if they're still in her room.*

Suddenly curious, she threw back the covers and strode down the dark hall. She reached for the doorknob of Charlotte's room and found it locked. "You've got to be kidding me. I know I didn't lock this door." Something brushed against her ever so softly in the darkness and Cami swore she heard a half laugh. Her mind instantly filled with Charlotte. Without thinking, she pounded on the door with her fist. "You know I have a key. You can't keep me out."

She walked back down the hall in a huff, pulled open her nightstand drawer, grabbed the skeleton key, and went back to Charlotte's room. Her footsteps faltered. Even in the dark, Cami could see the door stood wide open.

"Charlotte?" Cami questioned, but her voice rang out in the empty house, and goosebumps ran up her arms. How had the door opened? Before she could overthink it, she crossed into Charlotte's room and flipped on the light switch which turned on the lamps. She stood for a moment, taking it all in.

"If I were Charlotte, where would I keep my yearbooks?"

Her eyes scanned the room. She crossed to the nightstand and the open shelf. Squatting down, Cami reached for a stack of magazines. Under them, she easily found the yearbooks.

She set the small stack beside her and opened the first one. Sitting on the edge of the bed, she started at the beginning. She quickly scanned the faces of the faculty, then the seniors. Next were the juniors. She laughed at their individual pictures, especially Kevin's, as he had on a bow tie and a dorky smile. Then there were Brock and Luke. Without thinking, her finger traced an invisible heart around Luke's face. Trailing fingers ran over Joselyn, Tanya, and her sister's photos. They were all so young. "My, how time has flown." She flipped quickly through the sophomores and freshman. Took her time looking through the clubs, chorus, and the band. Paused when a picture of Charlotte in her cheerleading outfit caught her eye.

She turned to the drama club and saw her sister as a lead in Grease. She had looked the part of Sandy, but the director had cast her as Rizzo. *The perfect mean girl.* Aaron's words slipped through her mind.

She quickly flipped the page and laughed at herself when she came across the volleyball team. There were some great shots of her and Tanya in action.

Football was next. And there he was, front and center. Luke Warner, the high school quarterback. Thinking back to that quick kiss, she had dared to dream for a brief shining moment that maybe it was the start of something, but ten years later, there was still only that one stolen kiss.

She sighed and turned the page. Suddenly tired, she flipped through the rest of the book quickly, scanning, when prom pictures caught her eye.

She stopped and looked through them. Charlotte had gone with Brock, and she with Kevin, as friends. The theme was "A Night Under the Stars." There was a picture of her and Charlotte with their arms linked through each other in front of a black backdrop that glittered with silver stars and twinkling lights. Charlotte had on a long white flowing gown looking like she had just stepped off a cover of a magazine, while Cami had on a pale sage green, short and sassy dress. Right underneath the photo in red ink were the words *I love you*. Cami smiled, picturing Brock writing it.

Without warning, the lights went out. A chill ran across her bare skin and the room filled with the faint scent of roses. "Charlotte?" Cami whispered into the darkness, but there was no answer. She closed the book and lay it on the bed beside her. She crossed to the light switch and flicked it up and down. But the darkness remained.

"This isn't funny, Charlotte. Turn the lights back on." There was no response. Of course there wasn't. This is crazy. Talking to her dead sister like she was in the room. Cami went out into the corridor to turn on the hall lights, but still nothing happened. Must have blown a fuse. The electrical box is in the basement. Cami swallowed hard, thinking of the steep steps leading down to the dirt floor basement. It was a place she had avoided at all costs as a child, even in the middle of the day, filled with unexplainable noises, shadows, and spiders. She wasn't about to go down there now and fumble around in the dark. Surely it can wait until morning.

On edge, a chill raced across her arms and a shiver had her turning a quick circle to make sure she was alone. The house was quiet and locked tight for the night, she reminded herself. Just because the electricity was out shouldn't be a reason to be scared. And yet it was.

***

His bare feet were perched on the corner of his desk as he reclined in his chair, staring at the file he had brought home from work. The windows were open and a crisp breeze blew in. Luke sipped a beer, letting the tangy taste linger on his tongue despite the late hour, and listened to the soothing sounds of the crickets chirping, unable to sleep with the events of the evening running through his head.

Luke had been looking forward to the barbeque, and imagine his surprise when he walked in and saw Cami sitting there. It was a shock to his system every time he accidentally ran into her and prayed it wasn't obvious.

He had really enjoyed sitting next to her and getting to know her all over again. It made him wonder what it would have been like if she had never left. Would that one kiss have turned into something more? He was truly disappointed they had never had the chance to find out.

And what was with Aaron? Luke had never seen him react like that to anyone or anything before. Aaron was usually even keeled and easygoing, but something had set him off tonight.

Bobby had taken Aaron home and safely tucked him in for the night, but having Aaron react that way really made Luke stop and think about just how much Charlotte Parker's death affected all of them, and in completely different ways.

He and Bobby were both being recruited heavily during their senior year to play football. That was the sum of his plans: go to Penn State undeclared and play football. The night Charlotte Parker died changed everything.

His life was altered, his course changed. The need, the pull to be in law enforcement, took hold and wouldn't let go. The desperate need to help people and to keep them safe was something he couldn't articulate, but Bobby understood and felt the same way.

Then there was Brock Gibson. Brock had been affected the most by losing Charlotte. It had devastated him. His grades had slipped, which affected his eligibility to play football. He lost his scholarship and opted for a community college instead. Despite his shaky beginnings, it had turned out for the best. He transferred to a four-year college and majored in business. After graduation, he started his own landscaping company about the same time Aaron had returned home from the army. They joined forces, and that was the start of the Green Zone.

Only one of the guys out of their tight knit group had stayed the course and seen his original plans through. Kevin went to college and majored in financial planning, landed himself a job at the bank, and worked his way up quickly. In his position, Kevin had helped almost everyone in town to buy a car or a house, start a business, or helped keep them afloat through the hard times. Had Luke been asked ten years ago who would be the most successful man in town, his money would *not* have been on Kevin.

Kevin had been a goofball for as long as Luke could remember, always joking around, taking no one or anything too seriously. Yet somehow that fun-loving attitude had served him well in his field.

Luke took a long slow pull on his beer and reached for the file with the name Charlotte Parker printed neatly across the dog-eared tab and flipped it open. Some of the pages' edges were worn and there was a faint purple smudge that looked like a glob of smeared jelly in the middle of one. Luke smiled and thought of Swanson and his love of blueberry-filled jelly donuts.

Pulling out the photos first, Luke sifted through them. Even after all these years, it was still hard to look at Charlotte lying there, white as snow, looking like she was merely asleep. Harder yet was trying not to see Cami's face in her sister's.

CHAPTER 14

It rained all day yesterday. Despite that, the time had passed quickly as Cami busied herself with appointments and cleaning the house. She'd been happy to work inside when the rain poured down, shutting out the rest of the world and isolating herself in her own tiny bubble, not wanting to face anyone other than nameless contractors that came out for estimates. But today the sun was shining brightly and nature called to her, tempting her out.

Gathering cleaning supplies and a radio, Cami put them in a pail and went outside, determined to tackle the windows. The fall air was crisp, but the sun was warm, and the smell of autumn was on the breeze. She deposited her pail on the ground, turning on her battery-operated radio tuned into a pop station. Satisfied with the radio, she set it down and walked across the yard to the shed in search of a ladder.

An eerie feeling fell over her. The sound was so faint it almost didn't register until the tiny hairs on the back of her neck stood on end. Cami shielded her face from the sun, peering around the side of the little out-building into the woods. She stood still and listened. She couldn't hear or see anything but the distant sound of her radio and the whisper of wind through the trees, yet she couldn't shake the sensation of being watched.

"Hello?" she called and heard her voice resonate in the woods. She waited, anticipating something. Anything. But nothing happened. "Of course there's nothing. This is ridiculous."

A flock of birds shot into the air and swarmed past her. Gasping, she put her hand on her heart, laughing at herself. "Oh, my gosh! I'm such a scaredy cat lately. Get a grip," she scolded herself. "What was I even doing? Of course." She smacked her forehead. "The ladder."

Dismissing the sound, she turned her attention to the shed. The wooden double doors were held shut by a long two-by-four inserted into a slot. Cami tugged, pulled, and lifted the board out of the groove and leaned it against the side of the shed. The doors made a long, harsh creak as they opened. Entering, it took her eyes a moment to adjust to the darkness. Spotting the ladder deep inside, she carefully picked her way through the tools toward it. A creature the size of her fist scurried past her feet causing Cami to shriek, hopping from one foot to the other. She shivered as it disappeared behind a pot. The idea of something small, hairy, and beady-eyed crawling up her leg made her cringe. Turning a slow circle something fluttered next to her cheek and stuck in her hair. Swatting frantically, jumping over tools, she darted out of the shed with a yelp.

Safely back in the light, she bent over to catch her breath. Her heart hammered in her chest as she ran her hands through her hair and down over her body to make sure there was nothing on her.

Deciding she was creepy-crawly free, Cami took a deep breath and walked back to the edge of the shed. Standing at the threshold, she shivered as she peered into the darkness, looking for the culprit. Spotting a frayed cord swinging from the ceiling, the beat of her heart returned to normal. *That must have been what was in my hair,* she thought. "What's happened to me?" she asked herself. "I used to run through these woods every day, play in the dirt and squash bugs with my bare feet." Disgusted, she pulled out the clip in her hair, ran her fingers through it again, and twisted it back into a messy bun, fastening it. "I've been in the city too long."

Taking a deep breath, she stepped back into the dark

shed, making a beeline for the string. Tugging on it, she was disappointed when it didn't light. "Figures," she muttered. "Get the ladder and get out."

Carefully stepping over tools, ducking under hanging baskets, maneuvering between stacks of old paint cans and flower pots, Cami made it deep into the shed to her ultimate destination: the ladder. With the only light coming from the open doors behind her, the process was difficult.

She silently congratulated herself as she stood eyeing the sought-after object. At the moment it was being used as storage, holding small tools and an assortment of aerosol cans. It was covered in cobwebs and dust. *Ugh.* She shifted an old push mower, making space to work, stifling a sneeze as the dust stirred while she removed the spray paint. An ear-piercing screech came from behind her, struggling with the heavy metal ladder, she turned in time to see the doors slam shut, pitching her into complete darkness.

"No!" she shrieked and dropped the ladder. A stack of clay pots crashed to the floor and paint cans toppled over. She pressed forward, cursing the darkness, and crying out as she hit her shin. Stumbling through the black she focused on the thin strip of light that came from the crack between doors. She pushed, shoved, and finally made her way to it. The doors rattled in their frame when she pushed on them but didn't budge. Cami screamed in pure dismay from the darkness within, ramming her hip into the hard wood.

The shadow slipped through the trees, darting in and out, while muffled screams carried on the wind, only to die a soft death in the vastness of the woods.

***

The morning rush was in full swing as Joselyn scurried in, greeted by a line of customers and the rich aroma of coffee. "I'm sorry I'm late," she said over her shoulder, stashing her purse and grabbing her black apron off the hook.

"You'd better have a good excuse," Tanya said, pulling the freshly baked muffins out of the oven and placing them on a cooling rack. "You know I can't handle this crowd by myself with Malinda out on maternity leave."

"I wish I did, but my excuse is lame. I overslept."

Tanya gave her a sideways glance as she rang up a customer and noticed Joselyn looked a little frazzled. "You never oversleep. I want the real story."

Joselyn took the next customer's order, swiped the card and handed it back, tearing off the receipt. She poured coffee in a to-go cup. "It's the truth. Kevin and I were up late talking about the wedding and how much money everything was going to cost." She turned, picked up the plastic tongs, selected a blueberry bagel, and slipped it into a small paper bag with the Jolt logo scrolled across it in rich brown lettering.

"And?"

Joselyn shrugged. "Kevin knows how exhausted I've been lately trying to get the wedding details together on such short notice, so instead of driving home, I spent the night. Between both our schedules, my grandmother not feeling well, in and out of the hospital, we haven't had a minute to ourselves. He shut the alarm off after he got out of bed this morning so I could sleep a little longer." She shrugged. "Had I come over last night prepared to spend the night, I wouldn't have had to run home to get clean clothes and shower."

Tanya boxed a dozen assorted muffins for a customer and said, "That's sweet and considerate of him to let you rest." She pointed a finger at Joselyn. "But you'd better tell him if he does it again, I'll have to kick his ass if he leaves me shorthanded. I don't know why that man just doesn't give you a drawer or some space in the closet. It's not like you won't be moving in together soon, anyway." Tanya folded the top of the box and smiled sweetly at the elderly woman behind the counter. "Sorry about the wait, Mrs. Jefferson. I hope the ladies at the sewing club enjoy them."

"They definitely will, my dear. Your muffins are worth

the wait and your coffee is the only thing that keeps this old ticker pumping," Mrs. Jefferson said, patting her chest softly.

Laughing, Tanya handed her a double tall latte. "You're too kind. Coffee is on the house today since you were so patient."

"Why, thank you, dear. I'll see you tomorrow."

Joselyn took the next order without missing a beat as both women fell into an easy rhythm, but clearly, the conversation wasn't over.

"What he should have done was come in here if he was going to let you sleep in and take your place. To hell with the bank. They don't technically open until after nine for business, anyway."

Smiling, Joselyn handed an order to a customer. "You know as well as I do, you're better off alone than having Kevin help. He's all thumbs in the kitchen."

"That's probably true. But it still doesn't let him off the hook for you missing half your shift. And I don't know why you're so worried about finances. You're marrying a financial planner, for goodness' sake."

She shrugged, trying to play it off. "I really am sorry," Joselyn said, laying her hand on her friend's arm in a quick gesture of sincerity. "His heart was in the right place, he's worried about me."

"Worried about you? Why?" Tanya demanded. "What are you not telling me?"

Shuffling past her to the register, Joselyn leaned in close. "Gran's not doing well. The hospital bills are really piling up, and I'm afraid she won't make it to the wedding. We need to get married soon if I want her to be there."

Tanya let out a little gasp. "Oh, Joselyn. I didn't know she was that bad."

Joselyn's eyes watered as she reached for a carrier and filled the order. She swiped at a tear before it could fall.

Tanya gave her a quick hug. "I'm so sorry. Is there anything I can do?"

"Not really."

"If you need a break to call and check on her, let me know."

"Thanks. The hospital will call if there's any change. I just want to focus on work for now."

Tanya nodded, understanding. Both women turned as the doorbell jingled. "Looks like it's two of our favorite customers."

Tanya ran a hand over her hair, trying desperately to smooth it back into place. "Well, well. Look what the cat dragged in." She placed her hands on her hips and turned her big brown eyes up at Bobby. "A couple of coppers in for their coffee. Sorry, we *still* don't carry any donuts."

Bobby leaned on the counter and stared down at Tanya. "Warner, remind me why we come in here and take this verbal abuse when we can go across town and get coffee *and* donuts at the Quick-Stop without the attitude?"

Before Luke could answer, Tanya supplied, "I'll tell you why, because we have the best damn coffee in town, in the county, and I'll even go so far as saying in the whole state."

"She's right," Luke vouched for her.

"Plus," Tanya batted her eyelashes at Bobby. "We're way better looking than Carl."

He laughed. "That you are."

"The usual?" Joselyn asked.

"Yes, ma'am," Bobby said, not taking his eyes off Tanya's.

"Besides, I think you like your coffee with a side of attitude or you wouldn't keep coming back."

He smirked. "Maybe I do."

"Luke, whatcha' doin' hanging around with this guy?" Tanya jerked a thumb in Bobby's direction.

"Somebody has to hang out with him."

Joselyn took over Bobby's order. "Do you want a muffin to go with that drink?"

Luke walked closer to Tanya, cleared his throat and asked, "Besides my usual, can I get that cherry blossom concoction you made the other day?"

"You mean the refresher?"

He nodded.

She smirked. "Of course." Tanya eyed him suspiciously. "Since when did you like cherries?"

"I've always had a soft spot for them."

"Really?" She cocked an eyebrow. "Interesting."

"Can't a guy just try something different for a change?"

Tanya selected a tall, clear to-go cup and mixed the drink, pouring it over ice. "Maybe. I'm not a detective, but my guess is that you're taking this refresher out to a certain cherry-loving girl."

"What makes you think that?"

Placing the drink on the counter, she turned to make his. "You're not the only one clever enough to be a detective around here. I hear things, see things, and know things." Tanya tapped her temple. "And it's all stored right here. Plus, you're a creature of habit. So, when you do something out of the ordinary, there has to be a reason."

"Touché." He took out his billfold and asked, "Ever play poker?"

"No, why?" She took his money, rang him up, and held out his coffee.

He shrugged. "Just curious. The card game is a lot like being a detective. You need to read the other players, judge, and call their bluff. All the while knowing what cards you hold and whether it's worth the risk to keep playing. You seem like you could do that."

"I'll take that as a compliment."

"I meant it as one." Luke reached for his cup, but Tanya didn't let go.

"Are you gonna tell me who's going to drink that cherry blossom refresher?"

He smiled a wide, easy grin. "No," Luke said and gently pried the coffee from her hand. Raising his cup in salute to her, he said, "Cannon, let's roll."

CHAPTER 15

Luke turned into the lane, parked the Range Rover, lifted the refresher out of his cup holder, and got out. He heard the music first, then spotted the cleaning supplies, but didn't see Cami. *She must be inside getting something else*, he thought, and made his way to the front door. He rang the bell and waited. *Perfect day to be outside.* When she didn't answer, he rang the bell again. This time, when the bell went unanswered, he knocked and tried the handle. Not surprised to find it unlocked, he pushed it open and called out, "Cami? It's me, Luke. Luke Warner. Are you here?" He left the door wide and walked into the house. "I stopped by Jolt and brought you a refresher." His voice rang out in the house. Luke stood still in the center and listened for a reply, but there was only silence. The house felt empty.

He was about to walk further into the house when he heard a vehicle approach. Ducking back outside, he pulled the door closed and went to meet the truck.

"Gibson, surprised to see you here," Luke said as Brock climbed out of the pickup.

"I could say the same to you." They shook hands. "Cami around?"

Luke shrugged. "I think so, but I haven't seen her yet. Just got here myself."

"Since when do you drink refreshers?" Brock questioned.

Luke laughed. "I don't. Brought it for Cami. I wanted to check on her after what happened the other night. What brings you out?"

"Kind-of the same thing." Brock reached in the truck's cab. "And I wanted to give her this." He held up paperwork. "She asked for a bid on some landscaping she wanted done. Figured I'd bring it out myself and apologize." Brock looked around slowly. "Not sure if she's even going to want us to do any work here after what Aaron said."

"He should be the one apologizing, not you."

"He's my partner and I feel responsible. I did nothing to stop him from saying it."

"Well, I don't think she's in the house. I just peeked in and didn't see her. Guess she's outside somewhere. Couldn't have gotten too far. All of her stuff is sitting right there, including her cell phone and the radio is on."

The men walked over and Luke set the drink down next to the radio. "What do we have here? She has a hose, a bucket, window cleaner, and a squeegee. Looks like she's getting ready to wash windows, be my guess." Luke glanced around. "If that's the case, the only thing missing is a ladder."

"I hate washing windows. It's a daunting task." Brock glanced up at the massive house, and its many windows. "Especially here."

"Yeah, not my idea of fun either."

Brock slipped off his sunglasses and tucked them in the V of his shirt. "But I'd say that's a pretty good assumption on your part. If that's what she's doin' she only has the garage and that one little out building to store a ladder big enough for this job. She couldn't have gone too far."

"Let's take a look, see if she needs a hand getting it out."

They started around the house, following the little stone path that led back to the shed.

"Kinda weird being back here after all these years, don't you think?" Brock asked Luke as they walked.

"Yeah, it is. I don't know about you, but I've missed coming here, hanging out with friends, the bonfires, and playing all those games. We had a lot of fun here."

"We did." Brock stopped and pointed. "Looks like she

didn't come out to the shed. The door is still shut." He pulled off his baseball cap and ran a hand through his wavy brown hair. "I've been wonderin' something, so I'm just going to ask."

"What?"

"Do you still have a thing for Cami?"

"Do you hear that?" Luke asked.

Brock laughed. "Come on, Warner. You're just stallin', now. Answer the question."

"No, I'm serious. Listen." Luke turned and looked directly at the shed. Even from this distance, he would swear he saw the doors shake, and the sun glinted off something shiny. "I think there's something in there."

"What?" Brock glanced over and saw it, too. "I'll be damned. I think you're right."

Both men jogged the rest of the way. They could see the blade of a hand saw pop out at the top of the board that held the doors closed and steadily work back and forth, cutting a jagged groove into the two-by-four.

"What the hell?" Curious, Luke said loudly, "Cami? Are you in there?"

"Oh, thank God!" came the muffled reply. "Get me out of here, please."

"Pull the saw back in and we'll remove the board."

They saw the blade wiggle up, lift and disappear behind the door.

"Get me out!"

Rolling the estimate, Brock tucked the papers he had in his back pocket. Hands free, he rocked the board up out of the metal cradle.

Once the board was out, Luke pulled the doors wide with a loud screech. Cami came stumbling out, blinking from the sun. She was covered in dust and cobwebs, her hair was slightly mussed, but damn, if she didn't look cute.

"I'm so glad to see you guys," Cami said with a slight hitch to her voice. "I thought I would never get out of there."

Brock examined the board and saw a pretty deep groove

from where the saw had been. "You've worked your way almost halfway through. How long have you been in there?"

"Long enough."

Luke reached out and pulled a long, dusty strand of cobweb from her hair. "What were you doing in there?"

"Looking for a ladder."

"And how did you get shut in?"

"Good question. That's what I'd like to know." With a shudder, she deliberately brushed dirt and cobwebs off her clothes, and stepped away from the opening. "I opened the doors, put that board," Cami said, pointing at the one Brock was holding, "against the wall and went in after the ladder."

"Then how. . .?" Luke couldn't even finish the thought.

Cami shivered despite the warmth of the sun. "I'm guessing I didn't prop the doors open properly and the wind must have blown them shut."

"It's not even windy."

"And that doesn't explain the board being across the door," Brock chimed in.

Luke glanced at Brock and could see he had made the same assumption. "Someone had to have put the board back."

"I had that thought, too, but I called out, thinking maybe Mr. Bontrager came by and saw it open." She shrugged. "I know he's hard of hearing, but I screamed at the top of my lungs for a full five minutes. There's no way he couldn't have heard me."

"How long do you think you've been in there?"

"What time is it?"

Brock glanced at his watch. "It's just after nine."

"Almost three hours then," she said, clearly disgusted.

Whoever locked her in was probably long gone by now, Luke thought. *He'd have a look around, just to be safe.* He looked her up and down and noticed a dark stain on her jeans down below her knee, and pointed at her leg. "Are you bleeding?"

"No." She glanced down though and saw her pant leg was soaked through. "Maybe."

"Let's look." Luke squatted down and lifted her jeans up

slightly above her shin. "Looks like you scraped it pretty badly. Why don't you take a seat on the front step? I have a first aid kit in the Ranger."

"It's fine, really. I can get it myself."

Luke looked up at her, into those hazel eyes, and his heart skipped a beat. "Humor me, please?"

"Fine," she relented. "I need to sit down for a minute, anyway."

They started back to the house.

"Do you want me to grab the ladder for you?" Brock asked.

"That would be great. Thank you, Brock."

"You bet. I'll be right behind you."

"Be careful," she called over her shoulder. "I knocked over almost everything in the dark trying to get out. It's like a minefield in there."

He laughed. "I'll be careful."

"Don't take this the wrong way because I'm grateful you're both here or I'd still be stuck in the shed. But *why* are you both here?"

"We're both here for partly the same reason." They heard a crash come from the shed, followed by cursing. "Are you okay?" Luke yelled.

"Yep!" came the muffled reply. "Be right out."

They followed the little path around the house, and Luke pointed to the step. "Sit. I'll get that first aid kit and then I'll explain."

Brock came around the corner of the house with the extension ladder at the same time Luke came back from his SUV.

"There should be a sign on that door that reads 'Danger Zone: Enter at your own risk.'"

Cami laughed. "I tried to warn you. Try doing that in the pitch dark with things I don't even want to imagine scurrying past your feet." Cami shivered at the thought.

Brock leaned the ladder against the house placing it near

the cleaning supplies. Snagging the drink Luke brought, he took it over to Cami.

"Here."

"Thanks," Cami said, reaching for it, her hand trembling slightly. "My throat is scratchy from all the yelling. What is this?" She took the first sip. "Mmmm. A cherry refresher. You shouldn't have."

"I didn't. Warner did."

Cami looked at Luke.

Shrugging, he said, "I was at Jolt, knew I was coming out, so I thought I'd bring you something. No big deal."

Cami laid her other hand on his arm. "It is to me. Thank you."

He gave her that easy grin. "Any time. Gibson, why don't you tell Cami why you're here?"

"Uh, yeah sure. I brought out your bid." He pulled it out of his back pocket, tried to smooth it down against his jeans, and then handed it to her. Rubbing a hand across the back of his neck, he shifted his weight from one foot to another, clearly uncomfortable.

Cami glanced down at the papers, then turned her attention back to him.

He waited a beat as she held his gaze, then cleared his throat. "I would like to start by apologizing for the other night. Aaron shouldn't have spoken to you like that."

Cami raised her hand to cut him off. "You needn't do that. There's no reason for you to apologize. You didn't say it, Aaron did."

"Yes, but he's my business partner, my friend, and he was way out of line. I'm sorry."

"Thank you. I appreciate that. But seriously, you don't need to. You didn't say anything."

"And that's really the problem, isn't it? I should have. I should have defended you. I should have defended Charlotte, she meant the world to me. It wasn't your fault, or Charlotte's and yet I let him blame you and your family. Certainly, the police would ask us questions, that's standard whether or not it's an accident. Right, Warner?" Brock asked.

Luke nodded but remained silent.

"The cops wouldn't be doing their job if they didn't investigate properly."

"True," she hesitated, taking her time, trying to form the right words, clearly able to see he was struggling. "I'm sorry the loss of my sister hurt you. We were teenagers and apparently, the situation we were all thrust into wasn't handled well. I hope you know we were grieving and we, or at least I, did not know what was going on with any of you. If my parents knew, they didn't tell me." She swallowed hard, trying to keep a tremor out of her voice. "But that was ten years ago. I think it's time to move on. I want to, I need to, and I hope you want to as well."

He smiled hesitantly. "I do."

"Good." She gave him a smile. "Now, about my estimate? I can look at it now, if you don't mind?"

"Of course. Go right ahead."

Cami read over the estimate, and Luke watched the exchange quietly.

She flipped the page, scanning it quickly. "When can you start?"

Clearly surprised, Brock asked, "Are you sure you don't want to think about it? Take some time and get other bids?"

"I already did. Had a couple of other landscapers out yesterday. Your estimate is right in range with the others. Frankly, I'd prefer to go with someone I know. So, when can you start? Assuming you still want to take the job."

"We do. Let me check the schedule." Brock opened the calendar on his phone. "Looks like I have a crew that could be here Monday morning, if you'd like?"

"That works for me. I'm eager to get started."

"Great!" His fingers worked his phone quickly. "I'll put you on the schedule for first thing Monday morning." He finished typing and glanced up at her. "You're in."

"Perfect."

Brock glanced from Cami to Luke. "That's all I needed. I guess I'd better let you get back to it. Make sure you take care of that leg."

"I will."

Both were silent as they watched him climb into the truck, drive down the lane, and disappear around the bend.

Cami glanced at Luke. "You said little."

"What's there to say? You're both adults and handled an uncomfortable situation well." He shrugged matter-of-factly. "Now, let's fix up that leg."

"I got this. I need to clean up a little, get these dirty jeans off first, get the cobwebs out of my hair, then I'll clean the scrape. You have better things to do." She held out her hand. He took it, and pulled her up a little too fast. She fell into him and his other hand went to her side to steady her.

Cami was so close. Looking into those hazel eyes, he felt like he was lost in the deep forest, with all those colors mixing and blending together. His eyes flicked down to her mouth, lingered, and all the blood drained out of his head. Every ounce of him wanted to kiss her.

"Are you going to give it to me?" she asked.

"Give it to you?" he swallowed hard. What the hell? Could she possibly want him to kiss her as much as he wanted to?

Inching back, she held out her hand. "The first aid kit?"

You idiot. Of course, the first aid kit. How could he be so stupid? His IQ must have dropped when the blood rushed out. He stepped back, slightly embarrassed, and handed her the kit.

"If you don't mind, I wanted to look around the shed." He quickly backed up, making space between them. "I'll come in and check on you when I'm done."

"Of course."

"I'll be back in a few minutes."

She nodded and went inside.

It was all he could do not to follow her in. Forcing

himself to back up and follow the path, Luke went around to the shed. The minute he took a step off the path, he sank easily into the soft dirt. The ground was still moist from yesterday's rain. Luke squatted and saw a set of footprints leading to and away from the shed. He snapped a picture of them with his phone, following them with his eyes as they led into the woods.

Luke stood, punched in the number, and called Cannon. "I'm going to need your help with something."

***

Cami was carrying her cleaning supplies back to the front porch when the police cruiser pulled into the yard. It pulled up and stopped behind Luke's SUV. Luke and Bobby got out of the car.

"I thought you'd wandered off and had gotten yourself lost in the woods," Cami said. "You've been gone for hours."

Luke smiled at her. "Almost. I noticed you didn't come looking for me."

"I didn't know you wanted me to."

"You can come find me any day." He jerked a thumb at Bobby. "Instead, Cannon picked me up."

"I got a report of a suspicious looking white male wandering down Sawmill Road, and looky who I found."

"He's suspicious alright," Cami laughed. "I was just going to go in and make a sandwich. Do you guys wanna come in for a minute?"

"That would be great. Thank you."

The two men followed her into the house, across the foyer, under the sweep of stairs, and into the kitchen. "Have a seat," she said, indicating the long wooden table that occupied the length of the breakfast area. Always the hostess, she asked, "Can I get either of you something to drink?"

"Ice water will be fine."

"I'll have the same."

Cami nodded and pulled three glass tumblers out of the cabinet, filled them with ice and water, and placed them on the table. "Now, how about a sandwich?"

"The water is fine for now, Cami. Please," Luke pulled out a chair. "Have a seat."

She faced him. "I don't like that tone, Luke. What did you find?"

He gave her an easy grin, trying to relax her. "I'm sorry. I didn't mean to put any tone in my voice, but I need you to sit down and talk to us."

Cami slid gracefully into the chair. "Okay."

Sitting across from her, he said, "I just want to go over everything that happened this morning. What time did you say you went outside?"

"Right around six."

"Did you see or hear anything unusual?"

"No." She thought for a second. "Actually, that's not true. When I went back to the shed to get the ladder, I thought I heard a branch snap in the woods. You know, like someone stepping on it. I peered around the side but I didn't see anything."

"Was the shed closed when you got to it?"

"Yes. The board was in place. I worked it out of the slot and set it on the side of the shed, like I told you before."

"You were deep inside when the doors swung shut?"

"Yes, I was all the way in the back corner getting the ladder when the doors closed. I called out, but no one answered. It probably took me at least five minutes to make my way to the door because it's so dark in there with no windows, and the light is burnt out."

Luke nodded. "I noticed that. If you have extra bulbs, I'll gladly go out and replace it for you."

"Thank you, I would appreciate that. I'm not too thrilled to be going back in there without a light. Anyway, I knocked over almost everything because I couldn't see. I was making all kinds of noise. Plus, I was yelling. There's no way someone didn't hear me. Unless, like I said, it was Mr. Bontrager. He's kind of hard of hearing."

"We checked with the Bontrager's. They weren't home this morning. They had a doctor's appointment in Lancaster at eight, so they had already left by then. Mr. Bontrager said he hasn't been over here since you asked him to meet the electrician to work on the water heater before you moved in."

"Okay," Cami hesitated. "So, what are you saying? If it wasn't him, it had to be someone else."

"I found a set of footprints by the shed and another print back in the woods. With the rain yesterday, there was no way to totally avoid the soft ground."

"What does that mean?" Cami's blood ran cold, thinking of someone lurking around outside.

Luke leaned forward, took a sip of his water. "If it wasn't you or Mr. Bontrager... well..." His voice trailed off. "We followed a deer path out to the road, which would be the simplest and shortest path through the woods. There was no sign that a vehicle was parked there, but they could have easily left the car on the pavement and not left any tracks. Or maybe they had another way in and out."

She half laughed. "Or maybe it was a ghost." She sucked in a breath. She hadn't meant to actually say it out loud, but now that she had, she couldn't exactly take it back.

"I don't think that's what Warner's insinuating here," Bobby said, shifting in his chair. "It's more like they were careful, but not careful enough since they left tracks."

She could feel both men watching her. *Should she say anything? They had both just dismissed the comment like she hadn't actually said it.* Cami glanced from one to the other. *Cami wasn't sure if she believed it herself. She had no proof, really. And yet she did. What about Charlotte's door being constantly locked, even though she would swear she hadn't locked it? And then the door was open when she came back from getting the key. What about the smell of roses or the sensation running across her arm like someone touching her when she woke up dreaming of*

Charlotte? Or what about the electricity going out unexpectedly? Would they think she was crazy if she mentioned any of these things? But wait… could a ghost lift a heavy board and slide it in place? Or leave footprints? Probably not. This was completely two different things. Her pulse raced. *Better to keep her "ghost" to herself.*

Cami was suddenly acutely aware that several minutes of silence had passed without her saying anything. Clearing her throat, she asked, "Could it be the same person who threw a golf ball through the window the other night?"

Luke nodded. "It's a very good possibility."

She could feel his gray eyes on her, watching her every move. It was unsettling, unnerving.

"Is there anything else you've noticed over the last few days? Anything suspicious or out of the ordinary?"

She shook her head a little too aggressively. "No, nothing." Cami would swear he could see right through her.

"You're sure?"

"Yes."

A door slammed overhead.

"What the hell?"

Both men were on their feet, headed toward the stairs.

"It's Charlotte's room," Cami said, following close behind them.

"Are you sure?"

"I'd know that slam anywhere."

Both men drew their guns and made their way up the stairs.

"Stay behind me," Luke said quietly to her as he placed a hand on her side and tucked her neatly behind him, shielding her with his own body.

"It's nothing, trust me."

"Doors don't just slam by themselves, Cami."

She remained silent, standing at the top of the stairs with Luke as Bobby crept down the hallway, clearing each room. All the doors were wide open except Charlotte's.

Against her better judgment, she said, "I'm telling you, it's Charlotte's door that slammed. No one's here."

Bobby laid a hand on the knob. "It's locked."

"That doesn't surprise me," Cami pushed past Luke and deliberately went into the main bedroom and retrieved her key from the nightstand. "She's been locking it." Cami crossed to the closed door and inserted the key. "She thinks she's being funny, I guess."

"Don't open that, let Cannon," Luke said, taking Cami's arm and pulling her back. "There could be someone in there."

"I'm telling you there's not."

"Humor me, please?"

Cami looked into those turbulent gray eyes and relented. "Okay, Luke. You win. Bobby can go first."

Bobby turned the knob and released the latch, gun drawn, he kicked it open with his foot. The door swung in noiselessly, opening to an undisturbed room.

"Hang back a minute. Let him check it out first."

Bobby cleared the room and then nodded to them. "She's right, there's no one here." He holstered his weapon.

"Then what the hell was that noise?"

"I'm telling you, it was Charlotte's door slamming."

"Is there another way downstairs besides the main staircase?" Bobby asked.

"Yes, down the hall. The last door on the right, it's servants' quarters and has stairs that come down just off the walk-in butler's pantry."

"I'm going to check it out and just make sure they didn't sneak out another way."

Luke nodded. "Good idea."

Cami glanced around. "Wait. That's not how I left those yearbooks." She crossed to the bed. The one she had been looking at when the lights went out was open. She could have sworn she'd closed it when she got up to check the lamp.

"What's wrong?" Luke asked, coming up beside Cami.

She shrugged and reached for the yearbook. "It's

probably nothing, but I'm sure I closed the book the other night, and yet it's wide open to the page I'd been looking at when the lights went out."

Peering over her shoulder, he asked, "Can I see?" Luke took the yearbook from her.

"I love that picture of us."

"Did you see the message?"

"Yeah, so? I'm sure that's not the first time Brock told her he loved her." Cami picked up another yearbook that was open to the signature page. "I know for a fact that I didn't open these. I never had time to because the lights went out."

Cami read through some messages. She smiled. "Listen to some of these: 'Have a great summer! Your friend, Clarissa.' 'You were awesome in the musical! XOXO, Annie.' 'Will you go out with me? Here's my number. Love, Bart.' He even had the nerve to leave it, but then scratched it out."

"Or maybe Charlotte did."

Cami laughed. "You're probably right." She read some more. "'Keep reaching for the stars! Julie.'" Cami flipped the page. "There are a lot of 'have a great summer' and 'you're so talented.'" Cami softened. "And she was."

"Cami?"

"Yeah?"

"Look at this again."

"Okay. What? It's just Brock saying he loves her."

"That's what I thought, too, but look." He flipped to the back of the book. "Here's a message from Brock. Look at the handwriting. It's completely different." He went back to the picture. "This is the only message in the entire book not signed."

"Okay," Cami followed his logic. "Maybe it wasn't Brock. And if it wasn't, then what? Or should I say, who? Somebody with a crush? It could have been anyone."

"Let me see that message from Bart. Maybe it's a match."

She turned quickly, not realizing Luke was that close, and bumped into him. His hand came up to her waist to steady her, and a rush of heat covered her entire body. Cami couldn't control it, and her face flushed red. This was the second time today he had his hands on her. "Ah, here," she said, flustered, pushing the book at him.

Luke cleared his throat, dropped his hand from her waist, and took a small step back. "Let's compare."

Nodding, they bent their heads to peer at the page.

"It's not even close. Bart's handwriting is small and choppy. This is small as well but flows a little nicer."

"Okay, so Bart's out. Keep looking." He handed her another yearbook. "Look through this one. Let's see if we can find a match."

Cami sat on the bed and thumbed through the yearbook, and was all too aware of Luke as he sat beside her. She should say something, but what? She tried to think. Anything to break the silence. Instead, she started reading out loud. "A few more 'have a great summer.' 'You are so talented! Love watching you in the school plays. FF Tina.' Here's one that looks like a little poem and it's not signed: 'Roses are white, cherries are red, make fun of me again, and you'll be dead.'" Cami gasped.

"Let me see that." Luke placed an arm behind Cami and leaned in close, reading it himself. "Flip back to the prom picture."

She did, pulling in the seductive scent of him. "It's not the same, either."

"You're right, it's not."

For the third time today, she looked up into his gray eyes and almost drowned. The heat of his body engulfed her as she saw his eyes flick down to her mouth and linger. Once again, she wondered what it would be like to have his mouth on hers after all these years. The room darkened slightly and the scent of roses drifted around them. Cami imagined him pulling her in close…

Bobby cleared his throat, Cami jumped, and Luke's eyes snapped back to hers, caught. They both turned simultaneously to find Bobby leaning on the door frame, grinning from ear to ear.

"Am I interrupting?" he asked with laughter in his voice. "I can come back if you need a minute?"

Cami quickly stood, recovering her composure. "Don't be silly."

"What did you find?" Luke asked, suddenly all business as if nothing happened.

And nothing did happen, she reminded herself. But she had almost - oh God! She didn't even want to think about what she had almost done.

"Nothing."

"I didn't think you would," Cami said, closing the book she was holding, crossing her arms over her chest protectively, tucking it in close to her heart, trying desperately to conceal the sound of her heart thudding against her chest. Afraid both men could hear it.

"How did you know that for sure?" Bobby asked.

She shrugged, deciding she still didn't think they would believe her even if she told them. "Just a feeling I had." She turned back to Luke and felt the heat rise back into her face. She was making a fool of herself in front of him. *Parkers don't do that.*

"Give us a minute?" Luke said to Bobby with a look.

"You bet. I'll be downstairs if you need me." He whistled as he walked away.

"Here, you can take it with you," she said, thrusting the yearbook at him. "Take the other ones, too."

"If you don't mind?"

"Of course not."

Luke reached out to her, placing a hand on her arm. "Cami, are you alright?"

"Of course," she said, feeling like a swooning damsel in distress romanticizing the moment, when he clearly wasn't affected, at least not the way she had been. Or wanted him to be. "Now if you'll excuse me, I have taken up a lot of your time today and I have some other things I need to get done." She slipped from his grasp and paused in the doorway. "I can show you out."

CHAPTER 16

Cami drove exactly the speed limit because she knew Officer Cannon, Bobby, wasn't that far in front of her, and she wouldn't dare get pulled over by him after she'd seen that smug look on his face when he had caught her sitting so close to Luke. About ready to burst, she parked on the street, got out of the car, and bolted into Jolt.

Joselyn was behind the counter cleaning out the display cabinet, getting ready to close for the day.

"Hi, Joselyn."

"Hello," she answered back, gazing over the counter at her.

Cami stopped and took a deep breath, trying to calm her nerves. "Tanya around?"

"She's in the back, getting things ready for tomorrow." Joselyn closed the display, sending her a sharp look. "Please tell me you don't want anything to drink? I've already cleaned the machines for the day."

"No, thank you. I'm good. I need to talk to Tanya. Do you think she'll mind if I go back?"

"No, go ahead." Without giving Cami another second, she turned back to the task at hand.

Cami pushed through the doors and found Tanya bent over, sorting through a newly delivered box of supplies, pencil behind her ear and a clipboard close by. This was the first time Cami had been behind the counter, let alone in the back room, and was suddenly in awe of her friend's organizational skills.

Just the mere sight of the open shelves with all the

ingredients labeled and in alphabetical order was enough to calm her racing heart.

"Hey! I wasn't expecting to see you today," Tanya said, taking the pencil out from behind her ear and checking off an item on the clipboard. "What brings you in?" When Cami didn't immediately respond, Tanya stopped counting and really looked at her friend. "Wow, you look shell-shocked. What happened?"

Cami slunk down onto the only chair in the room. "I'm absolutely mortified!"

"That bad, huh?"

She nodded.

"Tell me."

The whole day had been a fiasco. "I don't even know where to start."

Tanya stood and stretched. "Do you want to sort and talk? Sometimes when my hands are busy, the words flow easier."

"Sure."

"Great. Grab that box of paper products. They go on that far shelf there. Everything is labeled, all you have to do is place and stack. Think you can handle that?"

"Yep." Cami stood, grabbed the box, and dug through it. She located the first item and blurted out, "I almost kissed him."

"Who?" Tanya demanded.

"Luke."

"Warner? You're kidding, right?"

"I wouldn't kid about something like this."

Tanya did a little dance. "It's about damn time! You've been in love with him for, like, *ever*."

"It is *so* not good. I made an absolute fool of myself. In front of Bobby and everything," Cami exclaimed, stacking coffee filters on the shelf.

"What the heck was Bobby doing there? Oh, wait. Le'me guess. I'm the best at this."

"No, you're not."

"Yes, I am. Quiet now, I'm thinking." She tapped her chin with the tip of her pencil, clearly getting ready. Tanya exclaimed, "I got it! They arrested you for something. We'll get to those details later." She waved her hand in the air like that part didn't really matter. "And Bobby hauled your butt in, kicking and screaming. Luke came out to see what all the commotion was. When he saw you in handcuffs..."

"Handcuffs?"

"Yes, don't interrupt. He immediately stepped in and stopped him cold. Before Bobby threw you in the cell, Luke pulled you into an interrogation room, still handcuffed, mind you. And in the dim, fluorescent light you threw yourself at him, confessing your undying love for him, asking him to spare you from a life in prison."

Cami stood with her hand in midair, holding the filters, and glaring at Tanya in disbelief. "Why did I come here?"

"Because you love me and I'm the bestest friend you've ever had."

Cami chucked the small box at Tanya's head. Tanya ducked and weaved.

"Ha! You missed."

"I won't this time." Cami snagged a half-eaten muffin off the little work table.

"Hey! That's mine." She narrowed her eyes at Cami. "You wouldn't."

"You wanna bet?" Cami whipped it at her friend, smacking her square in the forehead.

"Ouch!" The muffin smeared chocolate on her face, crumbled, and fell to the floor. Tanya stared at Cami in stunned disbelief, then doubled over in laughter. "I can't believe you just did that! You should see the look on your face!"

Cami cracked a smile and held back a laugh. "You should see yours! There are crumbs in your eyebrows and chocolate on your nose."

"What's going on here?" Joselyn asked, coming through

the swinging doors. "Tanya! Your face is a mess. What happened?"

Tanya pointed an accusatory finger at Cami. "She did it!"

"You sound like a little kid," Joselyn stated, an impatient tone in her voice. "Cami, did you throw that muffin at her?"

Caught, Cami said, "I'll clean it up."

"You most certainly will. Dust pan is over there," Joselyn said, pointing. "I'm going to lock the front door. I trust you two can behave for five minutes while I do that?"

"Of course," Cami said to Joselyn's retreating form. "When did she become no fun?"

"When Kevin put a ring on her finger. Now tell me what happened." She reached for a paper towel and wiped her face. "I want all the juicy details."

"We were in Charlotte's room sitting on the bed and his hand was on my side. His face was so close…" Her voice trailed off, as she bent down to sweep up the muffin crumbs. "Like a moron, I leaned in. I was lost in those gray eyes; I wasn't thinking. The next thing I know, Bobby's in the doorway clearing his throat, grinning at us like some stupid idiot."

"So it sounds to me that if Bobby had better timing, we would be dissecting the details of a hot, passionate kiss, not an almost kiss."

"Thank goodness he came when he did, so I didn't totally make a fool out of myself. If I had kissed him . . ."

"What? It would have been wonderful. There would have been sparks and possibly fireworks! Maybe even butterflies flying around your head, just like in the movies. Long-lost lovers, finally united." Tanya sighed as she pictured the scene. "This is a good thing, not a bad thing." Tanya came over to Cami, seeing her distress. She draped an arm around Cami. "How does almost kissing a good-looking, single, available, I might add, man become a bad thing?"

"I feel like I'm always messing up around him. Even after all these years, I feel like he can see how infatuated I am. I swear it's written all over my face. Bobby could certainly see it."

"To hell with Bobby. And to hell with these supplies." They both had completely abandoned stocking the shelves anyway.

"What am I going to do?"

"I'll tell you what you're going to do. You're going to act as if nothing happened. Let Detective Warner come to you. Let *him* make a fool out of himself in front of *you*. If he doesn't come to his senses and see what he's missing, then it's his loss, and he's not as smart as I thought he was. Or as good of a detective as he should be for missing all the clues." Tanya linked her arm through Cami's. "In the meantime, it's going to be a beautiful evening. Why don't we go to Finn's? We can get some food, maybe even grab some wine, and have a girl's night at your place."

"Sounds perfect."

***

Sitting at his desk, Luke thumbed through the yearbook. There had to be at least sixty entries and signatures in each yearbook, and as far as he could tell, none of them matched the three words under the prom picture or the poem. Both entries disturbed him. What really bothered him, though, was that if Detective Swanson had this information ten years ago, he could have pursued the idea of murder with a vengeance.

Luke closed the book, stood, and looked out the window, his back to the office door.

"Are you pissed off because you didn't kiss her when you could have, or because I walked in?"

Luke didn't turn. "You always had bad timing, Cannon."

Bobby pushed off the doorjamb and came into the office uninvited. "Hell, man. I'm sorry I interrupted, that was a long time coming, and I ruined it."

Luke turned and faced his friend. "No, you didn't. It's a good thing you came in when you did. I had no business kissing her at that moment. We were there on official business. It was totally unprofessional on my part."

"Wait just a damn minute. I was there on business. You were there on a social call, remember? You went out to check on her and bring her some sort of cherry bomb concoction."

"Cherry blossom refresher," Luke supplied dryly.

"That's what I said." Bobby ran a hand over his closely cropped hair. "By the way, what exactly did you find in that yearbook?"

"A couple of messages."

"Can I see?"

"Sure." Luke picked up the yearbook and handed it to Bobby. "I have the pages marked."

Flipping to the first tab, Bobby gave a little whistle. "Those two were gorgeous, weren't they? The same, yet completely different. Charlotte in her signature white, with her hair and makeup professionally done, sophisticated and untouchable. Cami in her pale sage green, looking like every high school boy's dream, naturally cute."

At Bobby's description, Luke peered over his shoulder. "That photo represents a whole lot of heartache and trouble.

"Trouble or not, you weren't the only one to have a crush on her."

"Yeah?" Luke questioned, surprised. "And why didn't you do anything about it?"

"Because she never looked at me the way she did at you. Still doesn't."

"I don't know about that. Anyway, it doesn't matter because I think I scared her off for good now. Did you see the look on her face? And the way she made a beeline for the door?" He shook his head, disgusted with himself. "Doesn't matter right now. Flip to the next tab."

Silently, Bobby did what he was told. "What am I looking for?"

"Bottom right-hand corner."

"I see it." Bobby read out loud: "'Roses are white, cherries are red, make fun of me again, and you'll be dead.'" He let out another whistle. "Geez, it rhymes and everything. And there's no question it's directed at Charlotte, with the reference to white roses. Everyone knew that was her signature fragrance and color." He handed the yearbook back to Luke. "I think you just found your first real clue in ten years."

"If this really is what I think it is, you know what this means, don't you?"

"Yeah," Bobby said grimly. "One of our classmates could be a killer."

CHAPTER 17

The timing couldn't have been better or worse depending on the point of view, but when Cami reached for the door of Finn's, Luke stepped up and said, "Allow me."

She froze.

"Come on, Parker. You're holdin' up the line," Bobby bellowed from behind her.

"Relax, big guy," Tanya said, patting him on the arm. "They won't run out of food."

"Thank you," Cami said to Luke, slightly flustered, the heat immediately rising to her cheeks. She tried to keep some distance between them. She didn't want to chance brushing up against him. The sting of the *almost* kiss was still fresh.

"Are you guys eating here?" Tanya asked Bobby.

"Not sure yet. Maybe we could be persuaded to eat with a couple of hot chicks."

Tanya tsked at the label. "You're hilarious, but if you're going to call us chicks, the answer is no."

A grin spread wide across Bobby's face. He pointed. "I was talking about those two wild hens that wandered across the road and are hanging out by that picnic table, yonder. See?" He pointed, and they all turned to look, sure enough there were two brown chickens pecking around the far picnic table. He elbowed Luke. "But if you two ladies want to join us, I'm sure Warner and I could make an exception."

Tanya let out a huff.

Luke stifled a grin, and Cami rolled her eyes. "Don't encourage him."

"Believe me, I won't. He doesn't need any encouragement. After you." He widened the door and followed Cami in. They debated over the menu, settling on burgers and fries, their usual at Finn's. They placed their order, paid, moved to the side, and prepared to wait.

"Seriously though, are you guys going to stay? It's a little crowded," Luke asked.

"No, we're going to take it to go," Cami said, unable to make eye contact with him, afraid her face would give away what her heart felt. Ten years and she still felt like a lovesick teenager with stars in her eyes when the high school quarterback glanced her way. She waved at someone she barely knew just to take a second, so she didn't come across desperate, asking, "How about you?"

"Not really sure."

Tanya watched the exchange, barely listening to Bobby rambling on, and finally butted in. "For Pete's sake," she said dryly. "You guys are so awkward. Grab your food and join us. We're going back to Cami's place. We're hoping to light a fire and hang out under the stars. It's a beautiful evening."

Cami glared at Tanya, but it didn't stop her.

"How 'bout it, Bobby?"

"Sounds good to me," Bobby answered. "We're game."

"Game for what?" Kevin asked, coming up beside them, Joselyn in tow.

"Hey, fancy meeting you here," Bobby said. "We're getting carry-out and heading back to Cherry Hollow. Wanna come?"

"Oh, no. We don't want to intrude," Joselyn said. "We have wedding arrangements to go over."

"You're not intruding at all," Cami said. "We'd love to have you both."

"That's right." Bobby clapped Kevin on the back. "The more, the merrier. But wedding arrangements? Come on, man," Bobby grumbled. "That's for women to do."

"What are you a caveman? Move into the 21st century

you male-chauvinist ass. First chicks and now wedding plans? Unbelievable."

Bobby clutched his chest. "That stung a little."

Ignoring Bobby, turning her attention back to Joselyn, Tanya said, "It'll be fun. You both should definitely come." Linking her arm with Joselyn's, she nudged her playfully. "And the girls can talk about wedding plans if the boys are too caveman-like to want to."

"But it's date night, right, Kevin?" Joselyn asked, her eyes pleading.

Cami liked that plan as soon as she heard it. The more people, hopefully, the less awkward it would be between her and Luke. But getting Kevin on board was the key. "What do you think, Kev?" Cami asked. "You'll come out, won't you? It could be a date night under the stars."

Kevin scanned the group, glancing between Josie, Tanya, and Cami. Relenting, he said, "Why not?"

"It'll be like old times," Tanya added.

"Wonderful!" Cami said a little too enthusiastically. She turned when their number was called, picked up their order, grabbed Tanya's arm, and started for the SUV. Putting on her sweetest smile, she said, "Head on out as soon as your food's ready. We'll be there." But under her breath, she said so only Tanya could hear: "If they don't hurry, you might not be."

Innocently, Tanya asked, "And why wouldn't I be there?"

"Because I'm going to kick you out of the car halfway there and leave you stranded on the side of the road for that. I can't believe you just invited them out!" she hissed.

"Somebody had to. Left to your own devices, you and Luke would never get around to it. You're like a deer in the headlights where he's concerned. Someone had to give you a push."

"Yeah?" Cami said, stowing the food in the back seat and climbing into the SUV. She glanced over at Tanya. "You'd better strap in because you might be the one getting a push, straight out of the car."

"You wouldn't dare," Tanya teased as Cami pulled out of the lot. "I'm your best friend. *And* I might add, the whole reason your high school crush is following in the car behind us." She patted Cami on the arm. "You're welcome."

Cami turned a hard glare on her. Tanya smiled wickedly, but fastened her seatbelt, just in case.

***

They all ate in the kitchen because she didn't have a table outside yet. Despite the large size of the room and the long table that easily sat twelve, they gravitated to the middle and divided up all the food. There was a heaping pile dumped in the center: fries, onion rings, boneless buffalo wings, cheeseburgers, and one salad. Cami provided the condiments and the drinks.

"Geez, Joselyn. What's with the salad?" Bobby asked, shoving an onion ring in his mouth and dangling a fry in front of her face. "I know you want one."

Joselyn turned up her nose. "Forgive me for wanting to look good on my wedding day."

"Please tell Josie she's fine, that she doesn't need to diet," Kevin said, grabbing a boneless wing. "She won't listen to me."

"It's true, Joselyn. You've never looked prettier than right now," Cami said sincerely.

"She's right. It must be all that mushy love stuff," Tanya added. "You have a glow."

"There. See?" Kevin said, looking from one woman to the other. "I couldn't have said it better myself." He leaned over and gave her a quick peck on the cheek.

"Thanks, you guys," Joselyn said, blushing.

"How 'bout that fry?" Bobby held another one out.

"Don't mind if I do." Kevin snagged it. "Oh, wait. Was that for Josie?"

Bobby laughed and pushed the fries toward her. "Not sure how you're going to live with this guy, Joselyn. You're going to have to fight for every crumb you get."

A large white globe hung over the middle of the table. The fixture was dated, but it kept the darkness at bay and bathed the kitchen in a warm light. Laughter filled the expanse of the room, and Cami realized it had been over ten years since they had filled the house with it. The mood affected her so much that she could almost feel the house sigh with relief.

Dipping her fries in ketchup, Cami glanced around the table. She couldn't believe she was really sitting here with her friends from high school. Once she had been forced to move away, she'd thought she'd lost them all for good. She had drifted apart from Joselyn, and nearly Kevin, too. She hadn't seen Bobby or Luke in ten years. Tanya had been her one true connection, her constant.

Her eyes filled with tears as she glanced from one friend to the next. She had missed them so much her heart nearly burst. Overwhelmed with emotion, she choked back a small sob.

Hearing it over the din of conversation, Luke cocked his head and studied her. "You okay?" he mouthed.

She nodded. "I'm fine." But she quickly got up. "Anyone need anything while I'm up?" Cami asked, going over to the counter and opening a drawer.

"Nope."

"We're good."

She kept her back to them, afraid if she turned around, she wouldn't be able to hide the tears in her eyes. "You guys keep eating. I'm going to go out and start the fire."

"Need any help?" Luke asked.

"No. I got it. I'll be back in a few minutes."

Pocketing matches, gathering newspapers, and a flashlight, Cami shrugged into a jacket she kept by the back door and slipped out, closing the laughter and fun inside.

The air was cool and crisp, making her cheeks sting where tears ran down her face. Wiping at them with the back of her hand, she followed the path to the clearing.

The firepit was stacked high with wood and encircled by three large logs honed down by weather and hands over the years to use as benches around the edge of the fire. She quickly set to work balling newspaper and tucking it under the pre-stacked wood in the firepit.

The Great Horned owl called out and soared high above her head. Cami watched the dark shadow against the inky black sky swoop gracefully over the outstretched branches. For a moment, she wondered if it was the same owl from her childhood. Shaking off her mood, Cami dug the matches out of her pocket, squatted, tucked the flashlight under her arm, and went to strike the match.

"Here, let me."

Cami jumped.

"Sorry, I didn't mean to scare you."

"You didn't."

"Really?" Luke chuckled. "You could have fooled me." He crouched beside her and took the matches from her hand, taking his time so the warmth of his transferred to hers in the exchange.

She relented. "Okay, maybe a little."

He smiled at that, then turned back to the firepit and frowned. He struck the match and held the tip to the newspaper and watched it ignite. "Did I put those tears in your eyes, too?" Luke asked.

The flame grew, white smoke curling up, and a twig snapped at the lick of flame. Without looking at him, she said. "No, memories did. I've missed this, you know? Being back here in the only place I've ever called home. Having friends here to enjoy it with. People from my past who knew me when I was young. Before."

"It must be hard."

"Sometimes it is. Others not. But tonight? In there, sitting around the table, laughing, eating... just living. It swamped me." She shrugged. "It's hard to explain. I just needed a minute."

"You don't have to explain it to me, Cami. You feel what you feel. No one can tell you what's right or wrong. But you need to, the good and the bad." He sat back on his heels and placed a hand on her knee. "And the sad. It's okay. What's that saying? 'Grow through what you go through.' If you do that, none of it is wrong."

She smiled, brushing away a tear that threatened to fall and tried to lighten the mood. "Are you a detective, or some kind of therapist? That was pretty deep for a cop."

"Ouch. That kinda hurt." He tapped a hand on his heart. "I can be deep when I want to." He turned those gray eyes on her and held her gaze.

She swallowed hard, desperate for something clever to say. "Actually, I always thought you might be. Of course, you were one of the high school elites, class jock, a little cocky and self-assured."

He laughed at that. "Why don't you tell me what you really thought?"

"Alright, I will. You might have been a little cocky and self-assured, but behind the shaggy blond hair and those intense gray eyes, I thought there might be a bit more happening than the average teenage boy. Maybe you noticed more than most and thought about things a little deeper."

He asked, "Think you had me all figured out?"

She shook her head. "Not at all."

"Good, I like to keep you guessing." An easy grin spread across his face as he reached up and tucked a wisp of hair behind her ear, his fingertips brushing her cheek softly. A deep longing ripped through her, and she felt him lean in. Her breath caught.

"Were you going to tell us the fire was lit? Or were you going to hog it all for yourselves?" Tanya asked, walking toward them, followed closely by the others.

He stopped just inches from her.

Cami stood quickly, like a kid caught with her hand in the cookie jar. "We were going to let you know as soon as the fire took off."

"Looks like it's taking off just fine to me."

Luke stood, too, tucking his hands into his front pockets, rocking back on his heels.

Tanya stopped and examined them both. "What just happened?" she demanded.

"Nothing," they said in unison.

Tanya wagged a finger between the two of them. "I don't believe either of you. Something's going on."

"Looks like the fire's going pretty good, Parker." Bobby sat on a large log and pulled Tanya down beside him. "Sit," he hissed.

"Hey! I was trying to . . ."

"I know what you were trying to do. Stop asking so many damn questions and let them be." He leaned in close and whispered in her ear. "I think we might have interrupted something long overdue."

Tanya looked at them, and then agreed. "I think you might be right."

Kevin and Joselyn sat, leaving the other log. Luke sat down and patted the spot beside him. "Have a seat, Cami."

She eyed the spot and wasn't sure if she trusted herself so close to him. "Does anyone want to roast marshmallows? I could go in and get some."

"No, we're good."

"I could go for a s'more," Kevin said.

"Okay, I'll be right back."

"Oh, for goodness' sake. Cami, no. Kevin's fine. We literally just ate. Sit down," Tanya ordered.

"I actually wanted one," Kevin murmured but was stopped cold by the look Tanya shot him.

Reluctantly, Cami sat down on the edge of the log, acutely aware that everyone watched her.

"I don't bite," Luke said. "Usually."

"You're funny," Cami replied, trying to relax, but it was hard when every eye was on her. She locked eyes with Tanya and silently begged for help.

On cue, Tanya asked, "Joselyn, did you pick a date for the wedding?"

There was a long sigh. "Not really. I wanted to have it on the first weekend of December, but that doesn't look possible now."

"Why not?" Bobby asked.

"Because. Every place that's remotely decent has been booked for months."

"Why does it have to be December?" Luke asked.

"That's the anniversary of our first date," Joselyn said, linking arms with Kevin and laying her head on his shoulder. "Also, I really want Gran to be at the wedding and she's in poor health. She's been in and out of the hospital these last few weeks."

"I'm sorry to hear that. I always liked your grandmother," Cami said.

Without missing a beat, Joselyn added, "And if I had it in December, I could have a winter themed wedding. I can picture it perfectly: the bridesmaids in dark green, the men in black tuxedos with matching bow ties. The flowers would be sprays of evergreen mixed with white roses, draped over white fur muffs with small touches of scarlet placed strategically."

"That sounds beautiful," Tanya commented.

"You could have pine trees along the outside strung with twinkle lights and luminaries with candles down the aisle," Cami added.

"Oh, I love that."

"I just had a thought." Tanya sat up straighter. "You could have it here."

"Here?" Joselyn asked. "At Cherry Hollow?"

"Yes, it would be perfect. You could be the first ones."

"I don't know." Joselyn asked cautiously, "Where would we have it? The house needs work and the grounds are atrocious."

Cami scooted forward eagerly, and ignored the last

comment. She had wanted to broach the subject of an engagement party with Joselyn and this was the perfect opening, thanks to Tanya. "I know it's a mess right now, but if you want to have it outside, we could. Brock is going to start on Monday working on the terrace and this area." Cami could see Joselyn was about to object. "Let me paint you a picture." She settled into her seat, relaxing. "The firepit will be removed. There's going to be a place for seating, and an arch over there." Cami pointed. "The arch itself will be made of wood and stone, and the columns square yet rugged and rustic looking. The arch will flow organically up from the columns, so the top of the arch looks like branches. It will blend with the surroundings. The path is going to be widened and flow organically to the arch."

She looked at Joselyn, trying to get her to see what she saw, excited now by the possibility of having the wedding. Cami didn't want to lose sight that the wedding should be about Joselyn. "You could have it at dusk with the fairy-lights twined through the branches, and luminaries lining the pathway. It would be so enchanting and romantic, especially with your color choice for the wedding party."

Joselyn let go of Kevin and leaned toward Cami, listening. "And what if it's cold? December in Pennsylvania is sure to be."

"We can rent portable heaters and place them around the perimeter. The reception can be on the terrace or in the ballroom," Cami shrugged. "Whichever you'd prefer."

"It sounds fabulous. Almost too good to be true. It could be the perfect backdrop for a wedding." Flip flopping, Joselyn frowned. "I don't know, though. How do we know you can pull it all together in six weeks?"

"She was an events coordinator at her last job, Joselyn, for five years. The hotel she worked at has events every week. Business meetings, job fairs, fashion shows, *and* weddings. On almost any given week there are multiple events going on. Cami can certainly handle one wedding," Tanya reminded her.

"Thank you, Tanya. And that's true, we generally had multiple events happening simultaneously. If it makes you feel better, I can call Brock in the morning and give him our timeline to make sure it's possible."

"I still don't know. What do you think?" Joselyn asked Kevin.

"How much money is this going to cost me?"

"I wouldn't charge you for using the space."

"Cami, you can't do that," Tanya protested. "You're just starting your business."

She held up her hand, cutting Tanya off. "I can, and I would let you use the space for free. I would need you to cover some expenses like staffing and food costs. Cake, drinks, dinner, just like you would at any other venue."

"That sounds reasonable," Kevin commented.

"I can work out the details with you."

"Are you sure about this? It's a little sudden," Luke asked.

"I need to get started on my business somehow. Someone has to be first, and as long as Kevin and Joselyn agree to letting me use them as a recommendation after and use photos from the event, I would be more than happy to do it for free."

Joselyn still hesitated. "It sounds wonderful, but…"

"But what?" Tanya asked. "It sounds like a no brainer to me."

She could tell Joselyn was on the fence. She wanted to, but was afraid to make the leap. Cami decided right there she would sweeten the deal, so they couldn't possibly say no. "How about I even throw in a small engagement party? My treat. We could have it in the ballroom. It could be a semi-formal affair. Simple. Elegant. Champagne and hors d'oeuvres." She paused and let that sink in. "If you need to think about it, you can. Like I said before, I'll call Brock tomorrow and verify a timeline."

Joselyn shifted on the log and looked at Kevin. "What do you think? Do you like the idea of having it here?"

Kevin smiled. "You had me at *free*."

Bobby roared with laughter. "Kevin the mighty financial planner strikes again!"

CHAPTER 18

"What exactly are we doing today that couldn't wait until noon?" Kevin asked, stifling a yawn.

Cami opened the door, flipped on the light, and turned around to face him. "We, that would be you and me," she said as she wagged her finger back and forth between them, "Are going to get carpets down from the attic."

"Tell me again why we need carpets?"

"We need them for the main hall and the ballroom."

"I got that much, but for what?"

Cami patted him on the cheek. "So that everything is perfect for the engagement party, silly." She started up the steep steps with him close behind her.

"But why does this involve me? You're the brains behind all this."

"I am the brains." She stopped and waited for him at the top of the attic stairs. He was eye to eye with her as he stopped one step short of the top. "And you're the brawn." Cami reached out and squeezed his upper arm. "Needs work, but since you're all I have, you'll do."

"Hey!" Kevin flexed his arm, slightly offended. "I've got more muscle than you think."

"Good, because you're going to have to prove it." Cami looked around the large expanse of the room. The endless space was as she remembered it: dark, dusty, and vast. The ceiling was low and peeked in the center, dormers flanking both sides, nooks and crannies lurking in the shadows as the attic followed the sprawling shape of the main house. At first glance, the space looked like it was a jumble of disarray, but there was a method to the madness. Stacks of boxes were stored off to the left, area rugs were rolled and stored in the center, and furniture covered in drop cloths flanked the outer rim.

The attic looked like something found in a horror movie. The shadows made the space feel cavernous and sinister, but Cami had always found it fascinating. It had been the perfect place on a rainy day as a child. She had played hide-and-seek with Charlotte up here and they explored the many treasures it held. After all, there was a rather large collection from five generations of Parkers stored under one roof.

Kevin ran a hand through his professionally styled walnut brown hair and asked, "Where exactly are we going to start?"

"Well, I have a crew coming Monday to pick up the runners and have them cleaned. They'll bring them back after the floors are finished. The rugs should be here." Cami pointed to the pile of carpets. "My mother had everything rolled, labeled, and stored up here before we moved out. When I called and asked her, she said what we are looking for should be on top."

"I'm surprised your mother was that forthcoming with information for someone that didn't want you to come back."

"Let's just say she didn't give up the information without a fight."

He laughed. "That doesn't surprise me. Gotta give Carol Parker a lot of credit. When she puts her mind to being a pure pain-in-the-ass, she does a good job of it."

"You can say that again," Cami agreed. "But she's an organized pain-in-the-ass." Good to her word, the hallway runners had been the last thing stored and were easily accessible. "Here they are, right on top."

It was a struggle as Kevin lifted one end and Cami the other. Kevin went down the stairs backward, holding his end. "Where exactly are we going with this bad boy?"

"First floor. I was thinking . . ."

"That's never good." He smirked at her over the rug.

Cami stuck out her tongue. "Be quiet and give me a minute."

"One, two, three."

"Are you counting?"

"Yes. Four, five."

"Why?" she asked, trying to keep from dropping her end as she came out of the stairwell and onto the second floor.

"You said to give you a minute. I want to make sure that's all you get. If I give you more, who knows what you will come up with?"

"Okay, wise guy. We're going to the study. Now pivot your end so we can take this next set of stairs."

"Not so fast," he grumbled, readjusting to take most of the weight as they descended again. "I'm losing my grip."

"We're almost there."

On the first floor, they turned toward the study.

"The door's closed."

"It shouldn't be."

"Well, it is. Hang on, let me see if I can get the handle without setting my side down."

Cami heard him swear under his breath.

"What's the matter?"

"It's locked."

"Are you sure?"

"Yes, I'm sure. I'm not an idiot."

"Oh, for goodness' sake. Let's put the rug down." They both set it down. "I'll have to go get the key. Be right back." Cami took the stairs two at a time to her room. Grabbing the keys out of her nightstand, she ran back down the stairs.

"Why didn't you unlock the door before we went upstairs?"

"I never locked them. The doors were wide open when you came this morning."

"Are you sure?"

"Yes, I'm sure."

"Then how do you explain that as we speak, you are inserting a key into the locked door?"

"I can't. Or if I did, you probably wouldn't believe me." She opened the doors and tucked the keys into her front pocket. "Grab the other end, please."

He bent as instructed and hoisted his end. "Try me."

"What?" Cami asked, struggling to do the same.

"Try telling me. I'm a pretty good listener, and I might believe you."

They put the rug down and walked back out of the room. Cami turned her hazel eyes on Kevin and pinned him in place. "I'm not ready to say just yet."

He laughed. "Okay, fair enough. Let me know when you are."

She nodded. "Think you're up for getting a few more rugs down here?"

"Sure. What else do I have to do today?"

"That's the spirit!"

They walked back up the stairs, side by side. They paused outside of Charlotte's room.

Kevin jerked his finger toward the closed door. "What's with Charlotte's room? Have you been in there yet since you've been back?"

"I have. Twice."

"And?"

"And what?"

"Did you look around?"

She shrugged. "A little."

"Did you find anything?"

"Like what?"

"I don't know." He rubbed his chin, thinking, his mood clearly shifting. "You said you wanted answers to what happened to Charlotte. If it were me, that's the place I would start."

Watching him, she wondered if she should mention

anything to him about the handwritten messages in the yearbook. She wasn't ready to discuss the possibility of what they might mean to him or anyone other than Luke. She tried to keep it light. "One of these days I'll get around to it." Cami linked her arm through his. "I've missed this." She nudged him.

"What, hauling rugs?"

"No, you and me. We used to do a lot of things together… before."

"I knew what you meant. I miss it, too. More than you'll ever know."

Changing the subject quickly, before she got too sentimental, she asked, "So, you and Joselyn, huh? How did that happen, exactly? I always knew you had a secret crush on someone in high school, but I never really thought you were interested in Joselyn."

Kevin shrugged. "I wasn't. I was into someone else."

"Okay, so what happened to the girl in high school? Did you go for it and get rejected?"

They stopped at the bottom of the attic stairs. Cami turned to face him, waiting.

"I never had the courage to ask her out."

"That's tough, Kevin." She watched him for a moment, took in the man, who, as a boy, had been one of her best friends, and still was. The quick wit, the tall build, the kind eyes. Her heart ached for him. She couldn't help herself, so she asked, "Do you have any regrets?"

His brown eyes softened and turned to liquid pools as dark as coffee. "Every day."

"Oh, Kevin." Cami reached out and gave him a quick hug, surprised when he hugged her back and held on tightly. "I think everyone has some regrets." She pulled back. "But at least there's a happy ending for you. You got Joselyn."

"Yes, I did."

"And?"

"And what?"

"And what happened? Geez. Do I have to pry every detail

out of you?"

"Things change."

"That's it? Things change. That's all you got? Soooo romantic." She rolled her eyes.

He laughed.

"Wow," she said dryly. "I have no words." Cami shook her head slightly, turned her back on him and ascended the attic stairs with him on her heels.

They grabbed the next rug, hefted it between them, and Kevin started down the stairs backward.

"I'll have you know I can be romantic when I need to be."

"Oh, really?" She raised an eyebrow at him over the rug. "Give me an example."

He was silent until they were off the stairs. "One summer I wrote a letter, or maybe a poem is a better word for it, every night to the girl I had a crush on."

"That's sweet. And?"

"And what?"

"What happened?"

"I put them all in a box and gave it to her for her birthday."

"What did she say?"

"Nothing."

"Nothing?" Cami asked in disbelief. "How can that be?"

He shrugged. "She never even acknowledged that she got them, let alone read any of them."

"Oh, Kevin. That's so sweet and completely devastating." Cami fell silent for a few minutes as they concentrated on carrying the large carpet. "I wonder what she thought. I wonder why she didn't respond. At the very least, she could have let you know she read them. You deserved that much after pouring your heart out." Cami sighed. "But it is definitely romantic."

"Guess we'll never know now."

He was silent for a long time.

Back down in the study, they walked in and laid the area

rug next to the other one. Changing the subject quickly, trying to bring the fun back into the atmosphere, she asked, "Do you remember what you gave me on my seventeenth birthday?"

He froze, watching her. "No, what?"

"A Chia Pet."

"No, I didn't."

"Yes, you did. I laughed so hard I nearly peed my pants."

His mouth twitched, and the corners turned up. "Hey, you know... that's the gift that keeps on giving."

"It was memorable, I'll give you that much." She prodded him along. "One more hallway runner to go."

Kevin nodded. "Yep. Then you're going to feed me, right? I'm starving."

"Of course." They walked back up the stairs headed to the attic. "I'll make my famous cheese and turkey panini for you."

"That actually sounds good. It's been a while since I had a home-cooked meal."

"Doesn't Joselyn cook?"

"Nope, she always wants to eat out."

"So, back to you and Joselyn. How did it happen?"

"Not much to say, really. I ran into her and Tanya one night at the bar. Didn't even know it was her at first. I hadn't seen her in a while. She'd gotten contacts and a new hairstyle. She looked cute." He shrugged. "Anyway, Tanya wasn't feeling well and wanted to go. I could tell Josie wasn't ready to go, so I offered to give her a ride. She was pretty tipsy by the time I got her home. One thing led to another." He picked up the end of the rug and Cami followed suit. "The rest is history."

They struggled down the stairs.

"Well, I, for one, think it's great."

The carpet was larger than the first two, and Cami was having a hard time holding on. They both fell silent as they struggled.

Kevin grunted as he came out of the stairwell, and Cami descended the last few steps.

"I'm definitely going to need a break after this one."

"Yeah, me too."

They walked in silence for another minute, both breathing heavily as Cami's hands and arms ached under the strain. At first, the scent didn't register with her, but the chill that brushed against her bare skin did. "Not now," she whispered, but it was too late. The surrounding air vibrated with energy.

Kevin exclaimed, "What the?" right before he toppled backward.

CHAPTER 19

Grabbing a bottle of water, Luke walked into his home office and sat down at his desk. The police scanner was on low in the background as he pulled out the Charlotte Parker file. He flipped it open and read through the coroner's report again.

Name: Charlotte Rose Parker
Sex: Female
Race: Caucasian
Age: 17 years, 2 months, 3 days
Height: 5'6"
Weight: 110lbs
Hair color: Blonde
Eyes color: Blue
Cause of Death: Trauma to the base of skull/exposure: subject appeared to have fallen backward, striking base of skull on a sharp rock. Subject lay bleeding and exposed overnight in sub-freezing temps. Rigor mortis was apparent when found. Time of death approximately between 11:00 pm on the 26th and 1:00 am on the 27th. Subject declared dead at scene.

Abnormal findings: Lips slightly blue, consistent with hypoxia. Green cotton fibers found in deceased mouth and airway. Green fibers consistent with deceased clothing. Deceased was wearing light green, cotton sweatshirt. Blood levels contained low amounts of oxygen. Possibilities: exposure due to extreme cold temps overnight, or asphyxiation. Slight bruising found around outside of mouth. Saliva was found on inside of the above-noted item of clothing.

Slight bruising found in middle of chest cavity. External only. No injuries internally.

Something about the report bothered him. He just couldn't put his finger on it. The radio squawked to life. Luke put the report aside and listened.

"Dispatch: we need an ambulance at 430 Sawmill Road. Twenty-eight-year-old male fell down a set of stairs and is unconscious."

"Dispatching an ambulance now."

Sawmill Road? Cami's house.

Luke put the photos back in the file, tucked them in his desk drawer, grabbed his keys, and ran to his SUV.

Less than ten minutes later, Luke pulled into the driveway right behind the ambulance.

He was crossing the yard when the front door opened and Cami emerged.

"He's in the front drawing room," Cami said to the EMTs. She held the door open and pointed when she noticed Luke. "I wasn't expecting to see you. I didn't know detectives answered emergency calls."

"I heard the address and let the station know I could respond quickly. We're a little short-staffed this weekend."

She nodded and ushered him in.

"What happened?"

"Kevin fell down the stairs. He's awake now and having a fit because I called. He was out cold for a good thirty seconds. Scared the heck out of me."

Kevin sat on the couch with an ice pack on his head, grumbling at the EMTs. "I'm fine. It's nothing but a bump on the head."

"Sit still and let them do their job, Kevin."

"What brings you out on an ambulance call, Detective?" he asked, glancing over at Luke. "You got nothin' better to do than gawk at the injured?"

"Heard some fool went and threw himself down the

stairs, had to come see for myself who it was." Luke reached for Cami's arm and ushered her back into the hall. "Let's give them a minute to properly assess him. Did you call Joselyn?"

"No, Kevin said not to. He practically grabbed the phone out of my hand while I was talking to 9-1-1."

"Tell me what happened."

"We were carrying an area rug down from the attic. He was on the second step from the top and just missed the next step." Cami shuddered. "You should have heard the crack when his head hit the railing. It was awful."

"And where were you when this happened?"

"I was on the other end."

"Did you lose your grip on the rug when he fell?"

She shook her head. "I hung on and tried to stop the momentum of his fall but the rug was so heavy I couldn't hold it back, just slowed it down a little."

He looked her over. "Are you hurt?"

"No, I'm fine."

One of the EMTs came out of the drawing room.

"How's the patient?" Luke asked, recognizing the EMT.

"Mild concussion and a big bump on the back of his head. Not much we can do. He doesn't want to go into the hospital and we can't force him." He waited for his partner to come out. "We're going to head out if there's nothing else."

"Thanks, Jasper."

"Yes, thank you for coming out quickly."

"Just doing our job. It would be best to monitor him over the next day or two. If he seems to act funny, like slurring his words, excessive headaches, sensitivity to light or sound, acts confused, clumsy or disoriented, then…"

"You mean more clumsy than usual?" Luke joked.

Jasper choked back a laugh and bobbed his head. "Yeah, more than his usual. Kevin has always been kinda clumsy."

"I can hear you; you know."

Unfazed, Jasper continued, "Then I'd suggest bringing him into the ER or getting an appointment with his provider.

He's going to be stiff and sore for a few days, that's to be expected." He looked over at his partner. "Got everything?"

"Yep, that's a wrap."

"Okay, we're heading out. Call us if you need us."

"Thanks again," Cami said, closing the door behind them.

"I'm not clumsy!" Kevin yelled from the drawing room.

Luke grinned at Cami. "Oh, yeah?" He winked at her and walked into the room. "Then how do you explain the fact that you just fell down the stairs?"

"I got spooked."

Cami tensed. There was just something in Kevin's tone that had her on edge. Deflecting, she pointed, "That ice pack is leaking. Let me go get a towel."

She wasn't completely out of the room when she heard Luke question Kevin.

"You got spooked? That's an odd thing to say."

"Yeah." Kevin cleared his throat. "I thought I saw something and I wasn't watching where I was going."

Cami didn't need to hear the rest. She hustled down the hall and into the mud room. She knew exactly what Kevin was going to say. She had smelled roses only seconds before Kevin fell. The question was, did Kevin know what he saw? Twice now, out of the corner of her eye, she too had seen Charlotte, or what she presumed was her twin sister.

It was weird. It was just the softest ripple in the air. Like a thin veil of semi-translucent smoke, or a whisper of a form that shimmered in place, disrupting the very fabric of the atmosphere. And then it was gone, leaving behind the soft scent of roses and a breath of cold air. She had mentioned it in passing before to Bobby and Luke, but now? Now there was a real possibility that someone else had seen it, too. The idea of it, the realization that it might actually be true and not just her imagination or long-forgotten memories resurfacing scared her. What if Charlotte really was here?

Cami grabbed a hand towel and hurried back to the

drawing room. "Here you go," she said unnaturally, thrusting the towel at Kevin. She wanted to ask him what he saw. Or thought he saw, but couldn't in front of Luke without looking suspicious.

"Are you okay?" Luke asked.

"I'm fine." Cami took a deep breath. *Stop acting crazy.* "Just concerned about what Joselyn is going to say when she finds out what happened. I don't want her to change her mind about the engagement party or the wedding." Cami reached out as Kevin stood up and placed her hand on his arm. "I so want to do this for you both."

"She doesn't need to know what happened. If she finds out, she'll just worry."

"Do you think you're going to keep it from her?" Luke asked. "The ambulance was here, and even if they don't mention it to someone, don't you think she's going to wonder where that bump on your head came from?"

"He's right, Kevin. She's going to find out."

"You let me worry about Josie. Keep things as planned. Nothing will change." Kevin rolled his shoulders and rubbed at the back of his neck with his hands. "Except."

"What's that?"

"I think I'm done for the day. I need a hot shower and some Icy Hot."

"That's completely understandable. You should take it easy. We'll walk you out," Cami said, taking the ice pack and towel from him. They walked to the front door, went outside, and stopped by Kevin's car. Concerned, she asked. "Are you alright to drive?"

"I'm fine, just stiff and sore."

"I think I should drive you home," Luke said.

"Stop worrying, both of you," he said pointedly. "Besides, if you take me home, I'll have to come back for my car, then Joselyn will know for sure." He dug his keys out of his pocket and opened the door. When he leaned down to get in, he fell forward, slightly off balance.

Luke reached for him, catching him by the shoulders. "Hold up. Cami, take his keys. You're driving him home. I'll follow behind in my SUV and bring you back."

"I'm fine."

"No, you're not," Cami said softly, the concern evident in her voice.

"Go around to the passenger side; Cami's driving you," Luke directed.

"I'm fine. Really."

"Stop arguing. I'm driving," Cami said firmly. "Let me grab my purse. I'll be right back."

Kevin sagged, defeated and hurting, he climbed into the passenger's side. He closed his eyes and leaned back.

When the driver's door opened and Cami climbed in, he cracked one eye at her and said, "Thanks. It would have actually been a struggle to keep it between the lines. My head really hurts."

"I'm sure it does." Cami started the car and drove out of the driveway with Luke directly behind her. They drove the distance in silence as Kevin rested his head against the window, Cami kept the music off. As she got close to his house, she glanced at him. "Kevin?"

"Yeah?"

"You're going to tell Joselyn, right? You really shouldn't be left alone for long."

He sighed heavily. "Yeah, I will."

"What's the big deal? She loves you."

"I know. It's just. . ." He sat up in the seat as she pulled into his driveway. "She's kind of a mother hen when it comes to me, a little obsessive. Always pecking around, getting under my skin. Sometimes I just want to be left alone. Especially when I don't feel good."

"Oh, you big baby, you had better get used to it because she's going to be around a lot after the wedding."

He squashed a grin. "You're right."

"Kevin?"

"Yeah?"

"Today on the stairs when you fell. What happened?"

"I told you I missed a step."

"That's it?"

"Yeah, what else would there be?"

"Nothing." Should she ask? "I just thought you might have..." She gave him a sideways glance and lost her courage. "That I was going too fast and accidentally pushed you down the stairs." Pulling into the yard, Cami parked.

"It wasn't your fault."

"Positive?"

"I am."

Cami got out of the car. Kevin moved a little slower, but he did the same.

"Need any help getting into the house?" Cami asked.

"No, I'm good."

"You're sure?"

"Yep."

She handed him the keys. "I'll call you later and see how you're doing. Okay?"

"Yep." Kevin waved at Luke. "Thanks, both of you."

"No worries. Just relax and get better," Luke said with his head stuck out the window. Cami got in the passenger's side and shut the door. They watched Kevin disappear inside, then backed out of the yard and headed toward Cherry Hollow.

Cami was suddenly very self-conscious as she sat next to Luke.

"Do you still have a lot of stuff to bring down from the attic?" he asked.

Looking out the window instead of directly at Luke, she answered, "A few more rugs, and I want to bring down a small breakfront for the foyer. I believe some of the crystal lamps are stored up there, too. They always look so nice in the corner of the ballroom. I want to bring those down. There are a few paintings I want to get back on the walls as well." She shrugged and watched the trees go by. "Stuff like that."

"Can I give you a hand?"

"Oh, no. There's no need. I can get most of it myself."

"And what about the pieces you can't?"

She hesitated. "I'll figure something out."

Luke pulled onto Sawmill Road. "I'm sure you could. But it will save some time if you just let me help."

Cami had no real argument. Part of her wanted to say yes so badly so she could spend as much time with him as possible, but the other half of her was afraid. Afraid of being rejected. Afraid that he wasn't interested in her like that. Not like she had been, and was still, after all these years with him. Ultimately, though, she needed help, and her only legitimate reason for not letting him was possibly a figment of her imagination.

Luke stopped the vehicle in front of her house.

"If you're sure? I could use the help," Cami said, sounding doubtful.

"I wouldn't have offered it if I wasn't." He smiled at her. "Cami, you need to remember you're back home now. When people offer, they do so with no ulterior motive."

She laughed, getting out of the car. Walking backward, looking at him, she asked, "Am I that obvious? Have I been in the city that long?"

An easy grin spread across his face. "A little. Although, I might have a motive other than the obvious bonus of getting to spend time with you."

"Oh? And what would that be?"

"Kevin mentioned something about getting a turkey and cheese panini."

She laughed. "That can be arranged."

CHAPTER 20

Shadows stretched long across the large expanse of the sprawling room as they sat dirty and exhausted on the top of the attic stairs.

"I don't think I can carry anything else."

"I hate to admit it but I'm tired myself." Luke rubbed at a kink in his neck. "Is there anything else you wanted to get out of here yet tonight?"

"There is one thing." Cami shifted, stretching her legs. "I was hoping to find my grandmother's china. She had an elegant pattern that would be perfect for something like an intimate engagement party."

"Any idea where it might be?"

"My guess would be off in the back." She pointed with her finger to the dark recesses of the attic, where the shadows hung low. "Tucked away to keep it from breaking easily."

Luke stood, held out his hand, and pulled her up. Surprised at the electricity that raced up her arm at the contact, Cami couldn't help but get lost in the feeling of the moment. He brushed against her and her pulse skidded. She swallowed hard and tried to keep her voice from betraying her. "I completely understand if you need to take off, I can get the box of china myself."

His free hand went to her face, his thumb brushed the dust off along the edge of her jawline. She shivered at his touch. Luke's eyes flicked down to her mouth, and it was all she could do not to lean in and kiss him.

Cami's face was flushed, her skin warm and soft, his

hand lingered on her face, and his eyes were on her full mouth. He wondered if she tasted the same after all these years. Luke felt her go rigid as his eyes lingered on her lips. It was all he could do to return his eyes to hers. Immediately, he was sucked into the realm of Cami. Eyes as intense as the deep forest tempted him. Without thinking, his hand released hers and dropped to her waist. Pulling her toward him, he leaned in and brushed his lips against hers. He felt her tense, then soften, relaxing into his embrace. Luke couldn't help himself. A sly smile crept across his rugged features, and he pressed in, deepening the kiss.

The lingering taste and scent of red ripe cherries still surrounded Cami, same as all those years ago. Suddenly he felt seventeen again, ready to grab her and drop down right where they were, but the man inside him took control. He wouldn't ruin this moment he'd waited so long for. Instead, he tasted, tempted with his tongue, felt her sigh into the kiss, and pressed her warm, willing body against him.

He was going down fast. A man drowning on land when he felt her hand slide between them and push him gently back.

"Luke, I need…"

His lips twitched. "What do you need, Cami?"

"Air."

He laughed. "Me too." Leaning back, he gave her some space but didn't take his hands off her. "I've been waiting to do that for ten years." Looking up at him with those intense hazel eyes, he was nearly undone. "What are you thinking?" he asked quietly.

"I… I," she stammered slightly. "So have I."

"How does it compare to the first time?"

She wanted to keep it light, needed to, so he wouldn't realize the effect he'd had on her. "Well, the first time was definitely more rushed, but the atmosphere was more romantic."

He chuckled. "Not a kiss-me-in-the-attic kinda girl? I'll have to remember that. Should have known you'd be the more outdoorsy type, liking it under the stars better. You always were."

Pleased he remembered and knew her that well, she eased back out of his grasp. *Keep it light,* she told herself. *Don't read too much into the moment.* "What were we going to look for?"

"China."

"Right." She side-stepped him. "Maybe over here." Cami moved back into the depths of the attic. She pulled a chain and a bare bulb lit over her head, pushing back shadows. "Looks like everything's labeled. The gray plastic totes are the more recent addition to the attic, thanks to my mom. The boxes are from the older generations."

"And just how many generations are we talking about here?"

"I'm the fifth. My great, great grandfather built this house, and they have passed it down to the oldest living male in the family for three generations. I'm the first woman and the youngest. Charlotte was born first, so I guess it would have been hers had she lived."

"Are you sure?" Luke asked.

"What do you mean?"

"If Charlotte was alive, would she want the house? I always pictured her as more of a city girl, myself."

"You're right. She would have loved New York, she'd always talked about going. I hated the city. Tolerated it for as long as I could, but it just wasn't me."

"Whose name are we looking for?" he asked, peering over her shoulder.

"Margaret Louise, my grandmother." She pointed. "There are labels on the corner of each box."

Luke glanced down. "Who took the time to label all these?"

"Probably my mother. Or at least the more recent ones."

"Who are some of these? They labeled this one Edith Marie."

"That's my great-grandmother on my mom's side." They both picked their way through the boxes. "Here's my grandmother's section," Cami said over her shoulder as she spotted the label. "My, she has a lot of boxes." Hands on her hips, Cami contemplated the pile. "If only my mother had written on the outside what was in them, we would be good to go."

"Let's think about this. Your mom would not put china on the bottom and stack heavy things on top. So it has to be on top, and probably marked FRAGILE, like that one." He pointed to the tote with big black letters.

Stepping past him, she said, "I'm impressed. Now I know why you became a detective so quickly."

He chuckled, a deep rich laugh, and it made her smile. Kiss or not, she enjoyed being with Luke. *No,* she scolded herself, *don't think about that kiss.* "Let's open the box and make sure it's china. I wish I had scissors. It's taped shut."

Luke pulled out a pocket knife and flicked it open. "Here, use this."

"Thanks." She slit the top and opened the box. "Bingo. Looks like these are the dishes." She held up a delicate, bone-white porcelain plate that had an embossed pattern of cherry blossoms around the edge. "Just as beautiful as I remembered. There should be at least one more box with serving pieces in it."

"How 'bout this one?" Reaching for another box with FRAGILE written on it, he handed it to her.

She slit the top. "Detective, we have a winner. Let's get this downstairs and call it a day."

"Hand me a box."

She did, and they worked their way back across the attic when a white plastic tote caught her eye. Hesitating, Cami set her box down.

"What's the matter?"

Pointing, she said, "That looks like a recent addition, but it's not with the others and not the same standard gray my mom used." Cami squatted. "There's no label." Popping the top of the container, Cami gasped.

"What is it?" Luke asked, putting his box down and coming over.

Cami reached in and lifted out a faded green sweatshirt. "It's my favorite hoodie." A wave of nausea swept over her. She swallowed hard as the memory swamped her. "The one...the one Charlotte was wearing when she died."

Reaching, he gently took the label that was attached out of Cami's trembling hand. "This looks like police evidence. It still has an id tag on it."

Someone neatly printed Charlotte Parker on the small label, along with the date and the word "evidence." Luke reached into the tote and found a pair of jeans with the same labeling. He didn't dig any further. Luke knew without a doubt. *That's what this is. Evidence.* "I'm sorry, Cami, this is your sister's belongings from that night. But you said it was your favorite hoodie, and I remember you wearing it a lot. So why was Charlotte wearing it?"

Tears blurred her vision. "We were standing in the woods talking, deciding which way to go, where to hide. Charlotte came running up and Joselyn turned, tripping. She stumbled and fell forward into Charlotte, covering her in soda. It was an accident, but Charlotte was pissed because she was wet and sticky. The only thing I had to give her was my hoodie. I hadn't been wearing it, just had it wrapped around my waist. So I gave it to her to put on."

"I see. What else?"

Cami shrugged, blinking back tears. "Nothing. She put it on and then ran off into the woods. That's the last time I saw her alive."

He wondered what else the container held. After all these years, could there be a clue in here that Detective Swanson missed? He itched to dig through the rest but wouldn't in front of Cami, and not without her permission. "Would you mind if I took this tote and looked through it?"

She nodded her consent.

The day and the mood had darkened considerably, and Luke needed to change that quickly. Snapping the lid back on, he placed the box marked FRAGILE on top of the white tote. "Let's get this china downstairs into the kitchen, where we can properly go through it. See if anything is missing."

Cami nodded, grabbed her box, and made a beeline for the stairs.

***

"Kevin, I'm home," Joselyn called as she walked into the darkened house.

He heard her and cringed, but didn't answer. She flipped on the kitchen lights comfortable in his space. Hearing her dropping her keys in the ceramic bowl on the counter, he imagined her shrugging out of her jacket, hanging it and her purse on the hook by the back door.

"Kevin?" she called again.

"In here," he replied.

Joselyn walked into the dark living room and reached for the lamp. "Why are you lying here in the dark?"

"I have a terrible headache. Please leave off the light."

"Oh, Kevin. I'm sorry, are you getting sick? You never have a headache." Joselyn came over and sat on the edge of the couch beside him and put her lips to his forehead. "You're not warm, so no fever."

"I'm not sick. I hit my head."

"At Cami's? I knew I shouldn't have let you go over there. How?" she demanded.

"Moving stuff," he said, then thought better of it when he felt her bristle. Thinking quickly, he added, "I wasn't watching where I was going, and bumped my head in the attic. The ceilings aren't very high. No big deal."

"Do you have a bump?"

"A little one," he lied. *More like the size of a goose egg.*

"Let me see."

He grabbed her hands when she reached out, not wanting her to touch his head. He kissed her hands instead. "It's nothing, Josie. Just a little bump." He could see her frown in the darkness. If she knew he fell down the stairs, she'd have an absolute fit. Or the reason he'd fallen in the first place, she'd never let him step foot back into that house. Right now he wasn't sure if he even wanted to, but he wasn't about to let Josie decide because the engagement party and the wedding wouldn't take place there if she knew. It could have easily been his imagination. Was it? Or had there really been something there? He shivered, despite himself. Pushing the image to the back of his mind, he feigned a smile instead. "Don't worry."

"But you know I do."

"I know." He sat up and pulled her onto his lap. "But there's no need."

"Other than your head, how did it go?" she asked, a little skeptical. "Is Cami going to have everything together for our engagement party, let alone a wedding, in six weeks? Or should we be looking elsewhere?"

"It went well. We got the hallway runners down. A cleaning company is coming Monday morning to get the rugs. Painters are coming first thing to paint the ballroom and entryway. They guaranteed they'd finish by Tuesday afternoon. Which is good because the flooring guys are coming Wednesday morning to refinish the hardwood."

"Wow, she really moved on this."

"Yes, she did. She wants it to be very special for us."

"And it will be good for her new business if she pulls it off." Josie sniffed. "That's really why she's doing this. You know that, right? It has nothing to do with us."

"How can you say that?" Kevin asked, slightly irked at Josie's attitude. "She's one of my very best friends, yours too."

"Used to be."

"What's that supposed to mean?"

Josie let out a huff. "You know Cami and I haven't been

close since she moved away."

Kevin lifted her chin and looked directly into her face, detecting a little jealousy beneath that innocent-looking face. "And whose fault is that? Cami tried, didn't she?" Josie looked away, staring off into the darkness. "You have to admit she tried. It was hard on her, but she didn't cut you off. You cut yourself off. Am I right, or am I right?" he asked playfully.

"Yeah, maybe. But you always take her side."

"No, I don't."

"*Yes,* you do."

He let the comment go. Kevin knew there was no winning this argument. He hadn't in the past and he wouldn't now. Even in the darkness, he could see the frown on her face and the crease between her eyebrows. She was brooding, and that was never good. If he didn't get her out of this funk, he'd pay the price later. Kevin slid her off his lap. "I'm going to grab some Tylenol, a quick shower, and then take you out for dinner. I'm starving." He thought of the panini he'd been deprived of because he'd fallen down the damn stairs. His mouth watered and his stomach growled. "Pick someplace that we haven't been to in a while." He didn't want to go to Finn's again and take the chance of running into anybody tonight. He wasn't in the mood to be social.

CHAPTER 21

The music started and an uplifting melody filled the air as Luke settled on the pew beside Bobby. The wooden doors to the sanctuary groaned loudly in resistance to being opened. He caught movement out of the corner of his eye and turned.

The sight of her hit him like a breath of fresh air. Simple and pure. She wore a moss green lantern sleeve print dress that dipped low in the front and floated mid-thigh. Swallowing hard, Luke noticed the hem brushed long, tan legs, and her hair hung loose in soft waves midway down her back. Cami slipped in the last row opposite them and threaded dark sunglasses into soft honey-brown hair.

Bobby leaned over and elbowed him. "You gonna take a breath soon? Or am I gonna have to call for an ambulance when you pass out?"

"What?" Luke asked, sucking in air.

"Damn if she ain't cute, but you gotta keep it together, man. I don't have any tissues if you drool."

"I don't know what you're talking about."

Joselyn glanced over her shoulder and hushed them.

"Look at that, now she's gotten us in trouble," Bobby chuckled, shaking his head. "Ten years later, and I'll be damned if the nickname still doesn't fit."

Luke forced his eyes to the front as the music ceased and a voice boomed from the podium, greeting them. Picking up his bulletin, Luke scanned the contents, dreading the next hour would drag now that he had the picture of her in his mind, or worse that she would slip out before the service was over and he wouldn't get to talk to her.

Heaven help him, Luke tried to concentrate on the service. He really did. He stood, sat, and bent his head at the appropriate times. He passed the plate and dropped money in, but for the life of him, no matter how hard he tried, he just couldn't keep his eyes forward and on the pulpit. His mind and his eyes kept wandering to the right. To her.

Luke let out a sigh of relief when the prelude started, and everyone stood. The preacher walked by and the ushers pulled the heavy doors open, letting in the fall air. As the music ended, everyone filed into the aisle. Luke saw Cami pick up her purse and slip out of the pew. She had just let go of the pastor's hand and walked out into the sunshine when Luke came up behind her.

"Hey, gorgeous."

Turning toward him, she smiled, melting his heart.

"Hey, yourself."

"Did you forget what time church started? Or did you oversleep?"

"A little of both, I suppose. But I made it before the first song was over. That has to count for something."

"Hey, Parker." Bobby looked her up and down. "Not sure you should be allowed in church looking like that. I think it might actually be a sin or a crime to look that good at church." Bobby grinned as Cami blushed. "Luke might have to haul your pretty little ass in." He tapped Luke on the shoulder with a fist. "What do you think, Detective?"

Luke was saved from answering with the arrival of the others. Aaron hung back, looking awkward. Tanya came up beside Cami and gave her a hug. "Girl, don't you look cute!"

"Thank you. So do both of you."

"Thanks," Joselyn said, giving a little twirl in her dress.

"If that ain't the truth," Bobby smiled at Tanya.

Doing a little curtsy, Tanya sent him a wink.

"Hi, Aaron," Cami made it a point to address him as he stood back behind the others.

"Hey, Cami," he managed to say.

Tanya filled the awkward pause. "I didn't see you come in. Why didn't you come up with us?" Tanya asked.

"I can't believe you didn't know she was here," Kevin said. "Everyone heard her come in late." He grinned. "Cami, you are *not* quiet."

"Don't blame me, blame those old oak doors. They're heavier than lead and squeal like nails on a chalkboard."

"That's for sure. I think they do that on purpose, so if the service goes long, you can't sneak out."

"Do you guys want to go grab some lunch?"

"Yes, I'm starving."

"You're always hungry, Kevin." They discussed options on where to eat, and Luke noticed Cami looking around as more people filed out of the church.

"Looking for someone special?" Luke asked, tucking his hands in his front pockets and leaning toward her.

"Actually, yes. I was looking for Detective Swanson. Thought maybe I'd see him here. I know he used to come when I was younger. Just wanted to say hello if he is."

Nodding, Luke said, "He sits up front. He's usually one of the last ones out." Pointing, he said, "Here he comes now." Luke stuck his arm in the air and called out, "Swanson!"

A short, thin man in his mid-sixties with white hair, wearing a suit and tie, glanced over and waved. He held up a finger, indicating he'd be over. They watched him thread his way through the crowd. He stuck out his hand to Luke and shook it heartily. Then Bobby's. "Warner, Cannon. I thought I heard snoring coming from behind me. Should have known you were both back there."

Taking it good-naturedly, Bobby laughed. "I'll have you know I was awake the whole service."

"That's a surprise." Swanson acknowledged the group, "Hello everyone. My, aren't you fellas lucky to be standing here with such beautiful ladies?" He looked from one to the other and recognized Cami. "As I live and breathe. Camilla Parker." He instantly reached out and hugged her. Then held her at arm's length. "What the hell brings you back?"

"Watch it, Swanson," an elderly man said, walking by. "You may not be in church, but you're in proximity."

Dwight waved him off and laughed, not easily offended. "My apologies," he said to the man. "Seriously, Miss Parker. Are you just in town visiting?"

"No, I'm back permanently."

"Really? By permanently, you mean living at Cherry Hollow?"

"Yes."

An ominous expression passed across the older man's face, so quickly, in fact, Luke wasn't sure if he'd just imagined it.

"I would love to sit down and catch up with you. I heard you've retired."

The moment was gone. Dwight nodded. "That's true. The old ticker is giving me some trouble," he said, patting his chest. "Had to ease back some if I want to be around for my golden years."

"Swanson! You comin'?" someone called from behind them.

"Be right there," he called. "I got brunch with the card club right after church every Sunday and they don't like to be late," he explained. "Are you busy this evening?" Detective Swanson asked, looking directly at Cami.

"I'm free."

"Why don't I swing by around seven? We can have coffee and I'll bring fresh baked banana bread. I make a mean loaf. Not to toot my own horn, but I even won a baking contest with it a few years back. It's award-winning." He winked at her. "Tempted?"

"How could I refuse? It sounds perfect. I'll see you at seven."

"Sounds like a plan." He stuck out his hand to the group, fingers spread in an all-encompassing wave. "Folks, you all have a nice Sunday afternoon. Cannon, keep up the good work."

Detective Swanson caught Luke by the arm. "Step into my office for a minute."

Luke nodded and moved away from the group. "What's up?"

"Congratulations on the promotion. I haven't had a chance to really congratulate you. I truly believe you'll make a damn good detective."

"Thanks, Dwight. I appreciate that."

Swanson ran a hand through his thinning white hair. "I know you just got the job less than a week ago, but have you looked through any of those files I left?"

"A few."

Dwight tilted his head slightly in Cami's direction. "Would love to talk to you about one in particular, now that my hands are no longer tied."

"I've wanted to speak with you as well. You were on my list to call, first thing tomorrow."

"Swanson! You comin'? You're holding us up!"

"I'm coming, gall darn it!" he bellowed over his shoulder. "Bunch of impatient…" he stopped himself. "They act like the food's gonna be gone if we don't go right over."

Luke grinned. "Why take chances?"

"Good point. Anyway, call me. There's a couple of things I'd like to discuss with you if she's back."

"You mean Cami?"

"Yep. Could be nothing, and then again…" Swanson shrugged but locked eyes with him, his meaning clear.

Despite the social atmosphere and the beautiful day, an eerie feeling crept over Luke as he held the older man's gaze, understanding. "I'll call you tomorrow."

"You do that."

Despite their discretion, the conversation didn't go unnoticed.

***

It was after five by the time Dwight Swanson headed home from the club. He was running slightly behind schedule because the card game had gone long. They had played three rounds of Progressive Rummy. His cards hadn't been worth a darn all day long. Despite that, his mood didn't sour. Once home, he threw together the ingredients for his award-winning banana bread. Showering quickly while it baked in the oven, he anticipated the evening ahead.

Swanson patted the still warm loaf lightly on the seat beside him as he drove the last few miles to Cherry Hollow. The sun sunk in his rearview mirror behind the Blue Ridge Mountains that ran the length of the horizon.

If he regretted anything about his time on the force, it was the death of Charlotte Parker and how the whole investigation was handled. Charles and Carol Parker had been a big part of the community and so had their daughters. *Maybe too much and that's why this terrible thing happened,* he thought. Everyone in town wanted to believe that Charlotte's death was an unfortunate accident, including the Parkers, so much so that most of the investigation had been restricted and swept under the rug.

Swanson would never forget the day the chief walked into his office and told him to close the Parker case. The Parkers didn't want to pursue it any further and the town would rest easier with an unfortunate accident, rather than a homicide. Because murder just didn't happen in their sleepy, little Pennsylvania town.

Shaking his head, he wondered, *were they right?* Was he the only one that truly believed it wasn't an accident? Ten years later, he still couldn't shake the feeling that they were letting a murderer walk around free.

He was glad he had run into Luke at church. It would be great to get Detective Warner's take on the case now that Luke had read the file and Dwight could fill him in on what wasn't in that folder. Swanson longed to get what he knew off his chest and finally put the case into someone else's hands.

Turning down the lane as dusk quickly approached, he wound through the woods, noting he was a little early. Hopefully, Miss Parker wouldn't mind. Parking the car in front of the fountain, he got out and mentally prepared himself to go into the house. The last time he was here, Carol Parker had screamed at him and thrown him out, accusing him of dragging the Parker name through the mud.

It was an accident, and how dare he say any differently? Who in their right mind would want to hurt her baby?

Dwight knew she was hurting and felt for her and the family, but he was there to do a job like it or not. Had it not been for the chief ordering him to back off… he mentally shrugged. Maybe things would have been different. Maybe there would be a killer behind bars, and this sick pit in his stomach would have gone away years ago, not just gone dormant. But now, seeing Cami? Now it was back in full force.

He got out of the car and started towards the front door when a figure in an upstairs window drew his eye. Looking up, he smiled and stuck his hand in the air. A second later he caught movement out of the corner of his eye.

Swanson only had a split second to react as the dark shadow came at him.

Turning, he swung. A flash of black. Metal struck bone. A sharp edge pierced. Pain seared through his head. A shriek of pain. Swanson didn't know if the guttural sound came from him or his attacker. The world spun. The bread dropped to the ground. Hands clutched the sides of his face, trying to keep the world from spinning. He swayed.

Blood oozed out, ran down his neck, and dripped onto the stone walkway. A wave of nausea swept over him. Swanson reached for the porch column to steady himself and missed. He staggered back. Hit the ground hard. Confused. Dazed. Disoriented, Swanson lay flat on his back staring up into the heavens as star after star winked on high overhead.

CHAPTER 22

The manor loomed large despite the trees as dusk fell quickly in the woods and stars became clearer. Sound carried easily through the woods, the crunch of leaves as Cami walked, the chatter of birds as they bounced from branch to branch, settling down for the night.

She thought of Detective Swanson, pulled her cell phone out of her back pocket and glanced at the time. It was almost seven. She should have turned on the outside lights before she went out for a walk in the woods, in case he was early. Picking up the pace, she covered the distance and went in the back door, flipping on lights as she went.

Cami shivered as a cold draft swept over her, leaving her feeling slightly rattled. "Go away Charlotte," Cami hissed to the still house. There was no response. Of course, there wasn't. Why would there be?

Night sounds and cool air drifted in through the open windows. "See, not Charlotte," she told herself. "Don't be so stupid." She'd opened the windows earlier in the day when it was warm and now the cold was seeping in. Distracted, Cami started her rounds, closing windows in the kitchen and the drawing room. She glanced outside and saw a car parked near the fountain. Smiling, Cami went to the front door and switched on the outside lights.

Opening the door, she called out, "Detective Swanson?" That's when she saw it. A dark liquid on the flagstone walk beside a rectangular lump wrapped in something shiny. *That's odd. What was that?*

"Detective Swanson?" Cami called again, her voice coming out in a croak as she reached down. "Banana bread? And is that blood?" Crimson as a red rose. Cami retracted her hand in horror as she stared at the pool of blood. Her eyes watered as she forced down bile, and followed the trail of blood droplets with her eyes. Taking a tentative step forward, Cami carefully stepped across the flagstones, past the loaf of banana bread, gasping as she saw a foot protruding from behind the car.

She ran to him and carefully turned him over, cradling his head. "Detective Swanson? Oh!" Cami retracted her hands as they came back smeared with blood. Her stomach jumped. She shook him. "Detective Swanson? Can you hear me?"

His eyes fluttered.

"Stay with me! I have to get something to stop the bleeding. I'll be right back." She ran to the house, grabbed a kitchen towel off the refrigerator, and ran back to him. She wadded the towel, lifted his head slightly and applied pressure.

"Detective Swanson! Can you hear me?"

His eyes fluttered. Opened. Closed. Open. Swanson whispered. "Danger...run."

"No, I won't leave you. You need help." Cami gripped the towel with one hand and dug her cell phone out of her back pocket with the other. Her hand was so full of blood she couldn't hang onto it.

Swanson grabbed her arm. "Keys..."

"What?" Unable to punch the numbers because the phone was covered in blood, Cami gave up and shouted, "Siri," she paused and waited impatiently for the automatic response.

"Yes?"

"Call 9-1-1, it's an emergency."

"Calling 9-1-1."

***

Black and white cars, red and blue lights, and the wail of sirens cut through the dark night. Turning in the winding lane, cars screeched to a halt in front of the manor. Men jumped out of vehicles and ran to the house.

Luke saw the loaf of bread and the blood. The stain of scarlet. The droplets of crimson and his heart clenched in his chest.

"We're here!" she yelled.

That's when he saw her. His heart skidded. Hunching over Swanson, Cami's arms were covered in blood, tears streaming down her face.

She looked straight at him and shouted, "Help me!"

Bobby shouted for the EMTs, and the sirens stopped. Their surroundings fell into deafening silence. The medics moved quickly, converging on Cami and Swanson. Luke came up behind Cami and gently wrapped his arm around her waist.

"Is he still alive?"

"Barely," she sobbed as the men pressed closer, assessing and evaluating.

"When they tell you, you need to let go so they can take over," Luke said into her ear.

She nodded slightly.

"We have a pulse."

"We need to move quickly."

"Cami," Bobby said forcefully to get her to focus on him. He was opposite her over Swanson's lifeless body. He locked eyes with her. "You did good, Cami. We'll take it from here. I'm going to count to three, and then you move your hand. Understand?"

Cami nodded again.

"Warner?" he questioned. "Ready?"

Luke bobbed his head.

"One, two, three."

In one swift movement, Cami was pulled away and Bobby's hands slipped in place of hers, cradling Dwight's head.

Luke extracted Cami from the scene quickly. An EMT handed him a blanket and he quickly wrapped it around her shoulders.

He led her into the house, away from the scene, through the house to the kitchen, placing her gently in a chair. She was covered in blood, shivering, and her hands were balled tight. She hadn't said a word since he had pulled her away from Swanson. Bending down so he was eye to eye with her, he looked into her pale face. "Cami?" he asked softly. "Are you hurt in any way? Do you need to go to the hospital to be checked out?"

Her head twitched slightly. "No," she whispered, and her bottom lip trembled. "I'm not hurt, but Detective Swanson. . ."

"I know. They're taking care of him. I need to ask you a few questions, then get you out of those clothes."

"He must have fallen backward off the step. Hit his head," she murmured, trying to make sense of it.

Wrapping the blanket tighter around her, he leaned her back against the chair. Despite being inside, Cami shook uncontrollably and stared aimlessly at the floor. Shock had obviously set in.

Luke wanted more than anything to reach out to her, pull her close, hold her until the shaking subsided, and tell her everything was going to be alright. But he couldn't. This was police business. She was a witness to an accident. Despite how he felt, he needed to treat her like one, at least until they assessed the situation and had her statement.

"Let's get you cleaned up. At least get the blood off your hands." He turned on the tap, running the water warm. "Can you stand and wash your hands?" he asked Cami, coming over to her.

She nodded slightly. He held the blanket as she shifted in her chair and stood. Guiding her to the sink, he held her in place with one arm while he tested the water with his other hand.

"Come closer, the water is warm."

The blanket pooled at her feet as it slipped off her shoulders when she leaned forward toward the sink, her hands still balled into fists.

"Cami," he said softly, approaching her like he would a stray puppy, his hand out, his voice calm. "Let me help you." He tugged her hands under the water. "Relax your hands. If we get the blood off, you'll feel better."

Trembling, Cami held her clenched fist toward Luke. "He told me not to give it to anyone but you." She choked back a sob.

"Who? Swanson?"

"Yes."

"Look at me, Cami."

She raised her eyes to meet his steady gaze.

"I'm going to hold out my hand and you let go, okay?"

She nodded slightly.

White knuckles and dried blood, Cami opened her hand and let a set of keys fall from hers to his.

"Where did you get these?"

"Detective Swanson's pocket. He told me to give them to you and only you. He said you need the smallest one."

CHAPTER 23

He insisted on staying, and frankly she was too tired to protest, but honestly, Cami didn't want to be left alone. Her stomach was in knots, her nerves were shot, and her body ached. She kept picturing Detective Swanson laying on the ground, the pool of warm blood seeping around his head, onto her hands. Cami could still feel the drum of his heart as she placed her hand on his chest, clutching the keys, trying to reassure him. Her ears burned with the harsh sound of Swanson's haggard breathing.

Completely clean after her shower, Luke ushered her into the drawing room. "Why don't you sit on the couch and I'll light a fire?" His hand on the small of her back, he guided her to the sofa. She stopped at the couch but didn't sit.

"Thank you. That would be nice. There's kindling on the left in the metal container. Matches should be there, too."

Squatting, he grabbed some kindling and a newspaper. He balled the newspaper and strategically stuffed it in between the wood. She stood stock-still and watched him strike the match, holding it to the edge of the paper. Mesmerized, she watched the tiny lick of the flame catch and grow. Once it had taken off, he stood, tossed the used match into the fireplace, and came over to her.

Softly brushing the damp hair from her face, he asked, "Why don't you sit down? You must be exhausted."

"I am, but I can't just yet. I need to do something, anything. I feel so helpless. Useless."

"There's nothing you need to do. You did everything

you could. Now," he put his hand to her face and caressed her cheek, looking deep into those hazel eyes. "We need to take care of you."

"I'm fine."

"You're not, but you will be with some rest."

"He brought his famous banana bread. Did you see it?"

"I did."

"It's ruined." Her bottom lip trembled slightly. "He was early. I should have been waiting in the house for him. If I hadn't gone for a walk, maybe..."

"Don't." He held up his hand. "Don't do that to yourself. You couldn't have known."

She wanted him to wrap his arms around her and simply hold her. But he didn't.

"Why don't you go up and grab a couple of blankets, sleep here on the couch tonight next to the fire?"

"I like that idea. I think I will." She stepped back and asked, "You won't leave, will you?"

"I'll stay as long as you want me to." His hand slipped down to hers and gently squeezed. "Go. I'll be waiting right here."

Nodding, she walked out of the room and up the large sweep of stairs, biting back tears as she fought to stay in control of her emotions. She wouldn't cry, not again. Luke needed her to stay sane. He certainly didn't need a hysterical woman. That was obvious, as he kept at least three feet between them, except for a moment ago.

In her bedroom, she grabbed pillows off the bed and blankets out of her closet. She hurried back downstairs. Relieved to see Luke stood next to the fire where she had left him.

Luke turned when he heard her, watching her cross the room with grace and poise despite what she'd been through. Cami deposited a couple of blankets on the sofa and moved to him.

Her eyes had gone quiet, and she looked pale despite

still having that summer glow. His heart ached for her, but he stood his ground and didn't move. Luke didn't understand what it was about Cami that made him want to forget he was an officer, let alone a detective on a case, correction, two cases, that heavily involved her. He had to get his priorities straight. Her safety was the utmost priority, but so were the two cases she was involved with. It didn't matter that the first was a case that had grown cold over ten years ago, and the second looked to be an accident. But until he was sure, he needed to keep his distance. He didn't want to let his growing feelings for her jeopardize the cases or her safety.

Clearing his throat, he forced a small smile. "This is a great room to crash in on a cold, dark night."

"I think so, too. I've always loved this room. It's warm and cozy."

He genuinely smiled at her this time and bobbed his head. "You're absolutely right. This room is inviting with its rich wood tones, plush carpet, comfy couches, and the large stone fireplace. It reminds me of a ski lodge you would find nestled in the woods, high up in the mountains."

"Exactly. It's the perfect place to curl up with a good book on a cold winter's day next to a roaring fire. Can I get you anything? A drink, or something to eat?"

"No, I'm good. Please," he indicated the sofa, "you must be exhausted."

"I am, but I'm not sure I can sleep. I keep thinking about Detective Swanson. I just don't understand how this happened. I keep going over it in my mind."

"I don't understand it myself, but I plan to figure it out."

"He must have fallen off the steps and landed on the flagstone, cracking his head," Cami said, arranging pillows and spreading a blanket. A wave of exhaustion rolled over her, and Cami sat on the couch.

She curled her long legs, tucking them underneath her, looking like pure sweet temptation. It was all he could do not to sit right next to her and…He couldn't think about the "and."

"If you don't mind, I'm going to go around the house and make sure all the doors and windows are locked tight for the night?"

Curled up like a feline, he tucked the blanket around her, her eyes already heavy with the pull of sleep.

"Thank you, I would appreciate that."

He nodded. "I'll be back in a few minutes. Get some rest."

In the foyer, he pulled out his cellphone, punched in Bobby's number, and headed to the kitchen to check the locks.

Bobby answered on the first ring. "Warner? Are you still at Cherry Hollow?"

"Yes. How's Swanson?"

"Not good. If Cami hadn't found him when she did, he might already be dead. He's lost a lot of blood. Too much. Head wounds always bleed profusely. He's in surgery right now. Doc's trying to relieve the pressure from the blow to his head."

Luke scrubbed a hand over his face. "I should have been there."

"What do you mean? You were there."

"No, not after the call. I should have offered to come over with Swanson. I just had this gut feeling that something was going to happen when he asked at church."

"Shit, Warner, it was an accident. You can't be everywhere. Besides, it's over and done with. We got the call, and we responded as quickly as humanly possible."

Luke flipped the latch on the kitchen door, slid the deadbolt in place, and moved on to the windows. "I know but. . ." His voice trailed off. *Was it simply an accident?* His gut told him no. "I should know by now to go with my gut."

"You're a damn good cop. You'll be an even better detective if you just cut yourself some slack. I don't think it's your gut that's the problem here."

"What the hell is that supposed to mean?"

"I think it's your damn heart that's getting in the way and got you all mixed up. You haven't been right since we ran into little Miss Trouble at Finn's. Don't think I ain't noticed."

"Whatever."

"How is she?"

"Cami's a lot stronger than I thought." He pictured her covered in Swanson's blood, hands clenched in the kitchen. *The keys.* He pulled them out of his pocket, held them in the palm of his hand, turning them over with his thumb. Three keys. One was definitely a car key, the other the house, but the small one looked like it could be for a safe deposit box or a small lock box. He remembered his grandfather having a key similar to it when he passed away. He'd have to find out exactly what it unlocked.

On autopilot, he made his way through the house, checking, jiggling, securing every door and window.

"What about the scene?"

"They've photographed and cleaned it up."

"Good. I don't want her to wake up to that mess in the morning."

"Are you staying there for the night?"

Luke stood in the drawing room's doorway and saw Cami fast asleep on the couch. Watching the soft light from the fire flicker on her face, he knew there was no way he was leaving her here alone tonight.

"Yeah, looks like I'll be sleeping on the couch."

***

Laying in the dark, his mind raced full of fear and dread. Sleep wouldn't come. Instead, images of the dark woods, the shadow of the trees, and the flash of green stirred. Sounds like the snap of a twig, the crack of bone impacting with stone, and retreating footsteps still haunted him to this day. *Had they been seen? Had there been a witness to the incident?*

His stomach turned. A mind filled with humiliation and rejection, betrayal and jealousy ended in a turn of events that was never seen coming. A mistaken identity, a hasty error of judgment, all these things kept sleep at bay.

And now Cami Parker was back, stirring up memories,

feelings, and digging into things better left buried. Fear bounced off every corner of his imagination and haunted his dreams in the dark. Someone had to stop her from finding out the truth, no matter what the cost.

CHAPTER 24

Yawning, Luke leaned back and stretched, trying to work out the kinks in his back after a long night spent on a short couch, too short for his six-foot frame. Showered, shaved, and freshly dressed with spare clothes he kept in the locker room, he typed up his notes on his laptop and took a swallow of his fourth cup of coffee. The caffeine pumped through his system making him feel human again. If only he'd had time to stop by Jolt and get a good cup instead of this mud they had at the office, he'd be doing much better.

Luke had stood on the front porch that morning, combing every inch of the bleached white flagstone walk to where Dwight's car had been parked. Trying to recreate how Swanson had fallen and moved from spot to spot. From there, he'd gone to Dwight's house.

Pulling Swanson's keys out of his pocket, he laid them on his desk. Luke searched the house, looking for a small lock box. When the search turned up empty he located Dwight's banking information at the house, made calls, and found out one bank Swanson banked with had safe deposit boxes, verified Dwight had one, and made an appointment with the branch manager to search it. He was waiting for the warrant when Officer Cannon knocked on his door, poking his head in.

"Got a minute?"

"Yes. What's up?"

Bobby dropped a couple of photos on the desk. "Look at those."

Luke straightened. Leaning forward, he gathered the

photos. "Boot prints?"

"Yep."

"Where were these found?"

"I found ones in the woods headed away from Cami's house toward the road." Bobby flopped down into one of the threadbare chairs across from his best friend. Propping his feet up on the corner of Luke's desk, he placed his elbows on the armrests and drummed his fists on his thighs, something he always did when he was deep in thought. Before Luke could ask, he said, "Men's size twelve hiking boots. Could be a hunter."

"Could be." Luke placed them side by side. He slid open the file drawer in his desk, pulled out the one he started on Cami that contained the broken window and the locked shed, and drew out the photo of the footprint near the building in the soft mud. He scrutinized it for a minute. Then slid it across the desk to Bobby. "Take a look at that."

Bobby took it, held it close, then selected another from the ones taken after Swanson, comparing. "Looks like the same damn print. Same size?"

"Yep. Men's size twelve."

"Coincidence?"

"Doubt it. Why'd you go looking for prints when last night you were sure it was an accident?"

Bobby shrugged. "Could be because my buddy had a gut feeling something was off, made me believe him, and I wanted to look around in the daylight. Then again, it could be a coincidence, like I said. Or from another time."

"Detective?" an officer said, sticking her head in.

Luke looked at her over Bobby's head. "Yes?"

Waving a piece of paper, she said, "Sorry to interrupt, but the warrant just arrived. Figured you'd want to know right away."

He held out his hand. She handed it to him. "Thanks."

"Yep." She disappeared as quickly as she'd come.

Scooping up the photos, he put them in the respective folders and tucked them in his drawer, locking it. He pushed back his chair, secured his weapon, grabbed Swanson's keys, and stood. "Looks like I'm headed to the bank."

***

The house was full of activity inside and out, which was beneficial because without it Cami probably would have crawled into bed and cried herself to sleep. She hadn't slept well last night. *How could she?* Every time she closed her eyes, the image of Detective Swanson lying on the ground came rushing back. The blood had seeped out of his head no matter how hard she tried to stop it. Scarlet red, running over her hand, pooling on the flagstone, and soaking into her jeans. The eerie sound of his ragged breathing filling her mind. Even now in the daylight she couldn't shake the image; it was seared into her brain.

She didn't think she would have survived the night if Luke hadn't been across the room, keeping her in check. He was a source of quiet support and safety, that without him... Well, she didn't want to think about what it would have been like without him last night. The house had been eerily silent, dark and cold. If she had been alone, the hours would have stretched on endlessly.

Luke had been reassuring and kind, building the fire, answering her endless questions, listening to her as she relived the terrible nightmare over and over, and yet content to just be still when the silence stretched between them. Not once had he said anything to let her believe she hadn't handled the situation correctly. For that she thanked him, and fell quiet at least to give him some peace, even though her own mind wouldn't shut off.

Exhausted but determined to get on with the day, Cami ducked underneath a blue tarp that had been hung and spoke briefly with the painter to verify the paint colors for each space. Scaffolding was erected in the center of the large expanse of the ballroom, twin chandeliers with teardrop crystals were lowered and removed, and the hardwood floor was covered diligently to keep any paint from dripping on it. Cami had selected a soft gold paint for the ballroom to accent the warm tones of the woodwork and reflect the soft light of the chandeliers.

She gave her approval, thanked the painters, and ducked back under the tarp heading outside in search of Brock.

The day was sunny and warm, and the air fresh. There was a flurry of activity as the landscaping crew was busy clearing away brush, pulling out dead plants, trimming and shaping shrubbery that could be salvaged, and preparing the beds all around the house. A large dump truck pulled into the yard with new shrubbery, followed by another truck hauling black mulch to be spread in the beds and along the borders.

More men from the Green Zone crew flanked the driveway, picking up fallen branches and sticks, clearing the long grass to be mowed. Cami could see Brock and Aaron unloading equipment from yet another truck. A little tickle of dread ran through her and formed a pit in her stomach. Cami wanted to go over and speak to Brock, but seeing Aaron stopped her.

She had tried to be friendly to Aaron at church yesterday, but he was still distant. Hanging on the edge of the group, he sat at the far end of the table at the restaurant, and got up to leave right away when he was finished. Maybe she should give him another day or two before trying to talk to him again. Decision made, she turned and went back into the house, determined to tackle her father's office and make it her own.

Once inside, she closed the door, sat down at her father's desk, and leaned back in the big leather chair, a little overwhelmed with where to start. She needed to clean the space, take out her father's papers, and arrange it to her liking, but for today, that would have to wait. Right now, she needed a plan, an outline of what she needed to accomplish before the engagement party, and where to get what she required. Cami already had a good start. The ballroom, foyer, and powder room would be done by the end of the week, and so would the landscaping in front of the house.

Now Cami had to plan for the actual engagement party. Reaching for the box she put in the office the other day, she pulled out her three-ring organizer. First things first, she wanted to create the mood. She flipped through photos of some of her previous events for inspiration. Each one was more beautiful than the last, but nothing seemed to fit the mood she wanted for Kevin and Joselyn.

Cami pictured them as a couple and focused on their best qualities. Inspired, she set the binder aside, raised the screen on her laptop and started a new file for them. As a couple, they were simple and casual. Having known Joselyn since second grade, Cami knew she'd want romance, too. Shades of white and soft lines, romantic lighting and soft instrumental music playing in the background.

The food would be light and airy. Hors d'oeuvres and tiny desserts that could easily be eaten with fingers and delicate plates. They would display everything on a buffet set with white linens off to the side for guests to gravitate to. Drinks would consist of seltzers, white wines, and champagne. Simple, refreshing, and clear.

Cami made more notes regarding everything from napkins to stereo equipment with surround sound for the ballroom. Hoping to use some of her past connections, as well as make some new ones, Cami started making calls.

The late morning turned to afternoon as the work outside and in progressed. The sun made a slow but steady trek across a pale blue sky, dipping to the west behind the fall foliage. Light filtered through the ever-changing pattern of the trees. Some branches were completely covered, others already bare, the scene changing by the minute as autumn edged toward winter as leaf after leaf fell silently to the ground around the men at work.

Brock knocked on the closed door and waited. Unable to hear a response from inside, he turned the handle and opened it a crack, peering in.

His heart skipped a beat as his eyes landed on Cami behind the large mahogany desk, talking on her cell phone. She looked so much like Charlotte it hurt his heart to look at her. *If only they hadn't played that damn game all those years ago, maybe Charlotte would be the one sitting here now, waiting for him,* he thought. *But she wasn't. She never would be.* A pang of grief so heavy washed over him. It was something so fierce, something he hadn't experienced in years, that it almost brought him to his knees. Brock reached out and grabbed the door frame to steady himself, causing the door to swing open further.

Cami looked up and blinked. "I'll email you the list as soon as I have it together." She waved Brock in. "Let me know if you have questions. And thank you. Have a good day." Cami put down her cell phone. "Hey, Brock. How's everything going?"

Pushing down his emotions, he crossed the room and smiled. "Good. I just wanted to update you on our progress and let you know we're packed up for the day."

Cami glanced at her phone. "I didn't realize it was that late already." She pushed back and stretched. "The day got away from me. I meant to come out and talk to you, but I got sidetracked with work."

"Can you take a break and walk around outside with me now?"

"Definitely."

Outside, they walked the length of the house. "As you can see, we cleaned up the beds, pulled out the dead or dying shrubs. Replaced them with boxwoods. Those are the small round ones that have that rich green color. Then we mixed in azaleas for the natural, wild look. They'll flower white in the spring." He pointed. "We used Golden Spirit for color year-round. It's a Smoke bush. Not sure if you are familiar with those or not?"

She shook her head.

"They emerge lime green, turning to gold in the summer, then the soft burgundy you see in the fall. The dense blue-green is a Dwarf Italian Cypress. They're easy to maintain, and hold their shape well, giving you some height and dimension to the front of the house."

"Simple, natural, yet beautiful. The black mulch really makes the colors pop against the dark, brown earth tones of the house."

Pleased she liked it, he moved on. "We managed to get the front half of the yard cleared, void of sticks and branches, and partially mowed. We'll finish mowing the front tomorrow and then the guys will work on the back." They walked the length of the driveway in silence, as they watched a leaf tumble across, tugged along by an invisible string.

"As you can see, we planted a few pine trees along the driveway for filler. We are also digging the trench along the edge of the drive to put in the lighting you wanted to illuminate the lane. They'll be on a sensor, set to come on as it becomes dusk, and off at dawn. That way, you won't have to remember to turn them off and on."

"I love that. Will they turn on for a rainy day?" she asked.

"I don't see why not. As long as it's overcast and fairly dark, they should be lit."

"I like what you've done so far."

They turned around and headed back toward the house.

"Any luck with the fountain?"

"Aaron took it apart and cleaned it up. He's going to add a heater so you can keep it flowing all winter if you want and put in some lights under the water to accent the statues in the dark. But first I need to check the electrical box. See if we have enough amperage. We might need to add another panel because of the volume of lighting we're adding outside, plus the extra pull from the fountain. Do you know where the box is located?"

"Yes, it's in the basement."

"Can you show me?"

"Of course."

"Let me grab a flashlight from the truck." She waited

while he did so, then he followed her inside.

"Basement is this way."

They went through the kitchen and into the large butler's pantry. Flipping a switch, she unlatched a worn wooden door. A single bulb hung from the slanted ceiling, barely illuminating the stairs.

"Watch your step. These stairs are steep, and not well lit."

Brock leaned forward, peering down. The steps disappeared into the darkness. He looked up at the lone bulb and saw dust and cobwebs across the opening. Out of the corner of his eye, he saw Cami shiver.

"Do you want me to go first?" Brock asked, turning on the flashlight.

"I thought that was a given," Cami said with a smile. "After all, you have the flashlight and you're a big, strong guy. Who knows what's down there?"

He gave her a lopsided grin. "I imagine, at the very least, spiders and mice. As long as it's not snakes or bats, we're good."

"There are definitely spiders, not sure about the mice, snakes, or bats." She shivered again. "After you."

He laughed. "Whatever happened to ladies first? It's your house, after all."

She huffed. "And they say chivalry isn't dead." Cami moved to go.

He caught her arm. "I was kidding, I had every intention of going first." Brock started down.

"Believe me when I say I had every intention of letting you."

Brock laughed heartily, the sound cutting heavily into the eerie darkness. "You're good, Cami. You are good," he said, realizing she'd conned him.

The basement smelled of damp, dust, and mold as they descended into darkness. "Spiders, snakes, and mice, oh my."

"Stop that," she scolded.

Brock said it again, only softer. "Spiders, snakes and

mice, oh my!"

Cami swatted him playfully. Reaching the bottom, she looped an arm through his, holding on tight. He glanced at her and grinned. "Scared?"

"No. I figured you were."

He laughed and enjoyed the feeling of her warm hand on his arm. His stomach did a little flip. Brock racked his brain and tried to remember if he had ever been this close to Cami alone in the dark, but he couldn't think of a time. Charlotte wouldn't have allowed it. Truth be told, he hadn't been interested either. Charlotte was a handful and with her around, he hadn't had time to look or even think about anyone else.

Cami's eyes were huge in the dim light, and she was soft and warm on his arm, he was drawn in, it had been a long time since he'd been affected by someone's touch, the way he was now. Was it the house? Or the thought of Charlotte? *Get a grip*, he scolded himself. This was Cami, *not* Charlotte. Shaking himself mentally, he moved the beam of his flashlight, slicing across the dark stone walls as they moved side by side in the dark.

"There should be another light hanging from the ceiling somewhere with a pull chain."

"I see it." He reached up and gave it a tug. The chain clinked against the glass bulb but didn't light. "Must be burnt out. When's the last time you were down here?"

"Not since before we moved out. I thought I was going to have to come down the other night and check the breaker because the lights went out, but I refused to go down in the dark alone. I waited until morning and luckily, the lights were back on."

"If the lights are going out on you, the breaker box definitely needs to be upgraded. Let's look. Point me in the right direction."

"Far corner." She pointed.

"I see it." They moved across the basement to the box. Brock unlatched it and the little metal door screeched open.

"That's what I thought. Looks like you need to add a subpanel."

"Can you fix it?"

He grinned. "It's not a fixable thing. It's adding something on or new. And no, I can't. I'm not sure if I mentioned it before, but Aaron is an electrician. He does this kind of work regularly. He can take a look, if you don't mind?"

"I don't mind at all."

"Good. While he's at it, I would get him to add some more lights to this basement. Looks like the whole house needs an upgrade."

"Really? I had a guy out and he never said anything."

"I mean, I guess it's fine if you just want to get by. But you want to have parties here. With guests in the house, you don't want to take the chance that the electricity is going to go out. You said yourself it did the other night."

"It did. And you're right, I don't."

"I'm actually thinking maybe we should put in a whole new separate panel out in the carriage house for the outside lighting and fountain. That way, if something happened to one, the other would still be okay. Aaron can even hook up a generator to the system that would run on propane. That way, if the lights go out during a party, you could still function with the back-up generator. We could have it tied in to automatically start if the electricity goes out." Brock scratched his chin. "You're on well water, right?"

"Yes."

"If the electricity goes out, you can't even flush a toilet, correct?"

"Correct."

"A generator would definitely be the way to go then."

"I like that idea a lot." Cami glanced around as they heard the skitter of little feet. "Do you need to do anything else down here?"

"No."

"Good, let's go. I think the natives are getting restless."

He closed the breaker box, bobbed his head as something

fluttered against it as they headed for the stairs.

Cami shrieked, "Mouse!" Grabbing his hand, she took off running for the stairs, pulling Brock along with her. They ran up the stairs, taking them two at a time, and pushed through the opening. Brock was barely through when Cami slammed the door behind him and flipped the latch clearly out of breath. "Mouse traps. I need them."

He doubled over in laughter. "You should see your face!" Damn if she didn't look cute. Cheeks flush and eyes wide.

"Whatever! I didn't see you staying down there," she huffed, clutching at her side.

Without thinking, he pulled her close and kissed her full on the mouth. The instant their lips touched, he knew it was all wrong. She smelled like cherries, not roses. She was soft and warm, but reserved. Charlotte had been hot and passionate. It almost felt like he was kissing his sister. He stiffened and reminded himself this was Cami, not Charlotte. *Her twin sister.* He pulled back and felt her stiffen. Her hand came between them and pushed him gently back. Pulling away, he saw her eyes were as big as saucers.

Guilt flooded over him. "Oh, hey, Cami, I'm sorry. I just… oh, hell."

"It's okay. I wasn't expecting that. I . . ." She swallowed hard. Her eyes shifted slightly to the left. The air behind him wavered like a soft mist rolling in. "It's Charlotte."

"I know. I'm sorry, I shouldn't have. Holy hell, this is awkward."

"Yes, but," she pointed over his shoulder, her hand trembling, and her other hand went to her mouth. She could see her. A mere mirage that wavered, then solidified. "Charlotte."

The name hung heavily in the air.

"It's not your fault, it's mine."

"Look!" she hissed between clenched teeth and pointed again. "It's Charlotte! *Behind* you."

Brock jerked, caught between guilt and desperation, and

turned in the direction Cami pointed. "Where?"

"She's standing right there!" It happened so fast. There was an image. Light. Wispy. A shimmer of blonde hair and blue eyes. A look of betrayal.

"I don't see anything."

As quickly as the image had formed, it was gone. Leaving Cami shaken and confused. "I saw her." A cold unlike any she'd ever felt before swept over her, sending chills racing down her spine.

"What the hell? Why is it suddenly so cold in here?" Brock stared at her in disbelief as a shiver racked his body. They both turned as the kitchen door swung open and banged against the wall.

"What the?"

In a voice barely audible, Cami whispered, "I saw her, but worse, she saw us."

"You're confused. Mistaken. It must be guilt from the kiss." He shook from the sudden cold, stomped across the kitchen and closed the door, turning the deadbolt.

Cami pushed past him. "You don't understand. She was there!"

"She's not. Cami, Charlotte's dead."

"I know that, Brock. Don't you think I know that?" Cami whirled on him. "Then how do you explain the door just now?"

Gaping at her in disbelief, he said simply, "It wasn't latched properly and a gust of wind pushed it open."

So simple an explanation. So believable, but she knew. *She knew.*

Brock followed her to the kitchen table. Cami sunk down onto a chair, head in her hands. "Don't believe me then."

"It's not that I don't believe you, but Cami? How is that even possible?"

She looked up at him. "I don't know, Brock, but she was there. I know what I saw." He stood awkwardly over her in the kitchen, filling the space. Too large. Too close. Her twin sister's high school boyfriend. She needed him out of her space, out of her kitchen, and out of her house. "You should go."

"I can't leave you after what just happened."

"Nothing happened. You said so yourself. It was just the wind."

"I meant between us. That kiss."

She stood, and he stepped back, like a man afraid of a snake. Cami just wanted him out. She couldn't think with him standing there looking at her like she was crazy. Forcing a weak smile, she gave a little laugh. "I know you didn't mean it."

"I did it without thinking."

Cami nodded, forced herself to remain calm and in control. She'd think about Charlotte later. "I know. It's okay, really." She laid a hand on his arm. "You should go." Ushering him to the front door, she said, "I want you to go. You were ready to go home before, so go."

Relenting, he walked out, turning to face her on the porch. He waved a hand between them. "Are you and I okay? I mean, I want *us* to be okay. I don't want one stupid lack of judgment to ruin anything."

"We're good. I think of you as a brother, Brock. Nothing is going to change that."

Visibly relieved, he grinned. Brock asked, "You got that vibe, too?"

She cocked her head. "What do you mean?"

"The kiss. When I kissed you, it was like kissing my kid sister."

"Oh, thank goodness." Cami was relieved that he was thinking about the kiss and not that she was crazy. *Get him out with that thought.* "I'll see you tomorrow." She practically shoved him off the porch. "And have Aaron bring his electrician stuff. I definitely want to make those upgrades." Before Brock could answer, she shut the door, closing him out, and turned the lock.

CHAPTER 25

Turning it over in his hands, Luke stared at the paper triangle. It fit discreetly into the palm of his hand when he closed it. *Precisely the point,* he thought, *easy to conceal.* He laid it on his desk and noted the paper was yellowed slightly on the edges. He took his time unfolding it, making sure not to rip or tear the paper. Unfolded, it was a full sheet of 8 ½ x11 college, ruled notebook paper with a perforated edge. The handwriting was a little sloppy and had a masculine tone.

> *I want you to know*
> *Exactly how I feel about you*
> *Before it's too late.*

"Is this a love letter or a warning?" he asked himself. He read it again out loud. Leaning back in his chair, Luke stared at the ceiling and followed a crack in the tile, and tried to think like the writer. He was so lost in thought, he didn't hear Officer Cannon come in.

Bobby stood just inside the door, looked up and asked, "Hole in the ceiling?"

Not looking at him, Luke answered, "Nope. Just thinking."

"'Bout what?"

He sat up straight and looked at his friend and fellow officer. "Come in and close the door."

Bobby nodded, did what he was told, then sat in the chair across from him.

"I went to Swanson's bank, used the key to unlock his

safe deposit box." Luke slid the paper across the desk toward Bobby. "This was the only thing in it. Besides, a small tablet with a couple of observations from Dwight."

Cannon didn't touch it. Just leaned forward and read it to himself. "Is that supposed to be someone confessing their love, or are they trying to warn them about something? Or both?"

"Those were my exact thoughts."

"And yet I'm not getting paid the big bucks or have the privilege of having the cool title of detective in front of my name. Go figure."

Luke frowned. "You help me figure this thing out and I'll put in a good word for you, if you want it."

"Naw. You know I don't. I'm just messin' with you. But seriously, what do you think? Confession or warning?"

"My first instinct is confession. Try thinking like a teenage boy. Not that long ago we were one." Luke was silent for a moment. "Did you have a high school crush?"

Bobby scratched his chin. "I mean, there were girls I thought were hot, like Tanya, Charlotte or Cami." Bobby grinned. "Charlotte was untouchable and Brock's girlfriend. Little Miss Double Trouble was a little too quiet and reserved for my taste. Seemed like she was always trying to be the opposite of her twin sister." He shrugged. "But there was no one that I was seriously crushing on. I was too busy playing the field to give one girl my undivided attention. I was more the love 'em and leave 'em type. If you know what I mean?"

"I know exactly what you mean. I had a front-row seat to the action."

"And you? Was it Miss Trouble the whole time or someone else?"

"Do I have to be honest?"

"Hell, yeah you do. I thought that's what we were doing here."

"Alright, it was definitely Cami."

"That's what I thought." Bobby leaned back in the chair and grinned. "It's a good feeling when you're always right."

When that didn't get a reaction out of Luke, he asked, "But?"

"I was playing it cool."

"Yeah, you were cool alright. And how did that work out for you?" Bobby asked with a chuckle.

"I thought it was working out pretty well, right up to the point Charlotte died." Luke was silent for a moment, picked up the football that he had sitting on the corner of his desk and tossed it in the air. "Then everything changed, and I wished like hell, I hadn't played it cool."

Bobby straightened and leaned in. "And now?"

Luke shrugged, palmed the ball, and looked out the window. How could he tell Cannon he still felt something for Cami? Even after all these years, his heart skipped a beat just thinking about her. He chided himself, *still playing it cool. Had he learned nothing?* "And now what?"

"What in the hell are you going to do about it?"

"Nothing."

"Nothing?" Bobby scrunched up his face, clearly put off. A crease formed right between his eyes. "Why the hell not?"

"Because Cami is a witness in a case of what looks like an attack of one of our own, and possibly to the death of her twin sister ten years ago. She's my key witness, Cannon. I can't pursue a relationship right now with her, no matter how I feel."

Bobby flopped back in the chair. "Okay, I get that. I don't like it, but I get it. So let's let that go for a moment. Back to the note." He pointed at the paper in question. "Did Swanson say where it was found?"

"Yeah, in the front pocket of the sweatshirt Charlotte was wearing when she died. It's here in Swanson's notes." He picked up the little tablet.

"Interesting. So, it could have been a warning."

"It's only a warning if you knew something was going to happen. How would anyone know we were going to play hide-and-seek that night? Or that they could get Charlotte alone? She was always the center of attention. Made it her life's goal to be so." Luke stood, paced back and forth behind his desk, and tossed the football at Bobby.

"Let's assume for a moment that it's a confession of love." Luke stopped behind his desk, picked up the paper, folded it back into a triangle, and held it out for Bobby to see. "Remember making these? We used to stand them on one point and flick them across the room, or hold up our hands and pretend we were kicking them through a field goal." Luke smiled at the thought. "That was the only way to pass time in Ms. Connor's creative writing class."

"Yeah, that and study hall. We used to launch those babies clear across the cafeteria to Aaron and Kevin. Remember when Aaron hit Principal McMillan in the back of the head? I laughed so hard I nearly lost my lunch trying to keep quiet."

The corner of Luke's mouth twitched into a smile. "Yeah, he put his head down so fast when McMillan turned around that he smacked it on the table, then tried to act like he was sleeping. McMillan didn't buy it for a second."

"Well, the big ass red mark on his forehead kind of gave it away. There's no way he could have done that in his sleep."

"I think he got a one day in-school suspension for it. Totally worth it in my book."

"Back to the triangle. Let's assume that any guy at the party could have made it." Luke sat down at his desk and flipped open Charlotte's file. "There were fifty-two teenagers at the party. Twenty-seven were boys and twenty-five girls. For now, let's rule out the girls. That leaves twenty-seven suspects. Minus two, which is you and me. Now we're at twenty-five."

"That's still a lot."

"Agreed."

"It's too bad we don't have a list of students that were in classes with Charlotte."

"We do." Luke pulled a list from the file. "Swanson had that in the file. He circled the ones that were in classes with her and were at the party." He handed Bobby the list. There were seven names circled.

"Well, that narrows it down considerably."

"Yes, it does." Luke flipped through the folder and pulled out a packet of paper stapled together. "Swanson pulled all the class roosters for that fall, even classes Charlotte wasn't in."

"He was thorough. I'll give him that. Any word on how he's doing?"

"They still have him heavily sedated. I was planning on stopping at the hospital on my way home tonight before poker and check on him. With regard to the note, I Googled poems, the types and styles. There's like twenty different styles. For example, Limerick, Sonnet, Ode, Haiku and a bunch of others."

"Does our love note fit any of the styles?"

"Yes, Haiku. The definition of Haiku is a three-line poem that has five syllables in the first and third lines, and seven in the second." He held up the paper. "This is written just like a Haiku. I remember Ms. Conner teaching Haikus in her class in the fall of our senior year."

"Yeah, I remember that, too. Only I had that class in the spring."

"This class list is a good place to start."

"Sounds like a good idea. You good then, man?"

"Yes."

"Guess I better get back to my paperwork if I want to be there when you guys show up tonight." Bobby stood. "For what it's worth, I think you're doing a great job. It ain't easy to step into someone else's shoes. I'd cut yourself some slack with Cami. It's difficult to get back your high school crush, then have to consider her a witness, and possibly be in danger all in a couple weeks' time."

"Thanks, I appreciate that."

Bobby tossed the football back. "See you later."

He waited until Bobby left, set the football down, then pulled out Charlotte's yearbook. Luke wanted to compare the handwriting, what little there was. He flipped to the page he had marked. The *"I love you"* under Charlotte and Cami's prom picture.

The three little words weren't much to go on, but he would swear the "I" and the "you" in both messages were the same. He flipped to the back of the yearbook and compared the note to the message or poem written in the back. Nothing looked similar. His guess would be two completely different people had written those entries. He would send copies off to the handwriting analysis lab and have them analyzed to be certain, but there was another way he might be able to find out easily. All he had to do was ask the right person.

***

"Did you bring beer?" Bobby asked Kevin as he came in the back door with a bag of ice and nothing more. Dumping pretzels in a bowl, Bobby scowled at Kevin. "It was your turn. I covered your ass last time."

"I know, I know. Don't get your panties in a wad. It's in the trunk. I bought it last week. I'll get it. I brought the ice in before it melted all over Josie's seats."

"What you're saying is the beer's not cold?"

"It can't be that warm. Temperatures haven't reached above sixty-five all week."

Kevin put the ice on the counter. "Where do you want it?"

"There's an Igloo in the laundry room, go get it. Pop the trunk and I'll grab the beer so we can get it on ice."

Kevin dug the key fob out of his front pocket, along with a check. He handed the check to Bobby. "Here's what I owe you from the time before."

"'Bout damn time." Bobby stuck the check in his wallet."

Kevin popped the trunk from inside. "There are sodas in there, too."

"I'll get 'em." Bobby walked outside to the car just as Aaron pulled in. "Care to make yourself useful?" he called.

"Yeah, what do you need?"

"Grab the soda out of the trunk while I get the beer."

"You got it, man."

Bobby leaned in to get the case of beer that had slid to the back, moved a pair of dirty boots, and grabbed the case, then Aaron jockeyed the boots around to get to the sodas, past the lone golf club. Bobby slammed the lid just as Brock and Luke pulled into the driveway. "You bring pizza?" Bobby called over his shoulder.

"Wow, glad to see you, too," Brock said, climbing out of the truck. "What's your deal?"

"Warm beer," Bobby said gruffly, lifting the case in question, "and a traffic stop on the way home, elderly lady that I had to give a ticket to. You know how much I hate that. Plus, I'm hangry and I barely had time for a shower."

"That's okay, we're used to your smell by now."

"You're hilarious," Bobby said dryly and disappeared into the house, following Aaron.

"Need a hand with the pizza?" Luke asked, coming around the truck.

"I got it. Where have you been? I would have thought you would have been here early, coming straight from work."

Luke waited until Brock had the pizzas out. "I stopped by the hospital to check on Swanson."

"How's he doin'? Wait, I almost forgot." Brock leaned back into the vehicle and snagged a bag of chips, balancing the pizzas in the other hand.

"He's still in serious condition. Swanson lost a lot of blood, head wounds bleed heavily and there's some swelling still in his brain. But they said he's holding steady, so they are going to try to reduce the sedation tomorrow."

"That's crazy, man," Brock said, shaking his head. "What happened? Did he just fall backwards?"

"I'm not at liberty to say at the moment."

"Fair enough." Brock tossed the bag of chips at Luke. "Carry those, will ya?"

Luke caught them easily. "Can I ask you a question?"

"Shoot." Brock slammed the truck door and tucked his keys in his pocket.

"Is it weird or difficult for you that Cami's back?"

Brock snorted. "I'll say. Weird and confusing."

Luke cocked his head in curiosity. "How so?"

"Can't stop thinking about Charlotte." Brock shifted the pizza looking slightly uncomfortable.

"Go on," Luke encouraged.

Brock shrugged. "Feelings I thought I'd buried with her have resurfaced." He smiled, but it didn't completely reach his eyes. "I was crazy about her. Charlotte always had me feeling all jumbled up inside and when a girl makes you feel like that, you can be sure you're going to do some stupid things. Unfortunately, her death and ten years haven't changed that."

They walked toward the house.

"What exactly is that supposed to mean?"

"It means, even though she's been gone almost ten years, the thought of her still makes me crazy and I've done something pretty stupid because of her."

Luke stopped Brock just outside the door. Raised an eyebrow, and asked, "What did you do?"

"I kissed her twin sister."

Surprised, Luke rocked back on his heels as a twinge of jealousy coursed through him. "You kissed Cami?"

"Yep."

Luke hesitated, trying to keep the brief surge of anger out of the next question. "When?"

"This afternoon."

"Why? I mean... what I meant to say is... how did that happen?"

"Listen, I can tell by the look on your face that you're not happy about this, but you have nothing to worry about."

"I'm not sure what you're talking about."

Brock laughed. "Okay, whatever you want to tell yourself."

"You didn't answer the question."

"Neither did you."

Luke scowled at him.

"Right. Long story short, I kissed her in the butler's pantry after we came up from the basement. We were laughing, she was close, I... she." He shrugged. "It just happened. But as soon as I kissed her, I knew it was a mistake. I can't explain it other than to say it was all wrong. From the way she smelled…"

"Fresh," Luke supplied, "like summer."

"Yeah," Brock answered, contemplating. "The way she tasted."

"Like sweet, ripe cherries?" Luke asked, unable to keep the longing out of his voice.

"Exactly. It was all wrong," he said again. "Almost like I was kissing my sister. And the guilt after."

"Guilt?" Luke questioned. "Because of Charlotte?"

"Yeah. We both felt guilty. So guilty that Cami even thought she saw Charlotte."

Surprised, Luke asked, "Was she joking?"

Brock shook his head no. "Not at all. She was so serious she almost had me convinced that I saw something, too." Brock shifted the pizzas.

"Did you?"

"Yes. No. Maybe. I can't be sure. It happened so fast. Anyway, I don't think that will ever happen again. That kiss was awkward for both of us."

Shaking his head in understanding, Luke said, "I'm sure. Especially since you've told her twin sister that you loved her, even if it was ten years ago. That kind of thing is bound to leave an impression on someone."

"Maybe, if I had, but I never did."

"You never told Charlotte you loved her?" Luke questioned, looking directly at Brock, looking for signs in his body language to see if Brock was telling the truth. "I find that hard to believe."

"Nope."

"Not even in a note, or maybe you wrote it in her yearbook?"

"Heck no. Not once. Don't act so surprised, Warner. I was a teenage boy full of hormones and angst. 'I love you' wasn't even in my vocabulary back then. Not sure if it is now, either."

Bobby opened the back door wide. "You two ladies coming in? Or are you going to stand outside all night gabbin' while our pizza grows cold?"

"We're coming," Brock said.

"'Bout time. Warm beer, cold pizza," Bobby grumbled, ducking back in the house.

Thinking of Charlotte's yearbook, Luke reached for Brock's arm and held him back just a moment. "Are you sure about that? You never told Charlotte once in any form, spoken or written? Like writing it in her yearbook. Maybe you just forgot?"

Brock shook his head, and a shadow of sadness flitted across his face. "Never. Not once, in any form. I'm positive. Not telling her is something I'll regret for the rest of my life."

Luke let him go. He stood there for another moment, contemplating. *If Brock hadn't written I love you under the prom picture, he didn't write the note either. But then who did?* That was something he was determined to find out.

CHAPTER 26

Cami put popcorn in the microwave, dumped M&Ms in a bowl, and set out sodas. She was getting cups from the cabinet when the microwave beeped.

"Want me to get the popcorn?" Tanya asked.

"Yes, please. There's a large bowl over the top of the refrigerator for the popcorn."

"On it." Tanya jumped up from the table, grabbed the bowl out of the cabinet, and snagged the popcorn from the microwave. "Hot, hot!" she said, holding the edge as steam escaped the bag.

"Well, duh," Joselyn exclaimed as Tanya shook white, fluffy kernels into the bowl. "Doesn't take a genius to figure that out."

"What do you want to do first? Watch a movie or go over some party plans?" Cami asked, putting napkins on the table.

"I say we get to the party plans. I've been up since four and probably won't last over twenty minutes into a movie."

"Yeah, let's do the planning first," Joselyn agreed.

"Great!" Cami grabbed her laptop off the counter and took a seat at the table. "Let's talk invitations." Cami opened a tab on her browser. "I wanted to show you the e-vite I sent out yesterday to the guests on your email list." She pulled up a folder, clicked on the email, and turned the laptop so Joselyn could read it.

"That's nice."

"I kept it simple and to the point. I already have ten replies." Cami opened another tab. "Now for the wedding invitations. Here are some choices for that. We can do actual paper invitations since we have over several weeks. Take a look. See if there's anything you like."

Joselyn leaned forward and scrolled through the page.

Scooping up a handful of popcorn, Tanya peered over Joselyn's shoulder. "That one looks nice. I love that one," Tanya said, pointing at the screen.

"Yeah, me too. That one really caught my eye."

"Let me mark it." Cami hit the check mark next to the invitation. "Keep scrolling."

"I like this one, too. And this one."

Cami checked them off, waited for Joselyn to scroll through a few more, then asked, "Do you want to keep looking? Or do you want to choose between those three?"

"Those three are good."

Nodding, Cami clicked twice, diminishing the ones Joselyn wasn't interested in and enlarging the ones she was. "Compare these three side by side. Which one most interests you?"

"Out of these three, this one is my least favorite."

Cami clicked, and the invitation disappeared. "The one on the left is whimsical and romantic. The right is simple and elegant."

"Oh, I love them both. What do you think?"

Cami looked at Joselyn. "In my opinion, the one on the right suits you and Kevin a little better. It would set the theme for your wedding. I picture your dress with straight lines, a minimalist gown that's long, fitted, with a plunging neckline. No veil, just a sweet kiss of miniature white roses in a silver clip sweeping your hair back from your face on one side. A small hand-held bouquet with long stem white roses, with tight blood red accents and trailing scarlet ribbons. The bridesmaids could be in simple, straight lined black dresses with bouquets of red and white accents, men in black tuxes and red rose boutonnieres. Or the handheld muffs you mentioned the other night would work as well with or without flowers. The only difference I think I would make to the dress is maybe with a high lace collar around the back of your neck, still leave the front of the dress open, if you went with the muffs."

Joselyn tilted her head, contemplating. "And what do you picture with the other invitation, the romantic, whimsical one?"

Cami settled back, completely in her element. "With your figure, I would still go with straight lines, but the dress should have a small sweeping train in winter white. See-through delicate lace across the décolleté, the area between your neck and breasts, showing just a hint of cleavage. The bridesmaids in similar style dresses made of a soft sage green, men in black. The bouquets should be short-stemmed, wrapped in the same sage as the dresses, blossoms in varying shades of white, peonies as the center flower. Soft. Full. Lush."

Tanya's hand went to her mouth. "Oh, Cami. Both are so beautiful. I can picture it perfectly."

Joselyn stood. Walked across the kitchen and stared out into the darkness, her reflection shining back at her. She was quiet for a moment. "What if I say I don't like either of those options?"

"Then I say, back to the drawing board."

"Seriously?" Tanya guffawed. "Joselyn? You can't be…"

Cami held up her hand and cut Tanya off. "Give her a minute. Let her think about it." Cami dipped her fingers into the bowl holding the M&M's and took a handful. Putting them on the table, she sorted them by their colors, and ate the brown ones first.

Tanya mouthed, "You have got to be kidding me."

Cami wagged a finger at Tanya, then placed it to her lips. Joselyn was a thinker, a planner. Maybe she had the event pictured completely differently in her mind. If so, that was okay. After all, it was her big day. Joselyn should have what she wanted, what she dreamed of. Every woman should. She moved onto the yellow M&M's, popping them in her mouth one by one, waiting patiently for Joselyn.

Tanya drummed her fingers on the table, then grabbed a handful of the candy-coated chocolate for herself. "The suspense is killing me!" she grumbled. "While we wait, tell me what's up between you and Luke?"

Eating an orange M&M, Cami asked, "What do you mean?"

"Anything since the big kiss?"

Sighing, she shrugged. "Not really. He spent the night last night."

"Really?" Tanya inched closer on her chair. "Do tell."

Cami gave half a laugh. "Keep your mind out of the gutter. He slept on one couch and I was on the other. It was definitely not romantic, but it was sweet. It was more like he felt like he needed to monitor me and that I shouldn't be alone after what happened. Luke was the perfect gentleman. I'm grateful he stayed."

"Did he at least put his arm around you? Or whisper in your ear?"

"Luke didn't get within three feet of me all night."

"Hmph." Tanya sat back. "Well, that's disappointing."

"He called tonight to check on me before he went to poker with the boys."

"Well, that's something, I guess. What did he say?"

"He stopped by the hospital and checked on Detective Swanson."

Joselyn turned around and came back to the table, sat down, grabbed a handful of popcorn, and asked, "How's Detective Swanson doing?"

"He's stable, but still heavily sedated. They're hopeful, but only time will tell." Cami tried to keep from picturing the older man crumpled on the ground, blood seeping out, his shallow breaths.

"I still can't believe that happened."

"I should have been in the house and maybe I could have prevented it," Cami said quietly.

"How?" Tanya questioned.

Cami shrugged. "I don't know. I just feel partly responsible. He came to see me and fell on my sidewalk."

"There's no way for you to know that was going to happen, Cami. I know it must have been terrifying, but you got him help as quickly as you could. You tried to stop the bleeding, and you stayed with him until help arrived. That's more than I could have done. I would have probably passed out right beside him."

"No, you wouldn't have. You would have helped, too."

"Maybe, maybe not. I hope I never have to find out."

"Detective Swanson's such a nice man, he didn't need this. It's been just six months since his heart attack."

"Let's not talk about it anymore. It's so depressing," Joselyn commented.

"You're right, it is. The good news is they're going to bring him off sedation in the next day or two, Luke said."

"That is good news."

Cami forced a smile. "Onto happier things. The wedding. Joselyn, if you don't like either option, it's okay. You won't hurt my feelings." Cami put her hand on top of Joselyn's. "I want your day to be perfect, so don't be afraid to tell me what you really want."

Joselyn nodded. "I think I've decided. Both ideas were wonderful, but I like the first one. It fits Kevin and me better."

"I agree," Tanya chimed in.

"Good." Cami clicked on the correct invitation. Dragging the option over into a folder marked "K&J." "I don't want to pressure you, but we need to decide quickly now. Although I do want to give you time to discuss it with Kevin. Could you let me know by tomorrow morning?"

"Kevin said for me to do what I want. So, I am. And I want everything, just the way you said it."

"Perfect. Let me make some notes. It will only take me a couple of minutes. Then tomorrow I'll get everything together. We need to go dress shopping, get you guys registered, sample cakes, visit the florist, the works!" She typed away as she spoke.

"I'll have the invitations written up and send them to your emails for you to proofread. Once you do, I can have them printed and overnighted."

Cami peered at Tanya over her laptop. "I have an order to place with Jolt for the engagement party: little cakes, cookies, some appetizers. I'll email that list to you right now. You should be able to handle it for Friday, right?"

"Yeah, no problem."

"Great! After the engagement party, Joselyn, I'll need you and Kevin to sit down with me and select a menu for the wedding."

"Sounds good."

"Go pick a movie," she encouraged. "I'll just be a minute more."

Joselyn grabbed the popcorn and scooped up the bowl of M&M's.

Tanya asked, "Got any wine in this place?"

"Yeah, in the butler's pantry," Cami said distractedly, still typing away.

"I'll get it." Tanya disappeared around the corner. "Which cabinet?"

"Bottom right-hand corner. There's a wine rack inside the cabinet."

"Where?"

"Right where Brock and I were standing when he kissed me."

Tanya's head immediately popped back around the corner of the butler's pantry and Joselyn stopped in mid-stride.

"What did you just say?"

Cami looked up sheepishly from her laptop and cringed. "I wasn't going to say anything but..."

"But what? And why the heck not?"

"You kissed Brock Gibson?"

The questions came at her in rapid succession. "I don't know. Because, and yes."

"You're not getting away with one-word answers here,

missy. Spill your guts. Wait." Tanya held up her hand. "Let me get the wine. I think I might need a drink for this."

Tanya disappeared around the corner, and they heard her mumble, "Kissed Brock Gibson, and she wasn't going to say anything. I can't believe it." She emerged triumphant, with a bottle in her hand. "Here it is."

Cami got up and retrieved three wine glasses. "It's really not that big of a deal."

"Silence!" Tanya said, cutting her off. "We," she wagged her finger between herself and Joselyn, "will be the judge of that. Now spill while I pour."

"Did you kiss him, or did he kiss you?" Joselyn demanded, setting both bowls back onto the table.

"Well…"

"Wait, start from the beginning. What was he doing here in the first place?"

"Landscaping."

"Right." Tanya nodded. "But why was he inside? There are no trees or bushes in here."

"It was after everyone had gone home for the day. We were looking around outside, talking about lighting, which led to the breaker box, which is in the basement." She waved off the looks she was getting from Tanya and Joselyn. "It doesn't matter. Anyway, we had just come up from the basement. We were laughing and joking, with no warning, he kissed me full on the mouth."

"And?" Joselyn narrowed her eyes at Cami and popped a couple of pieces of candy-coated chocolate into her mouth.

"And what?"

"Was there an explosion? Did fireworks go off?"

"Is he a good kisser?"

"I guess, but definitely no fireworks. More like an explosion of guilt," Cami said, shaking her head.

Tanya reached across the table and laid her hand on Cami's, her eyes clouded with sympathy. "She's been gone for ten years. You have nothing to feel guilty about."

"Wait. What?" Joselyn slammed her hand down onto the table. "You felt guilty kissing Brock because of Charlotte?" she asked in disbelief. "Why?"

"He was my sister's boyfriend."

"So?" Joselyn snorted. "I guarantee you she wouldn't feel guilty if it was the other way around."

"You don't know that," Tanya replied.

"Oh, really? Charlotte kissed plenty of other people's boyfriends or crushes and never thought twice about it."

"How do you know that?" Tanya raised an eyebrow at Joselyn.

"It doesn't matter," Cami said, reaching for the bottle of wine and pouring some into a glass.

"Why not?" Tanya asked. "Do you like him?"

Cami took a sip and shook her head. "I care about him, but like a brother. And that's exactly how I felt when I was kissing him, like he was my brother. And he felt the same way."

"He said that?" Tanya questioned.

"Yes, needless to say, it was fairly awkward."

"I'll bet."

"This is unbelievable. You've only been back a little over two weeks and you've kissed the two most eligible bachelors in town. How does this happen?" Joselyn asked in disbelief. "I guess you're more like Charlotte than I thought."

"Hey, that was uncalled for, Joselyn."

"Whatever. You of all people know it's true."

"What's that supposed to mean?" Tanya demanded.

Joselyn placed her hand on her hip. "Seriously? Bobby? Are you going to stand there and act like you didn't know?" She ran her fingers through her hair and scowled at Tanya. "I know you saw Charlotte kiss Bobby Cannon outside the locker room before the game homecoming night our sophomore year. You acted like it meant nothing, but deep down, you were hurt. And you," Joselyn turned and pointed a finger at Cami. "Your own sister was snuggling up to Luke every chance she could. Heck, she was sitting next to him at the bonfire the night she died."

"That's different," Cami came to her sister's defense. "She was going to tell Luke I liked him if I didn't."

"Whatever. Yet, you sit here feeling guilty for a kiss that didn't even mean anything to you. How does that happen? How does someone have that much power, even in death?"

The lights flickered overhead, all three women looked up.

"What the heck?" Joselyn questioned.

The lights went out, plunging them into darkness.

"It's nothing," Cami lied, trying to sound more confident than she felt. She could see the air shimmer and smell a hint of roses. *Charlotte*. Her pulse skipped as she clutched the table, bracing herself. Trying to remain calm, she tried to talk them through the situation. "My breaker box needs to be upgraded, I just told you that. Aaron's coming tomorrow to install it."

"Are you going to kiss him, too? Charlotte would." The question hung in the air as a wave of cold descended on the room, crawling down the walls like icy fingers.

Joselyn glanced nervously around, her breath funneling out in a plume of white. She gasped for air, visibly uncomfortable. The air shifted. Joselyn stepped backward and lost her balance. She cried out as she hit the floor hard. It was like a burst of air right before a storm hits. The lights flickered, and the cold seeped slowly away. As the heat returned, so did the lights.

"What the heck!" Tanya exclaimed, rubbing her hands up and down her arms to warm up.

Cami scrambled over to Joselyn, who was still sprawled on the floor, pale as a sheet, trying to catch her breath.

"Are you alright? You're shaking."

"What the hell just happened?"

"I'm not sure."

"I don't know what the heck that was, but that was so scary I almost peed my pants. It was as if..." Tanya scrambled to make sense of it.

"As if what?"

"I don't know. Like a ghost or something."

Her stomach was in knots. Cami tried to act normal. "Sometimes a cold draft blows through. I can't explain it. Grab the snacks, I'll build a fire, and we can put on a movie. Forget it even happened."

"I'm all for that!" Tanya grabbed the wine, took a big gulp from the bottle and followed on Cami's heels into the drawing room, glancing over her shoulder as she went. "What the hell was that?"

"That's some weird shit, Cami," Joselyn stated with an edge of fear in her voice.

Tanya plopped down on the sofa, clutching the wine bottle to her chest, wrapping a blanket around herself, still shivering. "I was going to suggest we watch something scary but after that, I'm already creeped out, so I say we go with a rom-com."

"Sounds good to me."

"I can't believe you two! Are you just going to act like nothing happened?"

Both women turned to look at her.

"Why?"

"Are you kidding me right now? You're acting like it's nothing. Did we just see the same thing back there?"

"There was nothing to see. I told you. It was just a draft. It really wasn't that big of a deal." Cami crossed the room and started stacking logs in the hearth.

"Maybe not to you because you're used to this old house and you're not the one that fell on your ass. Help me out, Tanya."

"I'm trying not to overthink it." Tanya shuddered. "The lights going out could be because of the breaker box, like Cami said. Falling on your ass, though, was all you."

"That was more than a damn breaker box or a fuse." Glancing around nervously, Joselyn added, "I'm leaving. This house is too big and empty for me. Besides, I want to be home when Kevin gets there."

Cami put the last log in place and crossed the room to Joselyn. Reaching for her, she asked, "I understand you're upset. That was freaky, and I can't explain it. Except to say it's an old house."

"That's a hell of an explanation."

"I'll get the fire going. Stay. It's over. I promise it won't happen again tonight."

Joselyn shook her head. "I can't. This whole thing with Detective Swanson kind of has me on edge anyway, and I'm not the one who even found him."

Reaching out, Cami grasped her hand. "That was an accident, Joselyn."

"Was it?"

"What makes you think it wasn't?"

Piercing her lips together, Joselyn fidgeted, clearly uncomfortable. "I shouldn't say anything. It's not my place."

"What do you know?" Tanya demanded, swinging her legs off the couch and coming over.

"Nothing."

"It has to be something or you wouldn't have said anything."

"What did you hear and from whom?" Tanya wouldn't let it go.

Sighing heavily, Joselyn relented. "Today, at work, while you were in the back, two EMTs that were on call last night came in. They weren't talking to me, so I'm not completely sure what they were saying, but I got the impression they felt it might not have been an accident." She put her hands on her hips and glared at Tanya. "Satisfied?" Joselyn asked.

"I guess."

"And now that just happened. I'm freaked and on edge. I'm going."

Cami squeezed Joselyn's hand. "You should go home then and be with Kevin, if it will make you feel better. We'll talk tomorrow."

"I'd lock the door behind me, if I were you." Turning on her heel, she walked through the grand foyer. Her footsteps echoed through the large space and faded as she opened the door and left.

***

The incessant beep of monitors echoed through the halls. The smell of bleach and antiseptic lingered in the air. Sidestepping the caution sign declaring a wet floor, feet tiptoed down the long corridor, a mere shadow in the darkened hallways at the late hour. Pausing outside the reception area to the critical care unit, eyes searched looking for nurses, doctors, or security. Patients slept heavily, and a skeleton crew worked the graveyard shift. All activity ceased on this level, as it should be in the middle of the night.

The nurse on duty sat with her back to the darkened corridor and watched a late-night re-run, the volume on low. The television light flickered eerily against the pale walls but held her attention. Watching. Waiting, the shadow held its breath and proceeded past the desk. Looking for one room in particular: Detective Dwight Swanson's.

The door stood wide, and the room was dark, except for the blue light that came from the monitor. The shadow moved about the room, unseen by the heavily sedated patient. With a gloved hand, the shadow fished out a small vile of medicine from a pocket, picked up a clean syringe that lay ready for the next dosage of medications to be delivered, and extracted the liquid from the tiny bottle. Without hesitating, the shadow inserted the syringe into the intravenous liquids flowing steadily into the patient. Once the poison emptied into the vinyl tubing, the syringe was carefully removed. The shadow dropped the evidence into their pocket and tiptoed to the doorway, disappearing into the darkened hallway as quickly as they'd come.

CHAPTER 27

Cami lay on the floor on the thick, plush rug in front of the dying fire. The wood was long gone, all that was left now were embers. Propped on her elbows, she flipped to the next page of her book, enjoying the enchanting glow and the soft warmth that emanated from the hearth.

She continued reading even when she realized she wasn't alone.

"Your nose is always in a book."

"I like to read, you know that." Cami didn't look up, but had to start the paragraph over.

"Scooch over. I wanna sit by the fire, too."

Cami sat up and slid over so her sister could share the rug. "There. Are you happy?"

Charlotte shrugged. "I guess. What are you reading? A romance novel?" She leaned over Cami's shoulder and peered down.

"No, a mystery."

"You always liked mysteries. Not me. If I read, I preferred romance. Funny how we can be sisters, even twins, and like different things."

"I like a good romance the same as you." Cami closed the book, knowing she wouldn't get to read any more until Charlotte got some attention. "What do you want?" Cami asked, looking at her twin sister.

"You know what I want."

Cami nodded. "I'm working on it."

"Not fast enough. You've had ten years."

"I've only been home two weeks. Give me a break, will you?"

"I won't. I can't. You need to keep at it."

"Why?" Cami asked her sister as her image shimmered. "Why do we need to know?"

"Because they've been here. Outside, in the shadows. Here in the house."

"Are they here now?"

Charlotte shook her head and her blonde hair shimmered like spun gold. "No, but they will be back."

"Who?" Cami begged. "Can you tell me who, Charlotte?"

"I can't."

"You can't or you won't?" Cami tried to keep impatience out of her voice.

"I can't."

"Then how do you know they'll be back?"

"I can feel the darkness when they're nearby. The jealousy. The hatred. And the fear."

"The fear?"

"Yes, fear. Fear that you will find out. Fear that they will lose everything. But the hatred and jealousy pour out of them like oil. Black as the night, thick and liquid, spreading out and covering everything it touches." Charlotte shivered and her image thinned at the vibration. "They were here last night. They were waiting in the shadows for Detective Swanson. The same person who killed me waited for him." She turned shimmering blue eyes at Cami. "They'll come for you, too. You're who they really want. It's only a matter of time."

CHAPTER 28

Armed with coffee from Jolt, Cami crossed the street at the light and walked down Main Street toward the police station. The sky was overcast, the sun completely hidden behind gray clouds. Looming in silhouette, the sun sat like a brooding mistress, exactly how Cami felt. She stopped just short of the door, not sure if she wanted to go in.

Was she thinking clearly? How could she be? Her nerves were shot. She hadn't slept well last night, or the night before. Every time she closed her eyes, all she could see was Detective Swanson struggling to breathe, his eyes rolled back into his head, and blood. Blood everywhere.

Then, at last, when sleep finally came, she dreamt of Charlotte. *Was Charlotte right? Had her death not been an accident?* She'd been relentless for ten years. The police had never proven it wasn't anything other than an unfortunate accident. One thing at a time.

A fall in the dark. A stumble backward. No one heard her cry out, if she even had. The dark, the drastic drop in temperature, and the elements too much for her.

But all these years, Cami hadn't believed it, Charlotte wouldn't let it lie or didn't want to. It was too simple. Too random. There was someone in the dark. A shadow. And now there was Detective Swanson with almost the exact same thing happening to him. Coincidence? She thought not.

"Hey, Parker."

Cami jumped at her name.

"Stand there much longer, I'm gonna have to arrest you

for loitering."

Cami turned and gave Bobby a ghost of a smile, despite her nerves. "What if I offer you a fresh cup of coffee from Jolt? Would you let me off with a warning?"

Bobby eyed the cup carrier in her hand. "Is one of them for me?"

"Yes, it is."

"Well, isn't that a nice surprise?" He took the cup she offered. "Wait. What did you do? Are you trying to bribe an officer of the law?"

"Maybe."

He took a tentative sip, testing the temperature with his lips.

"Did it work?"

"Maybe. Who made the coffee?"

"Tanya."

"Oh?" Bobby quirked an eyebrow. "She knows what I like. Regular with…"

"Two sugars and a shot of cream."

He took a slow swallow. "Ahhh, perfect. Again, I have to ask, what did you do?"

Smiling, she said, "Now why would you think I've done something?"

"Most people avoid the police station at all costs, and they definitely don't bring us coffee. That's a sure sign of guilt in my mind." He tapped his temple lightly.

"Well, your mind must be a little tainted. I've done nothing wrong."

"Yet," Bobby added and Cami laughed. "Seriously though, what brings you by?" He looked back at the carrier. "One of those coffees for Warner?"

"How did you guess?"

"Cops' intuition. You coming in then?" He snagged the door as it opened and an officer walked out, holding it for her.

"Sure," Cami said hesitantly, the nerves rushing back.

He escorted her in. The office was fairly quiet. A few

police officers sat at computers, while others hovered in the corner, deep in conversation. They walked down the narrow hall together. Bobby stopped at the half-opened door and stuck his head in. "You busy?"

"Kinda. Why? What's up?"

"I have a visitor for you."

Before Cami could change her mind, Bobby put his hand on her back and ushered her through the door.

Glancing up from his laptop, Luke smiled when he saw Cami. "Good morning, Cami. I was just thinking about you."

"You were?" Cami asked, trying not to blush.

"Yes, please, come in."

"Watch her, Warner. She brought coffee from Jolt. Says she's done nothing, but I have my suspicions."

Cami handed Luke a cup. "Tanya made it. Apparently, she knows exactly what you like. One black coffee with a shot of espresso."

Luke took the cup and checked it over carefully. Looking at Bobby, he asked, "Did you get one, too?"

"Yep, made perfectly, I might add."

Both men looked at Cami and said in unison, "What did you do?"

"What in the world is with you two? Can't a girl just bring two good looking police officers' coffee and not be guilty of anything?"

"Two things are wrong with what you just said."

"First, only one of us is good looking."

Luke looked at Bobby, who was grinning, pointing to himself, and mouthing "me."

"And second, your nickname is double trouble for a reason."

"I'm offended." She reached for the coffee. "I'll be needing that back now."

Luke took a step back. "Not on your life."

Bobby quickly licked the entire rim of his cup. "My germs are all over it. You wouldn't want it back. Would you?" His grin was wide as he held it out to her.

"That was gross on so many levels."

"I'll be going now. Thanks for the coffee, Parker." Cannon raised his cup in salute.

"Believe me when I tell you I won't be bringing you another cup."

"I'll savor this one then until the very last drop," Bobby said, walking away chuckling to himself. "Good luck, Warner."

"Sorry about him," Luke said.

"Him? You're just as bad."

Luke flashed her an affable grin, walked behind her, and closed the door. He indicated one of the chairs. "Please, have a seat."

Cami sat, put the carrier on the edge of the worn desk, and took out her own cup.

Walking around the desk, Luke sat across from her. "Thank you for the coffee. I appreciate it." Settling in, he really looked at her. "Seriously though, what brings you in?"

"A couple of things," Cami said.

"The first one?"

"How is Detective Swanson?"

Luke took a sip of coffee, stalling. "There's no easy way to say this and I am sorry to have to tell you, Cami, but Detective Swanson didn't make it. I got the call earlier this morning that he'd passed away."

Cami couldn't even say anything. There was a lump in her throat and pressure on her chest.

"The trauma to his head was just too severe."

She nodded, understanding. Tears threatened to fall, but she fought through them. Cami didn't want to fall apart in front of Luke. She knew she was on the verge of a nervous breakdown. The exhaustion, all the things happening to her at the house. Then there was the upcoming engagement party, and the stress of starting a new business, and now? Now losing a very sweet man.

"I know what you're thinking and don't. It's not your

fault, Cami. You did everything you could."

She heard him. In her mind she understood, but in her heart, she only felt responsibility and loss.

Luke leaned forward. "Cami, are you okay? You look tired."

Giving a weak smile, she said, "I am. I haven't slept well the past couple of nights."

"That's understandable. Anything I can do?"

"You can tell me I'm not crazy."

"Why would you be crazy?"

Cami shifted in her seat, suddenly very uncomfortable. She hadn't meant to say that out loud. She laughed nervously. "I mean, I was kidding."

"Of course, but you are here for a reason."

He looked at her with those intense gray eyes, and any nerve she had left quickly dissipated. She couldn't imagine what it would feel like if Luke Warner, of all people, thought she was crazy. "It's nothing, really. I should go."

Cami moved to go but Luke was faster, coming around the desk. Reaching for her arm, he held her gently in place. "Cami," he breathed. "Please, tell me why you're here."

She sighed, fighting an inward battle. Relenting just a little, Cami said, "It's probably nothing."

"Why don't you let me decide?"

"Try not to judge me too harshly, please."

"I won't." Perching himself on the edge of his desk, he gazed down at her intently.

Where should she start? *Start slow so he doesn't think you're crazy.* Shifting in her seat, Cami twisted the top of her coffee off, letting steam escape. "I don't know if you ever remember hearing that sometimes we, Charlotte and I, would accidentally wear the same outfit on the same day?"

Luke quirked a small smile. "I had heard that. I think I even noticed it once or twice. I also heard you kept an extra outfit in your locker for fashion emergencies like that. Was that true?"

Nodding, Cami smiled. "Yes, it is. Charlotte never wanted to match. Our mom sometimes dressed us identically when we were little and Charlotte would fuss about it the entire time."

"Then why would you buy the same clothes?"

"When we were older?"

Luke nodded.

"We didn't, at least not on purpose. Charlotte and I didn't always shop together. We bought items when we weren't together and didn't realize the other already had it. We had similar taste in some things."

"That's actually fascinating."

"Not to Charlotte. She hated it." Cami shrugged. "Anyway, there were other things, too. Sometimes when we were together, we would say the same thing or order the same food at a restaurant. Sometimes when one of us got hurt, the other would feel the pain, or just sense that something happened if we were apart." Cami fell silent for a moment, grasping her cup a little tighter.

"Like you did the night she died?"

Looking up at Luke, he held her gaze, and knew he understood. "Yes, exactly like that."

"Go on," he prompted. "I'm listening."

Swallowing the enormous lump in her throat, she asked, "Have you read Charlotte's file?"

"Yes, several times."

"Then you know I lead them straight to her body?"

His gaze never shifted from hers. "Yes."

"I was afraid they thought I might have..." Her voice trailed off. Cami didn't know if she could say it. Tears formed at the edge of her vision, she looked away from him, then back, hesitant. "That I might have been responsible, or had something to do with it."

"Detective Swanson never thought that."

"He didn't?" Cami asked as a tear threatened to fall.

Luke shook his head. "And neither do I."

"You don't?"

"I was there, remember? With you. I saw firsthand the reaction you had. How pale you turned. Hell, I don't think I'll ever forget the look on your face. I dreamt about it for weeks after."

"You did?" Cami asked, unable to think clearly with him looking directly at her.

He nodded. "I did."

"Me too."

Luke lifted an eyebrow in question.

"Well, not that exactly, but I dreamt of Charlotte. She would come to me in my dreams and tell me..."

"Tell you what?"

Cami stood quickly, accidentally brushing against him.

Both of his hands came up quickly, holding her in place. Luke asked quietly, "Where are you going? Talk to me, please."

She wanted to. Needed to. But could she? *Trust someone,* a voice whispered in her mind. "I dreamt of Charlotte. She told me it wasn't an accident."

"What wasn't?"

"The night Charlotte died, it wasn't an accident. She told me over and over. She haunted my every dream, turning them into nightmares. Over and over, she kept repeating it. She was relentless." Cami shifted slightly from foot to foot, uncomfortable, all too aware of his hands on her.

Taking a deep breath, she continued, "That's why we moved so quickly, only weeks after her death. I couldn't sleep, because I became afraid to. All I could see once I closed my eyes was Charlotte. And sensations. Sensations like I was trapped inside her body. I could feel myself fall backward, the blow to her head. Rock connecting with bone. The disorientation. Confusion. Anger. And a darkness. A darkness creeping over her. Me. Us. Her." Cami shook her head, trying to clear the images. "And then she can't breathe. There's this tickle of fear that races through her as she pulls in a breath. It's hard. The air is thick, clogged somehow. It's so very hard to breathe."

Without thinking, Cami places her hand on her chest as if she's reliving it. "Charlotte can't breathe. Everything hurts. Her head. Her chest. Her lungs. So dizzy. Darkness covers her." Cami stares off into the distance, past Luke, out the window into the gray day.

"Then what?" Luke asks softly.

"Then nothing. It's over. She's gone."

He knew he shouldn't, but he couldn't help himself. On a prayer, Luke pulled her in, wrapped his arms around her and held her tight. Cami relaxed into him. She was soft, warm, and smelled like heaven. "I didn't know you were going through this back then, reliving it night after night. No wonder your parents made you move. They probably thought with some distance and time, it would be better for you to heal." Without thinking, he said, "Now I understand why they wanted the case closed."

Cami pulled back. "What did you just say? Who wanted the case closed?"

"Of course, you didn't know. How could I have been so stupid?"

"Who closed the case, Luke? My parents?"

"Yes, I'm sorry. You shouldn't have found out that way."

Cami let go of him and sank into the chair. "I can't believe it. Why would they do that?"

Luke pulled the other side chair up and sat next to her, reached for her hand, and said, "My guess would be to protect you."

More mad now than sad, Cami looked at Luke. "More likely to protect Charlotte and the Parker name." Cami ran her hand through her long hair, brushing it away from her face.

"Let's backtrack for a moment. We started this entire conversation with you saying I would think you're crazy. So far, you have said nothing that would even make me think that." He reached over and picked up his coffee that she'd brought. "I know you didn't come in just to bring me coffee, as much as it's appreciated."

"No, you're right, I didn't." *It's now or never,* she thought. "So the dreams," she started.

"Did they go away?"

"Not entirely, but they lessened. More accurately, I learned how to shut Charlotte out. With distance, time, and keeping myself busy. I never wanted to leave, not school, not my friends, or the house. But when you're seventeen and have a very domineering mother, you have little choice. Charlotte was the only one that stood up to her. I guess that's why Mom loved her best."

"Cami, I'm sure that's not true."

"Oh, it is. But I'm not telling you that to get sympathy or anything, I'm just stating a fact. Anyway, Mom thought she could control me. She wanted to pick my friends, my clothes, and my school. I was shy, as you know, grieving, and completely heartbroken, so I let her. But once I went to college and got some distance from her, I made my own choices. My own career, one she didn't approve of, my own friends, and as silly as it sounds, my own clothes. Of course, that didn't stop her. Mom was very persistent when she wanted to be, so she picked her battles. She couldn't pick the career I had, but she could control the circle of men that were around me."

"What are you saying? Your mom wanted to pick who you dated?"

"That's exactly what I'm saying. She wanted the perfect son-in-law if she couldn't have the perfect daughter."

"That's twisted."

"I'll say. And so were most of her hand-picked men. The last one, Richard, was a real winner. He came off very polished and sophisticated, but behind closed doors he was arrogant, domineering, and belittling."

"Did he ever hurt you?" Luke asked in a low voice.

She could hear anger festering. "No. He didn't need to; his words were enough of a beating."

"How long?" Luke's blood was ready to boil. "How long did you stay with him?"

"Not long, but long enough." Cami gave a sad smile. "Within a few weeks, I saw his true colors. Richard didn't like to be questioned, or second guessed. He invited me to a cocktail party for work. I didn't want to go. I was already feeling the pressure of being with him. To look a certain way, or dress in a particular outfit, and I didn't like it. I tried to end it, but Richard insisted I owed it to him to go to this one last business cocktail party with him. Everyone knew I was coming. He was up for a promotion and by not attending, it would make him look bad. He even called my mother and had her convince me to go.

"Richard was relentless on the way to the party. My hair wasn't right, my dress was too short, my shoes didn't match. On and on. I couldn't wait for the night to be over. To be done with him for good. And I told him so when he dropped me off. He was too drunk to argue or even get out of the cab and walk me to the door. He didn't take it well, and neither did my mother."

Cami twirled the half empty coffee cup in her hand and continued. "He came over every night for a week, sat outside my apartment, waiting for me to come home. I stayed away. At my parents, then at friends. After a week, he quit. I thought I was in the clear until he showed up at work. That's the day I put in my two weeks. I could see he had no intentions to stop."

The worst of it was over now. Cami relaxed, a little exhausted from explaining. She didn't want Luke to think less of her because of the situation with Richard, but still wasn't sure if she could tell him the rest. Cami wasn't sure if Luke was ready for all that. She'd better stay with what was safe for now. "That's where Cherry Hollow comes in. It has always been my escape plan."

"Pretty good backup plan, if you ask me."

"Thanks, I thought so."

"Back up a minute. You said you learned to control your dreams about Charlotte, not let her in. But now that you're back, they've started again?"

"Yes, and no. They started before I came home when I was stressed about Richard, if that makes sense?"

Shaking his head, he said, "It does. Being under stress is associated with poor quality of sleep. Which can trigger more frequent dreams. It's a way for the brain to process emotions. We have dreams regularly and sometimes have recurring dreams about an event or a certain person. And in your case, because you've had a traumatic event, your subconscious may try to connect the dots for you to better cope with what happened to your twin sister. Therefore, your subconscious and conscious mind are working together, trying to help you cope. Do you follow me?"

"Yes, and in this case, I guess my subconscious mind has a name: Charlotte."

"Okay, fair enough. And what is she saying?"

"She's trying to warn me."

"Warn you about what?"

There was a knock on the door.

"Son of a… Hold that thought. Come in."

"Sorry to interrupt," Bobby said, sticking his head in.

"You're not," Cami said. "I was just about to leave."

"You were?" Luke asked, clearly surprised. "We weren't finished."

"I am," she said firmly, afraid she might have said too much already. But one look at Luke's concerned face had her softening. "At least for now. I've taken up enough of your time. Besides, I need to get going. We're going wedding dress shopping today with Joselyn."

"Can I walk you out at least?"

"No need. I can find my way."

"Can I stop by later? I'd like to finish this conversation."

Cami tucked a stray strand of hair behind her ear, considering. "I guess that would be okay."

"Maybe bring out a pizza or better yet, we could go get a bite to eat somewhere?"

"I'd like that."

"I'll pick you up at six."

"Perfect."

"Thanks for the coffee."

She smiled sweetly at him. "Anytime." Cami turned to Bobby, squinted her eyes, and pointed her finger. "But not you."

Bobby roared with laughter as she walked down the hall.

CHAPTER 29

Armed with his tools, Aaron knocked on the heavy wooden door. Despite Brock saying he had seen Cami leave for the day and the house was seemingly empty, Aaron would swear someone was home because every time he glanced up at the house, he saw movement in the second-story window.

He stepped into the darkened grand foyer as the heavy front door slowly closed behind him, cutting out the sounds of the landscape crew and what little natural light filtered in.

"Cami? It's Aaron," he called out. "I'm here to install a new electrical panel in the basement and upgrade what you have." He stood still, listening to the echo of his voice resonate throughout the space and waited for a response. When none came, he walked through the grand foyer, under the sweep of massive stairs, and into the kitchen. Flipping a few switches, he brought light to the space. He found the butler's pantry just like Brock had said, and the door to the basement. Aaron unlatched the old wooden door. A single bulb hung from the slanted ceiling. He flipped the switch and was disappointed by the light that barely illuminated the stairs.

Aaron couldn't believe he was in the house, let alone going into the spooky basement by himself. He had nightmares for weeks after Charlotte died; about the house, Charlotte, the woods, and about what he had seen. He tried to block out those thoughts as he turned on his flashlight and descended the stairs into the damp, dank basement. "Damn it, you're not a seventeen-year-old kid anymore. Just do what you came to do. Get in, get out. It's that simple."

Pointing the flashlight, he located the other light Brock had told him about suspended from the ceiling. Finding it, he set down his equipment and got out the new lightbulbs he'd brought. Changing the old for the new, he yanked the chain and was greeted with light. Feeling a little better, Aaron scanned the basement and spotted the electrical panel on the far wall. Beside it was the board for the new panel one of the guys had brought down earlier in the day. He threaded his way through the piles of junk across the basement.

Setting up his portable light so the panel was well lit when he cut the electricity, Aaron aimed the powerful flood light strategically so it swathed most of the wall in an eerie, fluorescent white light.

Making sure the service panel was completely dry before he opened the door to the box, he stood to the side and switched off the main breaker, shutting off electricity all over the house. Using a non-contact voltage tester to confirm the power was off, he set to work.

Aaron switched off each individual circuit breaker, even though it was redundant, and rocked the first breaker from the bus bar. "Don't be nervous," he scolded himself while he worked. "No one knows what you saw." But he was.

He couldn't stand the silence. Every little creek and groan of the house set his teeth on edge. He needed noise. A steady noise that would drown out the scurry of little feet that scattered when he moved, noise that would drown out his own heavy breathing and the pounding of his heart.

Pulling out his cell phone, he put in his earbuds that he carried in his front pocket and started his playlist. Heavy metal wailed away inside his head and made it impossible to think about anything other than the task at hand.

Loosening the terminal screw on the back of the circuit, he pulled the first wire and tried to put where he was out of his mind. He worked steadily through all the breakers, removing them and replacing them with new ones. It worked for a while, but then thoughts, memories, and images niggled their way back into his conscious mind. He didn't know what was worse, being outside where she died or in the house, alone.

Despite the dank and musty smell of the basement, Aaron would swear he could detect the faintest scent of roses mixed with mold. He shifted from foot to foot as he felt a cold draft wash over him. *It's just my imagination,* he thought, *which had been overly active since the minute they'd run into Cami at Finn's last week.*

Something he thought he had suppressed ten years ago came rushing to the surface. He thought about it at odd times during the day, like now, and it most definitely haunted his dreams at night. He didn't know what to do about it, or if he should do anything. What was that expression? Let dead dogs lie. Or, in this case, let Charlotte lie. She'd dug her own grave, so to speak, let her rest in peace in it. If that's what she was actually doing, not haunting this house instead.

He finished fastening the last wire in place, relieved that he was halfway done. Now for the new breaker box. Reaching down to get his battery-operated drill out of his toolbox, a shape passed in front of the light, casting a long shadow on the wall.

His heart literally stopped. A hand came down on his shoulder. Aaron yelped, turned and swung.

"What the hell?" Brock cussed, jumping back, dodging Aaron's fist.

Aaron stumbled back, away from him in pure horror, landing on his ass. His eyes focused on Brock's face and relief washed over him. "Damn, Brock! I was ready to lay you out. Don't sneak up on a guy like that." He put his hand to his heart and felt it bang relentlessly against his ribs.

"Take the damn earbuds out of your ears, and maybe you'd hear a guy coming. You nearly punched me in the face." Brock scowled at Aaron. Without warning, a grin cracked his otherwise serious face. "Holy shit! If you don't look like you've seen a ghost, I don't know who does!" Brock bent over and howled with laughter. "I bet you practically pissed your pants when I put my hand on your shoulder."

"Okay, jackass. Think it's funny? If my fist had connected with your face, you'd be the one on the ground right now. What the hell are you doin' down here, anyway?"

Brock extended his hand to his partner. "I'm here to help you. Everyone's knocking off for the day, figured if we both worked on this project, you'd be done quicker. Let me hold the plywood while you secure it." Brock reached for it, glanced at Aaron. "You ready? Or are you just going to stand there?"

"I'm coming."

"Let's get this done. This basement gives me the creeps."

"You and me both."

***

Driving with the windows down was something Luke always enjoyed after a long day. He loved the feel of the wind on his skin, blowing through his hair, with the fresh scent of fall surrounding him as he drove. The hum of the tires on asphalt, the twang of country pumping out of his speakers, and the roll of landscape around him always put him in a reflective mood. And with the loss of an old friend and coworker heavy on his heart, tonight was no different.

What were the two things he wanted most out of life? That was the question plaguing him lately. Luke thought of himself as a simple guy. And if he was being honest, there were really only two things he desired: someone to love, and a career that was fulfilling.

He truly believed that the key to both those things was at the end of this very drive. On cue, he came to the last road, made the turn, went around the long slow curve, and watched for the lane that led to her.

To say he was nervous was an understatement. Luke's stomach did a small flip as he parked the SUV outside the large stone house and made his way to the front door. Cursing his nerves, he tried to push down the nervous energy he had. It's not like he hadn't been here a half a dozen times in the last week or so. But tonight, was different. Tonight, he felt like he was crossing a line that he promised himself he wouldn't cross.

He was torn. Torn between wanting to take Cami out on a date to see where it could lead and trying to keep his professional distance, following the clues and solving the ten-year-old case. *Why couldn't he do both?* He asked himself. *Because it's a conflict of interest. You'll need to compartmentalize.* Praying he could, he rang the doorbell.

The minute the door opened, all hope he had of that vanished.

Cami stood just inside, silhouetted by the soft light of the chandelier. Her hair was hanging loose, framing her face in a golden caramel sheath. She wore jeans and a tight-knit moss green sweater, which pulled out the green in her eyes, making her look ethereal in the light. Simple and beautiful.

He stood still, staring, unable to form any cognitive thought. Except, "Wow." The word slipped from his mouth with no hesitation or thought of what her reaction might be.

It was slow at first, like the slow burn of a match, but the smile tugged at the corners of her mouth. And when the smile took over, it lit her entire face, making him pleased the word had slipped out.

"Wow, yourself," she said. "Do you want to come in or just go?" Cami asked, holding the door wide in invitation.

Luke contemplated the situation quickly. His eyes moved over her, then to the grand sweep of stairs behind her, and what lay at the top. There was a long curl of lust that surged through him. He wanted nothing more than to take her hand, lead her up the stairs and...He couldn't even complete the thought. Instead, he took a step back. "We should probably just go. If you're ready?"

"I am." She reached for a small purse, flipped the light switch, and locked the door behind her. "Where are we going?"

Luke wanted somewhere quiet, where they wouldn't be interrupted, where no one would know them. He had questions about the conversation they'd had earlier, about the case, and about her on a personal level. "Are you up for a drive?"

"Always."

"Good, because I have just the place in mind."

***

They drove over an hour, but the place was worth it. A three-story brick and mortar sprawling building that once served as an inn, the cornerstone read 1859 and sported a sign stating they had survived prohibition. Cami smiled as she followed the waitress to a corner booth away from the crowd. Ivory candles in mason jars dotted the tables as wax pooled in the bottom and the tiny flames flickered, giving off an enchanting glow against the black table cloths.

Luke's shoulder brushed hers as he slid into the curved booth next to her, giving her a warm feeling all over. The hostess handed them menus and disappeared, followed quickly by the waitress. They ordered drinks, debated over entrees, and finally ordered off the menu and sat back to enjoy their surroundings.

She'd been anxious when they started the drive, but he'd quickly made her relax. He was so easy to talk to, quick-witted and confident. Cami enjoyed everything about him, from the way he looked at her to the way he listened. It had been a long while since she'd been with a man that genuinely seemed interested in her, and not what her father could do for them or that her mother hadn't arranged.

Their drinks came, and she asked, "Why did you become a police officer?"

He took a sip of his Coke and contemplated her. "I'm not sure if you really want to know."

"Why wouldn't I?"

"Because it involves you."

She was quiet for a moment as they placed their entrees in front of them. Turning her plate slightly, she reached for her silverware, unrolling it and placing the cloth napkin across her lap, giving herself some time. "You mean, Charlotte?"

"Not just Charlotte, you and your family. All of you. I was there, remember? I know the feelings I had when I saw you almost faint, and the next day when we heard they had found Charlotte."

He reached across the table and placed his hand on hers. "I was at the funeral and saw what the loss did to Brock, your parents, and you. I wanted to help, but I couldn't. All I could do was answer a few questions, and that helped very little. I wanted to do more, needed to."

Picking up his knife and fork, he cut into his steak. She waited, watched him for a moment, then asked, "So until then, you what? What were your plans before my sister died?"

He shrugged. "Nothing important. I didn't know, didn't have a plan. All I wanted to do was go to college, have fun, and play football. But that night? That night changed everything for me. Bobby, too."

"Really?"

"Yep, I think he was going for accounting or something." Luke laughed. "Can you see Bobby in a suit and tie, sitting behind a desk every day?"

"No, I can't. Being a police officer seems to fit him. And you too."

"I'll take that as a compliment."

"I meant it as one." Stabbing a cherry tomato, she waved it at him. "I didn't realize how many lives that night changed." Cami took a couple of bites, savoring the tangy flavor of her meal. "Do you think it would have been different had she died alone?"

"What do you mean, alone?"

"What if Charlotte had just wandered off in the woods like she did and tripped, fallen like she did, but none of you were there?"

"I think..." He hesitated, clearly thinking it through. Luke leaned in close, looked her square in the eye and said matter-of-factly, "My guess would be that she'd still be alive."

Cami sat back, surprised. "You do?"

Luke nodded.

That hadn't been what she meant at all. She had wanted to know if he would still be a police officer if he wasn't there that night. Would it have left such an impression on him? But this was something completely different. She could barely ask, "Why?"

"There are just too many things that don't add up."

Cami was both relieved and shocked all at the same time. She'd felt since the night it happened it wasn't an accident, but no one had ever believed her, certainly not her parents. And now, sitting across from her, the very boy she had a crush on in high school, who had grown into the man that she might fall for all over again, felt the same way. "Like what?" she asked cautiously.

Luke glanced around. "I'm not sure this is the right time or place to discuss this."

"You're probably right. But Luke? I need to. There are still some things I need to tell you."

"Like what?"

"I told you earlier today about the dreams I was having about Charlotte."

"Yes. Are you ready to tell me the rest?"

"I think so. It's difficult to explain."

"Just try, that's all I ask."

"Do you believe in ghosts?"

His fork stopped midway to his mouth. He studied her, and decided she was serious. "I'm not sure."

Nodding, Cami started, "Fair enough." *There was no easy way to say it. She imagined it would be like ripping off a band aid. Do it and do it fast.* "I think Charlotte's in the house."

"What do you mean?"

"Her spirit."

Luke straightened. "What makes you think that?"

"Things."

"You'll have to be a little more specific than that." Putting down his fork, he contemplated her. "Foremost, I believe in facts, in tangible evidence. Can you give me any of that?"

Disheartened, Cami replied, "No, only feelings, sensations, and a specific scent."

"A specific scent?" he questioned.

"Yes, roses."

"Of course, Charlotte's signature scent. I smelled that the other day."

"See?"

"That's an easy one to explain though, Cami. We were in her room. The house, and specifically Charlotte's room, has been closed up a long time, it's bound to trap odors or scents in after being closed up with no air circulation."

"True. But then why don't we smell it all the time? It definitely comes and goes. Sometimes it's soft, just a hint, and others it's overpowering."

"I'm playing devil's advocate here, but maybe it's because you're thinking of Charlotte or something reminds you of her. Is it possible it's simply the power of suggestion?"

Cami shifted in her seat. Leaning forward, she said, "Then how do you explain the slamming door? You were there. Then there's the locking and unlocking of Charlotte's own bedroom door, and cold drafts that come out of nowhere. How do you explain all that?"

He started slowly, "First, the slamming door was the day you were locked in the shed. Someone had to have been in the house. There's no way a ghost locked you in that shed. Second, the cold drafts. Temperatures are dropping, summer's gone and autumn is leaning into winter. It's an old house, there's bound to be drafts. And the locked doors? Again, the house is old, wood expands and contracts, the house shifts and settles, making the doors seem locked, or maybe they've contracted just enough to swing open."

Cami leaned back, pushing her plate away, and crossed

her arms. "I know the difference between a door that's stuck and one I need a key to unlock. I'm not stupid, Luke."

"No, you're not, Cami, you're anything but. I think you've been under a lot of stress since you've moved back. A lot of strange things have happened in the short time you've been home. Maybe you just forgot that you locked it." He slid a little closer to her, brushed a strand of hair from her forehead. "All I'm saying is we need to keep an open mind and look at it from all angles. There's likely a logical explanation for all of it."

She looked into those gray eyes and almost wept. He didn't believe her. *Was he right? Was this all her imagination? Did she get up in the middle of the night and lock the door, or did she do it in passing without thinking?* Cami's stomach lurched, making her queasy. *She should have never told him. I'm such a fool.* Forcing a smile, she said, "You're probably right." Putting her hands in her lap, she balled up her napkin, clutching it tightly. "If I could get a box, I'm ready to go."

Luke nodded slightly. "Of course. Waitress," he called, flagging her down. "Check, please."

CHAPTER 30

Cami sat on the ground crisscross style, leaning against the tree, an unopened book beside her. The sun was warm on her shoulders and the blades of grass tickled the bottoms of her legs. Birds chattered in the treetops as her fingers absently toyed with the long blades of grass.

She didn't look up as Charlotte plopped down beside her.

"Are you still mad?"

"At you? Or Luke?"

Charlotte shrugged and flopped back in the grass. "Both, I guess."

"Yes."

"Yes, what?"

Cami groaned, exasperated with her sister. "Yes, I'm still mad at you *and* him."

"Why me? What did I do?"

Shifting in the grass so she could see her sister's face, she asked, "Really? You have to ask?"

"Apparently. So, tell me."

Standing up, Cami brushed off the seat of her pants. "I'm mad at you for dying!"

Charlotte leaned up onto her elbows so she was elevated slightly off the ground. "Go on."

"You want me to explain it?"

"Yes."

"You have got to be kidding me! Damn it, Charlotte! How could you die? How could you leave me here all alone? I needed you. You were my sister, my best friend, my twin."

Tears formed in her eyes as she glared down at Charlotte. "Everything changed after you died. Everything! You haunted my dreams, then my nightmares. Mom and dad thought I was crazy! We had to move, had to get away. I went to counseling for years because of you." Cami swallowed hard and tried to reign in her emotions. "I lost everything. You, my high school, my job, my friends, Luke, but worst of all, I lost Cherry Hollow. The one place in the world I felt safe. You took it all away in one fell swoop. How could you do that to me?" Tears streamed down her face steadily now.

"You're back now and he kissed you, didn't he?"

"What?"

"Luke. He kissed you, didn't he?"

"How did you know that?" Cami asked, surprised.

Charlotte didn't answer, instead stood, her eyes teary, matching Cami's. "Do you think I did it on purpose? Do you think I wanted to die?"

"No, but it's still your fault! You didn't listen. I told you we shouldn't play hide-and-seek. I told you someone was going to get hurt. But you always have to have your way! You just come in and steam roll everyone and look what happened! Look what it got you! Six feet under, that's what." Cami's voice hitched. "You always had to have the spotlight. You always have to be in charge."

"So what? Were you jealous?"

"Jealous? How could you even ask me that? I loved you! You were my sister. Just once, I wished you would have listened to me."

"This isn't my fault, Cami, I swear."

"Whose idea was it to play hide-and-seek?"

"Mine."

"Whose idea was it to go as far as they could in the woods so they wouldn't get caught by just anybody?"

"Mine."

"Who fell and hit her head?"

"Me."

"Exactly! Explain to me why this isn't your fault?" Cami pointed an accusatory finger at her twin.

"I did all those things just like you said, but it wasn't my fault. You have to believe me."

"Why should I?"

"I was caught off guard. I fell backwards. I was hurt, confused, and mad."

"Why?"

"Because it wasn't supposed to happen."

"What wasn't supposed to happen?" Cami demanded. "You'd better explain yourself because Luke Warner thinks I'm crazy. That I'm losing it. And once again, it's your fault."

"The kiss. It was all wrong."

"What kiss? Me and Luke?"

Charlotte shook her head. Her fingers brushed her lips. "No, my kiss. It was all wrong. Someone saw. I didn't want him to know."

"Who? What kiss? You're not making any sense."

"I don't know. My head hurts. Everything is jumbled. I have to go."

"Don't go, Charlotte!" Cami cried, "Not again!" But she could already see her sister's image shimmering.

"Tell Luke what you know."

"He won't believe me. Give me something. Anything, Charlotte, so I know it's real. That you're not just some figment of my deranged imagination."

Charlotte reached for Cami's hand, placing in it a few ripe cherries. It was their way of apologizing to each other without actually saying the words. Cami looked down at the three red berries in her hand. When she looked up, Charlotte was gone.

"No!" she screamed and woke up with a start.

CHAPTER 31

Luke stirred in his sleep, disturbed by a bang but settled back down, wanting five more minutes. The tug of sleep was heavy, but one eye popped open when the pounding returned. "Damn it," he hissed as he groped in the dark for his phone. He snagged it off the nightstand and swore again when he saw the time. "Whoever the hell this is, had better have a damn good excuse for knocking on my door at four in the morning." He tugged on jeans and padded barefoot to the front door. Flipping on the porch light, he scowled as he twisted the deadbolt.

"Who in the hell is it? And what do you want at this hour?" Luke demanded as he yanked the front door open. "Cami?" he said, clearly surprised. Softening his tone drastically, he asked, "What's wrong?"

"I know you don't believe me, and may even think I'm slightly crazy, but . . ." she thrust her clenched fist at him, uncurled her fingers and held her open palm up into the light, her hand trembling slightly. "How do you explain this?"

Quirking an eyebrow, he examined her hand. "Cherries?" Luke scrubbed at his face with his hands, trying to wake himself up, and looked again. "They're cherries. Three, to be exact."

"Exactly."

He didn't answer at first, looked at her instead, taking her in silently. She looked like he did, half dressed, hair hastily pulled back, and straight out of bed. But her eyes. Cami's eyes pulled him in and held him captive. There was fear in them, pure and raw. He didn't want to do or say the wrong thing and have her shut down like she had at dinner. Needing to tread lightly, he said, "I'm sorry, but I'm not following you at all." Shivering slightly as the frosty night air blew in against bare skin, Luke opened the door wider. "Come in, please, and help me understand."

She dipped her head and slipped past him, careful not to brush against him.

"Come into the kitchen. I'll put on some coffee."

Cami followed Luke into the kitchen and stood awkwardly at the edge of the room. "I'm sorry about the early hour. I should have waited. I should have called."

Pulling out a chair, he indicated for her to sit. "Don't be. I may not understand at the moment, but I want to. And it must be important for you to come over now."

Nodding, she slipped into the chair and placed the three cherries on the worn wooden table. Instead of making coffee, he pulled out the other kitchen chair, swung it around and sat straddling the back. Glancing from the fruit in question to Cami, he asked, "Care to explain?"

She sucked in a deep breath. "I want to preface this by saying whatever you may think of me at this very moment, confused, crazy, maybe even overly dramatic, believe me I've heard it all, but I want you to know I would never lie, especially to you."

Her entire expression was so serious, her statement so sad, he couldn't stop from falling a little further for her. Luke couldn't help it; he just had to touch her. Reaching out, he tucked a strand of hair behind her ear. "I'm listening."

"First, I want to say I'm sorry about dinner. I shouldn't have shut down. I know the whole concept of a ghost is hard to swallow, especially since that ghost is presumably my sister, but I didn't come to that conclusion easily. I've been to enough therapy sessions to know that I sound crazy, but Luke, I promise you, I'm not." She paused, waiting for a response.

"I'm sorry, too. I enjoyed last night very much, until I

made you feel like I wasn't taking you seriously, and I don't think you're crazy."

"Here goes nothing." Cami took a deep, cleansing breath. "You said you need proof or facts, solid evidence. I'm here to tell you that's what those cherries represent."

"I'm listening."

"I dreamt of Charlotte again. Only this time, we were fighting. I told her I was mad at her for dying and that it was all her fault."

"Why'd you say that?"

"Because it's true. I am, I'm furious. It took me almost ten years to admit it, to come to terms with it. And I finally said it to her face, even if it was only in my dreams."

"But Cami..."

She waved him off. "Think about it. She threw the party while I was at work. The party was in full swing by the time I got there. It was her idea to play hide-and-seek. I told her not to. Charlotte insisted like she always does. If she hadn't gone farther out-of-bounds then anyone else, she might not have fallen. If she hadn't fallen, she wouldn't have gotten hurt. Or if she'd been closer, maybe someone would have seen her, helped her up and we could have gotten her to the hospital." She swallowed hard and shook her head. "Everything that happened, happened because of her choices."

"So far I'm following you and what you're saying is true, but I think you're forgetting something."

"What?"

"I could say the same thing about you."

"What do you mean?"

"Didn't you technically go out-of-bounds, too? I mean, when I found you, there was no way to see the fire from where you were. Wasn't that the one rule? You needed to hide so that you could see the bonfire, or at least the clearing?"

Opening her mouth to deny it, she stopped herself. "That's different."

"Why?" He lifted an eyebrow. "Because you know the

woods better than anyone? Or because it was your place? Or maybe it was because you didn't want to get caught by just anyone?" He waited, baiting her. "Which of those statements is true?"

She waited a full thirty seconds before she answered reluctantly, "You know as well as I do, they're all true."

In a quiet voice, he said, "So the same thing could have happened to you."

She was still for a moment. "But it didn't."

"No, it didn't. But you're the one left here trying to pick up the pieces, and that's hard on a good day, let alone how difficult it is on a bad one. It's understandable to be mad, Cami, but don't blame Charlotte. No one deserves to die so young. You need to forgive her and let it go. It's been ten years."

Luke stood, moved his chair aside, and reached for her. Tugging her up out of the chair, he pulled her into him, wrapping his arms around her. She melted into him as a tear ran down her face. "You also need to forgive yourself."

In a voice that was so reedy he could barely hear her, she said, "I can't. If I had found her sooner. . ."

"Don't." He cut her off. "Don't even go there." Running his hand down her back, he tried to comfort her. He couldn't stand to see her in pain. Needing to change the mood, he pulled back, kissed her forehead, and looked down at her. "So, tell me why you brought me three cherries at four in the morning?"

She sniffed and wiped the back of her hand across her face to dry her tears. "As I told you, I dreamt of Charlotte. We fought, and she apologized." Cami pointed at the cherries.

Looking down at the table, he cocked his head. "I don't get it?"

Smiling, Cami said, "No, of course you wouldn't. Cherries are our way of apologizing to each other. It started when we were little. We had been out picking cherries with our father. Walking back, Charlotte darted in front of me, causing me to trip and fall, spilling all my cherries. My dad and Charlotte helped me pick them up, but most of them had scattered or were smashed when I fell. Dad told Charlotte she should apologize and give me half of hers. Well, you know Charlotte, she was never good at sharing or apologizing. So instead of giving me half, she picked out three and handed them to me, placing them gently in the palm of my hand. My dad asked Charlotte if she thought that was fair. After all, I had lost almost all of mine because of her. Charlotte looked my father straight in the eye and said those were her very best cherries chosen from her bucket just for me. He nodded at her, then turned to me and asked if I would accept her apology."

"And did you?"

"Yes, and from then on, whenever one of us needed to apologize, we would find three ripe cherries and give them to the other. No words exchanged, just cherries."

"And these cherries," he pointed at the table, and asked, "where did they come from?"

"They were in my hand when I woke up."

CHAPTER 32

Aaron was riding the mower, enjoying the fall air and the swatches of sunshine as he took the zero turn in and around the trees. There was nothing he enjoyed more than the steady hum of the motor and the whir of the blades. Relaxing back into the seat, he slid his sunglasses on and put his earbuds in, listening to hard rock as his arms worked the levers.

He still had to hook the generator up to the house, but it was so nice out he didn't want to waste time being in the basement when the sun was out. It was supposed to cloud over this afternoon. He promised himself he'd do it then. By then, he would be finished mowing and the crew would pack up for the day. They'd be able to load the mower and haul it back to the shop while he stayed behind and installed the generator. Satisfied, he concentrated on mowing.

Aaron hadn't been at it very long when he saw the car pull into the driveway. Kevin gave a little wave as Aaron rounded the tree and headed for the house. His stomach did a flip as he saw Cami open the front door and let Kevin in.

Aaron still wasn't used to seeing Cami, let alone her and Kevin together. It reminded him too much of high school and the bonfire, which he tried hard to push to the recess of his mind and lock it away, but for some reason it wouldn't stay hidden. And what he remembered made him nauseous.

In high school, Cami and Kevin had been inseparable, but Charlotte's death had changed all that. Cami had moved, and Kevin had been left behind. Aaron knew from poker nights that her leaving had hurt him deeply, even though Kevin had kept in contact with Cami. As the years went by, he spoke to her and talked about her less often. But now that she was back, it seemed as if they had rekindled their friendship. Aaron worked his way across the yard and wondered if Joselyn knew.

***

Two days. Cami only had two days to get this engagement party put together. Waiting impatiently for the coffeepot to fill, she rubbed her temples, trying to hold off the impending headache that pulsated right below the surface.

Scanning over her list, she checked off the tasks she had accomplished, listening to the steady drip of liquid gold. She'd emailed Tanya the list of desserts and appetizers, ordered the centerpieces, the standing tables, and the linens. The grand foyer, main hallway, and the ballroom were freshly painted, cleaned, and waxed. Even though Cami herself had cleaned the other rooms, she had a cleaning crew lined up to clean on Friday morning and again on Saturday after the party.

The favors had been delivered and the labels were printed. They just needed to be assembled. The invitations were on her table and needed to be stamped, stuffed, and mailed today. The installer was here now working on a new surround system for the ballroom, the landscapers were outside working, and the e-vites were rolling in for the engagement party.

Reaching for a mug, she sighed with relief as the last drops dripped from the coffee pot. Annoyed when the doorbell rang, with one last longing look at the pot, she set her mug down and went to the front door.

"Good morning, sunshine," Kevin said, greeting her.

"Kevin? What a pleasant surprise." She eyed the brown bag with the golden arches on it in his hand. "What do you have there?"

"Sustenance."

"You brought me McDonalds?"

"You betcha." He grinned. "Can I come in?"

Cami held the door wide. "By all means. Come to the kitchen. I was just going to pour myself a cup of coffee. I need caffeine." Her stomach rumbled at the scent emanating from the brown bag. "And apparently food, too."

Making himself comfortable at the large wooden table, Kevin unrolled the paper bag and produced breakfast sandwiches and hash browns, while Cami got out another cup and poured coffee.

"Cream or sugar?"

"Yes, to both."

Getting out a small serving tray, Cami arranged cups, a bowl of sugar, creamer, spoons and napkins. Carrying over the tray, she deposited everything on the table, sat across from Kevin, took a cup and her first sip of coffee. Peering at him over her mug, she asked, "I thought Joselyn had you both on a strict diet until after the wedding?"

Unwrapping his sandwich, he smoothed the light-yellow wrapper out with fingers. "Who told you that?"

"Joselyn did, when we went dress shopping."

"Hmph." Reaching for the salt and pepper that were in the middle of the table, he sprinkled both over his hash brown, then picked up his sandwich and asked, "Not gonna tell, are ya?"

Cami took another sip of coffee. "Your secrets are safe with me."

His smile spread wide. "I knew I could count on you." He sunk his teeth deep into the English muffin with sausage and egg, savoring the bite as yellow cheese oozed out the sides.

"Is that one for me?"

He nodded.

"Thank you."

"No problem," he said between mouthfuls. "I see you're wearing your signature color today."

She glanced down at her light green Boho print top and smiled. "Why yes, and I see you're not dressed in your usual business attire, Mr. Weller. You're casual in your polo and jeans. Not going into the office today?"

"Nope," he answered, wadding up his wrapper and tossing it into the trash. "I'm playing hooky. Wanna come? You look like you could use a little Vitamin D in the form of sunshine and relaxation."

"I can't. Too much to do here."

"You look tired. Everything alright?"

Cami hesitated, wondering if she should say anything or not. She quickly decided against it. Having to explain it to Luke had been hard enough. "It was a short night."

He nodded, pointed at her hash brown. "You gonna eat that?"

Sliding it across the table, she said, "It's all yours. The sandwich will be plenty."

"Thanks." He picked it up and took a bite. "You sure I can't talk you into it? After all, I brought you breakfast."

"Sorry, I have too much to do to get ready for the engagement party on Friday night. Tell me, though, what's on your agenda?"

"I was thinking of playing a round of golf with my best friend, but I guess I'll just have to go it alone," he said, acting a little forlorn.

"Hmmm, tempting. It is awfully nice out. But I can't, I have tables, and two new side-by-side industrial sized refrigerators being delivered today."

"For what?"

"The engagement party. I have to have some place to store the appetizers."

"Where in the world are you going to put two industrial size refrigerators?"

"For now, along that wall." She pointed. "I'm not using those cabinets for anything. They'll just have to sit out from the wall until I can get the kitchen remodeled. I have a designer coming next week to draw up plans."

"Isn't that kind of out of order?"

"Yes, but I need them now. It can't wait, and the kitchen will take six to eight weeks once we complete the design and get it ordered. The engagement party is on Friday night. Therein lies the dilemma."

Kevin drank his coffee, clearly contemplating the situation. "You're going all in with this, aren't you? I thought we were just a test run."

"Of course. This is something I really want to do. I've always wanted to have my own business. To have it here at Cherry Hollow is the icing on the cake."

"You're really here to stay?"

"I am."

"Good. I'm proud of you for chasing your dream and not settling."

He moved to go.

"You know, you could stay and help."

"I could?"

"It might be way more fun than golfing by yourself."

"What's there to do?"

"Invitations and favors."

"That's not really my forte. That's girl's stuff."

"It's simple. Anyone could do it. Even a sexist like you."

"I'm not a sexist. Far from it. I just want to golf."

Cami patted his cheek. "You thought if you offended me, I'd let you off the hook? Nice try."

"It was worth a shot."

"If you stay, I'll make it up to you."

"How?"

"I can put on music, we can talk, and I promise to feed you at lunchtime."

"Very tempting, but the sunshine and greens are calling me."

"We could sit out back in the sunshine and work."

He slid his chair back, then hesitated. "How long would all this take?"

"I was expecting it to take me three to four hours, but

with two hands, we could definitely have it done in half that."

"If I helped, and we were done by," he glanced at his watch, "say by ten. Would you go for a round of golf?"

"Sure, as long as I can be back here by three. The refrigerators are supposed to come late this afternoon, and I have to be here for that."

"Count me in."

CHAPTER 33

Not waiting for an invitation, Bobby knocked on Luke's front door as he opened it, comfortable in his friend's house. "Hey, Warner? You alright?" he called, walking in. "Haven't seen you all day."

"I'm back here. In my office."

"What the hell is all this?" Bobby asked, sticking his head in the room.

Luke turned around and looked at him, scrubbing his hands over his face. He'd been at it since Cami had left this morning. He had piles of papers stacked here and there. Class rosters were tacked to his bulletin board. Note cards with individual names pinned and connected with string. "This," he waved his hand, encompassing the whole of the room, "Is my lame attempt at trying to solve a ten-year-old case."

Bobby scratched his head. "Wanna walk me through it?"

"Sure," Luke said bitterly. "How much time do you have?"

"The rest of the afternoon and all evening if you need it."

"Okay, let me get something to drink first. I haven't stopped all day. Come into the kitchen a second. I need a break."

Cannon gave one last look at the wall and followed his friend down the short hall.

"Do you want anything?" Luke asked as he opened the fridge.

"I'll take a Coke if you got one?"

"Yep." Luke snagged two from the fridge and tossed one

to him.

Bobby tapped his index finger on the can to settle any bubbles, then popped the top. "What's with the cherries?"

Unable to wrap his head around it himself, Luke tried to figure out the best way to broach the subject with Bobby. "Can you listen without jumping to any conclusions?"

"That sounds ominous." Bobby frowned when he saw the look on Luke's face. "Let me rephrase that, I'm a cop, ain't I? I'm supposed to be impartial until I hear all the facts. Why would a story about three little cherries be any different?"

"Just wait." Luke grabbed a bag of chips and tossed them on the table, then selected an apple from the bowl, rubbed it on his shirt, and took a bite. Snagging a kitchen chair, he plopped down into it and ripped open the bag of chips.

"Let me guess, lunch?"

"Yep. Want in?"

"Hell yes." Bobby snatched the bag of chips and took a handful. Munching on the first chip, he said, "My mouth is full and my mind is clear."

Luke laughed for the first time today and felt a little of the tension in his neck release. "Well, your mouth is full. We will see about your mind." He hesitated, trying to decide where to start. "So, Cami came by this morning."

Bobby chuckled despite himself. "I should have known, cherries had to equal Cami. Which in my mind equals trouble."

Scowling at him, Luke grumbled, "I thought you were going to keep an open mind?"

Popping another chip into his mouth, he nodded. "No more comments, I promise. Scout's honor."

"You were never in the Scouts."

"True. Proceed anyway. Cami came by and brought you cherries. Continue please, I promise not to interrupt."

With his brow furrowed, Luke told Bobby the entire story, completely uninterrupted. When he was finished, he took a long pull from his can of Coke and let the story sink in.

"Well? Thoughts? I know you've got some."

"Give me another minute to process. I think you may have rendered me temporarily speechless."

Luke smirked. "That'll be the day."

Ignoring the dig, Bobby said, "Let's look at Cami for a second. Give me your unbiased opinion of her."

"Okay." Luke thought for a moment. "Cami Parker is intelligent, has humility, perseverance, and courage."

"If that's unbiased, I wonder what a biased opinion from you is."

"Personally, I think she's sweet, caring, funny, and sexy as hell."

Grinning, Bobby said, "I would agree with both statements. Let's go back to the first one, though, for argument's sake. The first thing you said was that Cami Parker was intelligent. I'd have to agree wholeheartedly."

Luke continued, "She was at the top of our class in high school, but she's not only book smart, she also has a good head on her shoulders with her career, business, and common sense."

Bobby eyed Luke knowingly.

"Don't look at me like that. I did my research on her. She left the hotel on good standing and comes highly recommended by anyone in her field. She is the best of the best. Their words, not mine."

"Fair enough. When she came to you this morning with cherries in hand, you took her seriously?"

"Yes."

"Why?"

"I can't explain it other than to say you should have seen her." Luke raked his hands through his hair, tossed the core of his half-eaten apple into the trash, and looked Bobby straight in the eye. "She was straight out of bed, dead serious, and filled with pure, raw fear. Her hand shook when she produced the cherries. I'm telling you she believed every word she said, and had me almost convinced, too."

"What do you mean by almost?"

"Don't get me wrong, I believe everything she said and I think it's all truly happening to her. The part that has me hung up is Charlotte as a ghost. That's hard to swallow."

"I agree. That seems far-fetched, but if it's not a ghost, who's doing all this?"

"That's what I'd like to know. Cami believes there is someone playing games with her, like throwing the golf ball through the window and locking her in the shed. She's not denying that's a real live person. We have the boot prints to prove it. The things that she is choosing to explain as a ghost are the scent of roses, cold drafts, slamming of doors, or the locking of them. She even claims to have seen Charlotte at least twice."

"Does she have any proof? Other than the cherries?" Bobby asked.

"Maybe some witnesses."

"Really?"

Luke nodded.

"Who?"

"Well, you and I both heard the door slam upstairs the day she was locked in the shed."

"That can be explained by the possibility of the person who locked her in being in the house."

"True, but you didn't find anyone."

"No." Bobby scratched his chin. "Who else?"

"Kevin. Cami's pretty sure he saw Charlotte, or something close to it, just before he fell down the stairs, although they never discussed it. And then there's Brock."

"Brock saw Charlotte?"

"He mentioned it to me the other night, but brushed it off as a guilty conscience."

"What's he got to be guilty about?"

"Kissing Cami."

"What the hell? How did that happen? And when?"

Just thinking about them kissing made his blood boil, even though Brock had said it meant nothing. But Luke couldn't help it, he still harbored a little jealousy. "Long story short, they kissed. It was awkward, like kissing his sister was his exact words. And they both felt guilty after. So guilty that Brock said Cami swore she saw Charlotte. He said he almost believed her, but was pretty sure it was the guilt that had her seeing things."

"Brock's not sure?"

"No, but he admitted to smelling roses inside the house and out."

"Well, that's something." Bobby looked down at the cherries, picked one up, and examined it. "This is pretty substantial evidence. Cherries aren't even in season. Where did you say Cami found them when she woke?"

"In her hand."

Bobby was silent for a moment. "If someone was in the house, that's pretty gutsy on their part to be that close to her, even if she was asleep." Bobby set the cherry back on the table with the others and stared at Luke. "If there was someone in the house, Cami could be in real danger."

"Those are my thoughts exactly."

CHAPTER 34

The house was a flurry of activity when he arrived. Luke stood off to the side and watched. She directed the appliances to the kitchen, the tables to the ballroom, and an older woman to her office, all with ease. It intrigued him. This was a side of her he hadn't seen. Cami spent just enough time with each so they didn't feel brushed off, knew exactly what to do, and where to go.

Dressed professionally in black dress pants, a crisp, white button shirt, small black heels, with silver dangling at her wrist and ears, she looked the part. Her face was flushed from a day spent in the sun and her hair was pulled back in a smooth, tight ponytail, making his hands itch to pull the tie from it, run his fingers through the silky mane, and let it hang loose, framing her face.

Those hazel eyes found his and locked. Her professional smile widened, and lit her whole face, making his heart dance.

"Luke? I'm surprised to see you." She frowned slightly. "Is everything okay?"

"Yes, I just came out to check on you, but I can see you're busy."

"Are you able to stay? I'm interviewing wait staff for the engagement party. It shouldn't take long."

"Of course, take your time."

"Why don't you hang out in the drawing room, Kevin's in there."

"Don't mind if I do."

"Can I get you anything to drink in the meantime?"

Shaking his head, he said, "No, I'm good. Go take care of business."

"I won't be long."

Luke watched her duck into the office, closing the door. Going into the drawing room, he found Kevin sprawled out on the couch, watching television. "Shouldn't you still be at work?"

Kevin glanced over his shoulder and grinned. "Nope, I'm playing hooky today."

"I can see that." Luke noticed quickly how comfortable Kevin was in Cami's house, and looked like he too had spent most of the day outside. He'd forgotten how tight Kevin and Cami had been in high school, and a twinge of jealousy tried to rear its ugly head. Luke quickly squashed it, remembering Kevin was getting married in a few weeks. "What have you been doing all day?"

"I stopped over here this morning to see if I could get a golf partner for the day, but instead I got roped into work. Can you believe it? And on my day off, too." Kevin didn't wait for a response. "I told her I would help if she went golfing with me after. So that's what happened. I stuffed envelopes and played golf. Now I'm just relaxing before I go home. What about you?"

"I came out to check on Cami."

Kevin wrinkled his brow, clicked off the TV, and tossed the remote onto the sofa cushions. "This official business or pleasure?" Kevin held up a hand. "Let me guess. By the look on your face, I would say pleasure."

Laughing, Luke grinned. "Am I that obvious?"

"Probably not to her, but to me? Definitely."

"Are you sure? I can usually bluff my way past you, and everybody else, when I have a lousy hand of cards."

"This is completely different. With Cami, your heart's on your sleeve."

Shaking his head, Luke glanced at the closed door. "I'll try to remember that."

"Remember this as well, she's my best friend, plain and

simple. Screw her over or crush her heart, and I'll beat the crap out of you. Got it?"

"I promise you won't even have to take a swing."

"I damn well better not." Kevin glanced at the time. "Guess I'd better be heading out. I wanna get home before Josie gets off work. She doesn't know I had the day off."

"I don't think you're going to hide the fact that you were out in the sun."

"Yes, I can. I'll jump on the mower and pretend like I spent all day at it."

"I'm pretty sure Joselyn can tell the difference between freshly mowed and last week's job."

"I don't know. She's pretty distracted with wedding plans lately. Right now, I might be able to get away with bloody murder."

"Keep telling yourself that."

"I will," Kevin said with a grin.

"I have a follow-up question, though."

"Always with the questions. I guess that's why you're a detective. Shoot."

"How is it you look like you just stepped off the golf course and Cami's dressed for business?"

"Because besides being naturally beautiful and organized, she's also a quick-change artist. You should have seen her fly up those stairs when we got home. She came down in less than fifteen minutes looking as fresh as a daisy and completely put together." Both men turned as the office door opened. "Speak of the devil, here she comes."

More like an angel, Luke thought. They both watched her escort the older woman to the door, thank her, and let her out. Turning toward them, she threw up her arms in victory, beaming. "We're in luck. We have a wait staff for Friday night. Guess I won't have to put either of you to work like I feared."

"I'm the guest of honor," Kevin whined. "Why would I have to work? Besides, I did more than my fair share today."

Cami came over and wrapped her arms around Kevin

and hugged him tight. "I appreciate it and I know as well as you that you loved every minute, even if it was girly stuff."

He hugged her back. "It was worth it to spend the day with you."

Luke tried to hide his envy as he watched the ease of the exchange. Old friends long since comfortable with each other. He wanted that, but Luke didn't want to be just friends.

As if realizing suddenly that Luke was still standing there, Kevin released her quickly. "Guess I'd better get going," Kevin said, reaching for the door. He glanced at Luke. "Warner," and gave him a nod. "Remember what I said."

Nodding, Luke said, "I will."

Kevin went out and Aaron walked in.

"Hey, Aaron. I wasn't expecting to see you this afternoon," Cami said as a way of greeting.

"Yeah, well, I got that part I was missing yesterday." Aaron shifted from foot to foot, looking slightly uncomfortable. "And I wanted to finish up in here since everyone is knocking off outside."

Cami glanced out the window and could see the men packing up for the day. "That's fine. Come right in and do what you need to. Do you need anything from me?"

"Nope." He tapped his toolbox. "Got everything I need right here. If you don't mind, I'll just get to it."

"Go right ahead."

"When I'm done, the fountain, the outdoor floods, and accent lighting along the drive should all work. The lights will come on before the fountain, though. Takes a little while to fill the basin. Once it's full, it should come on automatically."

"I can't wait to see everything. Thank you, Aaron. For all you've done and so quickly. I truly appreciate it."

"You're welcome." Aaron glanced at Luke. "You be around tomorrow? Like to have a word."

"Should be. Stop by the office."

"Will do."

Cami watched him go in silence. When he was well out

of range, she looked at Luke and asked, "Do you think he'll ever forgive me?"

"There's nothing to forgive. You did nothing wrong."

"Not in his mind. He blames me and my family."

Luke shrugged, wanting to comfort her but not knowing how. "I think it's more that he feels guilty and awkward for lashing out at you in front of everyone. Something I'm sure he wouldn't have done if he hadn't been drinking."

"Maybe not the other night, but it would have come out eventually. You can't hold something like that back forever."

***

By the time everyone left, the sun had dropped behind the Blue Ridge Mountains and shadows stretched long and wide through the trees.

He knew he should leave like the others, but he didn't want to. Luke wanted to be here with her. He pictured them all too easily snuggled up by a cozy fire watching TV or just talking, normal things; things people did when they dated or were in love. That last thought had his pulse jumping. He wasn't in love with Cami Parker, at least not completely…yet. But he knew damn well he was on his way. Head over heels and falling. That thought alone almost sent him running for the hills, because what if she didn't feel the same way? Last night when they had dinner, it hadn't gone well in the end because he had doubted her, but after this morning, he no longer did. She had come to him despite everything.

Luke wanted a do over. A fresh slate. He hoped she did, too. There was only one way to find out. He stood on the threshold of her office and asked, "Did you have plans for dinner?"

"I don't," Cami said as she shut down her laptop and filed the receipts from the deliveries for today.

It was now or never. "How do you feel about dinner and a movie?"

She hesitated. "I would love to, but I have so much yet to do before Friday. I really can't take that much time out tonight."

"What if we swing through a drive thru and eat on the way? Then we can sit, relax, and enjoy a movie. You need a break. You've been working hard."

Cami studied him for a hot minute, then decided. "I'd like that, but promise me we won't stay out too late. I have a full day tomorrow filled with appointments and set up."

"Fair enough. I'll have you home by ten."

"Before we go, I need to grab the birdcage while I'm thinking of it or I'll forget it."

Cocking his head, he asked, "A birdcage?"

"Yes."

"For what?"

"Cards for the engagement party. Some people might bring a card and I need a decorative place to put them."

"Where in the world are you going to get that?"

"Upstairs. We have one. Charlotte had a pet canary when we were younger. The cage is beautiful and would be perfect for this."

"That's an interesting tidbit I didn't know."

"Will you help me? It's very heavy."

"Of course. Lead the way."

He followed her up the stairs. "I don't remember seeing it in the attic."

"That's because it's not there. The bird cage is in Charlotte's room." They walked down the long hall silently, the only sound the click of Cami's heels on the hardwood echoing through the space. She reached for the door and found it locked. "Oh, for goodness' sake. I should have known." Cami turned on her heel. "I'll be right back. I need the key."

When she returned, he asked, "I'm guessing you didn't remember locking it?"

"I didn't lock it. Charlotte did."

She said it so matter-of-factly that he truly believed her.

Or at least believed that she believed it. He let the comment slide. Instead, he watched her insert the key, unlock the door, and open it.

Switching on the light, Cami scanned the bedroom quickly. "The birdcage used to sit over in the corner, but we put it away a couple of years before Charlotte died." She strode across the room with purpose, straight for the closet. Opening the door, she spotted it. "Here it is."

Luke came up behind her, close enough to notice how good she smelled. The scent scattered his thoughts and made it hard to concentrate on the matter at hand.

"It's behind a couple of boxes."

"Here, let me," Luke offered. He slipped past her, his arm brushing against her ever so slightly, sending an intense heat over him. "Take this," he said, handing her a decorative box.

Cami took it from him, and their hands touched. Quick and electric, had them both retreating to safety.

"I'll just put this on the bed for now."

He nodded and reached back into the recesses of the closet. Shifting a couple of other boxes and sliding clothes aside on the rack, he grabbed a hold of the gilded birdcage. "It's still in pretty good condition. A little dusty but no worse for the wear."

"I'll clean it up. That's not a problem."

"Whatever happened to her canary?" Luke asked as he maneuvered it out of the small space.

"It's a funny story, really. One day before we went to school, Charlotte fed Peaches. That was the canary's name." The corner of Cami's mouth twitched at the mention of the bird. "Charlotte didn't latch the door properly and Peaches got out."

"Let me guess." Luke set the four-foot, white birdcage temporarily on the ground, and regarded Cami. "Peaches got out of the room and somehow managed to fly out the front door into the woods."

"That would have had a happier ending if that had been

the case." There was a twinkle in Cami's eyes. "Did I mention I had a kitten? Solid white and fluffy as a cloud. Cutest thing you ever saw. She was the best: sweet, playful, and full of mischief. Her name was Sophie."

"Oh, no. Don't tell me. Sophie ate Peaches."

"Yep."

Luke couldn't help it. He laughed. "I'm sorry, it's not funny. Sophie really ate the bird?"

Cami's mouth twitched, trying not to smile. "Yes, and Charlotte was devastated."

"What happened to Sophie?"

"She's still alive and thriving, living with my parents."

"That's good. I was afraid she might have gotten the boot after eating Peaches." Luke picked up the birdcage. "Where would you like this?"

"Downstairs."

"Lead the way."

Flipping off the light to the bedroom, Cami made it a point to leave the door wide open.

***

The night encroached, and the shadows fell hard. Watching them from the safety of the trees protected by the long, outstretched darkness, he saw them get into the SUV and drive away. He didn't like it, not one bit. He didn't want them to be together, but he wasn't sure how he could stop it. Or even if he should. How could she even do this to him? What was she thinking? Did Cami think Luke could make her happy? Maybe, but not like he could. What he wanted, what he truly wanted, was her. Time was running out. He needed to make his move. Or it would be too late.

CHAPTER 35

The night had been perfect, Cami thought as she snuggled back in the leather seat while Luke drove, the radio on low, watching the passing cars rush by. True to his word, Luke had gone through the drive-thru and gotten them cheeseburgers and Cokes so they could make the seven o'clock movie, then drove straight to the movie theater, where they ate in the parking lot. He got points for letting her pick the movie, didn't flinch when she said she wanted the documentary, but let out a small breath when she settled on an action-adventure. Halfway through the movie, Luke reached for her hand.

If anyone ever asked her how the movie ended, she'd never be able to tell them, from the point his fingers linked with hers, she had lost all track of the storyline. All she could think about was how perfectly her hand fit in his, and the simple pure pleasure of it.

The cars thinned out as they left the highway and turned down the country road. The night was dark with only a sliver of moon, but quickly turned pitch black as the road narrowed and the trees crowded in.

"Hey, look," Luke pointed as he slowed to turn into her lane. The trees had lost enough leaves that part of the house could be viewed from the road. "Looks like Aaron has the accent lighting along the driveway finished."

Cami sat up straight in her seat and saw the soft patches of yellow illuminating the drive. "Oh, it looks wonderful and inviting, doesn't it?" Cami inquired as she peered out the window.

"It really does." Following the lane, the house came into full view. Spotlights shone up from the ground strategically placed to accent every peak and angle, playing off the stone and the roof lines. "The lane and the house look enchanting. Like something right out of a fairytale."

"Oh," Cami said breathlessly, putting her hand on her heart. "I think so, too. It's absolutely perfect." She reached over and put her hand lightly on Luke's arm. "Look, the fountain is working as well."

"That's pretty cool."

"Isn't it?" She beamed. "I love it." Glancing at Luke, she noticed his brow furrowed. "What's the matter?"

"It may be nothing but . . ." he pointed. "There's a light on in Charlotte's room. I thought you shut it off."

Cami peered up at the house and her blood ran cold. "I did. I know I did. I flipped off the switch and went out of the room before you. Remember?"

"I do."

Before Luke could say anything else, Cami unbuckled and grabbed her purse, digging for her house keys. She reached for the door, but Luke grabbed her arm. "Cami, wait, let me go in. There could be someone in there."

"There is. Charlotte."

"A ghost doesn't turn on lights."

"How do you know?"

"Because . . ." he hesitated. "Ghosts don't need lights, people do."

"I don't care what you believe or don't. I'm going in and proving to you once and for all that it's Charlotte."

"Damn it, Cami. At least let me call it in. Get Cannon out here in case we need to search the house and the grounds."

Finding her keys, she relented, "Fine." Even if she truly believed it was Charlotte, she was still scared. A ghost was a ghost, sister or not. Keeping an eye on the window, she saw the light go out. "The light went out, let's go."

He had just sent the text when she jumped out of the

car and ran to the front door. Luke was hot on her heels, his weapon drawn.

"If you insist on going in," he paused while he watched her insert the key, "and I can see that you do, you're going to let me go first, or I'm going to drag you kicking and screaming back to the SUV and not feel bad about it."

"Fine," Cami said haughtily, "but please note the door is still locked."

"There are other ways into the house," he fired back. The door swung in noiselessly, Luke moved Cami to the side, and crept in. "Stay behind me," he whispered.

"She's in her room. Go to Charlotte's room," Cami insisted. She nudged him along. "Hurry."

They were at the bottom of the stairs when they heard the door slam. Cami's heart hammered inside her chest, banging against her rib cage. "That's Charlotte's door," Cami hissed and darted past Luke.

"Son of a . . ." Luke growled as he took the stairs two at a time to keep up with her. They ran down the hall side by side, straight for Charlotte's room, not even trying to keep out of sight. Luke reached out and grabbed the doorknob. It was ice cold. Cursing, he yanked his hand back when he found it locked. "Do you have your keys?"

A waft of cold descended around them, and a sound almost like laughter echoed down the hall as Cami inserted the key. Shivering, Cami pushed the door open. Even in the dark she could see the room was a mess, paper everywhere.

"What the?" Luke questioned. He reached for the light switch and the lamps illuminated. There were full sheets of paper scattered all over the floor, some were crumpled into balls, others folded in half. "Where did all this paper come from?"

They both stood at the threshold, scanning the room.

"My guess would be the overturned box by the foot of the bed." Cami pointed. "That's the box you gave me out of the closet. I set it on the bed but never looked in it." Bending over, Cami picked up a crumpled piece of notebook paper. She smoothed it out on her leg and read the first line. "You are like the sun. Every day I circle you. Lost in your orbit," Cami paused, looking at Luke. "That was so sweet."

Luke picked up the next one, which was only folded in half. "This one says, 'You mean the world to me.'"

"That's it?" Cami asked. She peered over his shoulder.

"Yeah, just the one line."

Cami stepped into the room and picked up three more. "A lot of these are just one line. There's no name on it to who or from who."

Luke started collecting pages too. "Seems to be all in the same handwriting."

"Yeah, these too. It's definitely not Charlotte's. Hers was smooth, graceful, but large with big flourishes. This is small and choppy, like a guy's."

"Yeah, that was my impression, too. It looks like the handwriting in the yearbook as well as . . ." Luke paused.

Cami stopped gathering notes and glanced over at him. "As well as what?"

"Nothing. It's nothing."

"Detective Warner," Cami stood with one hand full of papers and the other on her hip. "If you don't come clean right now, I swear I'll . . ." Her voice trailed off as a grin spread easily across his face. "What are you smiling at?"

"You. Do you know how cute you look right this minute?" He crossed the room in three easy strides. Without hesitation, he tossed the papers he'd been holding behind her on the bed, circled her waist with his hands and tugged her forward into him. "God, I've wanted to kiss you again. That's all I think about."

She looked up into those gray eyes and melted. "Then why haven't you?"

"That's a good question." He ran his thumb across her bottom lip and almost lost it when he felt her tremble. "I don't have a suitable answer. Other than, I wasn't sure if you wanted me to."

"Hmmm, and here I thought you had the answers to everything."

He leaned in, hovering a whisper away from her mouth, a grin spreading. "I'm about to find out." His mouth touched hers, softly at first. Tempting, tasting. Her lips held a trace of cherry, her scent was like a hint of a blossom, and her mouth was ripe for the taking. He went down swiftly, filled himself with every bit of her like a boy gorging on ripe, wild fruit.

Satisfied, and a bit dizzy with overwhelming emotions, he drew back, his smile even wider than before.

Her eyes sparkled with emerald flecks, her cheeks were flushed, and her breath hitched. "What do you think now?" she asked, drawing in a sorely needed breath.

"I think I should have never stopped kissing you."

"Those were my exact thoughts."

He leaned in, put his palm on the side of her face, caressing it, ready to kiss her again when the lights flickered. Hesitating, he glanced at the lamp as the light dimmed and came back full force, then went out completely. The heady scent of roses filled the room.

"Charlotte," Cami murmured. "Do you believe me now?"

He tucked her in closer, whispering into her ear. "I do." A waft of cold air swept the room, as if someone suddenly opened a window, making the papers flutter. The sound they made as they danced and swirled rivaled a girl's laughter. The notes flew up as if pulled up by an invisible hand, like puppets on string, swirling, turning, spinning in an obscured vortex with a shimmering image barely visible in the center.

The minute the siren rang out through the still night, the image shifted and faded. Blue lights cut across the room and the vortex stilled, with the papers slowly drifting to the floor. The cold dissipated and the scent of roses vanished.

Bobby found them in the dark bedroom, huddled together, surrounded by papers.

***

Cami went to the refrigerator and got out a slab of Colby jack cheese, found the cutting board and a knife. She sliced thin layers of cheese, found crackers, and was arranging them on a decorative plate when the men returned from clearing the house. Placing the platter on the table, Cami selected a bottle of wine from the butler's pantry and three glasses. Grabbing napkins, she sat, and both men looked at her.

"What?"

Bobby cracked a smile. "Wine and cheese? You know this isn't a social call, right?"

"I know that," Cami said, choosing a cracker. "But I need something to calm myself, my nerves are frayed, and I don't have any bourbon in the house, so a glass of wine will have to do. And you can't have wine without cheese, even if it is just Colby jack." She waved a slice at him and put it on her cracker. "Besides, it's too late for coffee. I'll never sleep if I drink it." She contemplated Bobby for a minute. "But if you'd like some, I can make it."

He waved her off. "I'm good. Just hassling you a little. So, what's your conclusion, Detective Warner?"

Furrowing his brow, Luke scrubbed his hands over his face. "I just don't know what to think."

"Cami?"

"I shut off the light and left the door wide open. The box was in the middle of the bed when we left. When we came home, we saw a light on in Charlotte's room."

"Are you sure it was her room?"

"I know which one is my sister's," Cami said defensively.

He nodded. "Fair enough."

"We came in, went directly upstairs, found her door locked. I unlocked it, found the box overturned, and papers scattered all over the floor. The room grew cold, we smelled roses, and the paper started to fly, no, swirl around us."

Bobby glanced at Luke for confirmation.

Luke held up his hands in defense. "I know how it sounds, and if I hadn't been there myself, I don't know if I would have believed it either. But it's God's honest truth. It happened just like Cami said."

"How are you two not completely freaked out right now?"

"Who says I'm not?" Luke answered, rubbing his hand across the stubble on his face. "But . . ." There was a long pause. "Other than the initial shock of what was actually happening, I don't feel like this ghost or spirit . . ."

"You mean Charlotte?"

"Okay, I guess we can call it Charlotte. I don't think she means any actual harm."

"Charlotte wanted us to find these letters," Cami insisted, pointing at the stack. "But for what reason? I don't know." But what she knew, deep in the recesses of her heart, was who wrote them. Seeing the writing and remembering the conversation was a shock to her system. Like a knife to the heart, cutting deep and jagged. Cami suddenly felt like she was adrift, lost at sea. Reaching for the bottle of wine like it was a life preserver, she poured herself a glass. Filling it to the top, it splashed out and pooled on the wood table. Her hand shook as she raised the full glass to her lips and took a sip. She couldn't possibly tell either of them what she knew. At least not yet. Not until she talked to him herself.

"Are you okay?" Luke inquired as he reached for a napkin and wiped up the spilled wine.

Pulling in a deep breath, she forced the corners of her mouth to turn up. "I'm fine, really." Seeing the concern etched on his face, Cami reached out and put her hand on Luke's arm. "Don't worry so much. It just shook me a little. At least now I know I'm not going crazy."

The radio on Bobby's hip squawked to life as dispatch relayed another call. Cannon stood. "If you both are alright, I need to respond to this call."

"We're good. I can handle it from here. Thanks, Cannon," Luke said, standing too and shaking Bobby's hand.

"You bet." Bobby looked at Cami. "If you need anything, don't hesitate to call me. Let me know what you find out about the letters."

"Will do."

"There is just one other thing, though," she looked from Bobby to Luke. "Can we keep this quiet? With the engagement party tomorrow night, I don't want Joselyn to get freaked out and change her mind about having it here. She was scared enough the other night."

"You have my word," Bobby answered. "Now I really have to go."

"Thank you."

"I'll show myself out."

"Later, Cannon." Luke turned around when he heard the front door click shut and faced Cami. "Do you think that's such a good idea? Still having the party here?"

"I don't know what to think, but I know I can't back out now. I've already sunk a good portion of my savings into Cherry Hollow, and Kevin and Joselyn are counting on me." Cami stood up and put her hands on her hips. "I won't let them down. Besides, it's only one more day. After that, I'll get a priest or an exorcist or... something. I won't let her ruin what I've started."

Luke skirted the table, wrapped his arms around Cami, and held her tight. "If that's what you want?"

"It really is. It's what I've dreamed of."

"Then I'll help you anyway I can." He kissed her forehead gently. "I promise we will get to the bottom of this once and for all. Let's just hope Charlotte cooperates."

"Now that we have the letters, maybe she will behave."

"The question is why does she want us to have them and who are they from? And why does it matter?"

"I don't know," Cami lied. She needed to be absolutely sure before she said anything to anyone. Until then, her lips were sealed, even to Luke.

"You should go to bed. You have a big day tomorrow." There were dark smudges beneath her eyes. It didn't take a genius to tell she was exhausted. It was well past midnight, and they both had to be up early, but he didn't want to leave her alone, not in this big house where anything could happen. "Go on up. I'll lock the door and crash on the couch."

"You're going to stay?" she leaned back and took him in, clearly surprised. "I told you I'm alright. I'm not afraid to be here alone. Not at Cherry Hollow."

"Maybe not, but I am."

Cami threw her head back and laughed. "No, you're not."

"Maybe not afraid, more like curious and intrigued. Also, concerned."

"Concerned?" Cami held Luke at arm's length. "Concerned about what?"

"About you."

"Why?" she asked cautiously.

"Because there's still a ghost in your house. Even if it is your sister, there could still be real danger here. Especially since we know an actual person has been here several times. Lurking around, causing damage."

"You're referring to the broken window?"

"Yes, and you're being locked in the shed, not to mention that something or someone might have spooked Detective Swanson, causing him to fall backward. Foul play hasn't been completely ruled out where he's concerned."

"I wasn't aware you thought it was anything other than a terrible accident."

"It may not be, but my gut tells me there's more than what's obvious here. I'll leave nothing to chance."

"Did you have an autopsy done on Detective Swanson?"

"Yes, I pulled a couple of strings and got it pushed through. I'm hoping to get the results tomorrow. Until then, we're going to be extra cautious. I'm staying whether you like it or not. There are too many strange things happening, and I'm not about to leave you here alone tonight.”

CHAPTER 36

The leaves were falling fast, some branches were almost bare, and the night was as deep and dark as any moonless night. Cami padded out to the balcony in her fuzzy socks wrapped in a quilt from the end of her bed. The wind whipped past her, sending a chill down her spine, making her shrug deeper into her blanket. It was late, but sleep avoided her like a jilted lover. There were so many things going on inside her head, thoughts and images tumbled about, leaving her restless and on edge.

She wondered if Luke was asleep downstairs on the couch or if he too found it hard to rest with so many questions running through his mind. She clasped her hands together, remembering the thrill of his hand finding hers in the dark theater, the warmth, the contentment, the simple pleasure of it. Those gray eyes seeking hers, the warmth of his lips. Her fingers brushed against her own lightly, still able to feel him. Just the thought of him made her smile.

A shimmer of movement in the corner of her eye caught her attention a split second before the hairs on the back of her neck lifted. She spoke to the wind just as easily as if she spoke to Charlotte herself: "I know you're here. I can feel your presence, sense you, and I swear I can just see the slightest image of the girl you used to be." Sucking in a cold breath, she muttered, "I'm not sure if we convinced Luke yet or not but it doesn't matter anymore. You're real, I know that."

Cami swiped at a tear that formed in the corner of her eye before it could fall. "I've missed you." The wind whipped away the sound of her voice.

Forcing the lump in her throat down, she inhaled. "I think I've figured it out, Charlotte. I know who the letters are from. I know who wrote that they loved you in your yearbook." Blinking back tears, she continued, "It's hard to fathom that it could be him, but I know in my heart it has to be true. Too many things point to him."

She knew in her gut he would be revealed soon. It was inevitable. Just as it was inevitable that she would return after all these years to Cherry Hollow on the anniversary of her sister's death. But did the letters incriminate him in Charlotte's death? She wasn't sure. There had to be another explanation. She couldn't fathom that he was responsible for that, too.

One way or the other, she had to know the truth for her parents, for Charlotte, and for herself. The question was, could she face him alone? Would she be able to confront him before Luke made the connection? When she did, then what? What would he say? Would he deny it? If he was guilty, then what? What would happen to him? Her heart weighed heavy in her chest thinking of the inevitable. Cami shivered at the answers that crept into her mind, and it had nothing to do with the cold.

CHAPTER 37

He stumbled through the dark knowingly, going out of bounds to find her, knowing full well she would stretch the limits of her own rules. Seeing her slip quietly through the shadows, he smirked, crouching down and advancing slowly, careful not to tip her off to his presence.

He was curious, wanting to know if she'd found the note he slipped into her pocket. Reaching out from the shadows, grabbing hold of her light green hoodie, he turned her around quickly, pulled her in, and kissed her full on the mouth. Her lips were tight, not soft and inviting like he had imagined. She tasted like bubblegum and smelled like roses. That was when he realized his mistake.

She squirmed and pushed him back. "Get your hands off of me! What on God's green earth do you think you're doing?" Charlotte hissed, wiping her mouth with the sleeve of Cami's hoodie.

Stepping back in shock, he mumbled, "I thought . . . I thought you were . . ."

"Who?" She shoved him hard in the chest. Charlotte narrowed her eyes at him and pointed, the knowledge suddenly perfectly clear in her eyes. "You have a crush on her?"

He snorted. "As if."

She drilled her finger into his chest. "You do."

His heart dropped and butterflies swarmed his stomach.

"All this time I thought you were just friends, but now?" Charlotte smiled devilishly at him, clearly putting it together. "You're whipped, aren't you? You hang on to her like a little lost puppy dog. I can see it now. How could I have not noticed before? The box… it was from you!"

"You're wrong."

"Prove it," she poked him. "Or admit it."

"I don't have to prove anything. Or admit to something that's not true."

"Yes, you do. If you don't, I'll go back to the party and shout to anyone who will listen that you're pathetically in love."

His palms were sweaty, wiping them nervously on his jeans. He glared at her. "You wouldn't."

"Try me." She crossed her arms and smirked knowingly. "Better yet, I'll do it right now and go back screaming your name and hers." She opened her mouth to shout.

He lunged at her. "Stop!"

Everything happened so quickly. A flash of green. Flailing arms. Her falling backward. A log. The crack of impact of bone on rock rang out like a gunshot. Charlotte was flat on her back. For a moment, she didn't move. Stepping closer, he noticed her eyes were closed.

Tentatively, he inquired, "Charlotte?"

She moaned and tried to sit up. "You asshole!" Holding her head, she cursed at him. "Now I'm dirty and my head hurts."

He scrambled over the log to help her. "Here let me."

Charlotte held up her hand, stopping him. "Don't touch me! You've done enough damage for one night."

The pop of a branch had both heads turning.

He woke with a jerk, face down in the pitch black, and felt grass on his bare skin. Disoriented and head pounding, he ran a hand over his face, his fingers coming away with a warm sticky substance. Blood. His feet and chest were bare, his heart was racing, and he was drenched in a cold sweat. Where the hell was he? Scrambling to his knees, he reached out and felt something hard and rough. Bark. Trees. He was in the woods. But how? He turned a slow circle, trying to get his bearings. His pulse skidded to a halt as his eyes adjusted to the dark, and the house at Cherry Hollow loomed large.

CHAPTER 38

Gray wintery clouds moved in, the temperature dropped drastically, and the ground sparkled with a hard frost in the dim morning light. The weatherman was calling for six to twelve inches of snow to start later in the evening, but the bruised and swollen sky looked ominous and forbidding, threatening to start earlier.

Luke had moved every item, scrap of paper, and piece of evidence from his house to his office at the police station first thing this morning, needing every asset the precinct held at his disposal. He had a sick feeling that something was going to happen at Cherry Hollow, and soon, today being the ten-year anniversary of Charlotte's death.

Sitting at his desk, with his feet propped on the corner, staring out the window, Luke turned the football over in his hands. Placing his fingers along the seam across the laces, he tossed the ball in the air.

"Are you thinking about going outside and throwing a couple of passes?" Bobby inquired, sticking his head in the door. "Because I'd be up for that."

Luke didn't turn around, just tossed the football straight up and grunted. "Maybe."

Bobby came around the desk and perched himself on the large window sill. "I know that look." Reaching out, he plucked the ball neatly out of the air as Luke tossed it up again. "What seems to be on your mind?"

"Today's the ten-year anniversary of Charlotte's death."

"I know. I can't help but think about it every year. The

date is seared into my memory." Bobby threw the football to Luke. "What's your point?"

Reluctant to speak at first, he tossed the ball back. "I just have a bad feeling about the party tonight. Isn't it weird that after ten years, we'll all be at Cherry Hollow again?"

"It is weird." Bobby tossed the football back.

There was a long stretch of silence when neither man spoke.

"Do you have any news on the letters?"

"As a matter of fact," Luke's feet hit the floor. Placing the football on the desk, he selected a note at random from the box and handed it to Bobby. "Why don't you look at that?"

Bobby unfolded the paper and read it to himself. "Another love letter?" he inquired.

"Seems to be." Luke reached for the box and shook it. "There's a whole slew of them."

Cannon quirked an eyebrow. "Are those the letters you found last night?"

"Yep."

"Remind me where you found the box."

"Cami and I went up to get a birdcage out of Charlotte's room." He held up a hand and said, "Don't ask. Anyway, the box was in the way. I handed it to Cami. She set it aside."

"On Charlotte's bed?"

"Correct."

"At what point did you realize it was full of letters?"

"We didn't," Luke hesitated, then plowed ahead anyway, "Not until we walked into the room hours later."

"Tell me again what happened."

Luke ran through it quickly for Bobby, not stopping to take a breath. Knowing how it sounded, he heard himself saying it and couldn't believe it was the truth, either. Yet, he'd been there, and it was. Going over and over in his mind while he lay on the couch last night at Cherry Hollow, he tried to fathom another explanation for what they found, what they'd seen, felt, but he couldn't.

"Well? Say something… anything."

"Just a minute. I'm digesting the whole thing."

"You heard the same story last night."

"I know, but in the light of day, it seems even more far-fetched." Bobby took a deep breath. "Let's say for a moment, just for argument's sake, I believe you and that it really is possible Charlotte is talking to you from beyond the grave. What exactly is her point for showing this to you?"

"I'm glad you asked." Reaching across his desk, he picked up the top yearbook, opened it to the page he had marked, and held it so Bobby could see it. "The handwriting matches this entry under the prom picture."

Scrutinizing the yearbook and then one of the letters, Bobby agreed, "I think you're correct in assuming that. So, the same person wrote in her yearbook as well as all these letters. Seems to me it's a boy head over heels in love with Charlotte, wouldn't you agree?"

"Possibly. The other option is they're obsessed. An unrequited obsession is hard to handle after a while, don't you think?"

"One problem. We don't have any idea how old these letters are, do we?"

"No, we don't."

"They could have been written when she was a freshman or a senior, even somewhere in between."

"That's true. We know, though, that the yearbook entry has to be the spring of our junior year. That's when we got our yearbooks for that year."

"Okay, I'll give you that one," Bobby answered. "But there is the off chance it could have been lying around during the summer and someone could have added the comment then."

"True, but that widens our search to include all the people who went to Cherry Hollow over the summer. Which could potentially be a lot of teenagers. The twins always had parties. I'm not sure we could even determine how many parties they had, let alone how many teens attended accurately, and on which dates ten years later.”

“No, that’s near impossible.”

Luke stood and walked over to his dry erase board. Picking up a dry erase marker, he uncapped it. “Let’s assume, for the time being, that they signed it in the spring of junior year like we said.” He jotted down “junior year,” added “yearbook” and “box of letters,” circling the latter. “Those letters also match the letter found in Charlotte’s pocket the day she died. That had to have been new, at least within a few days of her death.”

“Could be more.”

“How do you figure that?”

“Well, when I was a teenager, I didn’t do my laundry every week. Did you?”

Grinning, Luke shook his head. “I can’t say that I did. I’d go a couple of weeks before my mom would complain that my bedroom smelled like an old gym, from dirty clothes and smelly socks.”

“See? That's my point.”

“And I would agree if we were talking about boys, but we're not. We're talking girls here. Very well-dressed girls. Girls that cared about their appearances. Plus, it was actually Cami’s hoodie, not Charlotte’s. She told me herself; she pulled it out of the dryer on the way to school that morning. She remembers it vividly because it was warm when she put it on, and that morning had been extremely cold, kind of like today.”

“At what point did Charlotte put on the hoodie?”

“Not until the bonfire when we were playing hide-and-seek.”

“That’s a pretty tight window of opportunity.”

“Cami told me, and it's in Detective Swanson’s notes as well, that Charlotte put the sweatshirt on when the girls went to hide because someone had spilled soda on Charlotte’s shirt.”

“That means . . .”

There was a knock on the door.

“Hold that thought.” Luke turned toward the door and

called out, "Come in."

An administrative assistant opened the door. "Please excuse me for interrupting, Detective Warner."

"It's okay, Meg. What can I do for you?"

"I have Detective Swanson's autopsy report. They expedited it like you asked. You said I should bring it to you as soon as I received it."

"Yes, of course, thank you."

Handing it to him, she said, "And one more thing. There's a message here from Aaron Phelps. He asked if you could give him a call this afternoon."

"Thanks, Meg."

Nodding, she ducked back out as quickly as she'd come, closing the door behind her.

Tossing the message on his desk, he slid the report out of the manilla envelope, scanning it quickly. His brow furrowed when he flipped the page.

Bobby waited patiently for Luke to finish reading. "What does it say?"

With a grim expression, Luke responded, "I thought there was foul play, and this confirms my suspicions. There are actually two separate contusions on Dwight's skull. One was caused by a blunt force trauma, leading to a contusion that's concave, most likely caused by a rounded tool or device. It's located on the top, back half of his skull in the parietal area. The other one is lower on the back of his skull, located on the occipital. Says here that it was most likely caused by a backward fall."

Pushing off the windowsill, Bobby stood and crossed his arms over his broad chest. "What you're saying is someone hit him first, and then he fell backward and he hit his head a second time?"

"Yes."

"Which head injury killed him?"

"Neither."

"What?" Bobby scowled at Luke. "Then what killed him,

Warner?"

"An overdose of morphine."

"What the hell? Are you kidding me?"

"I wouldn't kid about something like this. It's here in the report. See for yourself." Luke held the report out for Bobby.

Pissed, Bobby fired back at Luke. "You're telling me someone's carelessness killed him? Because you know he was in no state to do it himself, he was in a medically induced coma."

Luke remained calm despite his own outrage at the situation. "I don't think it was carelessness or a mistake. Someone obviously wanted him dead, enough to hit him over the head and put him in a coma. When that didn't work, I bet they decided to finish the job another way, not taking any chances that he might recover." Luke laid the autopsy report on his desk and picked up his phone. "I want to get over to that hospital and look at their security footage. With any luck, I can find out who went in and out of that room."

"What do you need me to do?"

"See if you can find out who might have had access to morphine, or if anyone is missing a couple of vials of it. They keep reports, quantities and such, and it had to come from somewhere."

CHAPTER 39

The house was bustling with activity despite the threat of inclement weather. A cleaning crew was scrubbing the house from top to bottom, tables and chairs were being placed in the ballroom, and flowers were being delivered. Staff swarmed the house like bees around a hive and Cami was the queen bee, orchestrating the whole thing when Tanya bustled in, her hands full.

"You're here!"

"I am, and I'm loaded down with enough ingredients to make all your culinary delights and wishes come true," Tanya beamed. "Where do you want me?"

"Go straight through to the kitchen. I'll snag a couple of staff to help us unload."

"Sounds like a plan."

Tanya disappeared into the house and came back out at the same time that Cami had two staff members there to help carry. They unloaded the catering van quickly and had everything deposited in the kitchen in a matter of minutes.

"I'll have someone move the van around to the carriage house so it's out of the way for tonight."

"Perfect." Tanya tossed her the keys.

"I thought Joselyn was going to help you get ready for tonight?"

"Not anymore, I decided against it," she commented, already arranging the workspace.

"Why?"

"Joselyn is working the morning rush at Jolt. I couldn't

afford to close for the whole day. She's closing at noon so she can get ready for tonight. You know, the usual: get her nails done, her hair, and just take time for herself today."

"That was very thoughtful of you."

"Not really," Tanya commented as she sorted out ingredients across the acre of counter. "She's been getting on my nerves a lot lately and I figured we were more likely to remain friends if she was out of my hair today. I love her to death, but I don't need her prickly attitude when I'm trying to present my best work tonight."

"I totally agree. You need to cut her a break, though. I think the wedding planning is getting to her. She's been pretty short with me the last couple of times I've spoken to her on the phone as well."

"That's what I figured, too. She most likely will be that way until the wedding is over."

Cami smoothed down her shirt. "I need to check on the crew, and finish a few things, but I'd be more than glad to help in the kitchen if you need or want me to."

"I'd love that. Let me get situated first, and I'll let you know."

Nodding, Cami left Tanya to it. She went into the ballroom, and noted the tables and chairs were set up, covered in ivory linens. The center pieces were delivered, needing to be unwrapped and placed on tables.

Cami quickly set to work unwrapping the delicate, compact center pieces of champagne colored hydrangeas, creamy white peonies, and full petaled quicksand roses in tarnished copper vases. The floral arrangements were soft, feminine, and romantic. Placing an arrangement at each table, Cami situated tapered ivory candles on either side.

The focal point of the room was the fireplace ornately carved out of cherry wood, with a light stain casting a gold patina over it and a heavy mantle to match. The florist had created a romantic swag of trailing greens overflowing with flowers matching the centerpieces. Cami layered pillar candles on either end of the mantle in varying shades of cream, ivory, and antique white.

Next, she lined the buffet table with candles and loose petals. Then she took out a package of fine glitter and sprinkled it like pixie dust over everything. She stood back and took in the entire room. *Perfect.*

In the grand foyer, Cami arranged peonies and hydrangeas in the same colors around the base of the bird cage they had retrieved from Charlotte's room and entwined them through the thin bars with greenery. Setting it on the large breakfront near the door, she put out the guest book and pen. Placing them just so, and adjusting the elegant chalkboard sign, they welcomed everyone to the engagement party.

Satisfied with what she saw, and all the little details seen to, Cami headed for the kitchen to see what she could do to help Tanya. She found her already sliding a tray of crab puffs in one of the new refrigerators.

"Those look delicious."

"Thanks," Tanya responded, grabbing another tray and sliding it on a lower rack.

"What can I help with?"

"The crab puffs are ready. They just need to bake for thirty minutes, and the crab Rangoon needs forty. I'll put them in the oven later this afternoon. I need to get the bacon cooked for the shrimp appetizers. Do you think you could handle that?"

"On it." Cami set the oven to 400 degrees, got out the bacon and a couple of baking pans. She cut the packages and started placing slices of bacon on the baking sheet. "I have a spot at the front door near the card drop and guest registry to put some of your business cards if you'd like."

"That would be great."

"I'm also going to have the florist and the photographer's cards there as well. I want to help promote as many local businesses as I can."

"I think that's a great idea, and I really appreciate you

doing that."

"Of course, we small business owners have to stick together."

"I would love to have a catering job like this at least twice a month."

"Same here. If I could have one wedding or party a weekend, that would be perfect." The oven dinged when it reached the temperature and Cami slid in the bacon, set the timer for twenty minutes, and then washed her hands. Wiping them on a towel, she asked, "What else can I help with?"

"I need to top the fruit tarts, but I need to get the fruit out and washed first. Can you give me a few minutes to get it set up?"

"Sure. I'll get out of your way for a bit. I'm going to make up the guest beds in case the weather gets bad tonight, or if you're just too tired to drive home afterwards."

"That sounds great. I might need to crash after. I heard the weather on the way over and the forecast doesn't sound promising."

"I know. Why don't you just plan on staying?"

"I think I will."

"Great. That's one less thing we have to worry about." She turned on her heel. "I'll be back in time to get the bacon out."

Cami was on her way up the stairs when the doorbell rang. "Now who could that be?" She opened the door only to find the older gentleman that had delivered the flowers. "Did you forget something?" she asked him.

"No, ma'am. I have another delivery for you."

He handed her a bouquet in an array of reds. There were Gerber daisies, carnations, poppies, and sweet williams with trailing greenery in a hand painted vase that had tiny cherry blossoms painted on it. It was cute, cheerful, and sweet.

"Oh my. Aren't these fun!"

He passed them to her and gave her a wink. "Enjoy."

"Thank you, I will." Cami carried them back to the

kitchen.

Tanya was busy washing the fruit in the sink. "Timer hasn't gone off yet."

"I know. I never made it upstairs."

Glancing at her, Tanya sucked in a breath. "Aren't those beautiful? Who are they from?"

"I'm not sure, but I have an idea." Cami set them on the kitchen table and plucked the card out and read it out loud. "Sending you warm wishes and positive vibes for a night of success. Thinking of you, Luke."

"Well, isn't he the sweetest?"

"Yes, yes, he is."

"Someone's got a boyfriend," Tanya said in a singsong voice.

"No, I don't."

"Yes, you do."

Touching the tips of the petals with her fingers, Cami couldn't help but smile.

"Oh, boy."

Cami blinked a couple of times and looked at Tanya. "What's the matter?"

"As much as I'd like to just stand here all day and watch you make doe eyes at those flowers, while you're in denial, we can't. There's too much work to do."

Cami straightened. "First, I wasn't making doe eyes at the flowers."

"Were you looking in the mirror?"

Confused, Cami answered, "No."

"Exactly." Tanya waved a wet hand at Cami and smirked. "I'm the one standing here watching you, not the other way around. I think I know what you look like more at this moment than you do. So, if I say you were making doe eyes at those flowers, you'd best be believing it."

Cami's mouth dropped open, but nothing came out.

Tanya laughed out loud. "Well, Camilla Parker, I don't think I've ever seen you speechless. There's no use in denying it."

Hesitating, Cami tried to think of a comeback, but she was at a loss. Was Luke her boyfriend? The thought warmed her insides and turned them to jelly. Saved from her own thoughts, the oven timer went off.

"Looky there, you just wasted twenty minutes mooning over flowers Luke sent you. If he's not your boyfriend, he soon will be. And if you don't get a move on, I'm going to fire your ass for standing around."

Cami grabbed the oven mitts, shut off the timer, and pulled out the bacon. "You can't fire me. I hired you."

"Lucky for you," Tanya said, grinning, "or you'd be up a creek without a paddle."

"Remind me again why I hired you to cater this event? I think I'm mad at you, you're such a brat."

"Ha!" Tanya laughed and draped an arm over Cami's shoulders. "You can't be mad at me because I'm your best friend, and the best caterer in town, and you love me."

"You're the best caterer alright, but as for best friend? That's debatable at the moment, but I do love you." Cami gave her a hug, and Tanya hugged her back.

Tanya leaned back and asked, "Am I forgiven?"

"For now."

"Let's get to work and make this the best damn party anyone in this town has seen in a while."

"That's exactly what we will do."

CHAPTER 40

Sitting on a folding chair in the square, windowless room next to a large man named Hank, the head of security for the hospital, Luke felt slightly claustrophobic. A screen ran the length of one whole wall above a rickety metal desk, a mini fridge hummed in the back corner adorned by a coffee pot and a toaster, and a metal filing cabinet made up the contents of the small room, which smelled slightly of Doritos and burnt toast.

Hank purposefully clicked the images on his laptop and diminished all the cameras except one. When he did, the image from the lone camera filled the entire screen. He went to the sidebar and selected the date, bringing the video to life outside Detective Swanson's room.

Luke checked his notes and stated, "The change in shift occurs around nine. Can we go back to a few minutes before and see if we can see them switch shifts?"

"Not a problem." Hank entered the time, and the video jumped backwards. He hit play, and they watched in silence as two staff members walked down the corridor together. They stopped just outside Swanson's room, making them both clearly visible to the camera.

"Can you pause it right there?" Luke asked.

"Yep."

Luke noted the time and identified each staff member from their photo ID's, checking to see which one was finishing her shift and which was relieving the other. "Okay, let it roll."

Hank nodded and let the footage advance. The two

women walked into the room together, out of sight from the camera, and spent all of ten minutes in the room. They exchanged a few words outside the door, then both went in opposite directions.

"Can you advance it until we see some movement again?"

"Sure."

Two minutes later, the night nurse returned with a new IV bag, disappearing into the room, only to pop back out a minute later. Nothing out of the ordinary. Luke once again noted the time and compared it to Detective Swanson's chart. So far, everything lined up.

"Alright, fast forward again."

As the night wore on, staff members bustled by in the hall, but no one entered Swanson's room. Staff in the corridor became nonexistent after eleven. Security stopped briefly at the desk, periodically checking in with the nurse, but then moved on. Around one, a figure dressed in dark clothing came down the hallway.

"Here we go," Hank commented, switching from fast forward to play. They followed the steady progress of the person down the hall, but noted how he stayed close to the wall, walking with his head down and hood up. He paused just outside of view of the nurses' station, glanced around the corner to see where the nurse was, and quickly darted across the hall and into Detective Swanson's room. He was out of sight for less than a minute, coming back out and practically running back down the hall.

"Stop, the footage. Roll it back and see if we can get a closeup on the face."

Hank froze frame after frame as the person dressed in black advanced down the hall. Not once did they look up, deliberately keeping their head down.

"He definitely knew there were cameras in the hallway. We know the time frame, so we can check the hospital entrance and the parking lot cameras. Let's see if we can catch this guy coming or going."

CHAPTER 41

They stood in Cami's bedroom in front of the full-length mirror, examining Tanya's dress choices. She held up a rich chocolate-brown, T-length dress that scooped dangerously low in the front and had a slit up the side.

"What do you think?" Tanya switched out the brown for a rose-gold, mini-length fitted sequin party dress.

Tilting her head, Cami said, "Both are beautiful. The brown brings out your eyes, the gold makes your skin glow, but I have to ask, what exactly are we going for here? Sophisticated yet flirty or look out, here I come?"

"Hmmm," Tanya held one dress in front of her, then the other, and debated. "Definitely, look out, here I come."

"Then I'd go with the rose-gold. Put it on and let me see."

Cami disappeared into the closet while Tanya changed, selecting for herself a simple black cocktail dress. Slipping it on, she examined herself in the bathroom mirror. It fit and flattered; the waist wrapped tight, the asymmetrical hem with slit showed a hint of thigh, and the neckline touched the edge of her collarbone, with just inches of the sheer material leaving her arms bare. Simple, elegant, and sophisticated.

She swept her hair up, put on small diamond studs, and applied her makeup with a light hand. Slipping on black heels, Cami found Tanya ready as well.

"Beautiful," she said, taking one look at Tanya. "You clean up pretty good."

"You're not so bad yourself. That dress will turn someone's head."

"I'm not trying to turn Luke's head. I'm simply trying to be a perfect hostess."

Tanya stifled a laugh.

"What's so funny?"

"I never mentioned Luke," she stuck an accusatory finger in Cami's direction. "You did."

Caught, Cami blushed. Waving her hand at her, she tried to brush it off. "I assumed that's who you meant. Anyway, are you leaving your hair down?"

"Nice segway." Tanya turned back to the mirror. "I was thinking about it."

"Those long black curls are perfect. Very sexy. Every man at the party will want to run his hands through it."

"I'm not looking to get everyone's attention. Just one would be fine."

"And which one would that be?"

Tanya wiggled her eyebrows. "Wouldn't you like to know?"

"I already have a pretty good idea. We'll just see how the night plays out."

"If we're lucky, maybe we will both get our man." Tanya linked her arm through Cami's. "Let's go get this party started."

***

The doorbell rang, and Cami went to let in the next guest. When she opened the door, Luke stood there dressed in a black suit, white shirt, and gray tie the same shade as his eyes.

He simply stood and stared at her. Looking her up and down, he gave a long slow, drawn out "Whoa." He inhaled deeply. "You're gorgeous."

Cami felt the color rise in her cheeks, and let a small smile flit across her face before she checked herself. *Control it,* she scolded. *Act casual.* She wasn't sure she could be with Luke. "Not so bad yourself, Detective Warner."

She leaned in to kiss him on the cheek, but he moved

faster and gently brushed her lips with his.

"If you're gonna make out in the doorway, can you at least let me go past? It's colder than a witch's wanger out here and the snow's falling."

"You always have the best timing, Cannon."

Bobby clapped Luke on the shoulder. "You know it. Nice move," he murmured. Brushing past, Bobby reached for Cami. "Hey trouble, looks like you could live up to your name tonight," he said, kissing her on the cheek.

She laughed. "Come in out of the snow and cold, both of you."

"Don't mind if we do."

"The house looks great, Cami. I'm not sure how you did it in two weeks."

Cami beamed. "Thank you, but just wait until you see the ballroom." The doorbell rang again. "Why don't you both head in and get yourself a drink? I have more guests to greet." With that, she left them.

They both watched her go.

"Any luck with the security footage at the hospital?" Bobby asked as they walked toward the ballroom.

"Yes, and no. We have a suspect on camera coming and going from the hospital and Swanson's room. The time of entry coincides with the time of death. The suspect was in Dwight's room for less than a minute. So not long, but enough time to give a couple of injections if he came prepared."

"What about the parking lot?"

"Cameras have him running out on foot, but didn't pick up any vehicle. He didn't park in the parking lot if he drove."

"Sounds like the suspect was careful."

"Yeah, he was quick, prepared, kept his head down and covered his tracks. If it wasn't for the cameras catching him coming and going out of Dwight's room, Swanson's death could have easily been ruled an accidental overdose."

"My, my, Bobby Cannon, I didn't know you owned a suit, let alone could look that good in one," Tanya declared, coming up beside them. "Luke, you look nice."

Bobby let out a little whistle. "Don't you look . . ."

"Beautiful," Luke finished for him.

"Why, thank you." Tanya did a slow turn.

"Yeah," Bobby loosened his tie a little. "Almost good enough to eat."

Tanya laughed. "If you're hungry, why don't we go get something? Everything you see was made by yours truly, and my trusty sidekick."

"You made Joselyn make her own appetizers?"

"No," Tanya shook her head. "Cami."

Both men looked surprised.

"What's the matter?"

"Nothing. I just thought Joselyn always helped you."

"She does, but this was different. This was for Joselyn. I couldn't expect her to slice, peel, and bake for her own engagement party."

"Of course."

"Geez, you guys act like I was replacing her."

"No, of course not. It's just you know she's touchy about those things, but I totally get why you didn't have her preparing for tonight."

"Speaking of, here comes the happy couple now," Bobby said, sticking out his hand to Kevin.

"Congratulations, you two. Can't believe you're finally going to do it."

Luke lost track of the conversation as he watched Cami work the room, mingling with the guests, introducing couples, greeting old acquaintances, and delegating to the wait staff, all discreetly done with poise and charm. She was born for this, he thought. Gone was the reserved, shy teenager he remembered from high school, replaced by a sophisticated, elegant woman. He had fallen easily for the quiet teenager, but was head over heels for the woman.

She crossed the room toward him with a waiter in tow carrying a tray of fluted glasses of champagne. His mouth went dry, and his heart hammered in his chest as she came closer.

Cami stopped short when she saw Luke's parents, instructing the waiter to go ahead then greeted them.

"Mr. and Mrs. Warner, so glad you could come." Leaning in to give them both a hug, he heard her ask, "How are you this evening?"

Unable to stop himself, when he saw the three people he cared about most in the world together, he crossed the short distance.

"You've done a wonderful job, Cami. I can't believe how beautiful everything is." Mrs. Warner turned to her son. "Hello, darling."

"Hi, Mom," Luke responded with a quick peck on her cheek.

"I was just telling Cami how lovely everything is."

"It certainly is," his father added. "You've outdone yourself."

"And in such a short amount of time. Your parents must be so proud of you."

"Thank you, both. I certainly hope they will be. They haven't seen the house yet, and may not for some time. My mother wasn't too thrilled about my new venture."

"Oh, nonsense," Mrs. Warner said, waving off the thought. "They'll come around, you'll see."

"I certainly hope so." Cami reached out, gently squeezing the older woman's hand. "I'm so glad you're both here, please get something to eat, the crab puffs melt in your mouth." Glancing at the entrance Cami made her excuse to go. "If you'll excuse me, I have a few new guests to attend to."

"Of course, dear. Don't let us hold you up."

She gave her hand one last little squeeze and walked quickly across the ballroom to greet the new arrivals.

"Welcome." Cami knelt down to be at eye level with an elderly woman wrapped in a blanket, snuggled into her wheelchair. Her lap and her escort were both dusted with snowflakes. "I'm so glad you could come this evening. I don't believe we've had the pleasure of meeting. I'm Cami Parker, your hostess this evening."

"Camilla Parker, I'd know you anywhere." The elderly lady lifted a shaky hand, reaching for Cami. "You used to play in my backyard. I'm Joselyn's Grammy."

"Oh, for goodness' sake, Mrs. Finch! I'm so glad you're here. I never expected to see you. Joselyn said you've been under the weather."

"Nonsense. Had a little scare a few weeks back, but now? The only weather I'm under is this dang, old snow that's falling outside. Way too early for this white stuff."

Amused, Cami answered, "You're certainly right about that. Can I take your blanket and get you a dry one? I'd be more than happy to pop this one in the dryer for you, so you can have it ready when you leave."

"If it ain't no trouble?"

"No trouble at all."

"That would be mighty kind of you, my dear."

"Of course." Cami gathered the blanket. "And who's the gentleman with you?"

"Oh, that's Randy, my driver."

Cami nodded. "Randy, may I take your coat as well?"

"Yes, please." Shrugging out of it, he handed it to her.

"You'll have to remind him to get both before we leave." Ms. Finch pulled Cami in close and explained, "He's a looker but he's forgetful."

"Oh?"

"Yeah, he'd forget his head if it wasn't attached. Why, the other day he misplaced the car keys and some of my medicine. Almost makes me think he hid them on purpose, but he doesn't need help sleeping and he's clearly not in any pain."

Trying to conceal a smile, Cami nodded. "That happens to everyone at one time or the other misplacing things. Looks like you found the keys, though."

"Thank heavens for that or we wouldn't be here tonight,

but unfortunately, not the medicine."

"I'm sure it will turn up." Straightening, Cami stood, gathering in the garments. "I'll just hang Randy's coat, put the blanket in the dryer, and I'll be right back with another."

"You take your time, dear. I see my granddaughter over yonder. I want to go say hello."

"Of course. Get something to eat as well."

CHAPTER 42

Soft classical music filled the air, enchanting candlelight surrounded him in an elegant atmosphere, yet Kevin felt like he was drowning. He retreated from the crowd and backed himself into a corner. His hand shook slightly as he downed the glass of champagne. Even the taste of the airy bubbles popping on his tongue and the cool liquid sliding down his throat didn't seem to take the edge off. Leaning back against the wall, he tried to fathom how he was at this house, in this room, in this uncanny circumstance. He absolutely couldn't believe it. How had he let it all happen? Kevin was at his own engagement party, surrounded by family and friends. He should be happy, ecstatic even at the thought of his future.

A waiter dressed in a white jacket and black pants glided across the room directly toward him, offering another glass. He downed the glass, deposited both empty flutes on the tray, and took two more, one for each hand. Discreetly, the waiter bowed his head and stepped away. Once again, Kevin was left alone in the corner of the room to his own devices.

He put the next glass to his lips and spotted the woman he loved across the expanse of the ballroom. His stomach pitched. She was simply beautiful, elegant, and sophisticated in a way that made his heart pine just looking at her. Kevin watched her glide across the room, stopping at different clusters of guests, making sure they felt welcome.

Guests. That word stirred something in him slightly. They were *his* guests, *his* friends, his family, and here she was entertaining them, like she was born to. She placed her hand on Brock's arm and flirted a little, laughing at something he couldn't hear. She smiled and turned her attention to Luke. Luke leaned in and whispered in her ear and a smile so shockingly beautiful creased her face. A spike of jealousy surged through him and he tipped back the flute of champagne, trying to drown it. His belly turned as the light amber liquid hit rock bottom inside his empty stomach. Did she have feelings for Luke? He'd never been one to be jealous, except with her. Kevin pushed the emotion to the recesses of his mind, locking it in a cold, dark corner, praying it would stay there. But how could it when he couldn't take his eyes off of her?

Feeling slightly sick, Kevin shook himself and decided the best thing to do was to get something in his stomach. He stepped out of the corner, determined to make the most of the night. After all, this was a party for him and his fiancée, even if it felt more like a funeral. He was drowning in his own thoughts and he knew it, killing himself slowly with the jealousy he felt when other men looked at her, talked to her, or touched her.

"There you are, silly," Josie said, coming up to him. "I've been looking for you everywhere."

He smiled sweetly at her. "You have?"

"Of course." She turned her attention to the lady beside her. "Kevin, this is the photographer Cami hired to take some pictures of us tonight."

Kevin took her hand and shook it. "Nice to meet you."

"Likewise." Getting down to business, the photographer said, "I would like to take a couple of photos of you and Joselyn over by the fireplace. Would that be alright with you?"

"Certainly," Kevin answered politely. "Just tell us what to do."

The photographer nodded and pointed. "Please stand next to the fireplace. Kevin, if you could go off to the side. Joselyn, put your back to him, and lean into Kevin."

They did as they were instructed.

"Perfect. Now Kevin, tilt your head slightly and wrap your arms around Joselyn's waist. Joselyn, put your hands on top of his, and tilt your head up slightly and to the left. Perfect." She raised the camera and centered them in the photo. "What a gorgeous couple you make." She clicked off a couple of shots. "And that ring, it's exquisite."

Joselyn beamed. "Kevin picked it out all by himself."

"It's the most beautiful ring I've ever seen. You have excellent taste."

The diamond sparkled in the soft lighting. "Thank you," Kevin murmured, glancing down at their joined hands, his heart in his throat. His heart whispered what his mind didn't want to admit. *The wrong woman was wearing it.*

***

Floating just above, the guests gathered in the ballroom around tables, congregated by the buffet, and clustered in groups, talking, eating, and laughing. She watched as champagne flowed, hors d'oeuvres were consumed, and decadent desserts sampled. Oh, what she wouldn't give for the tiniest taste of chocolate, or to have the briefest snippet of conversation again.

Descending into the mix, she slipped through the guests, reaching out to touch the sequins of their cocktail dresses, the scratch of lace, the slick of sheer material, only to have her fingertips brush against nothing, passing right through. There were too many of them for her to concentrate and make contact. Charlotte longed for anything and everything. The scent of roses following her was cast out by her own sadness. She was a mere wisp of air in a sea of suits and dresses, a phantom of the night, completely unnoticed, except by one.

Their eyes locked, just for a moment. The brief recognition in her twin sister's eyes. A shudder of fear, the swamp of grief, followed by a wave of love. So instantaneous, so electric, so overwhelming. The wave rolled through, washing over her, more than the mere shadow of herself could bear. Turning away from Cami, she moved on, wishing she could be one of them if only for a few minutes.

She walked through guests, saw the faces of what could be friends, neighbors, people she should know but didn't, feeling vibes, sensations, and emotions in her soul. Some were warm, happy thoughts. Conversation and gossip lingered around her, filling her mind. Overwhelmed by so much stimulation, she weaved her way across the ballroom, back the way she had come. The crowd had shifted, different guests mingled, and congregated.

Suddenly, everything went black. It was like hitting a wall, only one she couldn't pass through. It was pure, dark rage. Something she'd only felt a handful of times, but one she would never forget. A cold so piercing ricocheted through her, clawing, tearing at her soul. She inched back just enough to free herself from its clutches. Standing back, she saw a cloud of darkness, and could feel the pure, black hatred. Charlotte shuddered, vanishing from the room.

CHAPTER 43

The champagne was gone, the food devoured, and the crowd had thinned considerably. The music was low, and they had softened the lighting reflecting the late hour.

"I think we'll be taking off now," Mr. Warner said to his son. "Snow's coming down pretty heavy. Will you be staying a while longer?"

"Yeah, I'm going to hang around and help clean up."

Mr. Warner nodded knowingly. "Brock, Aaron, it was good to see you." He shook both men's hands.

"Here are your coats, Mr. and Mrs. Warner," Cami said, holding them out to the older couple. "I'm so glad that you could join us tonight."

"The evening was enchanting, my dear. I can't wait to see what you have in store for the wedding."

"We'd better get going, though, before the roads get too bad."

"I'll walk you out," Cami said, leading the way.

Tanya slid up beside the guys. "I hope you don't mind, but you offered to help, and the snow is really coming down out there, so we let the wait staff go."

"That's no problem. We can stay," Luke answered for the group.

"Cami has enough beds and couches for everyone so you can stay and not worry about the roads," Tanya said, casting a glance at Aaron and Brock. "Already bribed Bobby with leftovers. Can I do the same with you?"

"Lead the way. I could go for a few more of those crab

balls."

They walked over to the table that held what was left of the appetizers and desserts, and stood next to Bobby, who was sampling a cherry tart.

"By the way, they're crab puffs, not balls."

"What's the difference?" Aaron asked, popping one in his mouth.

"Big difference between puffs and balls, man. You ought to know that," Bobby grinned.

"Only you could make appetizers sound dirty." Tanya wrinkled her nose at him. She started combining half empty trays of food, condensing, stacking, and handed a stack of platters to Bobby, who had his mouth full, and another stack to Aaron. "Make yourself useful, will you? Take these empty trays to the kitchen."

"Certainly, Your Highness." Bobby bowed at the waist.

Punching him lightly in the arm, she shook her head. "Get out of here."

He laughed good-naturally and headed to the kitchen, followed closely by Aaron. Brock and Luke made the rounds to the tables and picked up the empty glasses, carting them to the kitchen.

Cami came back in the ballroom shivering after saying goodbye to the last guest and found everyone gathered around the buffet table devouring what was left of the appetizers.

"Snow's really coming down out there." She walked over to them. "Thank you all for helping. I just wasn't comfortable keeping the wait staff any later with the roads getting bad."

"It's fine. We don't mind pitching in."

"Especially when there's free food involved."

"Everything was damn good."

"Thanks."

"It was a perfect evening, Cami," Kevin said, slipping away from Joselyn to give her a hug. "Thank you."

"You're welcome. Anything for you," Cami whispered.

"I could capitalize on that."

"I think you already have."

"Hey, what about me?" Tanya questioned, feeling left out.

Kevin stretched out his arm and laughed. "Yes, you too."

"I want in on this," Joselyn said. "It's my night, too."

"Bring it in, Joselyn."

"Everyone come here," Cami said, motioning to the men. "Big group hug."

The room fell quiet except for the soft lull of the music in the background. Tears came to Cami's eyes as she reflected on the evening, the fun, the celebration of the start of Kevin and Joselyn's life together, but also the comradery she felt, the way they'd all pitched in with no hesitation. Cami was overwhelmed with emotions.

She'd had a great team to work with at the hotel, but this was different. These were her people, her friends first. She shared a past with them, childhood memories of fun and laughter, but also loss, and now a future.

"Who farted?"

There was a groan, then everyone started talking at once.

"Cannon, was that you?"

"Wasn't me!"

"So gross."

"Whoever smelt it, dealt it."

"That's so junior high."

"That's disgusting."

"Cami was about to cry. I had to do something."

"Kevin!"

"Hey, at least I didn't say pull my finger."

"Joselyn? Do you realize what you're getting yourself into?"

"Yes, I do," Joselyn said, shaking her head.

The smell slowly dissipated, replaced by the heady scent of roses. Luke caught Cami's eye, and she stiffened. The lights flickered, but stayed on. "I guess we'd better get to work cleaning up."

"I could really go for some tea. Cami, could you make me some?"

"Of course, Joselyn.

"Before you do that, there's one thing we should do first. Something that I wanted to do all night," Luke said, "but didn't get the chance."

"What's that?" Cami slanted a curious look at Luke.

"A long slow dance in this spectacular ballroom, with the most gorgeous girl I've ever laid eyes on. Come here." He pulled her free of the group and spun her out into the middle of the ballroom. She couldn't help but laugh.

"That looks like a great idea. Let's go, Your Highness." Bobby escorted Tanya out onto the dance floor.

They shut the lights off, the music was turned up, the ballroom was lit only by waning candles, softening the edges, casting enchanting shadows, creating a place where romance and dreams come true.

Cami's stomach filled with butterflies as Luke spun her out again, pulled her in close, and tucked her against him. She tried to focus, but with his hands on her, it was almost impossible.

"You smelled roses just now, didn't you?"

"I did." He kissed her lightly. "I've been wanting to do that all night." So, he did it again.

"You need to stop that for a moment. I need to discuss something serious with you, and I can't if you keep kissing me."

An easy grin, broad and wide, spread across Luke's face. "Now I really don't want to stop." He kissed her again, deepening it.

It was easy to let herself spiral down into what was Luke. Warm, kind, and all man. His hands skimmed over her bare arms, sending a delicious chill up her spin as she softened into him.

He pulled back, grinning, and asked, "Now, what did you

want to talk about?"

A smile flitted across Cami's face, then turned into a frown. "Do you think I'm crazy?"

"If anyone's crazy, it's me, because I'm crazy about you. Why?"

Her heart tumbled inside her chest. She smiled at that, but had to ignore the comment or she'd never get through this. "I'm serious. I would swear I saw Charlotte earlier tonight, walking among the guests."

He lifted her chin and looked into those turbulent hazel eyes. "I don't think you're crazy. On a night like tonight, a special night celebrating lifelong friends, I have to say part of me half expected her to make an appearance as well, this being the tenth anniversary of her death."

"I know. I've had this sick feeling all day that something was going to happen, but it didn't. The night was perfect."

"Yes, it was. All because of you."

Luke took his hand, placing it on her face. Cami tilted her head toward his palm, relishing the warmth of it. Sighing into him, he pulled her closer still.

She lay her head on his shoulder and he whispered into it. "I don't want to ruin this moment, but I feel I have to at least warn you, we have another problem."

"What do you mean?"

Luke cleared his throat slightly, hesitating. "Detective Swanson's autopsy report came back."

Cami pulled back and looked up at him. "What did it say?"

Luke gazed down at her with those storm cloud eyes. "This needs to stay between us. I'm only telling you so you realize you might be in real danger, and you'll be careful."

"Luke, you're scaring me."

He nodded knowingly. "It should."

"Tell me."

"There's no easy way to say this, so here goes."

Neither one realized it, but they had stopped dancing

and just stood in the middle of the ballroom.

"Swanson had two contusions on his head. It's apparent that someone hit him with an object. The other resulted from falling backward."

"I don't understand. He was hit from behind and then?"

"He fell backwards and hit his head again against the flagstone."

"That's why he said 'danger,'" Cami said more to herself than Luke.

"What did you just say?"

"He said 'danger' and 'run,' but with all the blood…"

"You never told me that."

"I didn't realize. I was so caught up in helping him that I didn't realize there might be real danger. I just thought he was confused, disoriented."

"Well, that's not all. He didn't die from either head wound, although he might have eventually."

"Then what?"

"An overdose of morphine."

"An accident?"

"No."

Cami's hand went to her mouth. "Oh, my God. I can't believe it. Are you serious?"

"Dead serious. And if what you say is true, he knew he'd been hit, and maybe he could have identified the culprit."

Cami shivered despite the warmth from Luke. "Do you have any suspects?"

Shaking his head, he said, "But we have him on camera. It's only a matter of time."

Bobby's cell phone went off across the ballroom. Luke turned as Bobby lifted it to take the call. His expression serious as he listened.

"There's been an accident," he stated loud enough for Luke to hear.

Seconds later, Luke's cell phone vibrated. He glanced down, reading the text message. "It's my parents. I'm sorry, I have to go. This conversation isn't over." He kissed Cami hard, trying to put all his emotions into that one kiss. "I'm sorry," he whispered again just for her. "My parents."

"Don't be. Go."

He nodded an understanding passing between them. He kept his eyes locked with hers and whispered, "Be careful," and called out, "Cannon! Let's roll."

Both men sprinted for the door.

CHAPTER 44

Joselyn sat at the kitchen table drinking tea as everyone else finished up for the night. Cami loaded platters into the dishwasher, Tanya stored food in the fridge, Brock hauled out trash, and Kevin and Aaron stacked chairs. One by one, they gravitated back to the kitchen and plopped down at the table that held the leftover champagne.

Cami got out glasses, poured the rest of the champagne and passed them out. "Let's have a toast."

Everyone held up their glass.

"To the happy couple. May all your days be filled with love and happiness."

"Here, here!"

Finishing her champagne, Tanya commented, "That's the perfect end to a perfect night." Tanya leaned over and hugged Cami tight. "You did good."

"*We* did," she corrected.

"Yeah, *we* did."

Cami looked around the table at her friends. "If you're ready, I can show you your rooms for the night."

Tired, they all climbed the stairs to the second floor, at the top Kevin plopped down, drunk. "Phew, that's a hell of a lot of stairs."

"Sit there a minute. I'll come back for you," Cami said, patting him on the head.

"Promise?"

"Of course."

"Fine. I'll wait right here."

"You do that." She turned her attention to Joselyn and the others, motioning for them to follow. "Joselyn, you and Kevin will be in here. Towels and washcloths are in the bathroom."

"I'm going to change then," Joselyn announced toward Kevin.

He waved an acknowledgment, but didn't move to get up.

"Let me light the fire in your room before you do. You're on the northern side and it's always been a little chillier." Cami grabbed the matches off the mantle, struck the match and held the flame to the pre-stacked wood. In a matter of seconds, the flame caught and took hold, creating a pleasant fire, making the room cozy and romantic. Cami used the poker and closed the screen, then returned it to the hook inlaid on the stone. "There you go."

"Send Kevin in, will you?"

"Of course."

Further down the hall, Cami opened another door. As it swung in, she turned to the guys. "Brock and Aaron, are you two okay sharing a room? This one has two beds."

"I guess I can put up with his snoring," Brock commented. "I put up with him all day long."

"As if."

"Bathroom's there," she said, pointing to another door, then stepped over the threshold and flipped a switch. "Extra blankets on the end of both beds. Next," Cami said, turning to Tanya and opening another door. "This one's you. You'll have to share a bathroom with the guys."

"No problem." Tanya hugged her, stifled a yawn, whispered, "Good night," and shut the door behind her.

Cami walked back down the hall and stopped next to Kevin. "Think you can make it now?" she inquired, holding out her hand to him.

"Not yet." He grabbed her hand and pulled her down. "Sit."

Sinking down next to him, Cami put her head on his shoulder, completely exhausted, in a good way. They sat in silence, looking out across the expanse of the grand foyer toward the large window, where they could periodically see fat snowflakes dance by the window.

"Ya done good."

"Thanks, but you think tonight was good? Just you wait until the wedding."

"I'm on pins and needles," he said dryly.

Cami laughed. "Okay, so fancy parties aren't your thing, but it's important to Joselyn." She sighed. "You'll have fun, I promise."

"Don't make promises you can't keep."

Lifting her head, she studied him from the side. "Is everything alright?"

He nodded slightly. "Never better," Kevin remarked, the comment dripping with disdain.

"I still can't believe you're getting married."

"Me either."

Cami stood. "Let's get you to bed. Your future bride is waiting." She held out her hand and pulled him up off the stairs.

Unexpectedly, he leaned in and hugged her tight. Holding on a little longer than necessary. He kissed the top of her head and whispered, "Goodnight, Cami."

Neither one heard the soft click of a door.

"Goodnight, Kevin." She released him and gave him a little push toward his room. She watched him go, smiled when he made a face before he went in.

The door shut, she turned slowly and went back downstairs. Taking a few extra minutes, she checked the ballroom, made sure all the candles were out, dampened the fire, and flipped off the lights. In the kitchen, Cami put the last of the bottles in the recycle bin, wiped off the counter, and turned on the dishwasher.

Exhausted, she glanced out the window as she saw the

snow continued to come down steadily, painting the world white. The lights flickered around her and then went out. The heady scent of roses filled the room. "I wondered if you'd show up again tonight." Cami shivered as the cold crept across the floor like a low-lying fog, curled up around her legs and made her shudder. A feeling of sadness swamped her as the fog rolled toward the door and escaped through the cracks. Cami watched in awe as it dissipated. Looking out the upper pane of the door, she gasped as she saw her own reflection in the glass. It shifted, changed, and morphed into her twin sister's face. In disbelief, she questioned, "Charlotte?"

Charlotte gave her a ghost of a smile, so sad that it tore at Cami's heartstrings.

The image moved away from the door, edging into the flurry of the snow, drawing back into the night.

"Don't go!" Cami croaked. She reached for a jacket and rubber boots, hastily pulling them on, flung open the door and raced out into the storm after her twin sister.

CHAPTER 45

Aaron lay in the dark listening to Brock snore, a gigantic pit in his stomach, staring at the vast ceiling, trying to wrap his head around what he'd seen. Cami in Kevin's arms.

Just like ten years ago, only then, it was the other sister. He should have spoken up, but he hadn't. All these years he had kept the secret, thinking he was a good friend by hiding the truth. Deep down, he knew, he was just a coward.

Brock's steady breathing should have calmed him, but it agitated him instead, leaving him wide awake and restless with what he knew itching to come out. Sliding out of bed, he retrieved his cell phone from the nightstand, wrestled into his pants, and quietly exited the room. He padded carefully down the hall and discreetly slipped into an empty room.

He waited anxiously for the phone to ring, and Luke to answer. When he heard the click, he immediately asked, "Warner?"

"Phelps? What's the matter?"

"I need to talk. You still at the hospital?"

"Yeah, I'm just heading to the station now. Why?"

Aaron heard the sound of a curtain rake aside, metal scraping metal, and the steady beep of machines. He took a deep breath, figuring he should inquire about Luke's parents first before he blurted out what he had seen. "How are your parents?"

"Pretty good, considering. Dad has just a few scratches, bumped his head."

"And your mom?"

"Didn't fair quite as well, but still lucky. She broke her wrist when she braced herself for impact and the snap of the seatbelt cracked her collar bone. Her side of the car took the brunt of the blow. They're going to keep both overnight for observation. Dad's blood pressure is through the roof. Doc believes it's just from the stress of the accident, but wants to keep him to make sure."

The sounds lessened. Aaron imagined Luke walking down the hall and out into the parking garage. He heard the double click of the key fob, the slam of the door, and the constant ding as Luke started the SUV until he fastened his seatbelt. The everyday recognizable sounds calmed him, kept him sane.

"Now I know you didn't call at this hour just to ask about them. Something's up. What happened?"

Taking a deep breath Aaron decided it was now or never, before he lost his nerve. "I saw something."

"You're going to have to be a little more specific. When?"

"Ten years ago," Aaron swallowed hard, and added, "and tonight."

"Which is it? Ten years ago, or tonight."

"It's both." He could hear the steady swish of the windshield wipers, the low hum of the engine, and the crackle of the radio station, and knew Luke only had a couple of blocks to drive to the police station. "I should have said something sooner."

"Why didn't you?"

"I was a dumb teenager, and at first I didn't think it mattered, not until the next day . . . not until they found Charlotte dead."

"And then?"

"I was scared. Frightened I'd been mistaken. Afraid I would accuse the wrong person, or that the police would think I was making the whole thing up, maybe even blame me." He heard Luke shut off the SUV, slam the door, and click the key fob.

"Hold that thought for a moment. I want to get into my office."

Aaron waited with bated breath. Now that he started, he yearned to get it out. All of it. The seconds ticked by and finally Luke spoke.

"Alright, I'm in my office, and the door is closed. Now, tell me everything."

Aaron wasn't exactly sure where to start. His heart was hammering in his chest, and he'd broken out in a cold sweat. Forcing the lump down in his throat, he began, "When we were playing hide-and-seek, I followed Charlotte. I had a little crush on her. She and Brock had broken up, or so I thought. I watched which way she went into the woods and headed in that direction as soon as we were done counting. Finding them in the woods was easy. The girls were talking, trying to decide which way to go. I was there when Joselyn tripped and spilled soda all over Charlotte, watched her strip down to her bra and pull on Cami's sweatshirt. I stayed hidden because I didn't want any of the girls to know I'd seen Charlotte without her shirt. I hung back and when she disappeared further into the trees, I went after her. Only I didn't find her first."

"Who did?"

"Kevin." Aaron let the name hang in the air and walked to the window, staring out at the swirling snow. The yard, the driveway, and the trees were coated with white. It was such a contrast to the dark house behind him he could see his own reflection in the window pane.

"Are you sure?"

"Positive."

"Alright, continue."

Running a hand across his face, he rubbed at his aching eyes, bone tired from a long day at work, a full evening, and ten years of pent-up secrets. "It all happened so fast. I was just going to step out of the woods when he came out of nowhere, grabbed her, spun her around, and kissed her. Charlotte went from cold to hot in an instant. She was furious and shoved

Kevin. She backed away, tripped, fell backward, hitting her head."

"Was it an accident?"

"Yes. Kevin tried to help her up, but Charlotte didn't want any parts of it."

"Was she mad about the kiss or something else?"

"Charlotte was expecting Brock, and didn't want him to find her with someone else. That sealed the deal for me. If she wanted Brock to find her, I didn't have a chance, so I hightailed it back to the bonfire."

"So when you left, she was alive?"

"Yes." Aaron caught a reflection in the window a split second before his world went dark. The phone hit the floor and skidded across the room.

***

At that moment there was a knock on the office door, and Luke waved in Bobby. "Okay. Let's hold that thought for just a moment. What happened tonight that made you finally come forward?"

Bobby stared at Luke, photo in hand, and tapped his foot impatiently.

"Phelps? Don't stop talking now. What happened tonight?" Luke waited a few seconds. When Aaron didn't respond, he asked, "Aaron? Are you still there?" A dial tone came on in his ear. "Damn it!" Luke clicked off and hit Aaron's number. It went straight to voicemail. "I lost him."

"Could be the storm."

"Could be. You're not going to believe this."

"Try me."

"After all these years, Aaron just admitted to seeing Kevin and Charlotte together minutes before she died." Luke waited for a reaction from Bobby, but it didn't come. "You don't seem surprised."

"I'm in shock."

"Aaron said it was an accident that Charlotte tripped and fell backward."

His brow furrowed Bobby asked, "Did he see it happen?"

"Yes, and when he walked away, she was still alive."

"The question is, what exactly does that mean? Did something else happen after he left?"

"That's the real question and brings about something else that bothers me."

"Which is?"

"There are green fibers found in her mouth and lungs." Luke reached for the report, flipped it open. "The coloring in her face suggests asphyxiation."

"If it was an accident, why didn't Kevin come forward?"

Luke shrugged his shoulders. "He was seventeen. He probably about shit himself when he heard Charlotte had died."

"Unless he didn't come forward because he killed her." Bobby held out a grainy photo. "Take a look at this."

Reluctantly Luke took the photograph, flipped on his desk lamp and held the picture under the pool of light. "What is this? What am I looking at?"

"It's a photo from the security footage at the hospital. It was sent over while we were at the party. It's zoomed in on the front left pocket of the black jacket worn by the suspect caught on camera going into Swanson's room."

"It's initials, just a shade lighter than the fabric. It looks like KW."

"KW," Bobby confirmed. "Could KW stand for Kevin Weller?"

"Son of a bitch."

"There has to be another explanation."

"Normally, I would agree with you, but under the circumstances we might have to accept that Kevin killed Swanson." This was one of their best friends they were talking about.

"The million-dollar question is, why?"

Thinking out loud Luke answered, "I guess he was worried that Swanson knew something."

"Dwight had ten years, and he hadn't been able to solve it. Why now? What changed?"

"Cami's back. Which means access to her, the house, and the past. Something Swanson never had before. Cami's parents had taken legal action to keep the police out of the house, not to disrupt their lives anymore, and back then it was because of the tragedy of Charlotte's death." Luke opened the yearbook, pulled out the note found in Cami's hoodie, and a random letter from the box. "I have it verified from the handwriting analyst that the same person wrote these. If only I had something of Kevin's to compare it to."

"We'll need a warrant to search his house. That'll take some time." Bobby flopped down in the overstuffed chair. "There's got to be some other explanation. This is fucking Kevin we're talking about, one of our best friends, one of the guys. *Our* guys."

"Believe me, I know. If we can prove that it's not his handwriting, that may help. If we only had a receipt or a grocery list, anything."

"Wait, I have a check from Kevin in my wallet." Bobby stood up, dug his wallet out of his back pocket of his suit, thumbed through it, and handed Luke the check.

Luke scrutinized the check and held it next to the other samples, but he knew the minute he saw the check that it was a perfect match.

Bobby didn't even need to ask. He could see it written all over Luke's face. "Don't tell me. I don't want to hear it. I can't believe it. I don't *want* to believe it."

"All this time." Luke shook his head. Leaning back in his chair, he picked up his football, twirling it in his hands. "Let's think this through from every angle. We can tie Kevin to Charlotte because we now have an eyewitness putting him at the scene of the crime prior to the victim's death."

"What's his motive?"

"Unrequited love."

"Damn it."

"My thoughts exactly."

"What's Kevin's motive for killing Swanson?"

"He killed Swanson because he was afraid he would find new information when he went over to Cami's. Maybe there was something in the house Kevin didn't want him to find, like the letters or the yearbook." Luke tossed the football to Brock. "We need substantial evidence to tie Kevin to Swanson."

"Like what?"

"The attempted murder weapon, and access or availability to get morphine. So far, none of the hospitals or nursing homes have reported any missing, and Kevin wouldn't have easy access to it." Luke scrubbed at his face, trying to think. "Hell, knowing Kevin, he probably hit him with a golf club."

Cannon sat up straight in his chair. "What did you just say?"

"He probably hit him with a golf club."

"A golf club...in the back of his car, along with muddy work boots."

"Muddy work boots," Luke repeated. "Kevin owns one frickin' pair of work boots and I've never seen him wear them, especially not to play golf."

"I'm telling you, they were in the back of his trunk the other night when Aaron and I retrieved the beer and soda out of his vehicle."

"Son of a bitch! What if he's the one harassing Cami? Locking her in the shed, breaking the window with a golf ball." Luke smacked his hand on the desk. "Golf ball. Cami." His heart slammed against his chest. "Shit! Kevin's there. That must have been what Aaron was referring to."

"What do you mean?"

"He started to tell me something, but I never got out of him, because we got cut off."

"Try calling Aaron again. See if he picks up."

Luke punched in Aaron's number.

Bobby continued, "Cami might not be in immediate danger or any at all. This is Kevin we're talking about. He loves her like a sister. More likely it's Aaron we should be concerned about. If Kevin finds out Aaron saw him, Swanson might not be the only one Kevin goes after."

Luke's blood ran cold. "What did you just say?"

"If Kevin finds out Aaron saw him, Swanson might not be the only one Kevin goes after."

"No, before that."

"He loves Cami like a sister."

"You're right."

"I'm right about a lot of things. You'll have to be more specific."

"Cami. What if he loves Cami, not Charlotte. Think about it." Luke grabbed the yearbook and pointed. "That 'I love you' is written under both their pictures. We just assumed it was Charlotte because it's her yearbook. Swanson found the love note in Cami's pocket. Charlotte was wearing Cami's hoodie, but Cami had been seen wearing it only a few minutes before Kevin found her in the woods. Heck, I remember seeing Cami with it wrapped around her waist that night, and the Parker twins can easily be mistaken for one another in the dark. What if all of this, the letters, the message, and the kiss, were meant for Cami, not Charlotte?"

Bobby pulled his keys out of his pocket. "I'll drive. You call Cami on the way."

"Let's roll."

CHAPTER 46

"Charlotte?" The wind whipped her words away the moment she opened her mouth. Cami looked down and saw footsteps leading away from the house, disappearing into the woods.

Cami took a step out and then another. She should get the others, a flashlight, and warmer clothes. Before she could make a decision, the door slammed shut behind her. Cami threw herself at the door, but it was too late. With a sickening click, she heard the deadbolt slide into place.

"Charlotte!" Cami beat on the door. "So, help me! If you're doing this!" Cami spun when she heard it. The crunch of footsteps on snow. *Follow the tracks.*

This was her home. These were her woods. She knew the area better than anyone. Whoever this was wouldn't get far. She took off, treading lightly, step by step in the tracks.

Relying on her senses, she strained to hear. The false gray light caused by the black night and the brilliant, white snow cast an eerie cloud as she crept across the frozen ground. Following the footprints, she wove her way back through the trees, past the outcropping of rocks, deep into the woods, until she could hear the babbling of the brook, now more a trickle over rocks as the edges froze and turned to ice. Struggling to stay on her feet against the wind and the deep snow, she trudged on, nerves skittering across her cold skin.

Darting in and out of shadows, quick on her feet, sticking out sharply as she passed into the open, black against white. Her dress caught on branches, snagging, ripping. She knew where they were headed, but not why.

As she neared the little clearing next to the stream, she came to a halt. He sat on what was left of the old hollowed tree, rotted, and snow covered. The log, the rock, and the frozen ground that had been her sister's deathbed now held him. His head was in his hands.

Her breathing was haggard and came out in small puffs. "Kevin?"

He didn't move, didn't look at her either.

She edged closer.

"Stop right there. Don't come any closer."

"Kevin? What's wrong?"

"I can't do it any longer, Cami. I just can't." He choked back a sob. "I thought I could go through with it, but I can't."

"Do what?" she asked, inching closer. That's when she saw the bottle of alcohol in one hand. "Kevin, talk to me," Cami begged.

"I can't marry Josie," he sobbed. "I don't love her. I never have."

"You don't have to marry her. The wedding is still weeks away. Plenty of time to cancel if that's what you really want. Is that what you want?"

Kevin looked up at her with tear-filled eyes. "That's exactly what I want." He shifted on the log, as snow accumulated on top of his head and shoulders. "You don't understand though, Joselyn won't call off the wedding." He took a long pull on the bottle.

Taking a step forward, closer to him. "It will devastate Joselyn, but she doesn't want to be trapped in a loveless marriage." She took another step closer, sat tentatively on the snowy log next to him. "Didn't you ever picture yourself getting married?"

"No, I did." He shifted, suddenly very sober, and faced her. "Just not to her."

Raising an eyebrow, Cami asked, "Then who?"

"I thought it would be you."

He was quick. His hands were in her hair, and his mouth sealed hers in a hot, passionate heat. His tongue plunged and pilfered. Taking and demanding more. Her hands shot up between them, struggling to push him back.

"Kevin!" she hissed, her mouth free at last. She shot to her feet. "Stop! What the hell are you doing?"

"Kissing you."

Lifting her hand to her mouth, covering her bruised and swollen lips. "Why?"

"Because I love you. Always have. Always will."

"No." She shook her head in disbelief. "It was Charlotte. You were in love with Charlotte."

"No. It was always you."

"But the box of letters."

"Were meant for you, for your birthday."

"But then. . . how?"

He shrugged. "The name tags must have gotten switched by mistake. The Chia pet was meant for Charlotte, not you." A hint of a smile flitted across his face. "Not you. Never you."

"Then I don't understand. If you don't love Joselyn, why did you agree to marry her?"

"She's blackmailing me."

Shocked, Cami asked, "Who?"

"Josie."

"Why?"

"I did something horrible, unthinkable, unforgivable, and she knows."

In a thin voice that was barely audible over the falling snow, Cami asked, "What did you do?"

"I think you already know. If you don't, I'm sure you can figure it out. Look around. Why else would I come here? To this spot?"

Her heart broke inside her chest. Shattered. She was silent for a moment as tears dripped down her face. The only sound was that of the virgin white flakes floating down around them. Her hands were numb and so were her toes, but she ignored the pain. "It can't be true," she whispered in a hollow voice.

Kevin stood quickly, trying to explain. "It was an accident. I thought she was you."

"So what? You attacked her?"

"No! Of course not! I kissed her, thinking she was you. She was furious, wanted no part of it. She stumbled backward, fell, and hit her head."

"Stop!" Cami put her hands on her ears, covering them. "I can't listen to one more minute of this."

He moved toward her. She stepped back, tripped, and fell backward into the snow. It was like slow motion. He reached for her hand but missed. The crack was like a gunshot. Bone on stone. Kevin cried out. His scream ripped through the darkness.

CHAPTER 47

"Cut the lights," Luke demanded. "The driveway is coming up on the right."

"I can't see a damn thing, Warner. I need the lights."

"Fine, leave them on, but hurry."

"I'm going as fast as physically possible and still staying on the road. No one knows we're coming, so the lights shouldn't matter. No one's answering their phones, remember?"

"I know you're right, but I just can't shake this feeling that something's happened and we're too late."

The snow was coming down at a good clip. The roads were covered, nearly a foot deep already, and there were no signs of it letting up.

"There's the stone fence and the opening. Turn here."

"Why isn't the driveway lit?"

"Maybe the snow has already buried the lights. It's deep."

Guiding the SUV through the trees with no visible path to follow was like trying to thread a needle. Soon, the house loomed large and dark.

"Not one light is on in the house. I wonder if they've lost power?"

"It's possible with this weather. Or maybe everyone's in bed."

Luke squinted through the snow, pointing. "There's Kevin's car. Pull up behind it. Block it in."

"We need to check that trunk." Bobby cut the engine, reached over and produced a couple of flashlights out of the glove-box, and got out.

"Kevin always leaves his keys in the car under the floor mat, tonight shouldn't be any different."

"Let's have a look."

They found the keys easily, peered inside the trunk, but it was empty.

***

From the shadows, she watched the scene unfold. The kiss. The push. The argument that ensued and then the inevitable step backward. Followed by the fall. The sickening sound. Then the world around them fell eerily silent. Exactly like before. A wave of deja vu swept over her.

Ten years she'd kept the secret. Locked away and buried. Buried like Charlotte Parker's body. Cold, dead, and forgotten. Until now. Until Cami Parker's return. Her return had set the wheels in motion. Somehow, she knew they'd end up in this exact spot.

She stepped out from behind the tree as the man she loved stood over another lifeless body. "What did you do?" she hissed.

Kevin twisted abruptly. "It's not how it looks! I swear!"

"That's what you said the last time. Look how that turned out. One dead girl. And now, ten years later, the exact spot, the same date. Only this time, the other twin."

"No!" Kevin crouched down as Joselyn approached, felt for a pulse. "She's still alive."

"For now."

"Help me, damn it!" He struggled to pull Cami up out of the snow. Scarlet stained the virgin snow beneath her head. "I won't leave her. Not Cami! Not this time."

"You'd rather go to jail for the death of Charlotte Parker than leave Cami here?"

"I won't go to jail. Charlotte was an accident. You know that. You're my witness. I'll explain it to them. Everything. Like

I should have before."

"So that's it then?" Joselyn asked, circling Kevin as he held Cami in his arms, rocking her. "You love her? Enough to give up everything. Your career? Me?"

"Yes. I'm sorry, but it's always been Cami. Not Charlotte, and not you."

The comment pierced like a knife. Twisting and slicing through her heart, ripping it to shreds, but Joselyn didn't cry. Not one tear. "I won't cover for you again."

"I don't care."

CHAPTER 48

The front door was unlocked. Luke and Bobby walked in with caution, flashlights scanning. Bobby flipped switches and produced light.

"The electricity is on. Everyone must be in bed."

"That doesn't explain why Aaron didn't call back."

"Let's check upstairs."

They took the stairs two at a time, saw a door open, and both drew guns.

"Holy cannoli!" Tanya's hands shot to the sky. "Don't shoot!"

"Tanya?" Luke called. "What the hell are you doing out of bed?"

"I have to pee. Too much champagne."

He quickly crossed to her.

"Are you alone?"

"In my room?"

"Where else would I mean?"

He deliberately pulled her away from her room and peered in.

"Of course. Who would be with me?" she asked, dumbfounded. "What's going on?"

Before he could answer, another door opened, and Brock popped his head out.

"What's going on?"

They heard a low groan coming from the right. The door to Cami's old room was ajar. Bobby nudged it to open with his toe. The beam of yellow cut a swatch across the empty room, landing on a figure crumpled in the corner.

They crossed the room, and Bobby rolled the body over. "Phelps? Aaron, are you alright?"

Aaron moaned, "My head."

"Shit, man, you've got a bump the size of a goose egg on the back of your head. How many fingers am I holding up?"

"Three... I think."

"What happened?"

"Last thing I remember is talking to Warner. Nothing after that."

"Cannon, stay with him. I'm going to check on the others."

Luke disappeared out the door, his pulse skipping, afraid of what he might find. His heart hit the floor when he found Cami's room empty. *If anything happens to her...* He couldn't even think about it, just had to concentrate on finding her.

By the time Luke came back, Bobby had Aaron up into a sitting position and he called for an ambulance.

"Anything?" Bobby asked.

"Cami, Kevin, and Joselyn aren't in bed."

They exchanged a look.

"He must have taken the women somewhere. We need to check the rest of the house." Luke glanced at Aaron, his brow creased heavily. "Brock? Can you and Tanya get Aaron downstairs on your own?"

"Yeah, we can manage. What's going on?"

"No time to explain. Just wait until I tell you it's clear to take him down."

"You finish searching upstairs. I'll start down." Luke ran from the room, taking the stairs quickly. At the bottom, the heady scent of roses waited for him. It overpowered his sense of smell, and a chill raced over him. He stopped cold. He felt silly, but he asked anyway, "Charlotte?" He waited a heartbeat. "Are you here?"

The scent increased until his nose itched, and so did the cold.

"Can you help me? Do you know where Cami is? Where he's taken her?" He made a long slow circle, searching for... anything. "I need some sort of sign, or signal, if you understand. There's a lot of area to cover, and I'm afraid I'm running out of time. Help me, please," he begged.

The scent dissipated, the warmth of the house returned.

"Charlotte, don't leave!" he pleaded.

The crash came from behind him. He spun. The vase from the antique breakfront shattered, water ran, and flowers scattered all over the hardwood floor. Without warning, a small, white rose lifted into the air. Luke stood stunned, his pulse spiking. *Was he really seeing this?* Rubbing at his eyes, he watched it hang in midair, suspended by an invisible hand. Then, one by one, petals dropped across the floor as if someone or something plucked them from the flower. Like a trail of breadcrumbs leading him to the kitchen, and ultimately, the backdoor.

What was left of the flower dropped by the back door next to a small pile of snow, pooled and melting. "They went outside."

Opening the door, he was pelted with sleet as the fury of the storm kicked up a notch. He saw footprints leading away from the house in mere inches of snow until a drift swallowed them whole. He zipped his jacket, put his head down, and ran into the storm.

***

"What did you just say to me?" Joselyn asked in disbelief.

"I said, I don't care. I won't hide anymore." He cradled Cami in his arms, but turned as Joselyn moved closer. A glint of metal in the pale light caught his attention. That's when he noticed the fire poker in her hand. "What the hell did you bring that out here for?"

Joselyn looked down, almost like she'd forgotten she had it. She raised it, gripped it like a baseball bat.

"Put that down and help me."

Her voice was eerily calm. "Cami's going to die out here. You know that, don't you?"

"No, I won't let her. Not this time. Help me. Please, I'm begging you."

"I'll help you. But I have one question first."

He struggled to stand, lifting Cami, cradling her in his arms as her eyes fluttered. Trying to get a grip, he moved forward, sinking into the snow. "What do you want to know that can't possibly wait until we get back to the house?"

"What happens if you're cleared, but Cami dies?"

"Then I might as well die right along with her."

"That's what I thought." The words came out devastatingly bitter. "I hope you know I loved you." She ran the sharp piece of iron right through him.

***

Sprinting across the knee-deep snow wasn't easy. He sunk in, struggled, fell down, but kept moving forward. He'd barely gone a hundred yards, the mere length of a football field, and he was completely winded. Luke didn't know which direction to search. He used the house as a point of reference, keeping it at his back, but it wasn't long before the darkness swallowed it whole.

Snow filled his shoes, cold stung his face and hands, and sleet pelted him incessantly. Deeper into the evergreens, he found little relief from the snow. The swirl of white was blinding, confusing his sense of direction.

It was a matter of life and death now, his and theirs. If Kevin didn't kill them, the conditions would if they weren't found soon. Luke was poorly prepared for the extreme weather and doubted they were much better off. His mind raced, trying to fill in the gaps. Kevin must have done it all, from the very first golf ball that broke Cami's bedroom window, to the love letters found in Charlotte's room, the note in Cami's pocket,

Charlotte's death, locking Cami in the shed, and Detective Swanson. It was all Kevin. It was so hard to fathom that Kevin would do such a thing. But why? He felt like he was missing something, but what?

A guttural scream ripped through the darkness. He ran at a dead sprint toward it.

***

The sudden jar from hitting the ground brought Cami around. Her eyes fluttered open. It was still pitch dark out and snow fluttered down around her. Something warm and metallic smelling covered her face. She struggled to sit up, but there was something heavy on top of her. She pushed, shoved, and screamed when Kevin's head lulled to one side.

His voice came out like a gurgle, "Cami." Blood spurted up, bubbled out of his mouth, sliding down his chin and pooling on the snow.

Cami screamed again, wiggled out from under him, terrified. Unable to comprehend what had happened, the back of her head throbbed and a wave of nausea swamped her. She struggled to sit up and focus.

Her eyes adjusted. "Joselyn? Is that you? Oh, God! Help me!" Cami crawled out from under Kevin on her hands and knees toward her. "What's happened?" she asked, confused. "How did I get out here?"

"I'll tell you what happened. Everything and nothing."

"You're not making any sense." Cami bit back bile. "I'm dizzy. I think I'm going to be sick."

"Shhh. Take it easy." Joselyn came over to her slowly. "You need to lie down. Flat on your back. That'll help with the nausea."

"Okay," Cami answered despondently, trusting her.

"Let me help." Joselyn eased her back onto the snow. "There. How's that?"

"Better."

"I'm c-cold. What happened?" Cami stammered, her teeth chattering.

"I'll tell you what happened." Joselyn crouched down beside her. "Kevin. That's what happened."

Confused, Cami asked, "Did he hurt Charlotte? He s-said it w-was an accident."

Joselyn stroked Cami's face. "Shhh, now don't fret. He's right. It was an accident. I saw the whole thing. Hid right in the trees over there." She pointed. "Your sister was alive when he left."

"That's g-good."

"I guess."

"Help me up. We need to ge-get out of the cold." Cami struggled to focus, felt a pressure on her chest, making it hard to move, and hard to breathe. "Then how did she die and why does Kev-Kevin think..."

"What Kevin doesn't know is after he left, your sister was on the ground, laying here. In this exact spot, just like you are now," Joselyn stated, with a stone-cold edge to her voice. "She, too, asked me to help her up. And I'll do for you exactly what I did for her." Joselyn shifted, lowered herself down, putting her knee right in Cami's sternum, pinning her to the ground.

"I can't breathe."

An evil smirk spread across Joselyn's face. "If you think it's hard now, just wait."

Cami gasped for air as Joselyn pinched her nose shut and placed her hand over Cami's mouth.

Joselyn smiled. "I actually used your favorite green hoodie to smother your sister, but I think this will do the trick. It might take a little longer."

Panic surged, a convulsion of fear rocked her body as Cami sucked in air that stank of lotion and sweat, clinging to Joselyn's damp skin. She flailed, swinging arms, and bucking wildly, but Joselyn was bigger, heavier and Cami was already weak. Cami saw stars, black and yellow orbs clouded her vision as she struggled for air. Her sister's face floated at the edge of her subconscious.

Fight, Cami! Charlotte cried. *Fight! Luke is coming! You have to fight!*

Cami groped in the snow for purchase, for leverage, for anything. She couldn't breathe. Desperate, she searched the frozen ground. And then she found it. Her hand closed around the half bottle of champagne. She swung with everything she had. Frozen glass connected with flesh. Tearing skin. Joselyn grabbed at her face, trying to protect and ward off the next blow. Joselyn shrieked as Cami's nails raked across her cheek. Shoving Cami, she ripped the iron shaft out of Kevin's chest and clambered away.

The urge to run consumed her, but she couldn't leave Kevin. She crawled slowly toward him.

Without warning, Luke silently emerged from the shadows, carefully tracking and assessing the situation.

He saw Kevin in a heap, unmoving, Cami scrambling backward over the snow toward him.

He moved closer, gun drawn. They hadn't seen him yet. Every bone, every muscle in his body was on high alert. It took all his willpower not to run to Cami.

Seeing the stain of crimson surrounding Kevin made him call out, "Stay back!"

She twisted to see him advancing quickly, and let out a sob. "Luke?"

"I'm here."

"He's hurt, Luke. He's dying. We have to get him back to the house." She held Kevin's head in her hands as tears ran down her cheeks.

"What happened?" He tucked his Glock in the back of his pants, under his jacket, so his hands were free. Then he ran them over her beautiful face, down her arms, and grasped her hands. "Are you hurt?"

"It's not me, it's Kevin. Joselyn..."

There was a crunch of snow, a blur of movement, and

Luke was hit from the side at full force. Metal pierced skin. Pain shot through his side. He felt his gun slip free, saw her face when she landed on top of him. It was red and distorted. Angry red slashes ran down the side, and a bump bulged just above her temple. Joselyn looked wild, like a demon possessed as they tumbled and thrashed in the snow, both their hands locked around the iron poker.

Cami crawled out of their path, unable to stand or run. Instead, she slipped free of her jacket, shivered against the intense cold, and pressed it against Kevin's chest. That's when she saw the gun directly at her feet.

Luke leveraged his legs and pushed, throwing Joselyn off. She landed hard against a tree, the poker still in her hand.

Luke tried to stand, but he was losing blood quickly. Pain shot through his middle and wrenched his gut. Out of the shadows, Joselyn came rushing, leading with the fire poker like a possessed knight charging with a lance.

The shot rang out. Blood spurted out across the front of Joselyn's chest. She stopped in shock mid-stride and fell to her knees. Joselyn crumpled like a used rag, face first into the snow. Blood bloomed out around her, tainting the virgin snow.

CHAPTER 49

The afternoon was mild for late November. The snow had melted, except for a few patches of ice that hugged the shadows and clung to the deep crevices. Cami and Luke walked in silence through the woods, the late afternoon sun already encroaching on the hills to the west. In one hand Cami held a shopping bag, the other Luke's hand.

Cami told him she could come alone, but he had insisted and was so thankful to have him by her side.

As the sun sunk down through the bare branches, Cami was all too aware that things could have turned out so differently. It had taken weeks to sort the whole mess out, but eventually they had pieced together what had happened.

Everything Joselyn did was carefully planned and calculated, incriminating Kevin at every move. Cami shook her head in dismay as the evidence rolled through her mind.

Following the deer path through the woods, they stepped over logs, walked along the small brook, around the outcropping of rocks to the small clearing where Charlotte had died.

Luke took the bag from Cami, handed her a wooden cross and a mallet he'd carried, and watched her crouch, driving it into the cold, hard ground in remembrance of Charlotte. The sound of the mallet hitting the wooden cross echoed through the trees, scattering chipmunks, and panicking birds. Then he handed her a second cross.

Kevin. Kind, caring Kevin. Memories flooded her as she pounded the stake in, tears streaming down her face. He had been one of her best friends since kindergarten. He had kept this one terrible secret from her but even so she'd known enough not to believe he could have killed Charlotte.

The night after the tragedy with Joselyn, that's what she was calling it now, a tragedy because she couldn't come to terms with the word murder. To call it anything else brought up too many emotions: guilt, fear, and loss to name a few. So many swirled around her even now, but she tried to focus on only one. Love.

Love for her twin, who wasn't perfect, by any standards, but she was still her sister. They shared a bond that could never be broken; even death couldn't break it. Charlotte had haunted her dreams for the last ten years, and was present in the house when she'd returned to Cherry Hollow.

Reaching up to Luke, he handed her flowers from the shopping bag, yellow roses for Kevin, and white for Charlotte. "Thank you for coming with me today," she whispered in a hushed tone. "Even though you probably shouldn't be here. Your doctor will have a fit when he finds out." She touched his side delicately. "You're still healing."

Luke gave her that heart-stopping grin of his and said, "Then we won't tell him, will we?"

Shaking her head, she said, "I seem to remember that you aren't very good at following the rules."

"You're right, I'm better at bending them, then following."

"Seriously, though," she pulled back and linked her hands in his. "It means a lot, so much more than you'll ever know, that you were here with me."

"I wouldn't want to be anywhere else."

"I never told you before, but Charlotte told me you were coming, that I only needed to hold on."

"And I never told you, without your sister's help, I may not have found you in time. She was there for you in the end."

"When Joselyn stabbed you...I thought I was going to lose you. That thought was more than I could bear." She choked back a sob.

"You're not going to lose me, ever. I'm right here. I'm not going anywhere."

Luke reached for her hand and turned to go, but Cami lingered. Digging deep into the pocket of her jacket she pulled out the cherished items. She opened her palm and produced three red, ripe cherries, bending and placing them beneath Charlotte's cross.

Cami promised herself that this would be a place that remembered the good, not the bad. A twin sister that she shared happy memories with and loved dearly. And a best friend who had been by her side growing up, and in the end, simply loved her. Love and loss were hand in hand in this peaceful place, only those things would be remembered here.

She stood, brushing her hands on her jeans and turned to Luke. A whisper of a smile played across her mouth as she looked into his gray eyes. He took his thumb, wiping away a lone tear.

"Ready?"

She nodded and they turned to go. With one last look over her shoulder they headed back. They walked in silence, both lost in their own thoughts. A cardinal flitted overhead, perched on a branch, then took off drifting on a breeze leading the way back to the clearing where the others waited for them.

Cami smelled the smoke before she saw the flames. In the center of the little glade Bobby had lit the fire and was bent over roasting a marshmallow, Tanya had grabbed blankets, and Aaron and Brock stood silently waiting.

They stopped next to the fire and Luke pulled her in close, hugging her tight. A warmth spreading through her like no other could provide.

His hand slipped from her, as Tanya walked over and linked her arm through Cami's.

"You okay?" she asked.

Cami nodded. "I will be, thanks to all of you."

They stood by the fire and watched Luke reach for a

stick, sliding on a marshmallow. He stuck it over the fire and toasted it lightly. When it was toasted to perfection, he pulled it out and turned towards Cami. "Want my marshmallow?"

"Yes, it's toasted perfectly, not burnt."

"It's all yours. But more importantly," a ghost of a smile played across his face. "I'm all yours."

She laughed.

He tugged her away from Tanya, pulled her in and kissed her. The scent of roses surrounded them as he pulled back, tenderly brushing a strand of hair off her face. Over Luke's shoulder Cami saw a faint, almost translucent image shift in the air. *Charlotte.*

The wind swirled up around them, playfully caressing her hair, swirling leaves, and lifting the scent, carrying it away and the essence of what was or could have been Charlotte. A loss so profound swept over Cami leaving only the forest, the fire, and her friends. Charlotte was truly gone this time. She felt it in her soul.

Swallowing hard, Cami looked around at her friends, the clearing, and the enormous house. The things that happened here didn't change her perception of Cherry Hollow, only made them more precious.

This was Cherry Hollow, the place she loved, the place she called home. It was where her friends were, it was a sanctuary, a place of refuge from loss and surrounded in love no matter the weather, the season, or the circumstance. Her place was here. Cherry Hollow had been her past, it was where she was at the present, and it would be her future.

THE END

Acknowledgments

I want to thank a few people for making this book possible. To my very first reader: My youngest daughter, Makayla. I love the fact that you read as I wrote, sometimes reading over my shoulder or sitting down at the computer when I walked away for a few minutes, frustrated. Your encouragement, your eagerness to see what happened next, kept me going. Then to Ryan and Kristy, who willingly read even though you know it's a rough draft, ignoring the mountainous volume of mistakes, able to see the story for what it is, in it's true form. I value your opinion and wait anxiously anticipating your reactions.

To Kate who encouraged me to dig a little deeper, explore my characters further, and test my ability to look at my story from another point of view. Without you, my book wouldn't be nearly as good. Thank you.

To Rachael, Pam, and Melisa, who found those last, little pesky typos and spelling mistakes, along with the rest of my ARC team: Amy, Melissa, Jill, Sue R., Erin, and Sue E. Thank you for joining me on this journey, your interest in my books and eagerness to read make it all worthwhile.

And then to Delaney who I run all my "stuff" past. Whether it's a book trailer, social media post, or a bookmark, it doesn't get made without her keen eye scrutinizing it or her approval.

I couldn't have done it without any of you. You have my sincerest gratitude, respect, and love.

To my readers: thank you for trusting me with your time and letting me be a little part of your entertainment. I love hearing from you - your feedback, comments, and questions. Keep them coming!

Last, but certainly not least, as always to my family for patiently waiting while I type one more sentence and believing I can accomplish anything. You have my eternal love.

Thank you for taking the time to read Cherry Hollow. If you enjoyed it, please connect with me at www.melissaroosauthor.com.

BOOKS BY THIS AUTHOR

You Can Hide

Jayde Walker is left for dead. Surviving, she is the only witness to the murder of her best friend. Fighting amnesia, she tries to get on with her life, with the killer still on the loose. Then one night she remembers, and the truth terrifies her.
Leaving behind everything and everyone she knows, she runs.

Halfway across the country, lost in the Midwest, Jayde makes a wrong turn, desperate to disappear.

The tall, green cornstalks in the vast fields of Iowa call to her. Without hesitation, Jayde steps in and disappears.

Who can save her? Her fiancé she left behind? The detective she trusted, or the farmer that finds her? Whom can she trust with her life? And her heart?

In The Shadow Of The Black Moon

Where would you go if you needed someplace to escape?
For grieving Bree Thompson, it was the East Coast.
Wanting time to heal, she thinks she's found the answer in the sand, the sun, and a place of her own . . . and Ryker James.
But just when Bree starts to believe it's possible to start over, trouble starts.

Watching, waiting, lurking in the shadows . . . she's taken

something from him . . . and he wants it back.

Can Bree deny her attraction to Ryker when all the trouble seems to point back to him?

Dive into this Mystery Romance filled with the perfect balance of romantic tension and suspense.

ABOUT THE AUTHOR

Melissa Roos

Melissa was born and raised in Iowa and grew up a true country girl at heart, having spent a lot of time outdoors and many summers working in the fields. She graduated from Iowa State University, and is a die-hard Cyclone fan.

Melissa previously lived in Maryland and now reside in Pennsylvania with her family.

Melissa's first novel, You Can Hide, was published in 2020. Her second book, In the Shadow of the Black Moon, was published in 2021.

Made in the USA
Columbia, SC
12 December 2022

73509523R00191